AUTHOR LIU, A.E.

CLASS A F A

TITLE Flash house

12

D0480298

FLASH HOUSE

Also by Aimee Liu from Headline

Cloud Mountain
Face

FLASH HOUSE

Aimee Liu

review

This edition published by arrangement with Warner Books, Inc.,
New York, NY, USA. All rights reserved.

The right of Aimee Liu to be identified as the Author of
the Work has been asserted by her in accordance with the
Copyright, Designs and Patents Act 1988.

First published in Great Britain in 2003
by HEADLINE BOOK PUBLISHING

A REVIEW book

10 9 8 7 6 5 4 3 2 1

All rights reserved. No part of this publication may be
reproduced, stored in a retrieval system, or transmitted,
in any form or by any means without the prior written
permission of the publisher, nor be otherwise circulated
in any form of binding or cover other than that in which
it is published and without a similar condition being
imposed on the subsequent purchaser.

All characters in this publication are fictitious
and any resemblance to real persons, living or dead,
is purely coincidental.

Cataloguing in Publication Data is
available from the British Library

ISBN 0 7553 0267 2 (hardback)
ISBN 0 7553 0255 9 (trade paperback)

Typeset in StempelGaramond by
Letterpart Limited, Reigate, Surrey

Printed and bound in Great Britain by
Clays Ltd, St Ives plc

HEADLINE BOOK PUBLISHING
A division of Hodder Headline
338 Euston Road
LONDON NW1 3BH

www.reviewbooks.co.uk
www.hodderheadline.com

For Marty
With honor, love, and laughter
Always

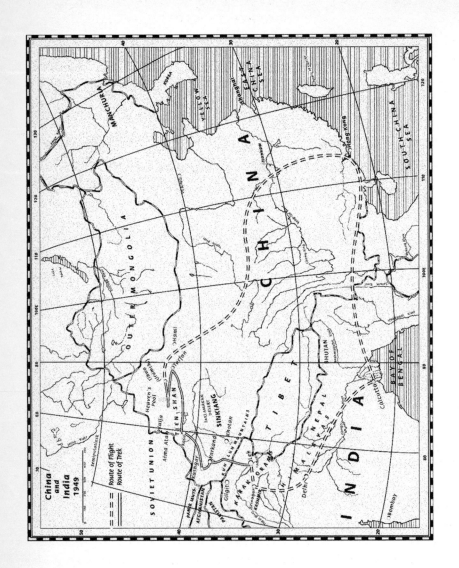

PROLOGUE
New Delhi, India

MARCH 1949

Joanna was dreaming of snow when Aidan kissed her goodbye. At his touch she came up fast and hard to a room too dark, hot against the phantom chill of her sleep. Her husband's closeness alarmed her.

Already dressed and seated on the edge of the bed, he smoothed the hair back from her face and kissed her again, longer this time, as if to imprint her with his leaving. He was off to Srinagar, he reminded her. Six a.m. flight.

She tasted the mint of his toothpaste, smelled his Burma Shave on her cheek. At once consoled and reluctant, she remembered why he was going to Kashmir. The Border War. UN observers. Proving himself an 'American.' Depending on what he came up with and when, Aidan would be gone from Delhi for at least two weeks.

'I wish you didn't have to do this,' she said.

He squeezed her hand. She knew as well as he that there was no point discussing what he did or didn't have to do, but it was unlike him to hold on this tight, this long. She could feel his wedding band pressing into her fingertip.

'What is it?' she asked.

'Will you say goodbye to Simon for me?'

'You did yourself, last night.'

'I know, but . . . he has a short memory.' The forced energy of his smile cut through the darkness. 'I'll be in touch, just as soon as I've got the right story.'

'No need to wait that long,' she said lightly. But as he released her, she added, 'Be careful.'

'You'll be fine, Jo. I've told Lawrence to see to it.'

'*That'll* make all the difference.'

3

'Be nice. He's a good friend, and we don't have many. Besides, Simon loves him even if you don't.'

'I hope you don't want *me* to love him!' She tugged her husband back down beside her, placed her lips against his ear to remind him of their lovemaking the night before.

'It's time,' he said, firmly turning his head. But again, that hesitation. He cupped one hand to her cheek. 'I love you. You know that.'

Neither forming a question nor a statement, the words seemed to wander between them.

'I could go with you,' she suggested, though they both knew Simon and her work made such impulses impossible.

He kissed her a third time, tenderly – briefly – then pulled back into his ritual preoccupation, reaching for his hat and bag, patting his pockets for wallet and documents: passport, visas, press certification, letters of safe conduct. Like a train edging cautiously but irreversibly out of the station, he moved toward the door. She started to get up, but he raised a hand. 'Stay there,' he said, 'just where you are. That way I'll know where to find you.' The half-light from the hall illuminated his smile, the determined tilt of his head. Before the door closed behind him, he looked back into the darkness and blew her one last kiss.

Moments later she heard the door to Simon's room open at the other end of the hall. Then it closed softly and the sound of Aidan's footsteps faded down the stairs.

Book One

March to June 1949

CHAPTER 1

1

From the beginning, we were sisters more than mother and daughter. Joanna Shaw rescued me in her way, and I tried to return the favor. I do not say this boastfully, but ironies are the way of the world, and now that I am an old woman I tell you with certainty that those who presume to lift another are most often in need of being raised themselves.

At the same time, those who appear the weaklings of this earth may possess strengths that overrule the mighty – that, indeed, may surpass even their own deepest longings and desires. I have seen this to be the case among women and children of my kind for as long as I can remember. Mrs Shaw, too, was of my kind, though on the now distant day when I first claimed her I did not know this to be true.

On the contrary, as I watched her making her way down G. B. Road in her stiff yellow dress and broad-brimmed hat with her handsome young Hindu escort I thought this must be some pampered *firenghi* who possesses no notion of pain. She looked younger than her thirty-four years, with a fire in her eyes that at once invited and warned me away. I was merely one of countless children of the red-light district. I owned nothing, not even my skin, but I knew why this foreign lady had come. The whole street knew. *Tongas* turned left instead of right at the sight of her. *Khas-khas tati* dropped over open windows. Smugglers bundled up their wares and trotted out of view. Women drew scarves across their faces, and the street became suddenly lively with dancing bears, monkey *wallahs,* and the calls of melon and *paan* vendors.

All for the benefit of the foreigner who would come to save us.

My keeper, Indrani, said that in the days of the British her kind were missionaries and bored commissioners' wives. In the past two years since Independence they had been attached to the new Departments of Health and Social Welfare, and usually they were Indian, but they remained the same. Women with hair like dust clouds and radish noses who had never enjoyed the touch of a man – or so Indrani said. Such women in India, it was well known, were so weak that for centuries they had required the almighty power of the Raj to stand guard over their virtue. Now this responsibility had fallen to India's own officials and police. We in the street could not know why these men should protect the dust cloud ladies when they freely preyed on us, but neither did we question such things.

Mrs Shaw was not ugly as the others I had seen. True, her body held hard juts and corners, and her lips were bare slivers against her teeth, but her eyes were large and filled with gold light, her skin and thick hair all the colors of honey. Her neck was long and slender and her ears shaped like perfect mangoes . . .

You see, even as early as that first day, I was viewing her in a different fashion. We were strangers, yet any stranger who is drawing such examination becomes something else, doesn't she? A stranger is strange, unknown, unexamined. When we study another we become familiar, and therefore cannot strictly be called strangers. I have often thought that of the thousands who pass in the streets each day, many hundreds may have passed before. Yet even if they pass two, five, twenty times, still they remain strangers except for those few who catch our eye, whose features we note and whose place in the street and day we remember – these are strangers no more but possessions of the mind. So in this way I, who was then called Kamla, claimed Mrs Shaw even as I hid from her under the shadow of a bullock cart.

It was easy to see that she was new to India. Her face was like a child's at a puppet show, while her feet and twinkling gloves behaved as if they belonged to the puppet. How awkwardly they plucked at earth and air as she turned this way and that! For although Mrs Shaw's small mouth rounded with evident pleasure at the sight of a tinseled altar or Bharati's little daughter, Shanta, with a red hibiscus in her hair, still she seemed to cling to herself, clutching her shiny white pocketbook to her waist as she stepped sideways past a dozing *pi* dog. Clearly she wished neither to touch nor be touched. Having claimed her, however, I dismissed this.

I could not help imagining how it would feel to press my small dirty face between those clean folds of her skirt, to rub my palms on the whiteness of her gloves. I pictured my wild black hair coming smooth beneath the answering strokes of her fingers. My heart would quiet to a purr as her foreign voice poured over me. I loved her foreignness. I adhered to it. I did not believe she would rescue me, but I believed that she could if she so desired.

At the same time, I did not desire rescue. Rescue, as it is understood in the red-light district, simply means greater suffering and risk. Oh, I had heard of girls who were 'rescued' by husbands and lovers and caring friends, but I also had seen the deadness in their eyes when they returned. And Indrani made sure I knew all the many, many reasons why other less fortunate girls never returned.

Mrs Shaw could not know these things. I imagined that her kind dreamed in black and white, as I was told they lived. Black was the dirt, the baby, the fly, the water she would not touch. White was the disinfected palace where she must sleep at night and the other *firenghi* home to which she would flee when her time in India was over. Home for Mrs Shaw must be a refuge, while home to me meant a dark place filled with blood and cries and madness.

For I, too, was a foreigner, my homeland also a world apart from Delhi. But I dreamed not in black and white but in colors bright as the waters of Holi. Fertile greens and dirt red, glacial blues and gold, these were the hues of my vision of myself, my life, my possibilities. These colors I had seen not only streaming in the riots of festivals and the bloodletting of India's Partition, but during my travels long ago away from that first place of fighting and death and what love I could recall. By the time I met Mrs Shaw I did not remember the place or the journey, only those colors and the sounds that accompanied them. Sounds of thrusting rivers and wind, skittering rocks and rain, but also the throat-swell of men's voices, the partition of vowels and guttural sighs, the language of my keepers. Whenever one from the hills came into the brothel, I would know it instantly and engage him with words from a buried poem, a song, a voice that once lullabyed me to sleep, a voice that had lost its face. And the man from the hills would roar. He would pull on his beard, cup his hand about my neck, and grope me with his eyes. He would talk at me a little and laugh, then set me down with a shake of his head, and Indrani would jerk her thumb for me to get back to my sweeping or go to the pump or fetch Mira or Fatya or Shahnaz for the hill man before he grew ill tempered. But then for a night or two my sleep would blaze with pink and gold, and the sounds would haunt me.

An odd thing happened after I claimed Mrs Shaw. Hers became the face of my dream voice, and the dreams themselves colored pale as her skin. Looking up through the yellow veil of her skirt I would see her head bent, the shadow shape of her nose and lips, that mane of hair. She would sing me the lullaby of the hills in low-drawn tones with a catch of the throat, and I would rock to and fro with her tenderness.

Some days later she returned to our lane. Her dress this time was a speckled orange like the petals of a tiger lily, her hair swept back under a man's hat, her pocketbook shouting out red. Her steps, too, were louder than before. This time when Bharati's child ran forward with her grimy palm outstretched, Mrs Shaw extended a gloved finger to brush the flies from the little brat's eyes. Immediately, the Indian servant gestured his disapproval. The two exchanged words. If you brush the flies from one child's eyes, he seemed to be saying, you must brush the flies from all. But even as he spoke, Shanta pressed closer, touching Mrs Shaw's skirt with her cheek and crying softly, grasping. The escort tried now to hurry Mrs Shaw away, but she reached back and dropped three paise into those pleading hands. When Shanta ran over to show off her treasure, I knocked her into the dust. Indrani, who had been watching from the doorway, dug her nails into my arm and lifted me off my feet, screaming that I should learn such skill from Shanta and then maybe I would be worth the fortune she wasted to keep me.

It had not always been this way. When I was younger, Indrani pretended to love me. A child of five or six, I had just arrived in Delhi, and she had recently a daughter who died. She would tell me tales of her own lost beauty. She had been a *nautch* girl in

Lucknow, singing and dancing her seductions. The house was a packrat's museum filled with artifacts of her wiles: A caged green parrot from the South African lover who had joined in Gandhiji's Great Salt March. The yellow gold bells with which she used to adorn her hands and ankles. Saris spangled with silver, headdresses dripping mirrors and pearls. Photographs taken by an Oxford-trained barrister of her Pathaka *mudra* portraying the sun. For a time she would take me into her bed and hold me, humming the ragas of her youth, petting my 'golden wheat-colored skin' and fawning over my turquoise eyes. But the house was hardly a business then. She had only Bharati. She still entertained customers herself, and her heart still possessed some measure of softness.

The madness of Partition changed Indrani. She had a brother in Amritsar who was mistaken for a Muslim. He and his two young sons had their throats cut in their own home. While the Muslim quarter in Delhi burned, Indrani took to drink. Afterward, as business improved and our house became more crowded, she grew fat and hard-hearted, and her tenderness toward me soured. I was a weight pulling her down. I was the biggest mistake of her days. I was the demon child from the north, but I would pay when I finally grew old enough. I would pay and pay and pay.

I knew what Indrani meant. I was the one who emptied the slop pots, carried the water jugs, washed the sisters' clothes and bed-clothes and monthly rags. I shaved their lipsticks and kohl pencils, tidied jars of powder and rouge. I combed the coconut oil through their hair, lit incense at twilight, filled their oil lamps, brought the clay cups from which they drank whiskey and gin with their *babus*. I took them their glasses of tea in the morning and swept up the occasional shattered bottle. Sometimes I tended their bruises and wounds after this *babu* flew into a drunken rage or that one chose to act out the part of the jealous lover Rama. Unlike Shanta, I did not lurk behind the slit curtains or crouch outside the barred windows. (Shanta was always competing with the *babus* for her mother's affections.) But even in my sleeping place in the kitchen I was surrounded by the sounds and smells, the undulations of brothel commerce.

'A woman's body is her implement,' Bharati told me once as we sat together patting out *chappati* for the evening meal. 'Like the

11

plow of the farmer, it is her means of livelihood and survival. Some say it is sacred. Others say it is evil. But it is a necessary vessel for spirit and for life. If as a girl you protect and use this vessel wisely, it may bring you comfort and wealth, a good husband and many sons. Once violated, however, a woman's body is forever diminished. Like mine, it will yield only daughters and the shelter of the brothel.' Knowing the secrets of the flash house, I did not see that the protection and wise use of a body was much under a girl's own control, but I accepted these words as a gift to hold in the back of my mind.

And now as I watched Mrs Shaw, I thought, yes, here is a lady who succeeds in using her body to secure a good life. Surely that is why she takes such pains to protect it from the violations of dust and beggars and the harsh midday sun. But even as this thought crossed my mind, she did something most unexpected.

There had been an accident. A boy named Surie in the next house had lifted his mother's sari while she prepared the morning meal. Somehow the fire got into the cloth, and both were badly burned. I had seen the victims with my own eyes as the flames engulfed them. They were lucky their faces and hands were spared, the legs not so good. By the time Mrs Shaw and her escort arrived, the excitement had died away. Plasters of mud had been applied to the wounds. But it was still the talk of the street, and the visitors were drawn in.

I went to watch from the communal tap a little down the lane as Mrs Shaw moved forward and dropped to her knees, not to help the boy as I had thought, but in front of the mother. I heard a cry. At first I thought Mrs Shaw was going to strike Surie's mother, perhaps for allowing such a thing to happen to a son. But no, she called for water – boiled water, she insisted, and finally accepted a vessel of tea, which she used to clean the wounds with her own hands. She removed her gloves.

I thought surely she must stop and instruct one of the other women to take over, but no, she lifted the leg of the woman – a Shudra – with her bare hands. The servant brought a large white box with a red cross on it, and in the next instant Mrs Shaw was stroking on the ointment with naked fingers, talking in a low murmur meant only for Surie's mother. No one could believe it. Mrs Shaw had the Untouchable's very blood on her hands. Many

12

of the onlookers turned away in disgust, but Mrs Shaw's daring only drew me forward. She was so intent, so confident and fearless! She bound the wound in a long white cloth, then turned and began to do the same for Surie. All the time squatting, her speckled skirt dragging in the dirt, her hat – a Western-style man's hat of straw – slipping from this side to that until finally she flung it back to her young escort, who put it on his own head and then looked around as if he hoped no one would notice. And we all laughed at him, and he smiled. I had come so close, however, that it seemed he was smiling straight at me. Mrs Shaw looked up and squinted through the light. She lifted a hand to shade her eyes. Quickly, I ducked back behind the water tank. My heart was racing, and my face was hot. I had claimed her, yes, but the very recklessness of her daring that had drawn me just instants ago now warned me away.

Mrs Shaw clucked her tongue and finished dressing Surie's burn. Then she and the young man went from house to house asking after other injuries and sickness. I tried to keep out of sight, but I could see Indrani looking out for me and scratching at her collarbone, which meant that she was angry, so finally I collected my water jars and brought them back. She would have cuffed me about the ears, but the foreigners were approaching our house. So instead she fit her palms together and raised them, *namaste*. No, no one sick, Indrani assured them, no one needing tending. Mira, crouching behind me in the doorway, pushed Bharati's child back into the shadows and held a finger at her lips to command her to silence.

Again my heart began to pound. This time I refused to hide, yet when Mrs Shaw herself pointed in my direction I was struck dumb. She wanted to know if Indrani was my mother. Her mother is away, said my keeper. I am her cousin. I watch her. She is a worthless girl, but I keep her out of goodness. She shook her pigeon-gray head and sighed.

Mrs Shaw and her escort looked at each other. Then they both looked at me, a firm look as if they were trying to tell me something with their eyes, but while I might speak with my sisters in this secret way, I could not understand these two.

Indrani pushed me inside. I heard the strangers asking more questions, and a skittering at the back of the house – Bharati's *babu* had stayed the night and was probably fleeing out the alley. Now the others were called, and each in turn said she worked for herself, the old lady just rented them rooms. No, no one forced them. Nothing illegal. They came and went as they pleased. The answers were well rehearsed. The laws did not prohibit women from selling their flesh of their own free will, as long as they were of age, which, of course, we all said we were. At last, with much shaking of heads and fumbling of hands, the young man and Mrs Shaw left.

That night, when the police came, I wondered if Mrs Shaw had summoned them. True, they often came. Indrani had known Inspector Golba since her days as a *nautch* girl. Sometimes, still, he let her dance for him, drink with him. In return, she let them pick, any girl they liked. I knew their smells, of hair grease and sweaty palms, of curry and onion and whiskey. Sometimes they gave me a sweet or stuck out their tongue. But never before had they picked me out. Never before spoken my name. This night Inspector Golba pointed his finger just as Mrs Shaw had done. Then his men took me away.

Indrani said nothing, did nothing to stop them. Mira cried out and Bharati cursed them. I struggled, but the two men holding my arms lifted me so that my *chappals* fell right off my feet, and my wails became whispers beneath the Hindi movie music squawking from loudspeakers at the back of their jeep. As we jerked forward I looked back at the many clusters of women watching along the lane. I remember so clearly, as if I'd never noticed and never would again, the glitter of the tinseled brothel lights, the brilliant colors those women wore, the casual relief with which they resumed their suggestive, welcoming poses. But most of all I remember the hot black silence of their knowing eyes.

The men took me straight to the police station and pushed me in through a back entrance. They marked me down as sixteen years old, though I was not yet near puberty. One of them joked they would call me China Blue – for my eyes.

I said nothing. Their talk was full of a swagger and heat that I knew full well from the brothel, but also from some more distant place buried deep within me. There were three of them. They placed me in a cell by myself. They bound my hands. Then they left me.

I was too frightened to call out. The men's hard taunts echoed in my ears. Not by way of the flash house now. No. Through a nightmare perhaps. Or a time long ago. The sliver of recall gnawed at me, filled me with dread.

I forced myself to push the voices away, to listen to the lizards *tsk, tsk*ing across the ceiling. A scorpion dropped on my arm, but it did not sting me, and I was grateful, told myself this was a sign that I would be forgotten. I slept, but soon woke to the rattle of the door, the stamp of boots, grunting, and a new smell over me, of police sweat and breath like rotten fish.

They yanked at the drawstring of my *kameez* trousers.

The bars of the cell's single high window divided the night into four flat blue-gray strips of sky encased in black. A crescent moon clung to one of these strips. By its light I could just make out the shadow shapes of three men leaning, heard the slap as they loosened their belts. One by one they pried my legs open and, wordless, shoved themselves inside me.

No recall now. No sweet dread. Only this. I felt my flesh tearing, burning, weeping as they pounded deeper. I did not mean to scream, for I knew it would do no good, but somehow the horror, not at the pain or even the raw physical invasion, but that sensation of their hot, sticky spill pouring over and out of me unleashed such revulsion that I did not hear myself. China Blue sings, they howled back, mocking before they gagged me.

When at last they left me alone, I thought, this is what it means to be rescued by Mrs Shaw.

2

As she woke to the second week of Aidan's absence, Joanna realized she was beginning to enjoy the slower pace of these mornings. Her husband had a habit of lurching out of bed the instant he opened his eyes, and if that didn't rouse her, the arthritic squeal of the plumbing as he showered and brushed his teeth surely would. Before her own eyes opened she could all but hear the roar of ideas, problems, assignments cramming Aidan's overactive skull, and by the time he emerged in one of his immaculate seersucker or white linen suits, she might have managed to sit up, might even

15

have her robe on, but he would already have set his day's game plan. This inner momentum and discipline, the sheer volume of purpose in his life were among the many qualities that Joanna admired in her husband, yet try as she might to keep up, she found his early rising a particularly hard act to follow in India's grueling heat.

She crossed the room and raised the grass blinds – *khas-khas tati,* she corrected herself, silently crisping the syllables in her mouth, or *tats,* as the British and Indians both called them for short – and stepped out onto the balcony. Their house was at the end of Ratendone Road, on the city's fringe. In the two years since India's Independence, Delhi had been expanding rapidly and this part of town would doubtless soon be swallowed by development, but for the moment, it enjoyed a curious double identity. At night, the quiet of the nearby wild lands lent an aura of isolation, yet by seven in the morning the street already was seething with *tonga* wagons, bullocks, rickshaw and bicycle traffic. A *sadhu* covered in ash squatted with his begging bowl on one side of the road. A belled elephant, draped in mirrored embroidery, lumbered along the other, while overhead a kite stretched its wings, riding the morning heat currents. Even after living here five months Joanna still marveled at the adventure of it all.

But she pushed aside the recurring question of where they would go – what Aidan would do if he did *not* come back with the story he needed to mollify his accusers. Right now she needed to get Simon off to school and herself to work by nine. And Aidan had assured her his lead in Kashmir was all but guaranteed.

Quickly she showered and dressed, then went in search of her son. For Simon, having absorbed both his mother's enthusiasm for India and his father's penchant for early rising, had already been up for ages. He'd been breakfasted and entertained and allowed to disrupt the chores of the entire household, from the gardener and cook to the bearer, Nagu. Joanna tracked him out to the garage turned servants' quarters where he was chasing lizards with Nagu's two sons.

Dilip and Bhanu were eleven and nine but, generous as their father, embraced eight-year-old Simon as a peer. He reveled in their company and, predictably, didn't want to leave this morning. Even after Joanna got him into the car and was maneuvering the second-hand Austin out of the driveway and into the flow of bicycle traffic, he couldn't stop talking about the krait that Dilip had killed behind the servants' quarters. The krait is a deadly poisonous snake, but the force behind Simon's story was not fear or awe but an almost clinical fascination with the undigested toad that tumbled out when Dilip slit the krait's belly.

Joanna kept her hands on the wheel and warned herself not to react. This was the same slight, tousle-haired child who spent his last weeks in Maryland huddled with his kittens under the dining room table, who had told her definitively that if they didn't have cowboys in India, then he wasn't going. The table eventually was collected by the packers, the kittens were distributed among the neighbors, and Simon's red Roy Rogers hat blew into the Atlantic four days into their voyage. He'd worn that hat – and slept in it – every day since he was three, but in the end Joanna mourned its loss more than he did. The cats, the hat, the good-hearted Bermans and Andersons next door, the house of cedar and fieldstone that Simon as a toddler had 'helped' to build, all were out of mind the instant they were out of his sight. And now he was playing with killer snakes. Let it go, she told herself. Danger is inescapable, but fear is a worse trap.

They reached Simon's school, and he grabbed his book bag, was about to scramble out when Joanna caught him around the shoulders. As she kissed him she tasted the salt of his skin, the morning dust in his hair. Then, before he could do it himself, she put out a thumb and wiped off her lipstick. By the time she reached the gate he was trotting yards ahead of her, making rushed *namaste* to his teachers, who were a mixed assortment of pinch-lipped Yankees and young upper-caste Indian women dressed in emerald and mustard and coral saris, with frangipani in their hair. The other children were already seating themselves on dhurries spread across the lawn under canopies dyed like circus tents.

Joanna paused to exchange small talk with two of the State Department wives who had founded this school as an alternative to sending their children to Indian-run institutions. The women addressed her with the same presumptive solidarity that she had come to recognize as an expat trademark, but as she walked away

17

she couldn't help wonder how their attitudes would change if and when the FBI's accusations against Aidan became public. Would they shun her as the wife of a 'Communist'? Or actively challenge her own political loyalties? Would they pressure her to pull Simon from school and forbid their children to play with him? Though she'd like to believe that some of these women might choose to defend Aidan, it would not help that she herself had sidestepped their clubs and bridge games, electing instead to take a job for the Indian government rescuing wayward natives.

Back in the car she squinted into the glare and, as she drove on to work, turned her thoughts defiantly to Aidan and their last night together. 'Lying in wait,' he'd joked when she tugged back the sheet and found him naked and preposterously ready. He'd gotten up onto his knees and slid her nightgown off over her head, then trailed his fingertips the length of her body, teasing her with affection and focusing all his restless energy into their mutual desire. Afterward, they lay cupped together drawing spirals on their sweat-slick skin and talking softly about the madness that seemed poised to engulf them.

Over the past few years J. Edgar Hoover and his friends with the China Lobby had repeatedly targeted Aidan, in part because he was half Chinese, but mostly for his articles criticizing Chiang Kai-shek's Nationalist Chinese government. After learning there were wiretaps on Aidan's phone and surveillance teams following him to and from the Washington office, the *Herald* finally assigned him to India to get him out of sight. But Aidan did not stop writing his stories, and just last month he sent off a particularly inflammatory piece, which his Australian friend Lawrence Malcolm archly dubbed 'The Generalissimo's Rag Team.' The highlight of the article was a description of fourteen-year-old Nationalist conscripts wearing rags for shoes as they stood in the snow guarding a restaurant where Madame Chiang Kai-shek was accepting personal 'gifts' of diamond jewelry and sipping French champagne with three notorious Shanghainese mobsters and their concubines. Joanna agreed with Aidan that this was one of the best pieces he'd ever written and she believed every word of it. But scathing honesty about the Chiangs was still out of fashion in Washington, so two weeks ago Aidan was demoted from Delhi bureau chief to special correspondent. With the demotion came a directive. As Aidan put it, 'Prove my Stars and Stripes and set the crusaders at ease.' His objective in Kashmir was to write something damning against the Communists in the UN peace commission.

'Or else . . .?' Joanna finally dared to ask.

'I suppose they'll order me home. Fire me. Send me up before the Un-American Activities Committee for one of their show trials, followed by the blacklist or jail. Or, they could just deport me. America, the beautiful.'

A shiver raced up Joanna's spine now as she recalled the bitterness in his voice. Up ahead a public bus had tipped over on its side and passengers were blithely scrambling out the windows as peddlers plied them with mangoes.

Farther on, a makeshift fair blared scratchy Indian film songs as two men hand-cranked a rickety wooden Ferris wheel stuffed full of schoolgirls in navy and pink, and all around the edges families camped under black tarpaulins or shreds of filthy matting. Lepers crouched caressing their wounds. Snake charmers held up cobras. And there, that old, old man in a soiled *lungi* curled down at the feet of a fat young dandy wearing movie star sunglasses. Joanna felt a surge of despair. Who exactly was in charge of doling out power in this world, and why did it always seem to wind up in the hands of those who deserved it least?

She braked to avoid a sauntering cow and squeezed the car between two battered cycle rickshaws in front of Safe Haven. In frustration she banged the heel of her hand, inadvertently tooting the horn. A child standing too close to the car jumped back as if struck, then immediately started forward again.

Joanna braced for the expected thrust of a palm through the open window, the stroking, pleading flurry of fingers demanding money or sweets – or perhaps delivering a trumped-up accusation that she *had* been struck. But though the girl was scrawny, bedraggled, and filthy as a beggar, her hair matted and her pajamalike *salwar kameez* stiff with embedded dust, she stood with dignity, watching and waiting as if expected.

In fact, on closer examination, Joanna did recognize her. Two weeks earlier she'd received an alert from the Vigilance Society about a 'blue-eyed hill child,' ten, maybe eleven years old, believed to be a kidnap victim living in a brothel in the red-light district. The rescue agencies kept an eye out for girls around this age because there was still a chance of taking them into custody before they were initiated into prostitution. Joanna and her assistant, Vijay Lal, had investigated and promptly located the child. There was no mistaking her identity; the eyes marked her, even from a distance. They were aquamarine in color, almost Chinese in shape, and they burned so brightly they might have been lit from within. Her skin was golden, and though she'd worn the same clothing and seemed familiar with the other girls of G. B. Road, she had looked distinctly out of place, solitary even in the crowded lane. The expression on her face – neither forlorn nor self-pitying, but strangely reserved – alerted Joanna that this was an exceptional child.

Unfortunately, she had not had the forethought that day to secure a search warrant. If the child had come forward and asked for asylum, all would have been well. But she ducked from their approach, and they were forced to leave without her. When they returned a few days later with the necessary warrant, the girl was nowhere to be found.

Now those same eyes trained on Joanna, waiting for her to get out of the car. Which she did slowly, closing the door with her hip. Without speaking, she extended her right hand.

The child stared at her naked fingers. No gloves. Perhaps this seemed too intimate, a brute violation of caste code, but just as Joanna was about to pull back, the girl snatched at her fingers, all but crushing them in her own small, powerful hands.

'I am called Kamla,' she said loudly in English. 'You are Mrs Shaw.'

3

Everything had changed after I was returned from the police station. Indrani beat me with a leather thong – as a warning, she said. I saw her as an old woman, but her greed and anger gave her strength, and the strap ate the flesh off my bones, so when she

20

had finished I could barely move. She locked me in the storage hut behind the house and refused to let Mira tend me, though I could hear through the wall Mira's arguments on my behalf. Why the child? my sister demanded. What can the child do? She cannot refuse. She would not dare to run away, and in any case, where could she go? She has no one, knows no one, is a stranger outside this house. But Indrani told Mira this was none of her concern.

Bharati had warned me, and now I knew. I was broken and worthless, yet only now was I worth the trouble of beating and locking. Now Indrani would take money for me. Now I had bled. But the bleeding had been forced on me. I was still a child. Still the girl they called Kamla. I told myself I had not changed, though I knew this was not true.

Days passed. The hut was mud-walled, tin-roofed, the floor packed dirt like an oven. During the day I could not move for the heat. My companions were old crates and packing boxes, scraps of cotton, a typewriter missing most of its keys, broken lamps, beer bottles, dented trays, a chair without a seat, a child's sandal with torn straps, rolled-up wall calendars six years old. In front, by the door stood sacks of *dal*, wheat, and rice, which attracted rats. I cleared a path through the rubbish into the farthest corner and made a nest of newspapers and cloth, but there was no way to stay clean. I tore rags from an old white mourning sari to sop the blood between my legs. Each time Indrani came for a cup of grain from her stores she would squint at me there in my corner before leaving a bowl of water and scraps. She would wrinkle her nose at my stink and make a noise of derision, but even when I called out to her, she did not speak. I chewed on bits of the raw grain, letting it soften in my mouth for many minutes before chewing and swallowing, and for the most part I kept it down. As my flesh healed, however, I grew weaker.

At night, when the darkness threatened to smother me, I first took comfort in the sounds coming through the walls. Calling, commanding, crying – they were alive. But soon I realized that these noises belonged mostly to men. They would shout out the full range of emotion as if megaphones were implanted in their hearts. Meanwhile the answering silence of my sisters seemed a dirge.

21

I thought of Mira and the way she would sometimes spy me passing and smile while a customer was on top of her. We conversed with our eyes, Mira and I. Hers were heavy and brown, brimming with her kindness. She had not been brought to the brothel, but walked in alone, and Indrani had accepted her with tenderness as she had me in my time. Eventually I learned that Mira, like me, had no mother or father, and the uncle who raised her had spoiled her for marriage, so she chose the only path left. Her debt was lighter than my own, but often I felt Mira's load to be weightier. When I asked her to tell me the colors of her dreams, she could not answer. When I asked her to sing me a song, she told me that she knew none. Yet I knew her secret smile. I knew that even when a man as hairy as a *pi* dog or as cruel as the demon Ravana rode her, he could not touch her smile. But I could.

Fatya and Shahnaz spent no smiles on me. They abided by themselves, sometimes even taking customers together. But though they had each other they were a joyless pair. Fatya's husband had sold her to the flash house before he left for Pakistan during Partition. Shahnaz had been tricked by a girlfriend's mother who said she would take her to the cinema and instead brought her to the brothel. Both were from Bengal and did not speak Hindi, but they chattered continuously between themselves and seemed to need no one else. When I crossed behind their screen I could see how they, like Mira, turned their faces as their customers heaved on top of them and the beads that jeweled their skin would slide away like tears.

I never saw any of my sisters actually cry, however, and now it was through their very silence that I felt myself disappearing. I realized that this was what Indrani intended. That she would take no chances until the last of my spirit was gone, and she could trade the body as she wished.

Then on the fifth morning I heard Mira calling softly outside the locked door. 'Kamla,' she whispered. 'Indrani says she will release you tomorrow. She has bought a new *charpoy*, raised a new curtain. You will stay beside me.'

This from Mira, my sister of smiles. Did she mean to warn, or reassure me? To this day I cannot say. But I knew from that instant, I must not allow Indrani to own my tomorrow.

I lay down to think, to make my plan. Instead, in the heat of the afternoon, I fell asleep. For the first time since my captivity, my dreams filled with color and song. I awoke clutching my own leg, but in my thoughts I was clinging to a hand that would lead me to safety. I had blamed Mrs Shaw. Even now I understood that my freedom would have stretched another month, perhaps another year but for her intrusion. Yet I knew in my heart that Indrani, not Mrs Shaw, had called for Golba. Indrani had witnessed Mrs Shaw's gesture, had seen her reaching for me. That pointed finger was not an accusation but an offer of safety. Surely Mrs Shaw had not meant to harm me! No, it was Indrani who wanted to teach me a lesson, and the police were only too happy to oblige. I must be taught to keep quiet. And so my situation was caused by Mrs Shaw and not Mrs Shaw. And perhaps she would never come again. But if she had extended her hand to me once, would she not do so again, even now? I did not know, but the thought of Mrs Shaw gave me strength. I remembered her bare hands against the white bandage, the sureness and quickness of her movements. I remembered the flashing amber of her eyes as they reached up and took me in. And I knew as suddenly as if she had spoken the words herself that my spirit was still intact.

Looking up I saw a crack of dusty light. Some days earlier, when I was still too weak to move, I had watched a rat nose through this seam in the roof. It was also a favorite passageway for lizards, and occasionally a pigeon would light here, pecking at the opening for bits of straw come loose from the mud brick. I was small, and the room was tall, but I thought if I could somehow climb up to that crack I might widen it enough to break through. I could not allow myself to wonder what I would do after that. I believed that Mrs Shaw's world was far from any I had ever known, and I had no idea how I would go there. But I did know what lay ahead if I stayed.

For the next hours, as the light through the crack changed from white to gold and finally dusky gray, I dragged the sturdiest sacks and boxes I could find into that back corner. All through the night, spurred on now by the same sounds of laughter and lust that days before had consoled me, I tested my ladder, climbing and tumbling, rising again until finally I succeeded in pressing my palm against the tin roofing.

The scraping when I pushed seemed as loud as a *tonga* horn, but gradually, bit by bit, I forced the gap wider. The dark morning air rushed through like water. I could hear the chug and shuffle of women rising to their chores, the wooden creak of bullock carts on their way to the river. Birdsong.

Fortunately, I was as narrow and light as I was weak. I felt for a chink in the wall with my toes and stretched my arms out and over the top. The sun was just coming up. A twist of smoke leaked from the stovepipe at the other end of the roof. That would be Bharati, starting a fire to cook breakfast for Shanta. Quickly, silently, I slithered down the outside wall until I hung from my fingers, then dropped the remaining distance to the ground. As I began to run I heard Indrani screeching for her tea.

Looking back, I realize that the only reason I was able to escape was the time of day. A few hours earlier or later, every doorway along the lane would have bristled with arms reaching out to catch me – friends of Indrani's, thugs visiting the brothels, *babus* trying to be helpful. As it was, the merchants who operated the ground-floor shops that fronted on G. B. Road were opening for business, and I could hear the grind of buses and horns barking from that direction. But most of the residents of this alley slept until late morning. Only Surie and his mother caught sight of me as I raced away, and they were not yet sufficiently recovered from their burns to give chase. Soon I was running along streets I had never seen before.

I had no plan, you see, no sense of the city. Although I had traveled hundreds, even thousands of miles to get here, in Delhi I was not allowed to leave our lane. *You will be kidnapped. You will be raped. The police will arrest you. Beggars will attack you.* These were the dire threats with which Indrani had kept me close. But now all but the last of these things had been done to me, and if I was myself a beggar, then why should other beggars attack me? The only fear I felt now was of Indrani and the *goondas* I was sure she would soon enlist to find me. There was a girl I had known from another flash house who was caught trying to escape, and when the *goondas* brought her back, the flesh from inside her body was hanging between her legs. I needed to get away from the red-light district as quickly as possible, but where would I go *to*?

24

The general flow of carts and bicycles led me first to the banks of the Yamuna River, where I found throngs of *dhobis* doing their morning wash. I was so tired and weak that the motion of the laundrymen's arms, the long white sausages of cloth arcing high and then smashing down on the wet stones, mesmerized me. The rhythmic sound, the unison, made me think of a flock of cranes, though I could not have named them as cranes but as birds I dimly recalled from a river buried in my childhood. Coming back to myself, I bathed and drank. I loosened my hair until it streamed about me in the water. I was free, yet this freedom was meaningless. I could beg, but as a beggar without protection, I would soon end up in another flash house or worse, one of the cage brothels I'd been told of, where girls were penned like animals. I could apply for work as a maid, but who would hire a scrawny child? The same for factory work. And in every case I would be at the mercy of men, though I no longer believed men had any mercy. Mira had mercy, but no power. Only Mrs Shaw possessed both.

I asked the *dhobis* if they knew where the *firenghi* lived and worked. They told me to go to New Delhi, on the other side of the city. By bicycle or bus only half an hour away. I had no bicycle or money for the bus, so I set off on foot. By day's end I had made my way to the white colonnades of Connaught Place. I had discovered the broad, tree-lined avenues designed in the time of the British. I had even tasted *firenghi* food, in the form of a sandwich dropped on the pavement by a small yellow-haired boy. That sandwich was all I had to eat until late that night, when I heard a commotion down an alley and found a group of street children scavenging scraps from behind a restaurant. I joined the group – four boys and two other girls about my age – and they led me to a park where the shrubbery was dense enough to conceal us as we slept. But when I woke, the others had left, and I was as lost as ever.

The size and strangeness of the city alone threatened to defeat me. Crossing the busy streets I would cleave to wandering cows so as not to be struck by the trucks and buses whirling past. When I came to the sweeping lawns near the government palaces I shrank like a mouse back into the hubbub of the smaller streets rather than risk walking in such open spaces. In one of the bazaars I picked up a yellow rag, which I wound about my head as a disguise. I pinched a salted plum here, a betel leaf there. I followed a group of passing foreigners in the hope they might lead me to Mrs Shaw. They led me to a street of white palaces just like the home I had imagined for Mrs Shaw, and even though I did not find her there, I discovered to my delight that I was slender enough to pass between the bars of certain private gates. For the next three nights I slept in the gardens of the rich.

These were cherished hiding grounds, so carefully groomed and tended that the very earth smelled privileged. Soft and rich and dark, the dirt held me like a mattress, and with summer arriving I was not cold. Sometimes, if the *mali* had watered late in the day, I would bury my hot feet in the mud, or scoop a cold pack of it onto my legs and arms where the skin was still raw. I would lie behind beds of cannas or underneath the drape of an oleander bush. Snails and centipedes would work their way over me, and through the foliage I would watch the lights of the house attached to the garden, the silhouettes of family and servants moving through their evening rituals. Sometimes there were children with loud, shrill voices, sometimes scolding, sometimes soothing ayahs. Once a foreign couple sat on their veranda not ten feet away, though it was so dark that I knew they would not see me, and they argued until the *memsahib* was in tears. I had been pretending that the couple were Mrs Shaw and her husband, and the lady's evident misery was causing me some distress until I realized that their discussion centered around a certain *fancy dress* the *sahib* disliked! No, I thought fiercely, Mrs Shaw would never waste her tears over such a thing. My indignation rekindled my desire to locate the real Mrs Shaw, and long before the *mali* could catch me the next morning I was on my way.

Mrs Shaw. I turned the name over and over on my tongue. I had heard her Hindu escort address her as they wandered through the district, and committed it to memory on the spot. The name was as much a part of her as the amber color of her hair or the emphasis of her smile. Little enough good it would do me. In those days I could speak bits and pieces of four languages – Hindustani, Urdu, English, and my native tongue – but I was penniless, and knew nothing of Delhi society. Today I might look in the telephone listings, or ask at the American embassy. I might go to the International School and ask one of the *chowkidar* if he had seen a woman of such and such description. But then New Delhi was to me a puzzle of walls and faces, glittering storefronts and meaningless signs. 'Mrs Shaw?' one old *mali* repeated, smacking his toothless mouth at the question. 'Why not ask for Mrs Singh, or Mrs Mukherjee, or Mrs Jain?'

'Are there so many?' I asked, incredulous.

'As many as there are *memsahib*,' replied the old liar. Almost certainly, he did not know even his own *memsahib*'s name, but I took him for an expert and went on my way quite undone.

I had only her image to go by. An image of matching hair and eyes, the color of dying fire. Of narrow bones and thin wrists, a bird's neck and big feet in black strap shoes. Of dresses that clung to the dampness of her skin and caught the breezes as she walked. I thought of the hollows of her cheeks, the deep settings of her eyes, the high square forehead and sharpened jawline with small knots of muscle that betrayed her tense nature. As I wound through the crowds, ducking out of the way of *tongas* and taxis, I practiced carving her image with words.

Meanwhile I strained to listen to the talk of the markets, the drivers for hire huddled outside big hotels, the schoolboys in their crisp white cricket uniforms assembling in the park. By nightfall of my fifth day on the streets I had found my way to a monument of an *angrezi*, very tall, with hat and waistcoat and sword in hand. Taller trees around him cast shadows in the twilight. A group of girls leaned against the statue, calling to one another, laughing.

They wore thin saris tied low across the belly and left their heads uncovered. The jitter of their glass bangles sounded like laughter through the groan of traffic. The road here was a small roundabout faced by compound walls, with other roads pulling like spokes of a wheel. So many directions to flee, I thought, as I worked up the courage to approach. A bicycle rickshaw slowed as if on parade, though I understood it was the girls who were on display, while the passenger, invisible in his covered cab, was the spectator. The cab stopped in front of a short, thick girl with round cheeks and flowing hair. A shirt-sleeved arm parted the oilcloth canopy. She climbed in, and the vehicle jerked away.

'Hey, little sister,' called a voice. 'Better shut your eyes or they'll fall out of your head.' The girls all laughed, but it was not malicious laughter, and when they summoned me to join them I crossed, dodging cows and bicycles and *pi* dogs. The scents of rose petals and jasmine floated from their skin. Their eyes were rimmed with collyrium, their mouths with vermilion, and the gems in their noses and earlobes twinkled. They sniggered at my rags, the dust in my hair. 'You will do no business like this,' they warned. 'Not even at your age.'

Their attention was warm and soothing as *nan,* and I wished I had returned to the river to bathe, only so that these girls might stretch a hand, might feel moved to pet me. To praise me. But perhaps this failure on my part was also my saving, for their disgust, the friendly joking that now turned disdainful reminded me of my true business here. Before the next customer could approach, before they had begun to tire of me, I called out the words I had rehearsed that day. I described the foreign woman with the kind, not beautiful face, the body of sharp turns and soft skin and ignorant gestures. I did not speak of rescue, did not call her Mrs Shaw. I only said she was known by the girls of the flash house and asked if she ever came here.

None knew her. In fact, a chill current seemed to sweep among the girls at the mention of a *firenghi* who would travel in their midst. I had not, after all, said what possessed her to seek their company. And then an automobile crept toward us, and the girls edged apart, each striking a pose like the cinema posters, hands on hips, lips pushed forward, saris draped to show off a comely throat or midriff or breast. But as I drew out of sight, a hiss beckoned me forward.

The eldest of the street girls hung back from the others. As I approached I saw that her eyes were so heavily blackened that they appeared like gouges in her skull. Her sari was threadbare and, beneath, she wore nothing. Painted shadows exaggerated the roundness of her breasts and hips, and rouge enlarged the nipples. She reeked of sandalwood. After the car had stopped by one of the other girls, she turned to me. 'This woman you seek,' she whispered. 'She is good *firenghi*?' At my nod, she said, 'Yes. I know her.

Mrs Shaw. I have seen her rescue home. There is nothing for me there. But you are still young.'

Quickly, she spat out an address, directions, which I committed to memory without understanding. Then she pushed me away.

I repeated the address to beggars, sweepers, rock pickers, ayahs on their way to work in the foreign houses. Two mornings later, I was waiting outside the gate of Salamat Jannat – Safe Haven – when Mrs Shaw stepped out of her small green automobile.

4

First she ate. In the relative privacy of Joanna's office, with the windows open to the courtyard and the ceiling fan doing its best, the child stuffed herself with *nan* and vegetable *bhaji* and *lhassi* and fresh mango. Joanna was both impressed and concerned by the sheer volume she consumed. She must not have eaten in days. But though she used her hands greedily and unabashedly, there was something dignified about the way she sat, erect and silent, shoveling rice into her mouth, catching the occasional stray grain on a fingertip, sliding it between her lips with an amused – yes, amused – glance up at Joanna. She was pleased with herself. That was it. After Joanna had made two trips to rescue her, she instead had come here on her own. Filthy, she was, too, and raggedly hollow-eyed, yet there was nothing needy about her expression. She appeared to believe she deserved this food, this attention and all the protection that Joanna wished she could give her, as if it were her due.

Joanna pretended to busy herself with papers while the girl ate undisturbed. Salamat Jannat was a 'Safe Haven' in name only. In reality it was little more than a dumping ground for girls remanded by the courts. There were sixteen of these inmates at the moment, all older than this child and most of them seasoned harlots, some wild and mean, some devious. As a newcomer to India and only recently appointed director of the home, Joanna had no choice but to temper her expectations. She could document the girls' exploitation and see that they received the necessary medical attention for the gonorrhea and syphilis, the abrasions and contusions, addictions and hysteria

29

that were the side effects of their trade. She could offer them the means and contacts to attempt a different livelihood, but despite her best efforts, the girls were loath to give up their lifestyle. Among her charges were two *devadasi*, 'temple girls' raised from birth to believe that sex was their spiritual calling. Another was a Beria, sent by her family into prostitution as a mandatory vocation – as were all the girls from her village according to centuries-old tradition. Still others had been lured to Delhi by friends or relatives promising easy money, or had fled alcoholic parents who would only beat them and send them back to the street if they went home. Hindu and Muslim cultures alike taught these girls that they were good for nothing but more of the same that had spoiled them. In the face of such teaching, Joanna knew that promises of hope must be made with care.

But this girl – Kamla – was obviously different. Her youth – and those arresting eyes – were the least of it. She stole another glance as the girl lifted her glass of *lhassi* with both hands and drank so deeply that her throat rippled. None of the other girls had come here voluntarily, let alone found their own way. And it could not be the home's reputation that had drawn her but some reading she had taken on Joanna herself. Joanna found it at once poignant and more than a little daunting to think how this child must have sized her up that day at the brothel, secretly marking her, then traveled the full length of the city to imagined sanctuary. How could Joanna not honor such faith? Certainly, she felt compelled to try.

Finally Kamla finished eating, wiped her mouth, and accepted a cup of milk tea. Joanna summoned her young assistant, Vijay Lal, to translate, and asked the child to tell them about herself. She had expected that 'I am called Kamla. You are Mrs Shaw' would exhaust the girl's English, but to her surprise, the tale that now tumbled unhesitatingly forth was studded with phrases such as 'under arrest,' 'flash house,' and 'break free,' which suggested either that the brothel she'd escaped had an unusually educated clientele or that the girl herself had been exposed to English earlier in her life. Joanna made a note of this, along with the core details of her story. Kamla, it seemed, had been sold by her family to the brothel keeper – or *gharwali* – when she was almost too young to remember. She had served as a kind of maidservant to the prostitutes, and she had never considered running away until one day recently when the police had come. She'd been used and beaten. Only then did she flee. She remembered that Mrs Shaw had helped the Untouchable boy and his mother. (So the police had taken Kamla *after* her own attempt to rescue the girl, Joanna noted with dismay.) Kamla thought Mrs Shaw might help her. It took seven days and nights but at last she had found her way here.

Vijay and Joanna exchanged looks. The young Hindu had a kind heart, but he was not one for complications. The girl's suggestion that the police had raped her was an indisputable complication. And Vijay clearly did not sympathize with Kamla. To him she was just another case to record, file, and dispatch. Neither the blue eyes nor the fair skin nor the defiance of her spirit shifted him out of his usual mode of thinking. More trouble than she is worth, his look warned.

Joanna held his gaze and shook her head. 'Tell her she is safe here.'

He spoke the words, but Kamla frowned. Her head wiggled in an Indian shrug, at once accepting and dismissing the assurance. Joanna leaned forward – they were seated across a low brass table from each other – and stroked the back of the girl's right hand. The blue eyes lifted as Joanna's fingers closed around the delicate wrist. She could feel the throb of Kamla's pulse lining up with her own. '*I* will keep you safe,' she promised.

Kamla smiled and nodded.

Joanna let her go. She felt Vijay watching, but turned away. She'd been warned not to get personally invested in people who were down and out, and not just here at Salamat Jannat. Over and over again, this lesson had been pounded into her by her teachers back in graduate school, by supervisors on her first jobs, at an adoption agency in Oakland, and later working with war refugees. 'We're like doctors,' one of her co-workers had observed. 'A certain number of losses are inevitable, and it's not possible to predict which they'll be. If we identify too closely with the people we lose, then we risk losing ourselves.'

'One step removed,' Aidan called it. In his profession this was considered journalistic objectivity. A margin of safety that divided rescuers from rescuees, observers from combatants. Aidan himself, of course, routinely crossed that line. This was, in fact, precisely what had gotten them into their current political fix. Yet even though Joanna sometimes despaired over her husband's stubbornness in taking such risks, she wouldn't have him any other way.

Well, this blue-eyed child was a risk she was willing – no, determined – to take.

She summoned the ayah to help, but attended personally as Kamla was bathed and deloused. Her body was emaciated, her back and arms covered with bruises and sores, and even though the girl did not make a sound, Joanna grimaced as she gently soaped the raw flesh. Afterward, Kamla lay rigid on the *charpoy* that served as an examining table while a public health nurse from the neighborhood clinic assessed the damage.

'Easy, child,' soothed the nurse, a Christian Dravidian with skin the color of bittersweet chocolate. Joanna held Kamla's hand. The tightness of her grip was the only sign the girl gave of fear, but the nurse gently coaxed even that to gradually relax. The smell of alcohol seemed sharper than her wince of pain at the slide of the needle into her flesh. 'Penicillin,' the nurse apologized, as if Kamla could have known what this meant.

What it meant was inscribed on her chart. *Rectal fissure, lacerated vaginal wall, ruptured perineum. Infection of reproductive and urinary tracts may compromise future fertility.*

Joanna closed her eyes and swallowed hard. If she'd rescued Kamla that first day at the brothel, this never would have happened.

'Such injuries are not uncommon,' the nurse said as Joanna helped Kamla into a fresh green cotton tunic and pants. 'But ordinarily, a child in this condition would be doubled over in pain.'

Joanna looked down at the small, insistent fingers threading through her own. She met those blue-green eyes. 'I do not think our Kamla is any ordinary child.'

Yet when she showed her to a quiet corner of the communal sleeping room, the girl would not release her arm. Joanna tried to reassure her, 'No harm will come to you here.' Her voice was strong and sure, but she remembered nights when Simon, aged three, would clutch her in just this way and demand that she console him about death. One of his cats had died, and for weeks he would ask when he, too, would die, and she and Daddy, and who would die first, and then would she promise not to die, or let

32

Daddy die, or him. And she'd promised, though she felt like a liar, for Aidan was still in China then, and what control, anyway, did one have over such things? Now, again, she was making a promise she could not guarantee. She'd already failed this child once.

She sat by the bedside, humming a lullaby as the girl curled herself into a ball and reluctantly let her exhaustion overtake her. What had happened to Kamla at the hands of the police might not be uncommon, Joanna thought, but the trust she showed in telling this story was. 'I hate this inspector,' Vijay said she had told him. 'He comes to the flash house, sits with *gharwali.* He drinks his whiskey, and when my sister Mira is passing he will take her flesh between his fat fingers, he will squeeze until she cries out, and he only laughs and says she is begging, then he must go with her.'

'And he is one of the men who forced himself on you?' Joanna had asked.

Kamla tipped her head, talking rapidly. 'In the night there is no light,' Vijay translated. 'She says, the men grunt and sweat and shove like animals.' He dropped his gaze. 'Like goats. Like pigs. Only one is smelling like fish.'

Kamla's eyes locked on Joanna's. Then, 'It is my first time, Mrs Shaw.'

The clarity and control of her voice as she uttered these last words in English had stunned Joanna all over again. She did not press for more. But she also knew that protecting this girl would not be a simple matter.

She stroked the sleeping child's forehead, smoothing tendrils of damp black hair behind one ear. She owed it to Kamla, and to herself. She would not fail her again.

Pulling the curtain to the sleeping room behind her, Joanna returned to her office. The bungalow was quiet, as the other girls now, too, settled to rest through the day's worst heat. Vijay had retired to his cubicle on the other side of the compound to review the home's account books. Joanna thought for a moment, then picked up the telephone and called her superior, Hari Kaushal. Typically evasive, he said he would be passing that way within the hour, and they could discuss whatever concerned her then.

Hari was no fonder of complications than Vijay, which was why he'd signed her on. Not a month after her arrival in Delhi, Joanna had attended an embassy cocktail party, and by way of introducing herself was telling Nancy Minton, the US Ambassador's wife, about her career as a social worker, especially how her work with refugee relief had saved her sanity when Aidan was overseas during the war. She'd like to find something like that here in India, she was saying when Nancy introduced Hari. The dapper Bengali sociologist had recently been appointed to head the government Social Welfare Committee's Moral Hygiene Programme. Before she knew it he was offering her the directorship at Salamat Jannat, a post that had been vacant for nearly a year. Joanna saw it as a chance to involve herself in the country. A viable defense against the stultifying teas and craft projects of the American Women's Club. In return, Hari had not balked at such incidental obstacles as her citizenship or her complete unfamiliarity with Indian habits, customs, and language, never mind the realm of prostitution. He had also not mentioned salary. Joanna, alone of the rescue home's staff of four, worked without pay, and five months later, this was still a bone of contention, though Hari insisted he had put in a request, and approval was 'most certainly just now coming.'

A broad voice behind her broke into her thoughts. 'Behold, the rescuer in her element!' She turned to find Aidan's friend Lawrence Malcolm leaning in through the low doorway.

'Lawrence!' She frowned in confusion. 'What are you doing here?'

'Sorry to surprise you,' he said. 'Won't take a minute.' He removed his solar topee and combed a hand haphazardly through his damp hair as he gave her one of his unsettling smiles. Lawrence's eyes were different colors – one a metallic gray, the other hazel green. Though Joanna had known him now a month and, up until Aidan's departure, had been seeing him almost daily, this singular feature still threw her off balance.

She got up and moved a chair for him, cranked up the ceiling fan. Sweat drizzled down her back. It was far too hot for company, but she tried to make light of this. 'Why aren't you sleeping like the rest of the world?'

He grinned. 'Little heat never bothered me.'

'No. So Aidan told me.' The two men had become friends in the war, during which they'd reportedly had more than a few 'heated' adventures, including a midsummer trek across Burma to escape the Japanese. Out of touch for seven years, they'd met up again by chance last month in Kabul, and Lawrence followed Aidan back to Delhi. 'He's been an aimless mess ever since his boy died,' Aidan told her. 'He could use some friends.' But welcoming him into the family was more than simple charity. Lawrence had worked with the Australian Foreign Office. He 'understood' politics, and Aidan felt comfortable confiding in him about his work, his career, even – or perhaps especially – about his troubles with the FBI. He actually said he'd trust Lawrence with his life.

Joanna couldn't quite see it, herself. Even now, Lawrence sat without looking, his chair too close to the desk. He hadn't left room for his knees, so he had to edge back, in the process tipping the bamboo frame, and when the legs came down again, they hit the stone floor with a crack. Joanna half expected the seat to splinter beneath Lawrence's clumsy weight. Aidan, by contrast, was a model of grace and poise. The two friends were an odd pair, to say the least.

Lawrence cleared his throat. 'I just happened to be passing this way.'

'The girls are asleep. Otherwise I'd give you a tour.'

'No. That's all right.' He looked past her to the studio photograph hanging on the wall. Aidan and Simon dressed as cowboys, Simon in his full Roy Rogers getup, Aidan in a ten-gallon hat, both of them leaning on toy rifles. They'd given it to her last Christmas. 'Cowboys in India,' Aidan had printed across the bottom.

Lawrence dropped his eyes. When he spoke, his voice was brighter than his face. 'I was wondering if I might collect Simon at school, take him to the Cecil for a dunk?'

Joanna hesitated. Before Aidan left, he'd picked up Simon from school almost every afternoon and taken him to the Cecil to swim. It was one of just three hotels in Delhi that had a swimming pool, and often Lawrence would join them. Lawrence, unlike Aidan, liked to swim himself, which had immediately won Simon over. But Simon had a reckless streak. The krait with the toad in its belly stuck in her mind. Along with the fact that Lawrence's young son had died in some sort of accident (Aidan either didn't know or refused to tell her the specifics) when Lawrence was present. If she

35

could get away herself to join them, she'd have no qualms, but she needed to resolve this new girl's status, and she wasn't sure how long that might take.

'That's kind,' she said. 'I'm sure he'd love it, but ... he's busy today ... He—'

She felt his eyes on her even as she refused to look at him. She hated lying. Why was she, anyway? If Aidan would trust Lawrence with his own life, surely he'd trust him with Simon. And if Aidan would, why shouldn't she?

But before she could reverse herself, Vijay popped his head around the door. 'Mr Kaushal is here, Mem.'

And in the next breath Hari Kaushal swept into the office, immediately taking charge.

As always, Hari was dressed after the fashion of Prime Minister Nehru, in a starched white *khadi* waistcoat with a red rose in the lapel. His thinning black hair lay smooth across the dome of his head, and his dark eyes snapped beneath a prominent brow. Vijay, who was in awe of Hari's authority, followed by several paces.

Hari clasped Joanna's right hand warmly in both of his own. 'So good to see you looking so well.' But this was his standard greeting. He had already turned to her other visitor.

'This is Lawrence Malcolm.' Then she added, 'A friend of my husband. Hari Kaushal, my boss.'

'Foolish me.' Lawrence shook Hari's extended hand. 'I thought Jo was the boss.'

'Indeed she is.' Hari beamed at Joanna. His standard trick. Paying in praise. She sighed, and Hari turned back to Lawrence. 'Are you also a journalist, like Mr Shaw?'

'Not quite.' Lawrence jiggled the change in his shorts pockets. 'More of a researcher these days.'

Hari waved them to sit down, so as Vijay scurried off in search of snacks they rearranged the three available chairs around the low brass table in the corner.

'What are you researching?' Hari asked.

'I s'pose you could say I'm revisiting my boyhood. Got hooked on the Great Game back in school – all that old Kipling lore, you know.'

Hari rolled his eyes. They were large round black eyes that bulged enough to make this a theatrical display. 'Spies and shadows.

36

Don't tell me you're another would-be Kim?' Joanna could see he was taken with Lawrence.

Lawrence smiled. 'Truth be told, I haven't half Kim's sense of adventure, nor Colonel Creighton's strategic omniscience. But I'm fascinated by the men that did have. The actual adventurers, explorers, spies – whatever you like to call them. Not just the British, but the Indians, and Russians as well, of course. Men who made their own maps, so to speak. I've fantasies of writing a book about them.'

In fact, this book was considerably more than a fantasy, and Joanna had spent more than her share of afternoons listening to Lawrence and Aidan arguing about the Great Game. The whole debate bored her; as far as she was concerned, Kipling had got it right, and this hundred-year 'game' between Britain and Russia for access to India through Central Asia really was little more than a contest between overgrown boys. But Aidan and Lawrence were hooked. Was it an example of colonial paranoia, as Aidan insisted, or a warranted defense against Russian expansionism? Did the benefits of exploration outweigh the imperialist mischief, as Lawrence maintained, or had British meddling permanently destabilized Central Asia? The last thing Jo wanted was to sit here while Lawrence dragged Hari down into it, but if she was to turn the conversation, she had better act quickly.

'I'm sorry to interrupt,' she said. 'But there was a business reason I called you, Hari. And thank you for coming so promptly, but the thing is, that hill child I told you about is here, and I'm not sure how to proceed.'

Vijay returned bearing a pitcher of lemonade and a plate of *pakoras*. Joanna hesitated. She felt uncomfortable discussing the particulars of this case in front of Lawrence. But Hari was rolling his hand for her to continue, so as succinctly as possible she described the alert they'd received weeks ago from the Vigilance Society, the two burn victims she had treated when she went out to investigate, and how a girl fitting the alert had come forward to watch. She told of the delays she and Vijay encountered at the magistrate's office before being granted a warrant to take her into custody, about their return, then, to G. B. Road only to find the girl vanished and no one in the neighborhood willing to admit she'd ever been there. And without going into intimate detail, she reported Kamla's rape and subsequent escape from the brothel.

When she finished, Hari merely shrugged as if to say, one more, one less, one had to be philosophical.

'But she came here on her *own*,' Joanna said. 'Don't you see? The reason she was so desperate to find us is that she was raped. By the *police*.'

Hari slid his thumbs together and tapped them against his glass. 'What do you wish to do?'

'What do you think! A crime's been committed – one of many, no doubt, but if it is the police—'

'I see several problems,' Hari interrupted. 'First, the judicial system is still in transition. Even if we bring this case before the courts now, it is bound to drag on for months. By then we will be governed by the new constitution that goes into effect this coming January. The case will no longer be argued by British advisors but by Indian prosecutors and advocates, and will bear the unique stamp of Indian reasoning. A legal action against Indian police so soon after the horrors of Partition, and over what many will consider such a trivial offense—'

'Trivial!'

'I am only telling you how the politicians will view this.'

'Damn the politicians!'

'Hear, hear!' Lawrence lifted his glass in a toast, then threw Hari a shamefaced smile as Joanna shook her head in exasperation. 'I've done a turn or two in government myself, so I know just how sorry a lot we are.'

Hari sat back and made a tent of his manicured fingers. Vijay poured more *nimbu pani*.

She tried again. 'I want justice for the crime that's been done this girl. I'm not asking to run for office.'

Hari shook his head. 'I try to remember what a short time you have been in India, Joanna. You did not live through last year, the year before that, or the fifty that preceded our Independence. You did not have to stand by as your best friends were rounded up like dogs and thrown into prison for daring to suggest that after two centuries of colonial rule, the British had overstayed their welcome. You did not bid your former schoolmates goodbye as they fled for

38

their lives over some arbitrary border that had yet to be marked by an Englishman who had never set foot in this country. Nor did you witness the insanity of Partition, when the border he drew was discovered to slice right through villages, towns, hospitals, schools, even individual homes, turning brothers against fathers, against one another. Co-workers hacking each other to bits, your own relatives hauling a machine gun to the corner and turning it on your neighbors. Women with no breasts, no hands, paraded naked through the streets. Wells overflowing with corpses.' He took a shuddering breath and raised his eyes to the ceiling. 'Barely two years ago . . . babies were nailed to the walls on iron spikes! And rape – you have no idea what is rape, Joanna. Yes, I called your crime a trivial one because next to what this country has suffered . . .' He snapped his fingers. 'It is nothing.'

In the thudding silence that followed, he shifted. 'Nevertheless, because this is India, even such a nothing case is political.'

Joanna kneaded a fold in her skirt. 'Are you advising me to ignore this?'

'I am merely telling you that your protests will do little good. The police today are local heroes. They are the survivors, the peacekeepers. We have no United Nations mediators here as they have up in Kashmir. We have been branded as savages by the entire Western world, and the British and friends are only too glad to be rid of their obligation to us. They have cut themselves a deal that allows them to continue dipping into our saucepots for profit, but they no longer have to clean up the messes or put out the fires that result when these saucepots overflow.'

Joanna thought of Aidan, also branded a kind of savage by the local heroes back home, now wandering around Kashmir trying to expose the treachery among those same UN mediators in order to save his political skin. The thought inflamed her all over again. 'Is that what this little girl is? A messy saucepot?'

Lawrence snorted, obviously enjoying Joanna's indignation. She tried to ignore him. 'You know, Hari, I can't tell whether you're eulogizing the British, or vilifying them. What am I doing here if there's no recourse for these girls?'

'You are protecting them. Perhaps, in a few cases, you will rehabilitate them.'

'But they're not what needs rehabilitating! What have *they* done wrong? You know, I give up. First you say there's nothing we can do against the brothels. They're old as the gods, you tell me. And there's no action we can take against the pimps and *goondas* that back them up, because that would be too dangerous. And the parents and husbands that sell these girls? No, too far-flung, too many jurisdictions. Besides, in some tribes, in some villages, in some castes daughters are expected to support whole clans by selling their bodies, so it would be against tradition to interfere!'

'You're getting yourself worked up for no purpose,' said Hari. 'You volunteered for this position, remember?'

'And have I done so poorly that you'd have me quit?'

Hari smiled. 'You've done a splendid job, Joanna. This is not at all what I am saying, and you know it.'

'What I hear you saying is, there's no point in doing my job at all!'

Hari leaned forward, took a pinch from the bowl of fennel seeds and sugar on the snack tray and chewed it thoughtfully. 'It is important to be realistic. I feel that already we have lost sight of this poor child even now lying in the other room. We are permitting ourselves to be dragged down into a debate of politics and police—'

'And justice,' interrupted Joanna. 'But who cares about that?'

'I do,' said Lawrence in such a tone that he might have been teasing, and he might have been in earnest. Joanna met his eyes briefly, caught a conspiratorial nod, and looked away in frustration.

She got up and went to the doorway. Beyond the veranda, the courtyard simmered, dusty green in the shade, blinding in the sun. The breeze generated by the wooden ceiling fan barely nudged the strands of hair pasted to her neck. It was simply too hot for argument, too hot to know for sure what was worth fighting for – or against.

Behind her, Hari warned, 'You'll need a remand order to keep her.'

'Is that a problem?' asked Lawrence.

She turned to see Hari wiggling his head. 'Remand orders come from magistrates. Magistrates depend on policemen, and in many cases are themselves former policemen.'

'And when *do* magistrates issue remand orders for these girls?' Lawrence asked.

'That depends. Alas, too often, it is a matter of this.' Hari rubbed his fingertips together. 'Usually there is some interested party agitating for a particular girl. Sometimes this is a sympathetic *babu* who wishes the girl well without wishing to accept full responsibility himself. By coaxing the magistrate to issue a remand order, he feels he has "rescued" her even if he never sees her again. Sometimes the petitioner is a missionary Christian who hopes to convert the girl. Sometimes it is a well-intentioned social worker such as our Joanna. But then, too, certain magistrates issue remand orders for highly desirable young women because they know that the brothel owners and pimps will pay a pretty sum to get their beauties back. This sum is then divided between the magistrate and the police who bring the girls in.'

Lawrence crossed his ankles, slapping the sole of one sandal against his heel. 'Seems a simple solution to pay the buggers off.'

'Wait a minute,' Joanna said. According to Aidan, Lawrence was no stranger to the brothel trade, and what else he was willing to pay for was an open question. But Hari had no hesitation.

'I am afraid,' he told Lawrence, 'that as a government appointee, I *myself* am not at liberty to pay the buggers off, as you say. Salamat Jannat also is a government facility, and it would be most inappropriate for anyone associated with the home to attempt even such a seemingly simple solution.'

'But I'm not associated with the home.' Lawrence raised his palms. 'And who's to say I'm not as sympathetic as the next *babu*?'

Joanna shook her head. Vijay was staring slack-jawed as if Lawrence were proposing to take on all the *goondas* in Delhi with one hand behind his back. 'Whose money will you use?' she asked.

Lawrence's forehead pinched into an exaggerated frown. 'I believe I've a few quid stashed away. Seems a worthy cause.'

Hari stood up, extending his right hand to Lawrence. 'You are a friend, indeed. I only hope Joanna does not take too much advantage of your generosity.'

'We're paying off the very men who raped her. You do realize that?' she said.

Hari clucked his tongue. 'Not the *very* same men.'

'It's the old means or ends game, Jo,' said Lawrence, skewering her with his silver eye. 'Decide which matters most.'

Joanna felt at once that he was toying with her and that he was deadly serious. According to Aidan, money was not an issue for Lawrence, as his family owned a large sheep ranch in New South Wales, and for a man on sabbatical from government service, as he claimed to be, the time it would take to play out this charade was hardly a sacrifice. But she still didn't fully trust him . . . Couldn't they *see* the principle at risk?

'For the girl's sake,' Hari prodded her, 'the order should be written this afternoon.'

Joanna thought of the child sleeping in the next room. The trust she had placed in her 'Mrs Shaw,' in spite of all she'd suffered.

'All right,' she said grudgingly. 'If you're sure there's no other way.'

'Excellent.' Hari nodded. 'It is settled, then. Vijay will take you over, Lawrence, and you specify to the magistrate that the girl must be remanded to Salamat Jannat.'

Lawrence rotated the brim of his helmet between his fingertips. Joanna waited for him to say something, but after a moment he clapped the topee back on his head and followed the other two out without speaking another word.

Half an hour later she was still wrestling with her conscience when the ayah banged on her office door. 'Mem, police! Come quickly!'

Even under the massive courtyard neem tree, the light had gone liquid with heat, and the rounded features of the policeman standing there shone as if shellacked. He was a sturdy man with a babyish face. He introduced himself as Inspector Golba and said precisely the words she feared. He had come to collect the blue-eyed child.

'I understand that this is a rescue home for just such fallen girls,' he said, waving his hand in the direction of the bungalow, where a few of these 'fallen girls' stood yawning in the doorway. 'But surely, Mrs Shaw, you are aware that certain procedures must be followed.'

Joanna felt herself floundering. How did this man even know

Kamla was here, let alone the unusual circumstances of her arrival? And why was he taking such interest in this case? She needed somehow to stall him, buy time for that remand order to come through. It occurred to her that her debt to Lawrence had just multiplied.

'As I am aware,' she said, working to steady her voice, 'this child has requested asylum here, and until I myself have thoroughly documented her case I have no intention of releasing her to you or anyone else.'

The man drew a rolled sheaf of papers from his back pocket and lifted it above his head, exposing an underarm stain that stood out like an inkblot against his faded uniform khaki. 'Madam, I have instructions on highest authority!'

Joanna scrutinized the paper baton and made a calculated guess. She positioned her hands on her hips. The slightest crack would give her away. 'I don't care if you're acting under the authority of God Almighty, which I've every certainty you're not.'

The baton came down. 'Certain homes are having licensed supervisor, Mrs Shaw, these are official permitted homes. You are not licensed, I think.'

She swallowed. 'Are you threatening me, Inspector?'

He hitched up his leatherette belt, and floated his large head on the stem of his neck. Neither-yes-nor-no-but-maybe-both. He had the velvet, self-satisfied gaze of a man used to getting his own way. Joanna suppressed a mental image of Kamla's bruises and wounds.

She stepped deeper into the shade of the neem tree. His informants could be anyone, from neighbors outside the home to her own staff. And whether his papers were official or not for the moment was irrelevant. Though Joanna wouldn't risk looking toward the knot of girls now watching from the common room window, she sensed Kamla among them. She hoped the child had the wit to hide. She also fervently wished that Lawrence were still here.

The inspector stabbed the papers with his finger and started in again. 'Salamat Jannat has not been renewing its permit for more than two years.'

She forced herself to meet his eyes. 'You might as well know, Inspector, that I have already alerted my good friend, the American Ambassador Minton, to this case. He has promised to investigate.

43

Police abuse of powers is a red flag in any democracy, and particularly in a new republic such as India, it warrants close review.'

This was a grotesque lie, particularly in light of the sermon Hari had just delivered, but Aidan had often remarked that America was regarded with awe in India as the Other Colony That Got Away and Showed Up England in the Wars. Based on this, she took the chance that the Ambassador's name would get a rise.

To her relief, the officer's moist face again began to float from side to side. His mud-brown eyes widened, and the soft lips stretched revealing flat betel-stained teeth. He muttered so incoherently that whatever he was trying to say got lost in the louder whine of cicadas and the splash and tangle of street sounds. One of which was the metallic thunk of a bicycle dropping against the gate.

When the blue-uniformed messenger came striding across the courtyard Joanna felt like hugging him. Instead she said merely, 'A moment, Inspector.'

The messenger held out the telltale yellow envelope. 'Please excuse, *memsahib*. I am bringing a telegram for Mrs Joanna Shaw.'

Consciously slowing her movements, she dried her palms on the thin white cotton of her skirt and signed for receipt. Then she dismissed the messenger with a generous tip and slid her thumbnail under the flap of the envelope. The cable consisted of just a few lines. She stared down at the first of them.

'As I thought,' she said, feeling herself go numb even as her voice reverberated inside her skull. Stay focused. 'Ambassador Minton will be back in Delhi next week, and he has alerted me that he would like to personally interview the child in advance of his meeting with Mr Nehru. In the meantime, I am under no circumstances to surrender custody.' She dropped the hand gripping the telegram to her side. 'I don't believe we have anything further to discuss.'

Golba frowned, stopped wiggling his head. He eyed the message in her hand with evident suspicion, but after a moment's consideration he must have decided that if he asked to double-check her paper she might just ask to see his. 'I am not forgetting this, Mrs Shaw,' he warned. They stood glaring at each other for several long seconds. Then he cleared his throat with a lugubrious rattle and strode out the gate.

Joanna managed to wait until he was gone, then groped blindly for the stone bench behind her. She sank down and finished reading the cable. She read it again. And again.

PLANE CARRYING YOUR HUSBAND DISAPPEARED LADAKH RANGE DIFFICULT TERRAIN WEATHER INTERFERE SEARCH PARTY DETAILS TO FOLLOW AS AVAILABLE
GEN PETER FARR

She looked up to find that the hill child had crept beside her. The girl had a hand on her arm and was staring at her with those wide blue eyes. A look of longing and unabashed will.

Joanna reached out and pulled her to her. Perhaps some of the child's courage would rub off.

CHAPTER 2

1

Mrs Shaw had indeed protected me! I was watching from the veranda when she sent Golba away. More than that, he had gone with a look of shock, like a bull who finds himself outsmarted by a goat. But after he had gone, the fear in Mrs Shaw's face warned that the message in her hand had nothing to do with me. A crack had opened in that white disinfected palace of her life. I did not know its cause or exact location, but I could see that if I was to hold my claim on her, I must act at once.

I was clean. She had bathed me, fed me, dressed me in a freshly washed *salwar kameez*. And I had seen her touch those dirtier than I. After all, I was no Untouchable! So I summoned my courage and dared to reach out, to stroke her bare arm. I moved my fingertips light as butterfly wings from the soft, smooth curve where her shoulder emerged from her sleeveless white dress all the way to the knob of bone like ivory jutting from her elbow.

At first I was not sure she even noticed, though through that brief contact I read so much. The dampness and firmness of her skin, the color of her, pale as ginger except for the perfectly round – and to me, mesmerizing – moon of her vaccination mark. Even in that split second, I imagined this circle was a kind of sign, that she was a member of some great elite with supernatural powers. Perhaps these powers possessed her in the same way Indrani had possessed me. But if I could break away from the flash house and come to Mrs Shaw – actually lay my skin against hers – then might she not reach back to me?

I saw tears. Then she drew me to her and held me against her breast. I hardly dared breathe. I, Kamla, in Mrs Shaw's arms! When at length she pushed me back she stretched her fingers to my cheek and looked into me so deeply I could feel her inside. But she shook her head. 'I'm sorry,' she said. 'Something's happened – ' Her voice broke as if a bone had caught in her throat, and she looked away.

A commotion at the gate drew her attention. She cried out, 'Lawrence!' and, without so much as a backward glance, started across the yard. The other girls spilled forward now laughing, calling, preening for attention as if this safe haven were itself just another brothel. I held myself in my own arms, but the sensation was lost. Reluctantly I let go and turned my attention to this man Mrs Shaw called Lawrence.

He was surely the largest I had ever seen. Not so much in height, or even necessarily in girth, his mere presence seemed enormous. He had so much hair, for one thing, springing out from under his helmet and shirtsleeves, cascading down his arms and from the open throat of his collar, coating those tree-trunk legs that showed beneath his British short pants. His hair glowed, not amber and fine like Mrs Shaw's, but orange as the skin of flame. And his flesh glistened, slick with sweat and bright pink in color, dotted with brown like a sprinkling of nutmeg. His face stretched, broad and muscular as his body, but what made him most remarkable were his mismatched eyes. One was a clear silver gray, the other muddy green, so that it seemed he was always moving in two directions at once. Smiling with one eye, sad in the other. Reaching forward and pulling back. Offering and taking away. He was so utterly foreign, and yet in this, my first sight of him, I had much the same feeling as when I'd first noticed Mrs Shaw. I knew that from this moment on, he, too, was my possession.

He removed his helmet and combed a hand through his hair. Mrs Shaw's aide, Vijay, danced about, waving the other girls back to the veranda. Curiously, though I stood just a few feet from this Lawrence and Mrs Shaw, the Hindu did not seem to notice me, or in any case did not push me back as he did the others. I had the peculiar sense that I had become invisible. But then I realized the man, Lawrence, was watching me even as he listened to Mrs Shaw. He appeared to recognize me, though I knew I had never before seen him. That I would have remembered.

Mrs Shaw was speaking too hard and quick for me to interpret all she was saying, but I gathered that someone for whom she cared very deeply had gone missing, and she did not know what to do next.

The man turned and put his hands on her shoulders. He spoke in a slow, strong voice with a wide accent that sounded British, but different from any I had heard before. It seemed to stretch, as if with the capacity to bind the space between them. I think Lawrence meant to calm Mrs Shaw, but she was inside of herself now in a way that not even he could penetrate. At first I had thought he might be her husband. As I watched her push him away, I realized I was mistaken.

In the same instant, however, I thought, if Mrs Shaw won't help me, and she will not permit Lawrence to help her, then perhaps *he* would help me!

'Please, *sahib*,' I said, appealing now in a new scramble of languages. 'I will work for you. Clean, cook, sweep, I take care of you. Please, *sahib*, I am telling the *memsahib*, this place is no good for me. I must not be safe here. Come,' and I reached up and plucked at his fingers, prying his hand from her shoulder, feeling her skin and his at once and gathering strength from a connection that was yet barely a ripple in my mind.

He stepped back from us both but looked at me, squinting against the rain of sun. I had succeeded in distracting him. 'She's the one,' he said, 'isn't she?'

I straightened up and lifted my chin. Mrs Shaw gave me a sad, brief nod. She studied me just for a moment, then hurried to her office.

Both the man and I watched, wordless now, as she moved about in the open doorway gathering up her belongings – the straw man's hat she had worn the day she tended Surie, a leather briefcase, her red pocketbook. As she recrossed the courtyard she said to Lawrence, 'Stay here. Take care of her.'

'Here! Jo, I'm coming with you.'

But she was insistent. 'It's all right. You'll be safe with him, Kamla.'

Her voice was too high, too loud. She reminded me of a spring wound to the breaking point. She turned away, and the sun caught her face, flashing against tears.

Lawrence took her arm. He would not let go, and before I could think how to keep either one of them, both had gone.

2

Joanna insisted on driving. 'If I just sit I'll go mad.' So Lawrence climbed in beside her and said nothing more.

Her shoulders hunched, she chewed her lips, leaning over the steering wheel as if negotiating a typhoon rather than the slow crosscurrents of Indian cyclists and *tonga* traffic. When the car swerved, narrowly missing a beggar who had hobbled into traffic, Joanna blinked behind her dark glasses and recovered control without touching the brakes. She gripped the wheel so tightly that her knuckles looked carved, and watching her Lawrence felt a pang of remorse.

Accidents happen, he told himself. Games can go wrong.

Abruptly, she raked a hand through her hair and yanked the gold clips from her ears. With her high cheekbones and angular face, there was a ferocity about her even in the grip of denial. When Aidan had asked him to 'keep an eye on her and Simon,' Lawrence had predicted this would not sit well with Joanna. But now she needed him. As he would need her.

She let him accompany her as far as the American Ambassador's anteroom. There, while a bobbed blond receptionist pored over her *Time* magazine, Joanna rummaged in her purse.

'I don't know how it's gotten so late,' she said holding out a fistful of rupees. 'Would you pick up Simon at school? Take him – I don't know – swimming or something. Buy him an ice cream. Just don't say anything about Aidan, all right? Not yet. There's nothing to tell, yet. Right?'

'Right.' Lawrence did not remind her that Simon was supposedly 'busy' that afternoon, or that he had originally offered to do just as she was asking. Instead, he gently pushed the money back at her. 'You sure you don't want me to drop him home and come back here?'

For a second he thought she might weaken. He had her hands between his, curling fingers over the wad of rupees. But she was a fortress, this one. Though he could feel that tremor of need run through her like an aftershock from an earthquake, it stopped abruptly.

She shrugged and stuffed the money back in her purse, looking down as his hands fell away. 'No. Thanks, but . . . I'll meet you at the Cecil?'

'Joanna,' he said, 'you have no proof that Aidan's even in danger.'

She nodded but still wouldn't meet his gaze. 'I'll be there as soon as I can.'

Outside the embassy a squadron of kneeling camels took up half the road. Indian traffic typically peeled around such obstacles, but a horse-drawn *tonga* stopped directly opposite made the bottleneck virtually impassable. The wagon was done up for a wedding with marigolds and rose petals, the white horse dressed in red and green and gold with a feathered headdress and mirrorwork blanket. The *tonga* driver and camel driver, deep in conversation, seemed oblivious to the honking motorists and cyclists.

Lawrence strode over to the elderly *tonga* driver and offered to hire the rig for an hour. The bottleneck promptly opened.

Luckily, the driver didn't speak English. Though he shot Lawrence occasional curious glances, he left him to his thoughts. Which were as confused as they were guilty. Aidan would never have gone to Kashmir if it weren't for Lawrence. Did that make him responsible? It would in Jo's eyes – if she found out. It would in Jack Battersby's, as well. 'Just send him to stir up a little mischief,' Jack had instructed him. 'Do your mate a favor.' But when favors went wrong there was hell to pay. Especially when the real favor was to Jack. During the war Battersby had once taken it into his head that a lad who'd given him a bum code in Hong Kong was serving the other side. By way of redress, he had the lad sent out to join the coast watchers in Guadalcanal. Poor bloke died of dysentery within the first month.

This time, stripped of the cover of war, Jack had even more at stake. Oh, he'd couch it in terms of honor. *International respect and cooperation. The defense of the free world. Serving the Alliance.* In reality, it was all about claiming position. Jack wanted to be recognized as a player by Washington and Whitehall, but to achieve

this recognition he had first to convince his own doubting government of the merit of an Australian foreign intelligence network. So
he'd appointed Lawrence as his 'free' agent and set Aidan as his
pawn. Lawrence had heeded grudgingly, Aidan unwittingly. If one
of them had to pay, it shouldn't be Aidan.

He could never let her know it, but Lawrence needed to find
Joanna's husband as badly as she did.

Simon was waiting by the school gate. Nothing if not obliging,
the lad let out a whoop of delight when Lawrence waved him
aboard, and began pelting his classmates with handfuls of rose
petals from the wagon's bed as they lurched out of the car park.
Then he climbed up front and the driver let him handle the reins.

Simon gave Lawrence a puzzled look but evidently decided not
to question a good thing. He took the reins and yelled a delighted
'Giddyap!'

He had sandy hair and light brown eyes, this boy, and teacup
handle ears. He looked nothing like either of his parents, really, and
yet was the image of both of them. Joanna's coloring had crept into
his skin and hair, and his eyes were the same elongated shape as
Aidan's. He had his father's lean build, his mother's candor, their
combined intensity. When they got down by the Kwality ice cream
cart in front of the hotel, Simon clutched the change Lawrence gave
him and was nearly sucked under by the surrounding swarm of
Indian schoolchildren, but when he eventually emerged he wore a
triumphant expression and held his cone high as an Olympic torch.

In the pool they splashed from one end to the other drawing
scowls from a cluster of Brahmins sitting on the deck. Lawrence
wiggled his ears at them, and Simon yelled his approval, kicking up
fat droplets of water that sparkled like coins in midair. Lawrence
threw him, shrieking, half the length of the pool, as once he had
tossed his own son.

'Watch, Lawrence!' Simon clambered out and up onto the diving
board. He stood backward, breathing hard, arms tight at his sides.
Lawrence watched from the shallow end expecting a backward
somersault, but suddenly Simon crumpled as if punched in the
stomach.

The water broke with a bone-chilling crack as he tumbled in
bottom first.

Lawrence held himself back. Tried to check his imagination. This was not his son. He counted, one . . . two . . . three. The surface began to resolve itself, but the boy remained below.

He took in a gulp of air and threw himself forward. Three long strokes, and he dove, got an arm under the sinking child. His own heart roared in his ears as he cradled Simon's limp body to the surface. 'Simon! Can you hear me!'

The boy's eyes flew open. The body squirmed.

'Gotcha!' He let out a whoop and pounded Lawrence's shoulder. 'You should see your face! Boy, oh boy!'

Lawrence felt a spasm of rage, convulsive as an electric shock. His grip tightened so that the child's laughter ratcheted abruptly into fear.

'Hey, Lawrence!' Simon gasped. 'Hey, I give up! C'mon, let go!'

But Lawrence could not let go. He found his footing on the ramp of the pool bottom. His hands closed on slippery ribs and shoulder blades – chicken bones, he'd once teased Davey. Were all small children so constructed, with this boggling union of fragility and recklessness? He pressed his cheek against the small forehead, smelled the residue of boy-dirt in the wet hair, chlorine seeped in the pores.

'Oh, Christ, I'm sorry, lad. I'm sorry, I'm sorry.'

For all that he remembered, he had forgotten this – the sensation of one small, brightly pounding heart, another complete universe pressed against his skin.

Simon went silent. He brought his slight, strong arms up and clasped them around Lawrence's neck, wrapped legs around his thick waist. They were still standing like this, rocking back and forth in the water when Joanna appeared at the far end of the pool deck, her gaze fixed on them.

She walked unsteadily but quickly past the Brahmins. Lawrence took a deep breath and gave Simon a squeeze. 'Here comes your Mem.'

The boy loosened his grip, turning to his mother.

'Simon!' she said in a voice too loud for her eyes. 'Are you all right?'

Simon gave Lawrence a conspiratorial glance. 'Sure. Why wouldn't I be?'

She frowned, lifting her head so her hat's shadow cut across her mouth. 'Of course. No reason. Time to get out, though.'

'*Why?*' But the boy climbed out obediently, and Lawrence followed.

'We've places to go and things to do.' She wrapped a towel around her son, pulling him against her. 'I need to talk to Lawrence for a bit. Can you get changed by yourself?'

' 'Course I can!'

As Simon pranced across the hot pavement to the dressing room, Joanna looked close to tears.

Lawrence drew a towel over his shoulders. 'What did he say?' he asked.

She faced him. 'I have to go up there. Aidan's plane didn't come back. Minton claims that's all they know, but a rescue team has been sent out, so it seems to me there must be more.'

'When will you go?'

'Tomorrow. There's a flight at eight in the morning.'

'Minton gave you a permit?'

She waved a hand. 'He tried to talk me out of it. But I can't just sit here twiddling my thumbs.'

'No,' he agreed. 'Do you want me to come with you?'

'Thanks, but there's no reason for me to make you crazy, too.'

'You won't make me any crazier than I am.' He smiled, but she wasn't having any of it. He said, 'Shall I stay with Simon, then?'

She shook her head. 'I'm taking him with me.'

'Joanna . . . are you sure that's wise?'

'I'm sure it's probably not. But Simon's never been away from me, and I don't know how long this could take. Besides . . .' Her voice broke as she looked in the direction the boy had disappeared. 'I couldn't leave him now.'

Lawrence reached for her arm, but she pulled away. 'Don't.' She met his eyes. 'I'm sorry. I don't do well with sympathy.'

He let it go. 'What are you going to tell him?'

'The truth. His father's lost. And we have to find him.'

Simon reappeared clutching his dripping swimsuit as he watched a flock of bright green parrots wheel across the sky.

'What *will* you let me do, then?' Lawrence asked.

She passed a hand aimlessly across her face. 'Keep things

together for me here. I called Hari from Minton's office, but I'm afraid I must have sounded like a madwoman. I'm completely abandoning my post—'

'I'll see that he understands.'

'And that little girl we rescued today.' She shook her head. 'She needs more help than Simon or I do.'

'If you say so . . . It's not sympathy, you know, Joanna. I feel . . . responsible.'

Her voice sharpened. 'For what?'

He hesitated. 'For you and Simon. I promised Aidan—'

'I know,' she cut him off. 'He asked you.' She picked up Simon's rucksack. 'Tell you what. I'll cable as soon as there's any news.'

He made one last stab. 'Aidan wouldn't want you going up there alone.'

But she forced a smile as the boy rejoined them. 'I'm not going alone,' she said slipping an arm around her son's shoulders. 'Simon will keep me company.'

3

The UN military observers in Srinagar were headquartered in a large square whitewashed building that seemed to give off an odor of institutional bureaucracy even before Joanna reached the front door. As she led Simon inside, that smell was compounded by the reek of cigarettes and mildew. Two armed guards listened impassively as she explained her mission, and waved her down a dimly lit corridor toward the last office on the right. General Farr's office. The source of the telegram.

According to the US embassy, the plane carrying Aidan Shaw also had been carrying three military observers, and even as he grudgingly issued her travel permits, Ambassador Minton had reminded Joanna that the cease-fire between Pakistani, Indian, and separatist Kashmiri forces was tenuous at best. Two years of war for control of this province, on top of the carnage here during Partition, had resulted in more than a million refugees and tens of thousands of murders, rapes, and 'accidents.' Foreigners were by no means immune, he'd cautioned, and it was no place for women and children.

54

Joanna looked down at Simon trudging the length of the hallway and gave his hand a squeeze. She knew she should not have brought him, but how could she leave him? All the way up on the plane that morning, he'd chattered as if they were going on holiday, and in answering his thousand and one questions about flight and clouds and the landscape below she had almost been able to push from her mind the true purpose of their trip. As long as he was with her, she would not allow herself to fall apart. And as long as he believed his father was merely waiting to be rescued, that really this was just an elaborate game of lost and found, then there was a chance she could believe it, too.

In spite of the smell, the corridors had a barren, hospital-like feel, and she caught herself fantasizing that Aidan was through one of these doors resting comfortably with a broken leg. A cracked rib. A fever. Something minor and finite, within her means to repair.

Unfortunately this was no hospital, and Aidan was not here. They had come to the end of the hall. She kissed the top of Simon's head and thrust open the heavy door.

A young male secretary with an Italian accent showed her to the inner office, where the Canadian general charged with overseeing the observer force stood and gravely nodded. In a glance she took in the sparsely furnished room, found an armchair for Simon next to an unlit charcoal brazier in the corner. She settled him there with a new comic book, then returned to the general's massive teak desk and reached across to shake hands.

General Farr was a narrow rectangular man with concave cheeks and fading blond hair shoved behind his ears, his blue eyes cool and brusque as his grip. He gestured for her to sit down. 'Mrs Shaw, I'm sure you want me to get straight to the point, but I'm afraid I have little to tell you. Our rescue team has not yet reached the crash site, and it could still be several days before we know anything.'

She dug her fingernails into the soft skin of her palms. 'I'd appreciate your telling me everything you do know.'

'Well, you realize, the possibility of sabotage and the delicate state of the peace agreement here in Kashmir mean that we must take seriously all reports of armistice violations along the cease-fire lines. A team of my observers was flying to the northern region to look into one of these reports. Your husband went along to cover the investigative procedure.'

'You've located the site . . .?'

Farr glanced over at Simon, now absorbed in his comic. 'Some wreckage was spotted on a slope just south of Leh. Unfortunately, it's not easily accessible.' He slid a map of Kashmir across the desk. Two strings of mountains – the Ladakh Range and the Zanskar – seemed to collide at the circled red star the general indicated.

Joanna tried to picture Aidan's face as the wall of rock hurtled toward him. Terror was not an emotion she had ever known in him. Even now she could only imagine him watching, recording – anticipating.

The image flickered, then, as if by a switch, went out. She asked, 'Are you positive my husband was on board?'

'I can assure you, Mrs Shaw, you would not be here if we weren't.' And, his tone implied, we'd both be spared this unpleasantness.

Somehow she managed to control her voice. 'I think it's obvious, General, that we'd both prefer this meeting never had to take place. I'm asking *how* you know.'

'Well, for one thing, he was seen boarding the plane.' Farr pulled an envelope from under his desk blotter. 'Before that, your husband checked out of his hotel here, but he'd left this for the desk man to post. The embassy in Delhi said you were on your way, so I kept it for you. I'm afraid circumstances necessitated our opening it.'

Joanna held the envelope as if it were alive. The rough slit across the top signaled Farr's intrusion, but at the same time her husband's confident script promised reassurance. To her dismay, however, it was the briefest of notes – like ones he used to send her at work early in their marriage, 'to keep you warm,' he would say.

April 4, 1949
Srinagar

Dearest Jo,
Just to let you know, the lead I chased up here hasn't panned out. I'm going to try to salvage the trip with a quick detour up

north – some human interest, if nothing else. In any case, I expect to be heading home day after tomorrow. Stars and Stripes will have to wait.

Meantime, kisses to both you and Simon.
I love you,
Aidan

Joanna ran her fingertip over his signature, the final line. She pictured him leaning over the paper, tips of his teeth lightly grazing his lower lip as he dashed this off . . . *home day after tomorrow*.

She looked up, determined not to cry. Simon had quit his comic and was busily rearranging with a metal poker the cold lumps of charcoal in the brazier. The general was flipping through papers on his desk, making a show of respecting her privacy. The very ordinariness of their motions should soothe her. If Aidan were really dead, she thought, nothing would ever seem ordinary again.

'The day after tomorrow was yesterday,' she said.

General Farr raised his head. She lifted the letter. 'That's true,' he agreed.

'General,' she said, 'what *were* the violations they were investigating?'

'If I knew that, Mrs Shaw, then your husband wouldn't be missing. Nor my men.'

My men. My observers. Farr himself had a stake in this disaster. That accounted for his defensiveness, she realized. After all, he was, as Aidan would insist, an 'international peacekeeper.' As Simon would say, 'a good guy.' And if this plane had crashed – fatally – then he had lost more soldiers than she had husbands. Aidan was the least of his worries. No. Aidan was *her* worry.

'I am sorry,' Farr said. 'There's nothing more any of us can do until we hear back from the rescue team.'

Joanna swallowed hard. Focus. She said, 'My husband was planning to interview members of the UN peace commission. The new head, I believe, was a Czech. Where could I reach him?'

Farr looked puzzled. 'I can't see what good that would do, even if it were possible. Most of them flew out last week. The head man's back in Prague by now.'

'I see.' She stared past Simon and out through the window. The sky was veined and pale as marble. Finally she returned to the general. 'You're not married, are you?'

'Why do you ask?'

'Because if you were married, I think you'd understand why I'm here.'

He smiled warily. 'I understand why you're here, Mrs Shaw. But journalists take chances. I didn't ask your husband to join that flight, and I don't think your being here is necessarily going to do him any good. However, if it makes you feel better, that's your business.'

'You won't mind if I ask one more favor, then?'

'That depends.'

'Could you help us find a hotel room?'

He pressed a buzzer on his desk. 'Cirino,' he said when his aide appeared, 'call over to the Shalimar and see about a room for Mrs Shaw and her son.'

Joanna detected reluctance in the Italian's reply. 'The *Shalimar,* sir?'

But the general insisted. 'You'll be quite comfortable there, I'm sure, Mrs Shaw. I'll notify you as soon as the rescue team reports back.'

It was nearly suppertime when the pedicab rustled up by the aide dropped them in front of the Shalimar. Immediately she understood Cirino's reluctance. The hotel was a pockmarked tenement occupied primarily by British war widows too impoverished, alcoholic, or alienated to go anywhere else. The deskman, unctuous and beady-eyed, rubbed his stubby hands at the sight of them as if welcoming new victims. He chattered nonstop in bastardized English as he led them up three flights of warped wood stairs to a large but unheated room with a bath that consisted of a tin tub and chamber pot. The furnishings looked as if they'd been scavenged from the street, and the lock on the door gaped so wide you could pick it with a comb. Joanna tipped the man sparingly and shoved a chair beneath the knob. She knew she should find another hotel, but what real difference would it make?

Simon, oblivious to the bleakness of their surroundings, hauled open one of the long frame windows and stepped out onto the balcony. The floorboards were rotted through in places and though the drizzle and mist obscured whatever view might exist, Simon immediately spotted three dead dogs and the carcass of a cow floating among the human bathers in the canal directly below. Joanna hauled him back inside. It was so cold and damp that their breath hung in clouds. Simon said he was hungry. Since leaving Delhi he had not once asked about his father, and for this she felt both grateful and dismayed. Still, she knew her son would sleep that night, which was more than she could say for herself.

After washing up, they picked their way back downstairs to the dining room, where the dozen tables all were set, though Simon and Joanna appeared to be the only diners. The deskman turned waiter grinned and bowed and brought large bowls of mutton swimming in grease and some cold Kashmiri bread. Simon started to turn up his nose, but when Joanna told him it was this or nothing, he wolfed it down so fast he could not possibly have tasted it. She forced herself to eat along with him, though what she really wanted was a drink. When she asked the man if he might bring her a little whiskey or wine, he clasped his hands and wiggled his head. 'I am very sorry, Madam. I am Muslim, you know, and this is being forbidden.' She cursed under her breath and doggedly continued her meal. But in the middle of this exchange an elderly woman with gray spit curls and the purple cheeks of a veteran wino had entered the dining room and seated herself at the next table. When the man was gone, she leaned across, rubbing her fingertips and thumb together. 'Don't believe a word he says, dear,' she advised. 'Just slip him a few annas. That's all it takes, and he'll be your slave for life. He's not such a bad sort, really, once you get used to him . . .' Her voice trailed off as she noticed a streak of grease on her knife and began fussily polishing her tableware with a napkin.

Joanna followed the woman's advice, and after supper as they were starting back up the stairs, Ali, as he called himself, beckoned to her from the shadows and slipped her a parcel wrapped in newspaper. 'Sundries,' he said with an oblique nod. 'I am putting the cost on your bill. Most pleasant dreams to you, madam.'

Under ordinary circumstances, the pint of local rum in the parcel would have been more than adequate to fuel those dreams, but these were hardly ordinary circumstances. She got Simon settled in bed under four blankets and their coats and lay with him stroking his head and singing lullabies from his infancy. After his body gave its telltale twitch and his breathing softened to a snore, she pulled her coat off the pile of bedding and drew it around her, then took a chair, her glass, and the bottle over to the window. She used her sleeve to wipe the grime from the window, rubbing a large circle through which she could see that the fog had lifted and stars glittered over the mountains and lake now visible in the distance. Closer along the canal, fruit and dogwood trees blossomed in ghostly clouds. Tomorrow would be April 8. The same day on which, ten years ago, she and Aidan had met. April fools, they called themselves. She lifted the glass to her lips.

Venice Beach, California. She'd grown up in nearby Mar Vista, and was only recently returned after graduating from Mills College up in Oakland. Aidan was en route from China to Washington, stopping in L.A. to visit friends. Those friends had brought him to the fun house on the pier, but when Joanna collided with him in the Hall of Mirrors he was alone.

As was she . . . moving too fast down a tunnel that appeared to stretch forever but in fact led to a blind turn, which Aidan was approaching from the other side. Her nose struck his chin, and she stepped on his foot. He caught her by the arms as she drew back blurting apologies and mortified laughter.

The mirrors tilted crazily on this side of the turn, multiplying his dark hair and elongated green eyes. In one reflection he towered with shoulders broad enough to stand on, in another he shrank to the height of a midget. But the true source of these images was a tall, slender man in an immaculate gray suit.

Mustering what dignity she could, she extended her hand. 'Joanna Dillon.'

'Aidan Shaw,' he answered evenly. Their hands touched, his grip steady and firm. He did not immediately let go – or release her from his gaze. Out of the corner of her eye, from five different angles and with growing distress, she saw what he saw. A girl barely out of school and so uncouth that she cropped her own hair, went without face paint, and wore an ex-boyfriend's Brooks Brothers shirt tucked into an old pair of jodhpurs. She knew from experience that the flecked gold of her eyes had a certain appeal for men, and she had, she was told, 'good bone structure.' But this man deserved true glamour – a woman like Merle Oberon or Dorothy Lamour. Joanna hadn't the slightest illusion about her chances in that league.

An overhead light flashed, startling her so that she stepped back against the mirror. Aidan Shaw ignored the clumsiness of her movement. His mouth shaped a smile as the honky-tonk music filtered in from the boardwalk. He seemed to have no inclination to leave. Instead, he said, 'Say, would you like to dance?'

She glanced over her shoulder, but none of the voices echoing through the chamber were heading toward their jog in the maze.

Not waiting for her answer, he stepped closer and placed his arm expertly around her waist. He smelled of starch and lime cologne, and sounded British but then again not quite as he spoke into her hair. 'Where are you from?'

He moved so gracefully in this cramped, glittery space. Without thinking she said, 'I live here.'

'*Here?*' He pulled back to grin at her.

And the maze suddenly seemed to widen. She breathed deeply, inhaling the closeness of the ocean and night. 'Why not?' She relaxed into his lead. 'All these mirrors, music, the sound of the surf. And you never know when you'll fall into the arms of a handsome man.'

'Ah.' He spun her. 'Have there been so many?'

She felt the blood rush to her cheeks, but the game was carrying her now. 'Thousands.' She dipped her head toward the mirrors and those multitudes of carelessly thrown together girls and their elegant dancing partners. 'Just look.'

'Hmm. How's a poor fellow to distinguish himself?'

The white light flashed again on its arbitrary pacer, but this time she hardly noticed. 'I was wondering that, myself.'

They stopped dancing and he studied her, in his eyes a sudden confusion. 'You know,' he said, 'I don't ordinarily do this. I mean—'

She said softly, 'That's the point, isn't it?'

He gave her a curious look and started to drop his arm from her waist. Then he changed his mind.

They emerged from the maze holding hands and eluded their respective friends. As the moon rose, they walked for miles down the beach, talking now. Effortlessly talking. He was a journalist – foreign correspondent. Asia was his beat. She learned that he was born in New York's Chinatown, raised in China, educated in Shanghai and Boston – all places that to Joanna sounded as distant and enticing as Shangri-la. His mother had been an Irish waitress, his father a Chinese merchant who succeeded against all odds in securing a degree in engineering at the turn of the century and returned to China with status and wealth. Aidan's sense of always being the outsider derived initially from his mixed heritage and his childhood – as he put it, 'with a foot in two continents' – but it had intensified with the Japanese occupation of China. He refused to go into detail, but she sensed that his family had suffered – perhaps more than suffered – as a result of the war in China while Aidan was studying in America.

Then the conversation shifted to Joanna, and Aidan seemed to find her life every bit as fascinating as she found his. Certainly it was different. Her father was a carpenter at MGM studios, her mother a bookkeeper. They'd emigrated to California from Minnesota in their twenties and never budged again. If they knew who Joanna's biological mother and father had been, they kept it to themselves, but she'd known even before her ninth birthday, when they admitted it was true, that she was adopted. She had always felt as if she belonged to an alien tribe. Her parents' complacency bewildered her. Their absolute self-certainty, the quiet rigidity of their patriotism and moral compass continuously seemed to be testing her, finding her wanting more and different approaches to thinking and to life. If it weren't for their similarly absolute love for her, she might have become a flagrant rebel – one of those girls who yanked up their skirts and turned down their stockings and sang throaty French songs on the boardwalk. As it was, she channeled her rebellious impulses into men's clothing and hikes up along the John Muir Trail. She tried to imagine what it would be like to walk around the world.

She and Aidan talked for hours that night, the only souls on the beach, the darkness above them a protective bell. He told her he believed in truth but not necessarily in God. She said she believed in love but could not decide between free will and fate. He confessed to a passion for mystery novels – Dashiell Hammett's *The Thin Man* was his favorite. And she said she preferred Jane Austen, but could be had for Agatha Christie.

'Do you mean to save the world?' he asked when she described her plan to go into social work.

It was a ludicrous question. This was 1939, and the world was poised to go up in flames. 'But of course,' she answered anyway. 'Save it and see it both. Don't you?'

Instead of answering he kissed her. The ocean roared in her ears. His hands cradled her head, and she felt a sensation of stillness and speed, as if she would never move again and yet she would never stop. The kiss lasted minutes, hours perhaps. When he pulled back she wanted to cry.

'Did anyone ever tell you you're a hopeless idealist?' he demanded.

'Is that a bad thing?'

He laughed and cupped her cheek in his hand. 'Hardly.'

'Then I'm afraid the answer is no,' she said.

'Well, allow me to be the first.'

The answer *was* no. No one had ever talked to her the way Aidan Shaw did, or seen in her what he seemed to, or asked the questions of her and himself that Aidan found perfectly natural. That night awakened something deep within Joanna that was the exact opposite of hopelessness.

Three days later Aidan flew on to Washington. Three weeks later she followed him. His gift on meeting her at the airport was a large silk scarf imprinted with a map of the world. He draped it around her shoulders and used it to pull her toward him. 'I don't think I ever officially answered your question that night at the beach,' he said.

'Which one?'

'Do I mean to see and save the world?'

'Well?' She leaned into him breathing his scent.

'I do,' he said, and kissed her.

They were married in Georgetown on Independence Day. Her parents flew all the way from California, and after the ceremony their friends hosted a party in their honor at the Hotel Willard. A party that she and Aidan forgot to attend.

We skipped our own wedding reception, Joanna thought, recalling the desire that had seized them like a flash flood. They had gone upstairs to their room to change and not come down for two days.

She crossed her arms now and held herself by the shoulders, remembering their haste and laughter, the delicious urgency with which they peeled off their clothes and discovered for the first time the guiltless wonder of each other's skin. That night, lying against his chest and listening to the fireworks exploding over the Mall, she felt beautiful in a way she never could have imagined before meeting Aidan. There was not the slightest doubt in her mind that they were the luckiest couple on earth.

She swallowed the last of her rum. Her teeth were chattering, and her skin felt blue. It was said that you always wake up before dying in a dream, that no matter how close to death your imagination might take you, it can never cross all the way over. That was how she felt about Aidan. But how long would it take to wake up?

4

The next morning, under a sun so bright it seemed a personal affront, Joanna and Simon made the rounds to everyone in Srinagar who might conceivably recognize Aidan's name. They spoke fruitlessly to the few reporters covering the cease-fire, tried without success to meet with UN officials, even appealed to individual soldiers as they patrolled the streets. 'But, madame,' one young lieutenant told her, 'in India just now we are seeing three hundred thousand Kashmiri refugees. Here in the camps outside Srinagar another two hundred thousand. And every one of them is wondering, where is my husband, where is my father, my mother, my son?'

It was true. The cease-fire had liberated hope in Kashmir. Painters and refurbishers clambered over Srinagar's famed but now vacant houseboats in anticipation of renewed warm weather tourism, and the bazaars boasted optimistic displays of embroidered leather, woolens, spices and dried fruit, intricate cedar and teakwood carvings, carpets and antique brass. Yet between the stalls ravaged men hunkered under greatcoats cupping cheroots in their callused palms. Women draped in threadbare head coverings tended babies in makeshift street corner encampments, and maimed boys on crude wheeled platforms propelled themselves with plaintive, demanding cries along the lakefront. Other casualties squatted, dead-eyed, their outstretched hands brushed aside by passing soldiers and foreign observers alike.

'Tuberculosis will kill those the fighting has missed,' Dr Ranjit Singh told her. This young Sikh doctor had ridden up on the plane with them. He had befriended Simon, leaving them with the address where he could be reached, and after exhausting all other avenues Joanna called him. They met in an open air tea shop near the bazaar. He immediately pulled out a painted wood yo-yo, which kept Simon amused.

Ranjit, as he insisted they call him, was in his early twenties, tall and gangly soft, the roundness of his face exaggerated by a ballooned red turban and heavily fringed brown eyes. His skin bore the pockmark scars of childhood disease, but he wore a spotless white shirt, navy trousers, and blazer, and spoke impeccable English. He was a medical researcher at Dharamsala Teaching Hospital and had been sent to Kashmir to document the spread of TB among those displaced by the war.

'Do you know Srinagar well?' Joanna asked.

'Well enough to do my work, to find my way about. My family used to summer here, before the fighting.'

In the street before them three little boys – younger than Simon – commandeered a thicket of sheep down the main market street. They faced horse-drawn carts, public buses, and irate merchants whose displays of goods and produce were at risk of tumbling under the sheep's hooves, yet the boys managed to maneuver their flock with unflappable grace and good humor. Joanna shook her head.

'I suppose you're wondering what we're doing here,' she said to Ranjit.

The young doctor sipped his tea. 'I believe you will tell me.'

Joanna directed Simon to a clear area a few yards from their table where he could play with the yo-yo without hitting anyone – and where he would not hear her. 'In point of fact,' she said, 'I'm looking for my husband. I was informed that a plane in which he was flying disappeared in the mountains near Leh four days ago. We've been to see the United Nations general in charge, and he's not very cooperative. I realize this has nothing to do with you or your business here in Kashmir, but frankly I'm at my wit's end. Is there anyone you know – any locals, I mean – who might be able to help us?' She showed him Aidan's press photo, the only picture she had thought to bring. It looked like a mug shot.

Ranjit sighed, abruptly grave, and Joanna realized how desperate she must seem. But the more she thought about it the more certain she was that Farr and the bureaucracy behind him were stonewalling her. If the downing of that plane had the slightest political implication, which in this climate it was sure to, then she'd be the last to know what had really happened to Aidan.

Ranjit put his fingers to his temples and rubbed in vigorous circles. Suddenly he snapped his fingers. '*Achcha!* I know just the fellow.' He glanced at Simon, who had stopped playing with the yo-yo and was staring rapt at an elderly peddler outside the tea stall. The man's wares consisted of daggers and swords, which he displayed in a large tin trunk.

'Come, come!' Ranjit called to Simon. 'Where we are going you will find all of this and more.'

'What do you mean?' Joanna asked warily.

But Ranjit looked pleased with himself. 'Well, you see, Dr Akbar is a bit of a collector.'

Specifically, he explained as they began to walk, Mahmood Akbar was an ethnologist, scholar of tribal customs and crafts. He had been at school in England with Ranjit's father but grew up in Kashmir and returned here after launching his career at the British Museum. 'He is a bit cagey about his current endeavors. Calls himself "an incorrigible antiquarian," but he knows everyone from Lahore to Kashgar, right down to the lowliest goat-herders. If anyone has information about your husband, Dr Akbar will know it.'

The ethnologist's home, a deceptively dark, weather-beaten structure located at the northern end of the city, itself resembled a museum. Tribal artifacts lined the entry hall. The walls glittered with mirrorwork, coral and turquoise jewelry, embroidered leathers and headdresses. A houseboy ushered them to a long parlor, where Dr Akbar welcomed them warmly.

A trim, short man, he wore spectacles, a dark mustache, and a black pin-striped double-breasted suit at least one size too big for him. He gave Ranjit an uncle's embrace, but was equally effusive in his greeting of Simon. Young boys, he informed Joanna, could be counted upon to appreciate his toys. He showed them his collection of Turki carpets and Ali Baba urns, his tank of purple and red speckled goldfish, and his five angora cats. But as Ranjit had intimated, Akbar's prize was his artillery treasury, which he kept in a small sitting room off the parlor. Crossbows, swords, blowguns, matchlocks. Soon Simon was happily occupied with an array of pistols – unloaded, Akbar assured Joanna – dating back to the 1700s. The houseboy brought a large samovar of coffee, but at this point Ranjit excused himself with apologies that he must return to his work, and so Joanna found herself alone with this unexpected host.

Akbar's manner was so unaffected – he had a habit of chewing intently on the end of his mustache as he listened – and his enthusiasm in greeting new guests so persuasive that Joanna soon let down her guard. She started to explain why she had come but had barely mentioned the plane crash when Akbar began to nod. As Ranjit had predicted, he knew all about it.

'Such news travels swiftly and widely here. Also, my work places me in contact with the hill people.' He lifted one bony hand, tipping it back and forth. 'There is difference between official and unofficial. For myself, I value more the unofficial reports.' Akbar paused, selecting his words. 'As I understand, all aboard were in uniform.'

'In *uniform.*' She searched the possible implications of this detail. 'You mean they've found the crash site . . . and he wasn't—'

'Mrs Shaw, were you told where this flight was destined?'

'All I know is the UN team was investigating some cease-fire violation.'

Akbar shook his head. 'Oh, yes. There were reports that a shot had been fired, and a man had been seen burying his victim. It turned out that victim was a mad dog. You know, I believe this team had completed its inquiry and was in fact already returning to

Srinagar when the crash occurred.' He smoothed the damp tip of his mustache back into a smile. 'How many did they say were aboard?'

'Including Aidan and the pilot, I think there must have been five.'

'Well, there you have it. I am told only four bodies were seen at the crash site. All, as I say, in uniform. It seems to me, Mrs Shaw, that your husband may have stayed on wherever that plane put down.'

Joanna exhaled, her heart racing. She *knew* Aidan was alive.

Through the archway she could see Simon kneeling on the floor, head bowed as if he, too, were giving thanks. She went in and crouched next to him. He held up a small red bow strung with catgut, pretended to ready an arrow. She said, 'Dr Akbar thinks Daddy's all right.'

Simon let the invisible arrow fly. Then he frowned. 'Does that mean we have to go home?'

Joanna flinched. She stroked his shoulder but did not reply. She turned back to the parlor.

'You are at ease now,' Akbar suggested.

But already she was not. Simon's question had hit its mark. 'How can we know Aidan wasn't aboard?' she demanded. 'He could have gone for help. He could be injured and lost.'

Akbar shook his head. 'Perhaps. But I am told the wreckage and terrain are both very bad. Survival would be unlikely.' His tone warned that even this was an understatement.

'Tell me,' she said finally. 'You seem to know this territory. If you were an American correspondent, why would *you* stay on in the middle of nowhere?'

Again Akbar's palm rose, equivocating. 'Perhaps he wished to report on the Ladakhi lamas? The area where the shots were reported is not far from Leh.'

'I doubt it. Aidan finds religion tedious, except when it's provocation for war. The Buddhists aren't inciting a war, are they?'

Akbar grinned, wrinkling his nose so that his glasses rode up. 'In Tibet, perhaps. Not at Leh.' But he quickly sobered, humming a low dirgelike melody as he outfitted a silver holder with a cigarette and lit it, then sat smoking thoughtfully.

At last he said, 'Leh is the last city this side of the Karakoram Pass. For thousands of years it has been the final supply station for trade caravans. Not many go through now, due to political instability both here and over the border in China, but some weeks ago I met another American journalist headed that way. She came to me with questions about the hill tribes. Were they friendly? Had I heard reports of bandit attacks in China? Were the rebels interfering with travel over the pass?'

'She?' Joanna thought she had heard him wrong.

'Indeed! A most lovely young girl. One of your yellow-haired beauties, though she dressed like a man in trousers and a leather flight jacket. Her name was Alice.' He studied Joanna as if seeing someone else. 'Alice James. I do not forget.'

Joanna glanced at Simon, now obliviously playing with the cats at the end of the hallway. 'You think,' she forced herself to ask, 'that this Alice meant to trek all the way to China?'

Akbar appeared not to notice her discomfort. 'I think she was most concerned by reports that the Chinese Nationalists have been mistreating the Turkestan tribesmen, which I assured her were true. Yes, yes, I said. Burdensome taxes, conscription of men and boys, raids and pilfering of the people's stocks and harvests. Everything you hear is true, but your government knows all this. Do they! Oh, Miss Alice James was most indignant.'

He paused. 'Perhaps you have heard the term, Tournament of Shadows? Or, Great Game?'

She looked at him sharply. 'Yes.'

'Then you know, for nearly two centuries Russia and England have competed for influence over these northern access routes linking India and China.' He selected a well-thumbed atlas from his wall of books, and opened it to a map of Central Asia. Above the stretch of mountains to the north of Kashmir floated a lengthwise yellow oval marking the Takla Makan Desert. The desert was rimmed by a string of names familiar to Joanna only because of Aidan and Lawrence's history chats. Khotan, Yarkand, Kashgar. These stops along the old Silk Road were also playing fields of the Great Game.

'In this century,' Akbar continued, 'the Tournament has been revised, contestants multiplied many times over. Sinkiang has seen many recent rebellions. The native tribespeople have been fighting for independence from Chinese rule. The Chinese Nationalists have been at odds with the growing Communist forces. The Soviets, too, have been sparring with the Nationalists as well as with the British. And now the Americans have been building an air base in the Sinkiang capital, Urumchi – Tihwa, the Chinese call it.' He chewed on his mustache. 'Urumchi is the old native name. It means Beautiful Pastures. But General Chiang Kai-shek prefers a name more in keeping with his true designs, so he calls the capital Tihwa, which means Assimilation. He would gladly rub out these ethnic minorities if he could do so without his Western allies taking note.'

He paused to smoke. 'Nothing is happening here in Kashmir. It is most distressing, but the situation appears to have reached a stalemate. If I were a foreign journalist in search of a good story, I think I, too, would prefer Sinkiang. The American press – perhaps not even the American government – wishes to admit that the Communists are winning the war in China—'

Joanna interrupted. 'This Alice. Whom did she work for?'

'Ah. She said she had an assignment for the *Washington Post*. I believe she called herself a freelancer, however.'

'But she left weeks ago?'

'Mmh. What is most remarkable of all, she was traveling alone.' He studied Joanna through a plume of smoke, then moved his fingertip along the line in the atlas marking the Karakoram Trail northward through the Kun Lun Mountains to China. 'Eastern Turkestan. Also known as Sinkiang.' Akbar tapped the map. 'You understand, the most direct route from India would be the lower six-week trail to the west through Gilgit. But since the line of control was drawn down the middle of Kashmir, Gilgit now lies in Pakistani territory, and to get there from Srinagar would mean crossing the line. So even though the Karakoram route has technically been closed since '47, the *dak* still occasionally struggles through this side, as does such trade as has survived. It is high and rough, and not closely patrolled.'

Joanna studied the twisting course. If everything this man said was true, then the prospect of Chiang Kai-shek's abuses so near could be as alluring to Aidan as it seemed to be to this Alice James.

But you didn't start a trek like this on the spur of the moment. And he'd promised to be home in two days!

'What you're suggesting is preposterous,' she said. '*Something must have happened to my husband.*'

Akbar turned his cigarette holder between the pads of his finger and thumb. 'I am sure you are right. However, you asked for my opinion.'

Joanna sensed it was time to leave, but she felt rooted to her seat. If Aidan's trip to Srinagar had in fact failed to produce the expected exposé of Communist dirty tricks, then all he could anticipate on his return to Delhi would be another round of recriminations and reprimands from Washington. Was it so implausible, then, that he would delay his return? He was no stranger to impulse. And his impulses were hardly predictable. Early in the war, in Burma, he had been out on a story when his photographer, Ben Eldon, tripped a land mine. The explosion threw Aidan clear, but ripped off the lower half of Ben's leg. Aidan carried the bleeding man and the severed leg two miles to the nearest medic, then returned to reclaim Ben's equipment. He proceeded to shoot six rolls of film from the perimeter of the mine's crater – of the nearby village and its residents, children, soldiers, women and old people, water buffalo and goats, the flies that swarmed the congealing pools of his friend's spilled blood. Ben survived, and much later discovered this film in his camera bag. 'It was as though he held nature to account,' Ben told Joanna the day he came to the house in Rockville to leave a set of the prints for Aidan. 'As though the camera were his weapon, and he was avenging the attack on us by shooting all the witnesses – even those who themselves had been injured in the blast.'

Your government knows all this, Akbar had said. *Stars and Stripes will have to wait.*

She lifted her eyes. 'How long is the flight to Leh?'

5

After Mrs Shaw left the rescue home, I tried to rest and not to think what the future would bring. I was the youngest of all the girls there, and without Mrs Shaw, I had no desire to stay. Yet this was a Safe Haven, even if in name only, and where else did I have to go? I thought, perhaps there will be another Mira here, who will care for me as a younger sister, console me with her smiles. This, however, was not to be.

Some at Safe Haven sat by the window and rocked endlessly back and forth. Others plotted fantastic escapes involving *babus* who had promised to marry them and take them off to Africa or Trinidad or New York. Still others occupied themselves with gossip and gambling or concealed jars of whiskey and petty theft, which led shortly to clawing, hair-pulling, eye-scratching fights. The constant clatter of glass bangles and the thickness of perfumed oil and sweat intensified the sensation of closeness that resulted from our crowding and the heat, but more than that, from the common pointlessness of our being there.

The only organized activity was the cooking of our individual allotments of chickpea flour and rice. This we did in shifts over a long iron stove in the kitchen. One small window offered little ventilation, and the billowing smoke led to tears and more quarreling among the inmates. I took my food away and ate by myself in a corner of the common room beneath a notice promising embroidery lessons. Along the opposite wall sat three large iron sewing machines, but when I asked, no one had ever seen a teacher. Another notice promised literacy classes, and though there was no sign of this teacher either, I did discover a stack of books in the passageway outside Mrs Shaw's office. They were shiny red with pictures of yellow-haired girls and boys. A Rajasthani girl who saw me eyeing them told me to be careful, they had been sent special by Mrs Shaw's friends in America and the ayah Suman said not to touch them. I waited until she left, then slid one under my tunic. As soon as others began going to bed I crawled under the covers myself and examined the book in shadow.

I was not illiterate. I could decipher those notices on the wall, and like the language of the hills, the words in this book remembered me. Long ago my father had taught me to read. He was a soldier and knew at least five languages, but he instructed me that my worth would be weighed in English. I was then only three or four, but he taught me using a book just like this one, with images of foreign children and stories about goblins and witches rather than Hindu deities or Muslim heroes. He called them fairy tales. However, on the last night he spent with me he read a tale from that same book in which the moon looks down not on a white child but on an Indian maiden burning her lamp by the Ganges. She places the lamp upon the stream and sets it afloat as a test. As long as the flame remains lit she will know her loved one remains alive.

I hunted through this book at Safe Haven searching in vain for that story, but as I stared at the words, I could not read for the picture that arose in my mind of a man I had nearly forgotten. A man with black eyes and the softest of beards who cradled me in his lap and held me with gentle words. His wide square fingertip traced the letters by flickering candlelight. 'He lives!' he taught me to read. 'She rejoiced, and from the hills came the echo, "He lives!"'

The walls were high around Salamat Jannat, and the windows barred. There were only two ways into the compound, and I had checked both and found them securely locked. In spite of my nightmare that Golba possessed the key and would come to me here in this bed, and even though the other girls slept fitfully and several cried out during the night, no one from outside disturbed us.

Six mornings passed, and Mrs Shaw did not return. But her friend Lawrence came each afternoon, bearing sweets and cinema magazines and words of encouragement for us all. It was Vijay who really took charge, but the girls much preferred Lawrence. They would swarm about him like bees to the hive. And he would laugh and play magic tricks, pulling an anna from behind one's ear, turning three bangles into four. I no longer begged for him to take me with him, but hung back waiting my turn. For on the second day he had pulled me aside. He lifted his eyebrows, which were like two short flames, and led me to the farthest corner of the court-yard, away from all the others.

Speaking in broken Hindi, he asked if I was Kashmiri. I decided he wanted me to say yes. So I said yes. He said, good, would I like to go back there? I took a large breath and, daring to trust him, nodded.

He continued to study me with doubt in his eyes. Mrs Shaw had gone to Kashmir, he said. He was thinking of joining her. If he did,

73

he would take me with him. But I must wait. I must not run away before he made the arrangements.

Of course, I promised to stay. What Lawrence proposed was more than I could have dreamed.

Some days later he spoke to me again, but this time – just a few words – in the language of my earliest years. He asked what they used to call me. Again I sensed this was some kind of test. I answered slowly, carefully, in the same tongue. 'I do not remember.'

'I knew it!' he said in English. Then, more gently, 'Where did you learn to speak Turki?'

Afraid now, I babbled something about my childhood, about my mother and father coming together from distant worlds.

'Do you know where you were born?' he asked.

I shrugged.

'Not Kashmir?'

I remained silent.

'Beyond Kashmir,' he suggested. 'Beyond the mountains.'

I began to cry. The tears were so large and unexpected that I felt as though someone other than myself must be weeping. But then Lawrence put his arm around my shoulders. Don't worry, he told me, Mrs Shaw was making plans to travel to my native place. Perhaps she would need some help finding her way or translating the local language, if my English was good enough. Lawrence's touch was clumsy and tentative as a skittish dog's. I stopped crying. Though we both knew the truth, I assured him my English was good enough.

He released me and offered his white handkerchief to dry my eyes. We had to keep our plans secret, he said, for there was no room for the other girls to come with us, and also Mrs Shaw might still change her mind and return straightaway to Delhi. I told him I could keep good secrets, and even if I wanted to tell, I would trust no one here. He said he was sorry to hear that, but it was just as well. I must be prepared to leave at a moment's notice, no time for goodbyes. Then he said he must go. He had work to do. I told him he was a great man.

He smiled and picked up my hand. To my astonishment, he lifted it to his lips and actually kissed my skin. I could scarcely breathe, but he seemed to think nothing of it. We grinned at each other and for the first time I felt the pleasure of conspiracy.

After that, I no longer feared Golba. I see now how foolish this was. The police might have come for me at any moment, and neither Vijay nor even Lawrence could have stopped them. But for the first time, I had too much hope to run away in fear. Lawrence and Mrs Shaw really were going to help me, and as the days passed and no Golba appeared, I was even able to sleep.

None of this made it any less terrifying to wake in the middle of the night and find a hand across my mouth. My reflex was to scream. That night in police custody raced through my mind, and I was already squirming to flee when Lawrence whispered in my ear, 'It's a'right, Kammy. It's time.'

CHAPTER 3

1

...the first person who presented himself was the native doctor ... who came to report that an orphan boy, a Yârkandee, had been left on his hands by the death of the child's mother in the hospital ... We sent for him, and he soon appeared, quite a rosy fat-cheeked boy, with high cheekbones and narrow eyes, very Mongolian in type, dressed in a curious combination of the garments of Mecca, India, and Toorkistân ... I cannot claim any great amount of merit for thus taking charge of the boy ... I confess the thought that had chief possession of my mind was, how much this would help my plans. Even with barbarians, it could not but be a good introduction for a stranger, to bring back an orphan of their race, found abandoned in a distant land. They could scarcely cut one's throat arriving in their country on such an errand!

So wrote the intrepid Robert Shaw (unrelated to Aidan by blood, though kindred in spirit) in *Visits to High Tartary*, 1871. Lawrence looked up from the book to the girl seated beside him, his own fortuitous orphan, enthralled by her first airplane ride. The Dakota's roaring vibration made it appear that her fingers were trembling as they clutched the armrest. Her rapt face hugged the window. Hard to know exactly what stock could have produced such a turquoise-eyed beauty, but her linguistic skill certainly hinted at birth somewhere in Sinkiang. She might actually prove a useful translator, and just as in Shaw's day, a mission to see a lost child home was likely to sit better with certain local 'barbarians' than a search for a foreign

76

trespasser. A show of goodwill and peaceful intentions. But more important, he hoped it would have the same effect on Joanna.

It was folly, of course, she and young Simon trekking solo over one of the highest mountain passes in the world. She'd cabled only that Aidan might still be alive. But she'd asked Lawrence to obtain money and visas, to arrange with Hari for 'indefinite leave' from her duties at Safe Haven, and to investigate whether the *Herald* had had any communications from Aidan.

He had cabled her, NO NEWS HERALD OK SAFE HAVEN MEET YOU SRINAGAR.

FLYING LEH TUESDAY, she flashed back. SEND FINAL PAPERS MONEY BY EMBASSY PACKET.

To which Lawrence replied, WILL ARRIVE LEH WEDNESDAY PM WITH ALL.

He looked past Kamla through the window to the successive walls of snow and stone rising ahead of them, and the narrow gap that would pull them down to Srinagar. From there it would be a military prop to Leh.

What the hell was Aidan up to? Lawrence had planted a simple thought: use his journalistic cover to publicly nail the Soviets for sabotaging the UN-backed plebiscite in Kashmir. Everybody wins, Battersby had said. 'Your old mate reclaims his patriotic stripes and Australia wins the prize for pinning a tail on the Soviet donkey.' And this prize, in turn, would win for Jack the glory of becoming his nation's first official spymaster. He did have a point, though: Aidan hardly needed to twist the truth, and he should have had the whole thing wrapped up in a week without ever setting foot outside Srinagar. The wire that came in last night from Jack was succinct. *Find your mate. Whatever it takes.*

Lawrence smiled at Kamla cautiously unwrapping another stick of the Juicy Fruit gum he'd given her, as if it were a royal delicacy. He wished it were that easy to distract Joanna. Leh was the start of the Karakoram Trail, and her request for Chinese visas suggested that she was prepared to follow it all the way into Sinkiang. Right now China was in the middle of a far larger civil war than Kashmir's. Refugees were streaming out of the eastern provinces by the thousands, and while the threat of Mao's Communists might seem more muted in the west, the Soviets in Sinkiang were entrenched. The American Ambassador, Minton, had understandably resisted Jo's trip to Kashmir. If he were consulted, Sinkiang would be out of the question.

But Joanna had grit. She loved her husband and thought she'd lost him. Who could fault her for wanting to find him? And if Lawrence, as a family friend, came along to lend moral support, would this not, too, make sense? So he'd tucked away a suitable amount of cash in various currencies, packed the necessary supplies, and set about securing the appropriate clearances for Joanna, Simon, and himself, and – as extra insurance – for Kamla, their orphan escort.

The visas had been no small feat. The Chinese Ministry of Foreign Affairs was jammed to overflowing with petitioners, some of whom had begun lining up at two in the morning in hopes of securing aid for relatives trapped in China. Lawrence had to bribe the desk officer fifty Nationalist yuan just to get inside the building, then spent nearly an hour elbowing his way through the teeming corridors before he spotted the clerk he was seeking.

At least fifty people stood in the queue ahead of him. Lawrence, however, stood at least a foot taller than the tallest of the Chinese. The clerk glanced up at his approach, and his face split into a grin.

'Lawrence! How jolly good to see you!'

'Likewise, Y.C. Got a minute?'

'For you? Always.' Y. C. Ng hurriedly stamped the visas of the couple seated in front of his desk, then waved Lawrence into one of their vacated chairs. He drew a folding paper screen across his cubicle, shutting out the mutinous line.

Lawrence had rescued Y.C.'s brother in '41, during the fall of Hong Kong to the Japanese. In actual fact, all Lawrence had done was to arrange a job for the fellow in a Sydney butcher shop, but that was sufficient to save his life, and the whole family judged themselves forever in Lawrence's debt. Money had been offered many times over. Lawrence never accepted. Now Y.C. sprang into action as if grateful to bend a few rules. No questions asked.

Inside the back flap of Lawrence's pass Ng wrote a personal tribute under official seal, referring to Lawrence as a 'Hero of the Republic.' He improvised visas for Joanna, Simon, and Kamla, and for good measure prepared four special Chinese passports plastered with chop marks. The whole process took exactly five minutes.

Guanxi, the Chinese called it. Connection.

2

The Leh airstrip dropped diagonally down the slope of an immense bowl rimmed with vertical mountains. It was paved in stone and ice and rubble, all but indistinguishable from the inclines to either side. No hint here of the spring that had been erupting in Srinagar. No trees, no grass, and only a bluish tinge to mark the distant fields stepping down to the swollen Indus. The road leading past the runway, the rectangular dwellings wedged into the mountainside, the peaks themselves with their crumbles of snow and even the cloudless but eerily reflective sky gave off so little color that when Joanna squinted, the whole scene merged into a single undifferentiated blur.

She had flown up with Simon the day before – a harrowing flight made more so by the specter of the crash that had lured them to Kashmir in the first place. Now she saw just how easily this could happen. Flying here meant navigating between rather than above the peaks, often with no more than a dozen feet of grace off either wing. On landing the plane tipped so far to one side it seemed they must have blown a tire, a sensation created by the steep downhill grade of the runway. Yet through it all, Simon had wiggled and bounced as if they were on an amusement ride, much the same way he was now finding entertainment in flag signal lessons from the Gujarati airman waiting with them for the plane carrying Lawrence.

Lawrence had strong-armed her, she decided, sitting down in the lean-to that served as a waiting area. Not that this plan wasn't risky, but Akbar had sworn by their Sherpa guide, and the lighter they traveled the faster they'd move. All she needed were the travel visas and a supply of money to get her over the border, if it came to that. What she did not need was another escort second-guessing her.

Three days after their arrival in Srinagar, the UN rescue team had relayed back word confirming that Aidan Shaw's was not among the bodies found at the crash site. That same afternoon

General Farr introduced Joanna to a UPI reporter who had heard that a foreigner fitting Aidan's description was seen trekking north on the Karakoram Trail four days after the crash. Only rumors, the UPI man cautioned, but there were also reports of a serious avalanche in the same area, and no one had seen this foreigner return.

Farr eyed Joanna as she took in the meaning of the reporter's words. 'Now don't go off half-cocked,' he warned. It was a chance phrase, one of millions he could have chosen, but the words sent her reeling. *Don't go off half-cocked.* Aidan had used those exact words when he returned from Chungking in '45.

He'd been gone seven dangerous months that trip, and even as they stood in the international arrivals terminal upon his return, with all the happy distractions of peacetime and reunion and four-year-old Simon's well-rehearsed appeals to 'Daddy,' Joanna could taste the betrayal in her husband's kiss. She knew from the way he held her, spasmodically alternating between an embrace like vapor and a guilty, yanking clutch. She smelled it in his skin.

That night, when they were alone, and before he felt compelled to touch her again, she confronted him. It was characteristic of Aidan that he did not try to deny it. Sometimes she thought her husband constitutionally incapable of telling a lie.

'Now, don't go off half-cocked,' he'd said instead, his eyes weighed down with sadness. 'I'm home, Joanna.'

She'd felt as though her internal organs were made of paper, which he was slowly, methodically, shredding. They would not survive a confession stocked with name, place, and physical description, so she asked only if he saw the other woman's face when he closed his eyes. She knew they were in for it when he didn't answer. But she also watched the glint of alarm when she said, more out of calculation than truth, that she could see herself doing the same in another place and time. She had hit her mark, and retreated before more damage could be done.

She did not go off half-cocked, but sought out the friends of Aidan's whose judgments she believed. The international press pool in those days, especially among China Hands, was a loose-knit group who drank together, traded information, and watched each other's backs. In Chungking they'd lived clustered in the official Press Hostel. No affairs went unnoticed, and it didn't take Joanna long to find among the recent returnees mutual friends who had witnessed her husband's indiscretions. Why the picture of the willowy redhead with a slight lisp and knock-knees and Irish surname was more bearable, even intriguing, coming from neutral observers, Joanna could not say. But it was.

The redhead was married. An adventuress playing at journalism. After Hiroshima and Nagasaki, she reportedly went back to her wealthy husband and manor house in Kildare. There had been tears, one public scene in the hostel barroom when Aidan threw his whiskey in her face. That night he kept on drinking, talked loudly about 'women too stubborn to know when they needed rescuing.'

Joanna could count on one hand the number of times she'd seen her husband drunk. Never had she witnessed him so passionately misbehaving, and the very thought of his despair now made her feel hollow inside. What pleasures must this woman have offered that Aidan should feel such anguish at the loss of her? She tormented herself with the inevitable images. And the inevitable question. How could she – his dutiful wife – possibly compete? She who had known all too well that she needed rescuing.

Their estrangement only came to an end after she sought out Ben Eldon, the photographer whose life Aidan had saved in Burma. Ben had gone back out to Chungking to cover the end of the war. He'd been a witness to the affair. But as he sat with her drinking coffee in a brightly lit delicatessen in Georgetown, he said he believed this had been Aidan's only infidelity. Joanna was trying to decide whether this made it better or worse when Ben leaned down and began to rub the trouser covering his artificial knee. He worked at his leg unconsciously for several seconds, and suddenly his face changed – he had one of those fair Southern faces, almost frail, that altered like a cirrus cloud with every passing thought. He hoisted his prosthesis onto the vinyl seat of their booth and scrunched up his pant leg to show her the works. 'It's been almost four years since this leg was real, but I still feel it itch and ache.' He rapped on the mechanical knee with his knuckles. 'It's like part of me died ahead of the rest, like I'm already part ghost . . .'

Joanna shook her head. She liked and admired Ben, but she could not imagine what he was driving at. 'All right, forget it if you think I'm cracked,' he said, 'but when you're out there sometimes you get into some funny chats with folks. And this one time Aidan started telling me about his mama. I'm sure you know how he felt like he's kind of responsible for her dying back there in China?'

Joanna considered. Aidan always referred to his mother as a 'beauty scarred by history and betrayed by optimism.' She and the family had moved to China in 1920 when Aidan's father went to work for a Belgian firm surveying railroad routes in the interior province of Shansi. They arrived in the middle of a peasant revolt against the local warlord, and in the melee the severed heads of their steward and amah were tossed onto the Shaws' front doorstep. The family retreated to Shanghai, and Aidan's mother began a long, bitter spiral into madness. Over the next dozen years she became convinced that the servants, local politicians, even the teachers at the children's school were all scheming to poison her. She filled notebooks with her suspicions that there was ground glass in her soup, bamboo shavings in her oatmeal, deadly nightshade in her tea. She pled with her husband to send her home to Ireland.

Aidan's Chinese grandmother maintained that the ghosts of the servants in Shansi had possessed her daughter-in-law's spirit. Finally Aidan's father gave in to his mother's demand that she take his younger son home with her to Nanking. But by this time Aidan was seventeen, had completed his schooling in Shanghai, and was angling to go to university in the States. It was 1933. Reluctantly, his father agreed, though he would not permit Aidan to take his mother with him. 'There will be time for that,' the old man promised. 'As soon as you have established yourself.'

Five months later Aidan received news that his mother had died after swallowing a cake laced with rat poison that the gardener left under a backyard azalea. Aidan, it seemed, had not established himself soon enough.

Ben said, 'Aidan first told me about his family way back in Burma, but then in Chungking one night he was talking about . . .' He hesitated, and Joanna stopped him with a look. She didn't want to know the woman's name.

'Anyway,' he continued, 'he said she reminded him so much of his mother it was spooky, and I thought, uh oh, something else is going on here, something maybe Aidan can't even see. You understand what I'm trying to say? It was like he was still fixing to rescue his mama . . .'

Joanna didn't know if Ben was right, but she found it impossible to accuse her husband after that. Given time, his promises regained their ring of truth. Gradually the familiar smooth spice taste and smell of him returned, the sorrow retreated from his eyes, and she would feel him touching his hand to her back or watch him gently stroking Simon on his lap as he read his newspaper, and she knew her husband was really home.

'If I'd been there,' she dared to ask him one night, 'in Chung-king, if I'd been there *with* you, would it . . .?'

They were sitting in the darkened living room, winter, watching the snow come down. He reached across the distance between their chairs and took her hand. His fingers threaded through hers. 'No,' he said, finishing her question for her. 'It would never have happened.'

Simon hove into view, up on the airman's shoulders, oblivious to the altitude and pumping his arm like the leader of a band while his new friend sang the Indian national anthem. It was because of Simon that she'd stayed home in '44. He was still so little then, still Simon of the cowboy hat, who clung to her hand in crowds and wept when she left his sight. There could be no thought of taking him to China, but neither could she leave him. Simon had come first. He was her baby. How could it have been otherwise?

The whir of an engine sounded in the distance. Though the plane was not yet in sight, the airman deposited Simon back in the lean-to and marched out with his flags at the ready. Simon's face was chapped pink by the wind and cold, his slight body doubled by the bulk of the long sheepskin jacket they had acquired in Srinagar, but he could hardly contain himself as he showed her the signals the airman had taught him. He was older now, sturdier, more resilient. He needed her less – she encouraged him to need her less. As if to prove it, when Joanna tried to hug him, he impatiently squirmed away.

This time, it might just be that Aidan needed her more.

'When do you think Tot will get here?' Simon asked.

'He promised by tomorrow.'

Tot was the Sherpa guide Akbar had recommended. Dr Akbar, bless him, had not made a peep when Joanna said she meant to go after her husband. On the contrary, he announced that if he were younger and not suffering from the gout he would accompany her himself. But he knew she'd be better off with Tot and insisted on introducing them.

The nickname was minted by a British mountaineer who'd hired the Sherpa years earlier, but it stuck because Tot liked the sound and because every foreigner he met said it suited him. He stood hardly more than five feet tall with bright eyes, big ears, and a childlike giggle, but also powerful shoulders and huge hands and a joyous air not the least undermined by his supreme but understated confidence in his own ability. He wore a red Ladakhi robe, green felt Himachal cap, and English plimsolls with red and blue leggings. Dr Akbar told Joanna that Tot's expeditions had never lost a man. She couldn't help asking, 'What about women and children?'

That startled Akbar. Evidently he had not understood that Joanna meant to take Simon along on this rescue mission. After a thoughtful pause, he said, 'You are welcome to leave Simon here with me, Joanna. He is young, after all. And China is at war.'

'So's Kashmir,' she pointed out. Dr Akbar's generosity did not entirely preclude the possibility (always present in Asia – and probably the world over) that he had befriended her for some less savory motive of his own. But the offer was already moot because even as they spoke, the Sherpa was entrancing Simon with a series of rope tricks. Joanna interrupted to hire him. They would travel the Karakoram Trail, she explained, as far as was necessary to determine the whereabouts and condition of her husband.

Tot grinned broadly and said that in that case, he must start right away. He assumed that she and Simon would fly as far as Leh, but since he did not like his feet to leave the ground, he preferred to trek. It would take no more than four days, he assured her, and they could start after her husband as soon as he arrived.

Again now she wished Tot alone were accompanying them. She dreaded having to explain – to justify – her decisions to Lawrence. But she had no choice. Simon pointed to a glittering speck that had

84

just emerged from behind the low peak near the end of the runway. 'That's him!' he said.

The plane banked steeply and dropped, one wing several feet lower than the other. It met the ground in a series of hops, brakes screaming as it shuddered to a halt.

Simon started forward, waving frantically. Joanna yanked him back for fear he'd run straight into the propellers. She reminded herself that Simon loved Lawrence. And Aidan trusted him.

Then the door swung open and he appeared at the top of the air steps, his bulk seeming to dwarf the fuselage. Bareheaded, wearing only a dark green sweater and no overcoat, he created a burst of fog with his breath, yet appeared not to notice the cold. He lifted a hand to shade his eyes, and Simon dashed forth, yelling. Lawrence grinned, and in spite of herself Joanna felt a spasm of relief. The sheer solidity of him, the familiarity of that smile, even the strange dance of those mismatched eyes promised reassurance.

Simon was just reaching the bottom of the steps when Lawrence turned back into the plane. A second later a much smaller figure appeared beside him, huddled inside a black leather flight jacket. Joanna blinked, thinking the altitude must be distorting her vision. But no. It was a child. Lawrence put his arm around her, started her down toward Simon. Celery green fabric flowed beneath the flight jacket. A black braid draped over one shoulder. The child held her chin up, aquamarine eyes reaching toward Joanna.

Her heart turned over. My God, she thought looking from the girl to Lawrence. Have we *all* lost our minds?

It took them close to an hour to walk back to the rest house, with Simon exuberantly clinging to Lawrence and singing songs to impress the girl. The boy clearly had no reservations about these new companions. Indeed, he could hardly wait to show Kamla their rest house and bedroom, which he unilaterally decided she should share with him and Joanna. And for her part, the girl seemed to take Simon as much in stride as she took her reunion with 'Mrs Shaw.' She smiled and nodded at both of them, and when they reached the rest house she obeyed Simon's command to sit while he showed off all the wooden tops and puzzles he'd picked up in Srinagar. Joanna couldn't imagine what

85

Lawrence must have told her to set Kamla so at ease.

But she waited until the children were engrossed in their play before steering him back to the outer room. 'What on earth possessed you?' she whispered.

'C'mon, Jo. Aidan would never forgive me if I let you and Simon set off alone.'

'You know what I'm talking about. Bringing that child here is insane and probably illegal.'

'No more illegal than anything else she's been through. Besides, I knew you wouldn't want me to leave her back.'

'You're a mind reader, are you?'

'Call it a hunch, but I believe, one way or another, she'd have disappeared by the time you got back to Delhi. Hari's put Vijay in charge, and while the lad means well—'

'You actually think she's safer *here*?'

He hooked his thumbs in his belt. 'I do . . . actually. And she can serve as a translator.'

'Her English isn't good enough to translate a nursery rhyme!'

'She's a bloody quick study. And she knows Turki. I'm pretty sure she's originally from Sinkiang.'

'I mean to find Aidan long before we reach Sinkiang!'

'Then why'd you have me bring those Chinese visas?'

Joanna faltered. 'Insurance . . . I don't plan to need them.'

'And I hope you're right. But in any case, I've promised Kamla to see her home.'

'*Home?*' She sat down at the long plank table where her maps were spread, showing Sinkiang to be more than three times the size of France. 'Did she tell you where exactly this home is?'

He gave her a hard look. 'I like the challenge of lost causes.'

She watched him reach toward her, cup his hand over her ear. Thinking he was going to touch her, she flinched. Instead he opened his palm. She felt a shiver of air travel the length of her neck. Between his right forefinger and index finger he held a small paper rectangle. 'I found this as I was heading out the door.'

She took the piece of paper, a photograph of Aidan she'd never seen. He was grinning, relaxed, the sun in his eyes. His hair hung shaggy around the ears. The shadow of a beard outlined his chin, and he looked as though someone had just told him a joke. Joanna's stomach clutched. 'Where did you get this?'

'I had my guide shoot the two of us in Afghanistan. It's the way I remember Aidan in the war, how he is in the field. How he would be now. That press photo you're carrying makes him look like a bloody spy. I'd show this instead.'

She ran her finger along the rough, scissored edge where Lawrence had cut himself out of the shot. 'Why'd you do that?'

' 'Cause you don't need a picture of me.' He paused. 'I'm the one that's here.'

She felt his eyes simultaneously holding her back and drawing her forward. 'I suppose I should thank you. For being here.'

'That's not what I want.'

'What *do* you want, Lawrence?'

'I want this not to be a lost cause.'

3

After we joined Mrs Shaw and her son in Leh, I began, like the others, to call her Mem. It seemed strange, at first, as if I must be addressing someone new or changed. But I sensed that something had changed, or would very shortly, and so I did as she requested, for it was she who said, most abruptly, 'No more Mrs Shaw, Kamla.' And the son, Simon, explained, 'I call her Mem. Like Mom. Like *memsahib*. Like Mom in India.' He told me to do the same.

Lawrence had warned that Mrs Shaw might not approve of my coming, but I knew when she returned my smile at the airfield that my claim on her was still good. She took my hand. She touched my hair. She shook her head and asked how on earth Lawrence could have brought a child like me to this 'godforsaken place.' I could hear in the softness of her voice that she was not truly angry. And while I could not have explained why, I knew that in her secret heart she was content that I had come. Her son did not bother to keep his pleasure secret, but danced around me like a young monkey.

Simon and I were friends from the first. He reminded me of the boy Surie who lived near the flash house – spoiled as a son had every right to be, but also innocent and eager. That evening Simon made a game of splashing his soup and gobbling sweets until Mem sent him from the table, yet he was not at all contrite and later, while Mem and Lawrence pored over maps, he showed me the rope tricks his new friend in Srinagar had taught him. He knew enough Hindi and I enough English that we just understood each other. I called him Little Brother and taught him a song my father used to sing about the rustle of *chikor* in the grasses under the gleaming moon.

As I sang I recalled how this melody would bring tears to my eyes in Indrani's house. Here in Leh the old words filled me with joy. For Lawrence had promised to take me home. We would all travel into the mountains to find Mem's missing husband, he said. And I would find my father. In the meantime I was given a cot in the very same room as Mem and Simon. This room was little more than a whitewashed cell with a gray cement floor and red and blue Ladakhi rugs pinned up over the windows, but the cot was more comfortable than either Indrani's kitchen floor or the *charpoy* at Safe Haven, and I lay with my father's song in my mind long after the others were sleeping.

I awoke the next morning to find Mem and Lawrence in the main room. There was argument in their voices. I did not understand all the words, but I heard my name once or twice, and the name of Mem's husband, Aidan. Mem looked worried and angry and frightened. She would not meet Lawrence's eyes and he would not turn his away from her.

As I stood in the doorway, I noticed a new man seated by the fire listening intently. I saw at once that he was a hill man with wide, flat features and a strength of muscle and bone far greater than his height. Neither old nor young, he winked at me and made *namaskar* with his hands. I returned the greeting. Then the argument stopped and Simon came up behind me rubbing the sleep from his eyes. Mem introduced the stranger as Tot, 'our Sherpa guide.' Simon explained that this was the very friend who had taught him the rope tricks. The Ladakhi owner of the rest house, a woman who melted about us like a shadow, brought a plate of dumplings, *momos,* and cups of thick buttered tea, and after we had eaten we walked together into the bazaar like a tribe of newfound friends.

The marketplace seemed to crouch beneath the walls of Leh's great palace, which sat up on the hill like an old squat toad. The palace, the road, the buildings and mountains all were of the same chalky gray, and yet there was no shortage of color. Buddhist prayer flags flapped their bright reds and blues along the road, and the stalls were piled high with rich brown grains, purple cabbages, slab apricots and eggs, goatskin capes, and Ladakhi neckpieces made of silver and turquoise and orange-red coral. Simon held my hand, and we swung our arms, our voices echoing between ancient stones. I wore a set of his clothing – Western jeans and a red flannel shirt. This made me feel free and new. Soon we were skipping through the narrow alleyways, and I realized that I had not skipped since I was a small, small girl.

Lawrence bought a threaded top for Simon and a new blue felt jacket for me. Mem strode ahead, with Tot to carry her purchases of yak-wool blankets and caps and leggings, leather boots and water flasks, and dried meat and rice. The bazaar was thronged with hill men, Turki traders, Buddhist monks spinning prayer wheels, and peasants selling the crafts they had produced over the long winter. The morning was warm and fresh, surely cause for celebration, yet the marketplace produced so little noise that it seemed, except for ourselves, Leh must be a city of mutes. Only later, listening to Simon pant as we struggled up a steep rock hill, did I remember something I was told long ago – that when air is brittle and thin, talk is a waste of breath.

It was then that Mem turned to me and asked if I had ever been here before. And I realized, quite dumbstruck, that I had.

4

'Kamla was here before. Did she tell you?' Joanna passed a mug of tea to Lawrence across the table. It was late. The children had gone to bed, the innkeeper off to her own lodgings. Tot had just left for town and the hostel where he was staying.

When Lawrence didn't reply, she went on, 'She remembers the palace, the silence of the bazaar, all the red and blue and yellow prayer flags. And Srinagar, too. The *shikara*. Water lilies. Just in the short time you stopped to change planes it all came back to her. Did you realize?'

He shook his head. 'Not in so many words.' He watched her draw her elbows tight against her chest, press her mug against her cheek. Only her hair fell loose and relaxed, swimming with light from the kerosene table lamp. Over the few weeks he'd known her Lawrence had seen that hair in knots, trailing strands from the cover of hats and scarves, twisted up the back of her head, or caught with combs so that it seemed to strain with a restive will of its own. This was the first time he'd seen it freed.

'She says she walked into India over the mountains. No pack animals. Nothing. And I believe it. The altitude seems to have no effect on her.'

'Anything else?' he asked quietly.

She lowered a hand to the map in front of her. 'There's only one trail over these mountains. If we follow it back she's sure to remember more. If she could make it at – what? Four? *Five?*' Her voice spiked.

'If survival were a sure thing, we wouldn't need to go at all. I'm as eager to be off as you are, believe me, but Tot knows what he's doing.'

Her shoulders twisted, her eyes darting to the ceiling. She bit down so hard on the corner of her mouth that blue tooth marks formed in her lower lip. This had been building ever since the Sherpa's arrival that morning. Joanna had her heart set on starting after Aidan as soon as Tot appeared, and when he refused she tried every angle to persuade him. Prods, orders, pleas, demands, and regular sidelong glares at Lawrence to back her up. Tot, however, was not trying to thwart them. His grin never wavered as he insisted his first concern was for their safety. On his trek from Srinagar, he'd heard continuing rumors of bandits along the Karakoram route and of more avalanches. To reach the Nubra Valley, where Aidan had been sighted, was only a few days' march from Leh, but if they then decided to continue over the passes, they would need some sort of escort to get past the border guards, and considerably more provisions than Joanna had now – more than they could acquire in the Nubra. Tot assured them it would take no more than a day or two to find a caravan and fill out their equipment. In any case, this delay would help their bodies adjust to the altitude. He was not asking permission.

Joanna didn't dare force Tot's hand – not with the children at risk – but all day Lawrence had sensed her frustration. She needed to release some of that fury, and he didn't mind her venting it on him. If anyone deserved it, he did, whether she realized that – would ever realize it – or not. Now, however, her defiance wavered as she came back to him and tried to stare him down.

He might have warned her. Primitives he'd encountered in New Guinea during the war thought his eyes marked him as a god, or witch doctor at the least. And in the Foreign Office, it had derailed his opponents more than once to look up and find this split image glaring back at them. His ex-wife refused to fight with him because she said his eyes gave him an unfair advantage. Only Davey loved this defect. As a baby he would cover the green, then the gray – their own brand of peek-a-boo – to see which color would appear when he pulled his hand away. Later, when Davey began to pick up tunes from the ether around him, 'Jeepers, Creepers' became his personal favorite. 'Jeepers, creepers, where'd you get those peepers?' The high, reedy voice would taunt and tease, luring his father down to meet Davey's own merry eyes, matched and dark as two licorice slices. Forehead to forehead, they'd have staring contests as his son kept humming the question to which there seemed no answer. Still later, he would grill Lawrence, taking a more scholarly approach – did he see different colors from each one, what made the color in an eye anyway, why was he the only person in the world to have two different eyes, was that a good or bad thing, what would Lawrence think if Davey became an eye doctor when he grew up? Lawrence told him anything Davey did was sure to make his dad proud. Then Davey died and now, as he watched the squirming in Joanna's gaze, he hated his mismatched eyes.

'I'm sorry.' He looked at the floor.

There was a long pause. Then she said softly, 'I am too.'

At length she asked, 'What would you do in my place?'

He thought of Davey. 'I'd be there with bells on, love, if it made a difference. But that's a bloody big if.'

91

5

That same night Tot learned of a caravan destined for Kashgar with a cargo of Indian hemp and jute. The leader had already taken on a Muslim merchant and his wife returning with their newborn daughter from a two-year pilgrimage to Mecca. Why not a band of foreigners?

When they all met the next day Joanna thought the caravan leader bore an unnerving resemblance to Rasputin, and she worried that the size of his load would make them impossibly slow, but Tot said they were ready to start in the morning, and any forward movement was better than none. She agreed with Lawrence to meet the headman's demand of one hundred Nationalist yuan.

The sky as they set off was cobalt blue, the sunshine so crisp and sheer it seemed to vibrate in the high mountain air. Behind them the pallid sprawl of Leh stepped down to the newly sprung green of the Indus Valley, and beyond that, layer upon white and blue layer of Himalayas licked the far horizon. Even the ragtag team of caravan men, with their unwashed beards and burning eyes, seemed touched by a degree of splendor. But while the Muslim merchant took his place up front with the headman, his anonymous *begum* lurched behind them sidesaddle, her child hidden in the folds of her voluminous black *burqa*. If she took any pleasure in this day, none of them would know, for her face and even her eyes were hidden behind the cloak's net window.

Lawrence and Tot chose to walk the first stretch, leading the children's ponies, but Simon and Kamla soon proved adept at handling their own mounts and could be allowed to move ahead. Simon raised his arm like Roy Rogers spinning a lariat, while beside him Kamla smiled good-naturedly, her face shining in the clear thin light. Joanna knew what they were feeling, this strange, almost addictive blend of freedom and anticipation. The risks of this expedition were countless, yet if *she* were missing, she told herself, Aidan wouldn't think twice about going after her. Like Lawrence, in fact, he'd keep copious notes in hopes of getting a book out of it.

Lawrence used cheap Indian copybooks for his journals. He liked to make lists. Yesterday he'd asked the children to help him name all the foods that were different in Ladakh from Kashmir and in Kashmir from Delhi. Said he found a certain poetry in lists. The beauty as well as the challenge was in the arrangement, he said.

Aidan, too, once organized his notes with meticulous care. Then the FBI's first 'blind memorandum' hit home. She remembered the bonfire they'd made of his journals in the fireplace back in Maryland. Twelve years' worth of interviews and observations that spanned the war and the globe. 'They can find incriminating evidence in the Lord's Prayer if they want to,' Aidan said as the flames died down, 'but they're not going to stop me.' He tapped his forehead. 'From now on, the notebook's in here.'

She shook out her hands and quickened her step. Lawrence dropped back beside her as they passed a crumbling stone and mortar structure, which Tot identified as the Temple of Guardian Deities. The vibration of the air seemed to repeat in the low cyclical chants of the lamas inside. Like the prayer wheels the lamas spun as they sang, the chants marked the constant revolution of life and death and life. 'What must it be to believe like that,' Joanna wondered aloud. 'To immerse yourself in perpetual devotion.'

Lawrence answered by turning to Tot. 'Correct me if I'm wrong, but isn't the idea to escape what it is they're singing about?'

The Sherpa trudged in time to the lingering rhythm. He replied, 'The object is to achieve release from the worldly cycle of rebirth. To achieve nirvana.'

'Precisely,' said Lawrence.

Pre-soyce-ly, Joanna repeated to herself.

But for once he was serious. He tugged his topee down over his eyes and said in a tone that put her on notice, 'To escape all this blasted devotion.'

6

KARAKORAM LUGGAGE
  Meade tents, kapok sleeping bags,
  Tarpaulins, blankets, paregoric.
  Flasks of whiskey and canteened water,
  Fodder for beasts of burden.

Matches, rope and iodine,
Lanterns and leather gloves.
Sheepskin hats and long johns,
Primus stoves and kerosene.
Twenty pounds of flour, rice,
Tinned meat and biscuits and cooking oil,
One trusty Sten Mark II,
Notes in warring currencies –
US, Russian, Chinese, Turki.
Now on to the roof of the world!

Lawrence wrote this on the inside of a Cadbury's wrapper. He'd brought one dozen candy bars with him from Delhi and rationed us to one every three days. Mem said she would never forget the expression on my face the first time Simon persuaded me to try this dark, ominous food.

'You look as though you've fallen in love.' She smiled in a way – wrinkling her nose – that let me know she was truly smiling and not merely fixing her face in a smile. Then she clenched her hand to her heart and licked her lips to demonstrate her meaning. Lawrence and Simon nodded in agreement, and after that I would forever associate chocolate with happiness.

For I recognized that I *was* happy among these people, even as I came to see just how little any of us had to be happy about. Mem's husband, Simon's father, was missing. Simon told me that Lawrence had a son who recently had died. And I myself had been missing from my own father for so many years and across so many miles that I hardly dared to believe that Mem and Lawrence could succeed in rejoining us. Yet I took strength from their promise.

As we climbed higher the weather turned bitter cold. The trail was hard, and the clouds slunk down like low gray hats around the mountaintops. The air tasted of stone coupled with the warm, dank smell of the pack animals. I frequently heard Mem and Simon gasping for breath, and often we stopped for them to rest. At night Lawrence taught us the stars, by day the names of plants and rock formations. Tot taught me and Simon to shoot pebbles across the streams we passed (never down the trail, for fear of sparking an avalanche). Mem helped me with my English. The Muslim woman in her *burqa,* or upside-down bag, as Simon said, let me hold her baby sometimes while she moved off to relieve herself. And every few hours the father in his embroidered blue skullcap and thickly padded coat would step to the side of the trail, roll out his prayer mat and drop to his knees, and bow and bow in praise of Allah as the rest of the caravan marched past. Tot told us that the Muslim family had walked all the way from China to Mecca to make their *hadj* and now were on their way home. Their baby was born on the road; they'd been walking for two years. At night when I lay in the tent with Mem and Simon packed in close beside me – the time I loved most of all – I would try to imagine our trek continuing for two years, and I wondered, if that were to happen, would this make me part of Mem's family?

The caravan drivers kept to themselves. They wore sheepskins and heavy beards, high leather boots, and astrakhan hats with earflaps. They did not change their clothes or bathe. Crumbs nested in their reddish brown beards, and their laughs shot forth without warning, like flames. They used no tents but piled pack boxes to create rough windbreaks. They liked to rise late, linger over tea, then march well into darkness – all habits that made Lawrence shrug and angered Mem. Simon's only complaint was the men's treatment of the animals – they drove them with prods and whips, and bellowed curses when they slowed. Food and water were given only as afterthoughts at the end of each day's march, and if Simon tried to pet or feed one of the ponies himself, the men would surround him with arms folded high, eyebrows bristling. Some sheathed daggers in their boots. Some were Kashmiri freedom fighters when they were not working as drivers, and none shared this foreign boy's concern for the welfare of animals, which anyway were expected to die before long. The leader, who went by the single name Muhammad, muttered that Simon would do better to worry about his own health, and predicted that he would weaken before the first pass. I chose not to translate this prediction for the others.

Fortunately, with Lawrence about, Simon had little need of the drivers' approval. Lawrence had an unmistakable gift for entertaining young boys. He noticed a small cleft in Simon's left earlobe and proclaimed it a magic door. Coins, sugar cubes, dried beans, and biscuits poured from this 'slot' into Lawrence's hand, much to all our delight. And Lawrence loved to tell stories about the seemingly endless array of characters he carried in his head. The nightly telling and retelling of these stories taught me his language as we all learned of men such as Colonel Alexander Gardiner, who disguised himself in tribal robes and found 'adventure through sword and spear.' Or the Indian Pundits who dressed as pilgrims and hid surveying equipment in their prayer wheels that they might secretly map the farthest reaches of the Himalayas for their British masters. Or George Hayward, a British political agent who spent twenty days in the mountains in winter without a tent. Unable to build a fire for lack of fuel, Hayward finally killed his pack yak and ate the meat raw in order to survive. All part of the Great Game, Lawrence would say.

At first I thought by this term, Great Game, he meant something like the Hindu term, maya, which my flash house sisters had taught me refers to the illusion of earthbound desire. But no, Simon said, the Great Game was more like a secret war. It was real, had taken place in these very mountains over the last hundred years, and Lawrence was writing a book about it. The men whose stories he told to us were all players in this war. Lawrence called them spies, opportunists, and zealots – terms which, he explained, meant they were up to no good, but I could see he admired these men. Perhaps he envied them. Then Simon told me his father was equally handsome and smart and brave, and I found myself wondering if Mem's missing husband, too, were a hero in this Great Game.

7

'Tell me about him,' Lawrence asked.

'Why?'

'Because it's starting to feel like the rhino in the parlor, Jo. The one that everyone knows is there and no one ever mentions.'

'It. You mean Aidan.' She wedged her hands between her knees and studied the campfire embers. That crushing sensation in her chest, she told herself, was altitude.

'Yes.'

'What do you want to know that you don't already? He's your friend, Lawrence.'

'He's *your* husband. You know him better than anyone. Tell me. If Farr hadn't cabled you about that crash, how long would it have taken you to start worrying?'

'You mean, how long is his leash?'

'I wouldn't put it like that. But he's a correspondent. He goes off. It's what they do. You're the first wife I know to charge after one of them.'

'Call it woman's intuition.'

'Call it anything you like. My question is why?'

'He's my *husband*, for Christ's sake! Why shouldn't I?'

'Fair enough,' Lawrence said quietly. 'But I'm asking why you should.'

'Because he promised. He . . . he warned me.'

'Warned you?'

'Before we got married. He said, "It's not going to be an ordinary life. Making a home, putting down roots. I'd rather die in my tracks." '

'He said that?'

She reached into the embers with the toe of her boot and attempted to stir them back to life. 'I remember we were driving through Rock Creek Park in the old blue Buick I bought when I first arrived in Washington. We were fording a stream. The sunlight cast this dappling like gold feathers spinning through the air, and the water splashed up over the running board, and I opened my door and dragged my hand in it. Silly, really. Aidan just watched me with that smile on his face – the indulgent, affectionate one.'

'I know it.'

'And that's when he warned me: no ordinary life. Only I took it as a promise. We had a picnic that day of Chinese sausage and dumplings that he'd bought in some hole in the wall and kept warm in a thermos, of all things! And a shaker of martinis. We lay on our old tartan blanket most of the afternoon getting pleasantly smashed and talking about all the adventures we'd have, all the places we'd live once the war was over. And I could hardly wait. I imagined . . . Well, you know the absurd thing is, I imagined being in places just like this.' She batted the cold with the back of one hand, a forefinger indiscriminately cocked at the moon-drenched trail and pale, scattered tents, the tilting immensity of the darkness. 'Hard situations. Impossible, even. But we'd be together.'

Lawrence let out an inscrutable laugh. 'You're an unusual woman, Joanna.'

'Why? Because the notion of an unconventional marriage excited me?'

'Because you're undaunted.'

'Am I?'

'Looks that way from where I sit.' He shifted his camp chair as if to improve the view.

She dug her heels now into the ashes. 'Aidan's the one who's undaunted. We'd have bang-up fights sometimes about my work, how I could ever expect to accomplish anything meaningful working with one child, one family at a time. I'm sure you've heard him talk about the Big Picture.'

'It has a vaguely familiar ring,' he said wryly, but she was serious.

'There always has to be a larger scheme. Saving one life isn't enough if by pulling a few more strings you can save a thousand, or hundreds of thousands. I told him that's how wars get fought, reducing human lives to numbers, but afterward it's individuals who have to pick up the pieces.'

'What strings was *he* pulling?'

'Why, his articles, of course. Each time he skewered Chiang Kai-shek, in his mind he was championing the millions who'd been robbed or maimed or killed by Chiang and his warlords. Same when he was writing about Hitler or the Japanese.'

'We live in large times.'

'We still suffer one by one – especially children.'

'He didn't support your work?'

She drew in her legs and arms sharply. 'I didn't say that. But he saw it tying me down, holding me back. Occupying me.'

'Was he jealous?'

'God, no! I don't think so. But it was as if he spent his days looking through a wide-angle lens, and I spent mine at the microscope. He said I rescued children because I was still trying to put the pieces of my own childhood together.'

'And he wasn't?'

'That's what I said! He refused to talk about it, but losing your entire family in the space of six years *must* be worse than never knowing your parents at all. I felt like I could never get to the bottom of him, you know?'

'Aidan's a fascinating man, Jo. If you understood him, he'd bore you, and we wouldn't be here now.'

'I suppose . . .' Her palms fell open on her knees. She stared at their moonlit whiteness. 'He was forever searching for evidence that someone in his family had survived. They'd been living in Nanking when Chiang Kai-shek bolted. But after the Japanese were through, the family home was destroyed and every name Aidan tried to contact was either dead or missing. He blamed the Chinese Nationalists and the Japanese equally. I think that's what's really behind this fixation with his so-called Big Picture. Why I always let him win that fight.'

'Why?' Lawrence asked.

'Because he *is* the child left behind. One way or the other, he'll devote the rest of his days to picking up his family's pieces. Naturally, he wants revenge on some larger scale than one life at a time.'

'Naturally,' Lawrence repeated. 'You loved him for that.'

'For his hatred?'

'No. For his sense of mission. Even if it was based on revenge.'

'I *love* him. Present tense. What does it matter why?'

'Sometimes the people we love reveal who we are.'

'So who am I?'

'A crusader, just like Aidan.'

'I'm nothing like Aidan.'

'But you wish you were . . . In fact, you envy him.'

'Yes. I guess I do.'

After a long pause Lawrence said, 'That makes two of us, then.'

8

For three days, the route crisscrossed the rapids and sand flats of the Shyok River. The ponies, submerged to their withers, had to be roped together so the torrents of glacial melt wouldn't sweep them away. The caravan camped on what flat ground was available, and at every stage Joanna searched for evidence that others had been there ahead of them. But though they found plenty of old wrappers and tins, there was nothing to prove that any of these had been discarded by Aidan.

By the third day, tempers were flaring and the first of the pack animals had to be shot when the rocks beneath him shifted, trapping and breaking his leg. Yet, Joanna observed, the river also gave back life. Eagles and hawks soared overhead, mountain goats, marmots, and wild sheep dotted the hillsides, and cottonwoods, willows, poplars, and wild roses crowded the sloping banks. Human life, too, returned to the landscape as the Shyok dropped to join the Nubra in a long green river valley strung with irrigated fields and whitewashed villages. It was easier to breathe, to think, and after the desolation of the higher trail, the sight of children's faces, women bending over cook fires, even the tousled glare of a madman seemed to Joanna to signal hope, the possibility of survival against all odds.

Panamik, the last of these villages, was where the rumors of Aidan's sighting – and of the subsequent avalanche – had originated. Tot questioned the villagers. Yes, they replied, many, many foreigners were coming through the mountains now. Large groups, small groups, all buying food, ponies, hiring guides. Yes, foreign men, foreign ladies. They grinned, offering eggs and vegetables for sale. Yes, they emphatically nodded, they had seen a man matching Aidan's picture. Yes, he looked very well, bought many eggs and breads and vegetables. Joanna suspected they would have said anything to make a sale, but Tot brought forth an elderly woman who insisted that her son had gone with Aidan to serve as his guide.

The woman came up close to Joanna, talking in a near shriek. She was dressed in a long black dress and a pink stocking cap. Most of her front teeth were missing, and her heavy turquoise and silver earrings shook as she demanded payment for the extra days she was being deprived of her son's labor.

'She says he is hired for five days but already is gone ten,' Tot explained. 'These men go to look. There is an avalanche near the trail, but no sign anyone is killed.' The old woman shook a brown cotton purse in Joanna's face. 'She says she gets no money now, she

100

has no one to chop wood for her . . .'

Joanna recoiled from the sour smell of the woman's breath and body. She fumbled in her pocket, let Lawrence nudge her aside to negotiate the compensation himself.

The woman, still grumbling, was about to leave when Joanna forced herself forward again, caught up the grimy hand in her own. 'Tell her,' she said to Tot. 'Tell her I need my husband just as much as she needs her son. Tell her I understand, and we'll find them.'

The old woman glared at the two clasped hands. Then she looked up at Joanna as Tot translated. Her whole face seemed to pull forward as she spat out another string of words, then yanked her fist back and strode away.

'What did she say?' Joanna demanded when Tot hesitated to translate.

He gave an apologetic shrug. 'She says that foreigners never talk truth.'

The beauty that only minutes ago had taken Joanna's breath away now seemed oppressive. Lawrence touched her arm, started in about this being a ploy for guilt money, but she fled from him to find Simon and Kamla crouched at the edge of the river.

They were making boats out of leaves and sticks. Thoroughly engrossed, they set each vessel in turn afloat, waited to see it into open water, then gravely waved goodbye.

That afternoon the caravan set up camp in a grassy orchard long used as a regular way stop for Karakoram travelers. Now that the trail was officially closed, the site's only other occupants were a middle-aged doctor, Reggie Milne, and his ten-year-old son, Ralph. Milne was a tall wiry man with gentle blue eyes, wheat-colored hair, and a dense russet beard, who welcomed the newcomers with the casual ease of one accustomed to befriending total strangers in the middle of nowhere.

From Wales originally, Milne and Ralph had been living in the Sinkiangese city of Yarkand for the past three years, working with a Swedish mission. The people of Sinkiang were delightful, he said, but the politics had finally become untenable. Communists, Nationalists, Uighurs, Tibetans, Kazakhs, Kirghiz, Mongols, Tungans – every time you turned around someone new was either calling for independence or being shot for doing the same. And now with the news of Communist advances in China's eastern provinces, they'd decided the time had come to return to Srinagar, where Milne owned a houseboat.

Milne talked a steady, good-natured stream, and after that morning's encounter Joanna was reluctant to force the inevitable question, but the children appeared tongue-tied, and Lawrence simply stood there with his hands in his pockets as if waiting for Milne to run out of air, which could take into the night, from the sound of him. Finally Joanna could stand it no longer.

She held up Lawrence's photo of Aidan and blurted, 'This is my husband. He's missing. Have you seen him?'

Milne looked at her. Then he examined the picture politely and handed it back. 'I'm sorry. We haven't seen but one other foreigner, and that was a woman, nearly three weeks ago.'

The light seemed to change, becoming harsher, whiter. Joanna squinted against it. 'Alice James,' she said.

'Yes!' Milne lifted his eyebrows. 'You know her?'

'Only of her. Was she really traveling alone?' She deflected Lawrence's questioning gaze.

'She had a guide, a couple of men,' Milne said, 'though you'd hardly call it a caravan. Strange girl. Acting so tough – she laughed and joked with the men as if she wished she were one of them, and she was a study with the language, too. But young . . . she couldn't have been much over twenty. What do you know of her?'

She shook her head. 'I only heard about her in Srinagar. A reporter looking for a story. Apparently thought she'd find one in Sinkiang.'

'One!' the doctor hooted. 'More like a thousand. There's enough intrigue back there to spin your head around.'

'We have a story,' broke in young Ralph. He drew himself up with an air of importance and beckoned Simon and Kamla closer. 'Some bandits robbed us up in the passes. They took our best ponies and three rifles – and we didn't hear a peep!'

'True,' his father verified. 'We had no idea until morning, when the man who was supposed to be on guard woke up and saw what trouble he was in!'

'How do you know they were bandits and not just hungry villagers?' Lawrence asked.

'Believe me,' Milne said, 'there were no villages within weeks of us. These were either bandits or soldiers, though in this part of the world that's small difference.'

'What sort of soldiers?' Simon asked.

'Why, any sort you like. Every tribe in the province seems to have its own army. Though the Chinese Nationalists set the standard. Bloody thieves. I can't say I blame the locals for getting up in arms against them.'

'Dr Milne,' Joanna interrupted. 'Is it possible that my husband could have left the trail somewhere between here and the border?'

'Not likely.' Milne stroked his beard, lowering his eyes. 'Not intentionally, anyway. There are no branch routes, if that's what you're asking. If he didn't want to be seen, of course, there are plenty of places for a lone man to take cover.' He returned his gaze to Joanna. 'I wish I could assure you that your husband is safe, but in reality if he met with some sort of accident, we would not necessarily have found him. I suppose the most reassurance I can give you is that we ourselves came over without a scratch.'

'Dad,' Ralph said. 'Can we take them to the hot spring?'

Milne put a hand to his son's shoulder. He paused as if to let the air clear, then spoke in a tone noticeably brighter, addressing the children. 'I think that's a brilliant idea. It's just down the track, and I'll wager you could all do with a scrub.' Then, to Joanna and Lawrence, 'I'll just take the kids off to fetch some towels. Wait for us here?'

Joanna nodded, watching Simon reach out and catch Ralph by one hand, Kamla by the other. Then the three of them, linked together – for safety? for comfort? or simply because one of them acted on impulse? – trotted off after Milne.

'What now, boss?' Lawrence asked when the others were out of earshot.

She folded her arms, holding her elbows. 'He wasn't looking for Aidan. He could have walked right past him, lying at the bottom of some cliff.'

Lawrence smoothed a patch of grass with the toe of his boot. 'Why didn't you tell me about this Alice James?'

103

'What was there to tell? You heard Reggie. She left Srinagar over a month ago. Akbar mentioned her in passing. It made an impression, that's all.'

'I see.'

They stood in silence watching Tot and the caravan men making camp on the other side of the apple orchard, tethering the animals under branches weighed down with late, white blossoms. The men moved with such practiced confidence that they resembled mechanical dolls.

The hot spring was a mile or so down the trail. As they set off, Ralph and Simon raced forward in a game of kick the stone, and Milne engaged Lawrence in a rambling chat about the eccentricities of missionaries. Joanna hung back and Kamla sidled up beside her. They walked, swinging arms. She began to hum, and the little girl picked up the tune. 'Amazing Grace.'

At the hot springs a crude wooden shack, divided, leaned out over the steaming pool. Lawrence and the boys disappeared in one door, and Milne directed Joanna and Kamla to the other side.

The hut was damp and warm and abruptly dark as they entered. The only illumination came from two spears of dust-filled sunshine that dropped between the uneven ceiling boards. A thick wooden partition blocked the other side, where the boys, from the sound of it, were engaged in a towel-slapping contest. The whole place, not much bigger than a closet and smelling pungently of sulfur and damp cedar, reminded Joanna of the bathhouses of her childhood. Although in those old Pacific beach cabanas, the pounding of the surf had been a constant, and the smells had been of sea salt and redwood and were inseparable in her mind from the splinters that lodged in her toes as she stretched to view herself in too high mirrors. Here there were no mirrors.

Only, she realized, Kamla's uncertain gaze. The child hung back in the doorway with her arms hugged to her sides. She looked up at Joanna, then at the dividing wall. They could not see to the other side, but they could clearly hear the male shouts and laughter.

Joanna smiled and motioned for Kamla to join her on the platform that edged the water. The child's fingers spread, grasping the khaki fabric of her trousers. Her small sharp chin pressed

104

against the throat of her camp shirt. She wore no ornaments, no nose or ear jewelry. The reasons for this were obvious enough, given her background, but now, as she raised her face into the sunbeam and lifted those blue-green eyes, it was equally clear that no jewels were necessary. Joanna held the child's gaze like a vow. For all her own preoccupations, here was one whose life hung even more precariously in the balance.

The men's voices splashed between them as Joanna removed her boots and socks. She unbuttoned her shirt, undid her belt and trousers, folding each item before placing it in a pile in a dry corner. As she loosened her hair from its knot and peeled off her brassiere she saw each fret of her rib cage, the slackness of her small white bull's-eye breasts, even the immunization circle on her right arm reflected in the child's eyes. Joanna was realistic about her body. Aphrodite she was not, but neither was she self-conscious. This was not difficult for her, only necessary. A conscious demonstration of trust.

She stripped off her underwear in one clean motion, and dropped down over the edge. The dark water lapped against her crotch, bubbles clinging to her skin. Curls of steam rose from the surface, and she gasped with pleasure, gliding into the heat, her hair like streaming seaweed.

She came up slick and turned around, propping her elbows on the floorboards. Four feet away Kamla stooped, clothes dangling, agape. Their eyes met. She'd been watching Joanna as she raced to finish undressing unseen. Now caught, she halted as if conceding a bet. A return to poise, the hasty child banished, she resumed at an imitating pace, carefully folding each garment as Joanna had done, removing, stepping, turning until she, too, stood naked before her equal. It was an act of pride and courage – and defiance. *I will prove myself,* she seemed to be saying. *One way or another, I will prove myself to you.*

Joanna was humbled. She had not intended her nakedness as a dare, but this was clearly how it had been received. Kamla felt obliged to present herself as deliberately as she, Joanna, had revealed herself to the girl. But oddly, the result was not parity. No. In some barely perceptible way, the tables had turned. This child's innate grace made Joanna's naked truth seem insignificant by contrast.

Less than three weeks had passed since the day Kamla appeared at the rescue home in Delhi. Since Joanna had examined this same child's body and noted a bruised sternum, lacerated hands, and welts across the buttocks. Since she had clenched her teeth and forced herself to memorize the exact hues of green and yellow and purple – the flesh tones of brutality. Yet in these weeks she'd discarded that memory. She had allowed her own lesser horrors to drive it from her mind, had satisfied herself without reexamination that the child's clear smiles and stamina on the march meant that she was healed. Such wishful thinking was inexcusable in one trained to know better. Joanna did not excuse herself. And yet, as the girl stood before her now, she could see that Kamla had indeed healed. And this healing was more than skin deep. Oh, the body was miraculously straight and smooth, narrow hips unscarred, and her flesh had evened to a golden bronze, brighter where the dusky light fell across one slender shoulder. But the truer healing was in her face, the clarity of her regard, the calm with which those blue eyes rested, measuring Joanna.

Kamla smiled as the boys on the other side let out a gleeful yelp. Then she stepped to the ledge and slid seal-like beneath the dark surface of the water. It was immediately apparent that she couldn't swim, and she sputtered as Joanna lifted her up. Even so, she laughed with pleasure.

That night after putting the children to bed Joanna came out to find Lawrence alone by the riverbank. She sat down in the grass, stretched her legs in front of her. 'I wish I knew their secret.'

'Whose?'

'Kamla's and Simon's. It's as if they have a second skin.'

'Childhood, you mean.'

'I guess that's it. I always used to think children needed extra care and protection. Now I'm wondering if they wouldn't be better off if we just stepped aside.'

'You don't believe that.'

'Or deputize certain adults as parents. Reggie Milne, for example.'

'Milne! He's dragged his poor kid backward and forward over these mountains, exposed him to war and bandits, and that's just what we learned in the first few minutes!'

'He kept him safe through all of that.'

Lawrence didn't answer.

'You never talk about your son,' she said softly.

'What good does talking do?'

'It might make him seem closer.'

'He's dead, Joanna. Not lost.'

'I'm sorry.'

He leaned back and skipped a stone across the moonlit water. 'Tracy – my wife – couldn't stop talking about him.'

A wolf bayed somewhere above them. The sound, both mournful and alarming, raised the hairs on the back of Joanna's neck. 'I'm told some people find comfort in religion,' she said.

'You're *told*?'

'I wish I could say I believed it myself. But Aidan persuaded me years ago that religion is a lie. It pretends to offer protection when really it's robbing the flock and setting it up for slaughter. The church is the maestro of war, he used to say, and faith is ammunition. I cursed him for making so much sense. The idea of a benevolent all-powerful Father had real appeal to me.'

'It's like you were saying about children. The parent is so often either the problem or a lie.'

'Which were your parents, Lawrence?'

'Both. At Davey's funeral they had the gall to tell me it was God's plan. As if my boy were a pawn in some cosmic chess match, and we were simply spectators. I haven't seen them since.'

He crossed his arms in front of his chest, then abruptly turned. 'It's late and we have an early start tomorrow. I'm going to turn in. G'night, Mrs Shaw.'

Joanna could see him just well enough to make out the change in his face, the pain that dulled his eyes. 'Good night, Mr Malcolm,' she said softly, and watched him walk away.

9

The caravan departed Panamik shortly after dawn, leaving the Milnes to continue on their homeward journey via Leh to Srinagar. Tot had acquired a squadron of yaks from the local herders, and with these capable, surefooted beasts to serve as porters at the higher altitudes (the half-dead ponies had all they could do to get themselves up and over), Lawrence predicted the caravan would cross Saser Pass by midday.

But as they climbed away from the river, the landscape hardened and became more foreboding. Thunderheads were massing over the summits, and for the first time they encountered the shattered downhill streaks and tumbled debris of recent avalanches. These leavings all appeared at some distance from the trail, which to Lawrence looked unscathed. Still, Joanna stood scanning the slope, peering down at the steepest drops, shading her eyes with one hand sharp and stiff as a salute.

Two nights before Aidan departed from Delhi, Lawrence had met him for a drink at the Imperial. They were talking about his preparations for the trip and his problems with the FBI. Abruptly, Aidan turned the conversation to Joanna. 'I know it's unintentional,' he said, 'but I feel the question every time she looks at me. "What are you going to do? How are you going to beat this? How can you let them do this to us?" She never says it out loud, but it's always there. I have to tell you, I'm not altogether sorry to be going away.'

Up ahead, Joanna paused to talk to the children. She had her hair pulled back from her face. The ends were tucked under a pale green slouch hat, leaving her nape exposed. Unscathed, that's what she was. Oh, she wore the scratches from childhood brambles, surface scars and congenital bruises. She was not unblemished, but she was unhurt. And she defended this tentative innocence like a prized virginity. Lawrence imagined this was the very trait that originally had won Aidan over – before it started to drive him away. He knew Aidan meant to warn him that night, but the warning said more to him about Aidan than it did about Jo. And it didn't resonate with Lawrence at all. If he could, he'd distill Jo's admittedly simplistic passion and pump his own veins full of it. Or, he'd just take her as she came.

Her chin now lifted toward the threatening sky, a gesture of false bravado like a child's defiance, and in spite of that bulky sheepskin jacket, he was aware of the whole slender length of her quavering in the ongoing struggle for oxygen.

All that morning they stumbled through slate moraines, skirted girders of ice several feet around and boulders the size of elephants. The sky hung damp skeins of fog above them, and the lush green of the valley gave way to shafts of rock that tore into their feet and gradually numbed their eyes.

The altitude became an invisible vise, the wind a perpetual drone in their ears, and the cold ate through hats, gloves, boots, and bone, cracking flesh and freezing blisters. Only the yaks were immune as they plowed doggedly forward, leather *yakdans* swelling their barrel-round sides while the burdenless ponies quivered. All human movement was brittle and sore. Thought soon became an uncertain ordeal, the effort of speech excruciating.

Poor Simon had the hardest time. He complained that his muscles were burning. Tears had frozen on his lashes. He was staggering, and on the turn of the fifth switchback he squatted and retched. Joanna wanted to stop with him, but the rest of the caravan had already cleared the top of the pass. Kamla and Tot, both of whom seemed to have the constitution of mountain goats, waited with their own pack animals a dozen yards up the trail. Lawrence warned Joanna that halting here would only intensify the boy's discomfort.

'What do you suggest?' She gripped her son as if Lawrence meant to snatch him away.

This was not, of course, what he meant at all, but before he could say so, Simon tried to stand. His legs swayed beneath him. Will or no, he could not make it up the pass on his own, and this narrow precipice was no place to battle the point. There were only a few more switchbacks, then Tot had told them the trail would relax to an easy descent on the other side. There was still a chance Simon might acclimate if they could just get him over the hump.

Lawrence waved to Tot and Kamla to resume their climb. With Joanna's help Simon climbed onto his back, and they began again. 'One, two. One, two,' he heard himself mutter beneath the howl of the wind. The trail was barely two feet wide. One stumble, a lurch to the side . . . a drop of several hundred feet. It was like piggybacking along the ledge of a skyscraper. The greater danger, though, Lawrence well knew, was to continue if the boy did not acclimate. Although he had started strong enough, Simon now seemed to be caving in on himself. His skin had turned clammy, the color of paste, and he was wheezing, his grip listless, as if he could not concentrate even enough to keep his arms around Lawrence's neck.

Finally, they cleared the top and started down the other side, which was, as Tot had predicted, an easy descent. The sky thickened, dripping snow in thin plumes, and they caught up with the caravan resting under a series of high ledges that angled over the trail, forming a sort of canyon.

Lawrence set Simon down and began rubbing his arms and cheeks. Tot caught his eye and shook his head.

'Can you walk?' Joanna asked her son.

Simon's shoulders were shaking, but he nodded, shamefaced, glancing at Kamla, who stood with her hands jammed into her pockets, not even out of breath. Up ahead the caravan men were cursing their animals, and a distance apart from them the merchant knelt in prayer beside his wife.

'Just take it easy,' Joanna said, but the quaver in her voice gave Lawrence the opening he needed.

He signaled Tot to look after the boy and drew Joanna out of earshot. 'The next passes are higher,' he said. 'People die of altitude sickness. You realize that.'

She crossed her arms over her chest and dropped her chin inside her collar. 'I don't understand,' she said. 'Ralph Milne's the same age. He made it sound like a lark.'

'Ralph Milne was raised in this climate. Being the same age means nothing. Look at Kamla.'

But instead her eyes trained through the curtain of snow at the *begum*'s black sack figure. 'If she can take that *baby*—'

'Neither she nor that baby has a choice, Jo.'

'What do you want me to do!' Her head snapped back and she stared out from under the brim of her hat. They were standing in the open. Snowflakes glistened on her lashes and skin.

'It's nothing to do with what I want,' he said quietly.

'Isn't it?'

And for a moment he was certain she'd figured him out, that whether or not she understood how, she knew he'd played a hand in Aidan's disappearance.

But the moment was obliterated by a series of loud metallic pops that rang out down the trail. The caravan men yelled back and forth, and the Muslim merchant's prayers terminated abruptly as everyone scrambled for cover. After the first stunned instant Joanna needed no instruction. She raced back toward the children as Lawrence darted forward along the stone outcropping to the alcove where Tot had tethered the pack animals. The crackle of gunfire did not let up, but the shots were intermittent and distinct. Single-shot rifles, maybe a pistol or two. No automatics.

Tot had drawn the children behind a boulder well out of the line of fire. Lawrence saw Joanna reach them safely just as he found the yak on which he'd stowed the Mark II. He pulled it from its case and snapped in a clip of ammunition. The Milnes had warned of Hunza bandits, Kirghiz rebels, and soldiers, but the warning had seemed melodramatic. No more real than the shots that now spattered ahead of them. Lawrence took off the Sten's safety.

Brave, woolly heroes that they were, the caravan men could hardly wait to wave their white cloths of surrender. Their shrieks of professed neutrality echoed up the pass, but the flags were no more visible than their assailants through the flurry of snow. Looking back, Lawrence saw Tot with his hand visored over his eyes.

'Chinese!' Tot called across the trail.

'Soldiers?' Lawrence demanded.

Tot strained to interpret the cries ricocheting backward. After another staccato burst of gunfire he nodded.

Lawrence pressed the button that converted the MII from a single-shot to an automatic and stepped forward. Joanna shouted, 'Get down, Lawrence! Are you mad?'

He glanced across the few feet that separated them. She crouched like a cat about to spring. Behind her the children held hands, and he grinned at them in a sudden flash of appreciation. 'Absolutely blooming,' he said.

And with that he pointed the weapon skyward, fired briefly but with a deafening report. As if on command, the snow ceased, and an uncertain volley of fire replied. Lawrence strode down the trail to an open area where their assailants would have a clear view of him brandishing the Sten gun. A white man. An attractive but historically dangerous target.

111

'All right, you cowards,' he yelled. 'What exactly is it you're after?' Again he shot into the air.

The pass was still reverberating with echoes from this final fusillade as he watched the soldiers scurry away. There were no more than a half-dozen of them, clad in the khaki drill of the Chinese Nationalist Army. Impossible to tell whether they were strays, renegades, or dispatches assigned to clear the trail, but in all likelihood their intent would be the same: to prey on the caravan for their own advantage.

'Gutless wonders,' Lawrence muttered under his breath, and whistled to let the others know it was safe.

But something was radically changed in the scene that greeted him when he turned. At first he couldn't say what it was. A low moaning filled the air. Joanna and Kamla were squatting with their backs to him. They seemed indifferent to the cessation of gunfire. Lawrence was about to address them when he noticed Simon's blue cap on the ground.

Tot had been hidden from view by Joanna and Kamla, but now he emerged from his position crouching before Simon's outstretched body.

Lawrence moved one step. Two. Simon was lying on the ground, just as he'd lain in the pool at the Cecil Hotel. Playing dead. He wouldn't fall for the game this time. He walked forward grinding his teeth.

But there was blood, a gash in the cloth. The unmistakable lividity of torn flesh. He could see for a fact the child was not pretending.

He was not dying, either, however. Simon moaned, craning to see his leg, and Lawrence exhaled.

'Don't look,' Joanna commanded. 'You're in shock, darling. Just lie back.' She glanced up. 'Lawrence, for God's sake. Help us!'

Her eyes ripped through his own dread, releasing him to come forward, pitch in. First he soothed Simon, praising the child for holding his tears and acting like a man. Then he examined the wound. It had gone straight across, missing both bone and muscle. The damage was only skin deep. But there could be no more thought of Simon going on. Joanna dispatched Tot to return to Panamik and bring Dr Milne. Lawrence fetched the whiskey, blankets, and bandages, and helped her clean the wound. Then Kamla stood in for Tot as translator while Lawrence notified the caravan leader.

Muhammad stomped his foot and glowered over his mammoth beard. As far as he was concerned the boy's injury was a scratch. If they went back down the pass not only would they lose a day's march, but the soldiers might think they'd retreated in fear. Lawrence urged him to go ahead, then, but the *firenghi* would not go with them. The boy needed medical attention. They were going back to wait for the doctor at a lower altitude. He knew the caravan leader was trapped. He and his men carried the crudest of pistols and knives. Lawrence's MII – as well as his physical size and race – had established him as the group's protector. The caravan would wait.

Only after he had Simon readied for the descent, with Joanna and Kamla both busy tending him, did Lawrence return to the ledge where the wounding had occurred. He considered the angle, found the stain in the rock. The bullet must have ricocheted off the side of the canyon. It had grazed the boy, then continued on. After several minutes, Lawrence found it wedged beneath the boulder where Simon had taken cover. He examined the battered Parabellum casing, noting its shape and substance and markings.

The bullet was one of his own.

CHAPTER 4

1

The snow gave way to an icy rain as they moved Simon back down the pass, but they reached the base without incident and found shelter in a shallow cave. Simon, by now anesthetized with whiskey, decided to teach Kamla the William Tell Overture, which he knew as the Lone Ranger theme song. 'Hi-Ho, Silver, away!' The two of them flapped their arms in unison. Joanna made an effort to smile.

He was not badly hurt. Her heart had gone out of her at his first cry, the sight of all that blood. But it could have been so much worse. This was really only a nick.

She turned to Lawrence, who stood speaking to her from the mouth of the cave, a distance of perhaps twelve feet. With the rain's heavy gray light at his back and his face in shadow, he seemed gargantuan. She had to step closer to hear him over the pelting water. 'I'll take Kamla and go on with the caravan,' he was saying. 'We'll find Aidan, one way or another, Jo. Don't worry.'

Aidan. She hadn't thought of him in hours. Hadn't allowed herself to think of him. Now her husband's name went through her like a fist. She looked away to Simon, who was showing Kamla how to make a church and steeple with his fingers – as if the girl would know what a church and steeple even were.

Lawrence hesitated, then came closer and put his arms around her. His grip was so tight she could feel his knuckles through the bulk of her jacket, digging into her shoulder blades.

Less than an hour after they reached the base, Dr Milne and Tot

114

arrived, accompanied by two Ladakhi porters carrying a litter. Immediately Milne set to work, touching Simon on the shoulder, the hand. He spoke in a soothing, nonstop patter as his fingertips circled the zone of damage, and Simon lay as if mesmerized, answering questions about cowboys and magic and snakes. Joanna was stunned that Milne had zeroed in on her son's three reigning passions. Then she realized he must have overheard the two boys talking in Panamik, or else Ralph had filled him in. Still, he was clearly a man who paid attention, and the care he took with Simon touched her. When he told her son, 'You'll soon be good as new,' she believed him.

'He's a lucky boy,' Milne said with a glance to Joanna and Lawrence. He poured sulfa powder onto the wound and prepared a dressing. 'A little rest is all he really needs.'

She watched Simon flip his hands, distracting himself by teaching Kamla the 'Eensy Weensy Spider.' Joanna had taught him this finger game while Aidan was in Chungking. 'Again!' Simon used to cry, over and over and over again until sometimes she thought she'd go mad. She looked away.

'I'm going out to help Tot,' Lawrence said. He pressed her shoulder lightly as he passed behind her.

'Only trouble,' Milne went on, 'he'll be a bit sore, and there's always the risk of infection if the dressings aren't properly tended. Especially at altitude.' He stood up and led her to the opposite side of the cave, wiping his hands on a clean white cloth.

Here it comes, she thought. About-face. Lawrence was already out there segregating the packs.

The doctor gave the cloth a shake, folded it lengthwise, and tossed it over his shoulder. The gesture reminded her of a mother preparing to tote her infant. He spoke in the same easy tone he had used with Simon, but just loud enough now for Joanna alone to hear. 'I could take the lad back to Srinagar with me and Ralph. That way you can go on with your mission knowing he's safe, and he won't slow you down.'

The proposal caught Joanna mid-swallow, and the fist slammed through her again. Her mission. She stared at the doctor, his words refusing to seat in her mind.

In Panamik, Milne had never returned to the subject of Aidan, but then, a man like Milne wouldn't have to. He had absorbed what he needed and wished them Godspeed. Then today he had trekked back miles to help them.

'You live and travel in war zones awhile, these things happen,' he said. 'Tot explained your situation.' His blue eyes rested on her, somber. Generous. 'I shouldn't presume to influence you, Joanna, but I do understand.'

She discovered her hand at her mouth, though she didn't remember putting it there. Nothing was a foregone conclusion, even now. Especially now. She lowered her hand. Her heart was picking up speed.

Milne looked over his shoulder at Simon and Kamla. 'Our houseboat's plenty big, and I plan to remain there at least through the summer, while Ralph and I decide our next move. Simon's welcome to stay with us as long as you need. Ralph would love it.'

But, surely what he proposed was impossible. 'I don't think you understand,' she said. 'He's never been away from me.'

He fingered the end of the cloth. His eyes traveled back to the rain now dropping in vertical threads. 'I lost my wife ten years ago. It wasn't . . .' he groped, 'an unusual death. She came down with pneumonia. Ralph was just born. I'd never experienced such helplessness. Nothing we gave her made the slightest difference. Worst of all, I'd never fully realized how much I loved her until I watched her die. At that point if I'd had the means to go after her, if I'd had even the slightest hope of fetching her back before it was too late, nothing could have stopped me.' He cleared his throat. 'Not even Ralph.'

Joanna took a step forward, out from under the cave. When she lifted her chin, the rain met her face. She closed her eyes. The wet traced a black chill against the heat of her skin, and her pulse roared in her ears. Once she and Aidan had made love in the rain. It was an unseasonably warm October shower for Maryland, and she'd dared him to come out to the backyard naked, to lie with her in the grass under the pouring darkness. A simple adventure. He held both her hands as he slid inside her and licked the rain from her breasts. Through the rustle of water she heard him murmur, 'How I love you, Joanna.' She suspected that was the night they conceived Simon.

Behind her Milne called, 'It's letting up!'

She opened her eyes and saw Lawrence striding toward them, pearls of water latched to his beard. His rawhide hat the color of soggy tobacco bobbed forward as he acknowledged Milne's comment. The air still swam, thick and wet as glycerine, but they were right. It had stopped coming down.

'Yes,' she said, more to herself than to either of the men. She let the word settle before looking back at Simon. He was sitting up, leaning on one hand and laughing at Kamla and, behind her, the two Ladakhi porters, at their brave attempts to sing along with the chorus of 'She'll Be Comin' 'Round the Mountain.'

'All right,' she said firmly.

Lawrence joined Milne under the lip of the cave. He removed his hat and slapped it against his thigh to shake off what water he could. His hair clung in straggles to his forehead and neck. His gray eye seemed transparent in this light, his green one penetrating yet quizzical as he studied her out in the wet.

'Ralph will be ecstatic,' Milne said, though he sounded tentative, as if still testing her resolve.

She pictured Aidan now lying face down at the bottom of a chasm. Behind Milne, Simon giggled.

'I'm going on with you and Kamla,' she told Lawrence. 'Reggie's offered to take Simon back to wait for us in Srinagar. We'll move faster this way. And he'll be safe.'

Lawrence's jaw slid sideways so that his face appeared momentarily dislocated. She felt a wave of disapproval, but couldn't be sure how much was his, how much her own.

She came in out of the mist. 'I wish I had more time to think about it, but I don't know if that would change anything.'

A cord of muscle like a thick rope stretched from Lawrence's jaw to his collar. Still he didn't speak. Milne waited another few seconds, then signaled across the cave for the porters to prepare for the trip back. He placed his fingertips briefly to Joanna's sleeve before retreating to Simon, whose skin was now flushed, his nose bright pink. The boy's head bounced to a rhythm only he could hear. 'How does it go?' he asked too loudly, and hummed a tune she didn't recognize. Kamla interrupted with a tune of her own. Simon grinned. 'Silly. *That's* not it!'

'You really intend to do this.' Lawrence's voice sounded brittle at her side.

'*He* understands,' she said, following Milne with her eyes.

'What could he possibly understand? He's a total stranger.'

'Simon can't go on, and I *have* to go on.' She realized suddenly how close Lawrence was standing and moved away from him. The back of her head struck the overhanging rock. Lawrence saw, and reached out a hand. Though blinking back tears of pain, she batted his arm away. 'If you're so concerned about Simon, why don't *you* go back with him?'

That stopped him. For several long seconds he was silent, staring out at the watered air and stone. Then he said slowly, in a pitiless tone she'd never heard before, but that she found strangely reassuring, 'I can't force you, Joanna, but I'm sure as hell not going to let you go on without me.'

'Well, I guess that makes two of us.' She met his look.

'What are you going to tell him?'

'The truth. We'll be back as soon as we can.'

'That should keep him warm at night.'

'*Lawrence* – ' But her voice cracked. She wiped her eyes with the back of one wrist, blinked two, three times, hard. This time he made no move to touch her.

'You'd better do it, then,' he said.

She told him, as best she could, but whether due to the whiskey or the shock or the toll of altitude, or the simple fact that this level of abandonment was beyond his ken, Simon seemed immune to the words and smiled mutely in response. Even as he was repositioned and belted to the litter and she pulled the oilcloth hood of his jacket up over his head. Even as she kissed his cheek and touched his hair, as she clung to his small, damp hands, still he could not grasp what was happening.

Finally the porters picked up the litter, and she moved along with them out onto the trail. The wet rock stretched black and slick, draped with fog. Two steps became five, then ten. Milne led the way as the path narrowed, forcing a single file.

Suddenly Simon's eyes rolled back toward her. She'd begun falling behind. Now she stood perhaps twenty feet away, stopped cold in the center of the trail. Her arms stiffened, her hands clenching and unclenching at her sides. She was still close enough to read his face, saw tears, the first flash of bewilderment. Those brown eyes grew larger, impossibly round. His head twisted in the same anguished contortion as when she'd left him the first day of nursery school. Yet there was no comparison. This time he didn't make a sound. Even as the distance thickened, and she stayed back and he moved forward until the fog drew a wall between them, he said nothing. Nothing.

2

I waited to tighten my claim on her. With Simon gone she was sad and quiet, no longer Mrs Shaw. Only Mem. My Mem. I spoke these words to myself in secret: *My* Mem – mimicking Simon.

Please understand, I enjoyed Simon, but I could not ignore his weakness. I had watched him squirm and kick in his sleep, heard him gasp and cough his way up the passes. He complained of hunger and pain, the cold wind in his ears. He begged to rest. Lucky boy, Dr Milne had called him. Lucky in spite of his weakness, I thought, or perhaps, among the *firenghi*, weakness brought luck? I was not a *firenghi*, and experience had taught me long ago that I could afford neither to show my own weakness nor protect the weakness of others. Still, I kept turning the question in my mind. How much to hide? How much to reveal? What would I have to do to become a lucky one, myself?

The mountains grew fiercer and much colder as we marched on, and Mem and Lawrence exchanged few words. During the days I kept closer to Tot, saying little and demanding less, but when the sun fell and everyone settled around the fire, Mem and Lawrence seemed to expect me to take a place between them. As Lawrence told his stories of the mountains and men who had climbed here before us, he made me follow along in his books. He commanded me to stop him when I did not understand. In this way my English improved, but sometimes his breath was so sour that it pushed me away from him. Sometimes his voice rose unaccountably or he would burst for no reason into laughter. Often Mem watched him with an expression of mistrust.

119

One night after the caravan drivers and the Muslim family had retreated from the fire, Lawrence was reading from his notebook about the many, many bones we were passing along the trail. Some, he said, dated back to caravans hundreds of years ago. And not all belonged to animals.

To my surprise Mem reached out and curled an arm around my shoulder. 'Can't you see you're scaring the poor child to death!'

Lawrence shut his book with a slap. 'To death,' he said. 'Well, what's wrong with 'at? Least I've heard it's warm down there.'

His breath was fouler than usual, and he leaned right into her face.

'You've been drinking!' Mem pulled me away from him.

'S'alright,' Lawrence said. 'Just a snippet of Muhammad's hooch to boost the furnace. He doesn't much like to share. You know' – he winked – 'good Muslims don't drink, so it follows the skin's nearly empty. Then I'll be sober as a judge, though I can't say I've known many sober judges. You, Kammy?'

I didn't dare speak. I had known plenty of men who drank liquor in the flash house. Some became jolly. Some became cruel. I could not imagine Lawrence becoming cruel, but the way Mem drew me to my feet told me she thought differently.

'Why are you doing this?' she demanded.

Lawrence remained sitting. He ran a hand over the thick beard that had grown across most of his face. He had purchased a rawhide hat in Panamik, which he wore low over his eyes. His nose was as red as a chili pod and the layers of wool and sheepskin clothing made his shoulders and chest as massive as a bear's. Yet he had never looked more gentle to me.

He folded his arms around his knees and rocked backward. 'I haven't touched the whiskey, Jo. It's yours if and when you need it.'

The softness of his voice seemed to melt into the hiss of the embers. I felt Mem's grip on my shoulders loosen. There was a long silence. Then she asked, 'Would you like me to comb your hair, Kamla?'

I nodded even though it saddened me to leave Lawrence sitting alone.

Inside our tent that night, I nudged and rolled and sidled so close that finally Mem opened her arms. She said, 'You poor thing, you're freezing. Why don't you come into my sleeping bag with me?' I moved so fast she could not think of changing her mind.

With our sheepskins and felt boots, the English long underwear and thick woolen sweaters that we wore day and night, there was hardly room for the two of us in that kapok cocoon. I do not pretend it was comfortable, and in truth I was not cold sleeping alone. But I nestled against her, and she wound her arms around me. When later I woke to feel her crying secret sobs, I lay very still in the scoop of her body. I let her think I was sleeping. Her tears became my secret, too.

In the days that followed I often thought of the *firenghi* lady I had spied in Delhi weeping over her fancy dress. The loss of a child, of a husband to me seemed far better reasons for tears, yet still my Mem concealed her sorrow. I had known all along she was not like the others.

No, I thought. She was like me.

And yet she had one vanity, which I loved. Every morning she applied a drop of perfume to the inside of each wrist and the hollow of her throat. Then she would touch me with that same moistened fingertip, and I would feel again the thrill of closeness, of daring and trust I had felt the day in Panamik when we stood naked before each other. That bath had been our last, and we had not changed our clothing since. The freezing cold and lack of water made washing nearly impossible, and the smell of human dirt and sweat hung heavy over the entire caravan, yet each morning Mem and I would step from our tent wearing the stinging clean scent of carnations. 'Our secret weapon,' she called it.

Now sometimes on our marches I would steal close and touch Mem's hand. Her fingers would close around mine and I would look up into her face. Over our weeks together her skin had browned to the color of cinnamon. The tip of her nose peeled to pink. Her hair had lightened with the sun, and her eyes now looked into me as if seeing some great distance.

Often, as Mem held me this way, I would catch sight of Lawrence watching, and I felt as if a silken thread bound me to these two. As long as this thread held, I was safe, yet I knew that once it was broken, I would be cast away. You see, I pictured my guardians like the Hindu gods my flash house sisters had taught me. Lawrence took the form of the great Protector, Shiva, so powerful yet also ascetic and sensitive. Mem could only be Lakshmi, the goddess of good fortune. But her husband was not Lakshmi's bird-god Garuda. Instead he appeared to me on a white horse as Vishnu's tenth incarnation Kalkin, destined to bring the present age of the world to an end.

I knew that if we found Mem's husband, she would immediately return with him to Simon and everything would change. While Lawrence said that he and I would continue on in any case, that he would do all in his power to help me find my father, I could plainly see that Mem, not I, was the reason he made this journey. So I did not join Mem at the edge of the trail as she studied the rocky hillsides. If I saw a biscuit wrapper or tin that Mem or Tot had failed to notice, I turned my head away. And when Lawrence handed me his binoculars, I trained them not on the nearby streams and gullies but up to the tops of the mountains where not even birds could fly.

At the same time, I believed that if I were good in other ways, at least I would not break the thread myself. So each night I helped erect our tent. I worked with Tot to prepare our supper of lentils or rice. I kept myself as clean and uncomplaining as possible and pleased Mem by learning to read the words she would draw for me in her notebook.

To please the gods I also helped the others in the camp, bringing water to the ponies or searching for dried bits of dung for the fire. While the *begum* cooked her husband's food or saw to their encampment, I would rock and sing to her infant daughter. This last was not solely for the gods, of course. I loved the way those tiny fingers wrapped around my own, the strength with which they grasped me. The baby's face was soft and pink, her eyes like narrow seeds of light, and I could just imagine her traveling each day, buffered by the darkness, snug against her mother's breast. I envied her safety and protection. But I should have known better.

As we descended from the high passes all the rivers we encountered were swollen with melted snow. The Black Jade, however, was by far the wildest. It ran so green and swift that it seemed to boil over the jagged bottom. This would not have mattered except that the gorge was very narrow. The trail would vanish on one side of the water and pick up on the other, forcing us to cross back and forth, and the yaks and ponies, still weak from the passes, would lose their footing and be swept downstream, screaming and kicking, their boxes floating like wings to keep them from drowning.

The *begum* always rode with her baby folded into her *burqa*. Together they rode behind her husband, and because of her many garments, she sat sideways on her mount. Holding the child she had only one hand free, and with this she clung to her pony's mane as if in constant terror. The animal must have sensed this, because he was often skittish. As we made our way along the Shahidulla Gorge I heard the *begum*'s husband scold her to relax, but I cannot imagine that *he* could relax if forced to ride in such a way. And she had safely ridden over the highest of the passes and crossed many rivers already. So they went on as before.

We made the last and most dangerous crossing at three different points of the river. The caravan men split into groups, the first crossing upstream with the pack animals, and the others divided between the Muslim family and our group at the lowest point. This way, if a pack animal were swept away, the lower men had a chance to catch it. But the ponies we rode carried no floatable boxes, and Tot warned us to look out for each other, lest we be pulled under.

In our group, Lawrence crossed all the way first, then I started, with Mem and Tot behind me. Almost immediately the water rose to my pony's belly, covering my boots. The current felt like hands of ice beating and grabbing my legs. It was so cold and so loud, but also exciting. As I reached the middle of the river I felt the spray on my cheeks, saw Lawrence grinning from the far shore. I looked up at the walls of stone, the sky a thin wedge of turquoise above us. Then I turned my head and saw the *begum* tip sideways into the water.

The rapids had swept her pony's legs out from under him. If the caravan leader had not been riding alongside, the *begum*, too, would have been swept away, but Muhammad reached over and seized her by the shoulders, hauling her like a great black fish over his saddle.

It all happened so quickly. I saw the pony spin around and under, hooves pedaling out of the water, the foam tinted pink. The *begum*'s husband shouted from shore, but the crash of the river drowned his voice. Behind me Tot yelled for me to move on, it was too dangerous to stop.

Suddenly I saw two small pink hands reaching through the foam. The river rose as if opening its mouth and spat out a misshapen bundle of rags. I glimpsed the baby's coal-black curls, then the rapids swallowed her again, perhaps a dozen yards directly upstream from where my pony stood swaying beneath me. He had found secure footing and seemed as unwilling to move ahead as I was to have him do so. I curled my legs around his belly and leaned sideways, opening my arms to the currents. Again I caught sight of the baby, much closer now and hurtling toward me. Her swaddling had come loose. Lengths of white cotton spread in a web. Then I touched her skin. The surface felt hard and slippery as eggshell. Impossible to grasp.

When my fingers closed I was holding only cloth. Still, I thought it must be fastened around her. But as I drew the swaddling toward me, the pull of the river was stronger. I could not see the baby now for the spray, the green-black water, the canyon's deafening echo.

3

Kamla couldn't swim. When Joanna saw the torrents pounding through this section of the gorge, she had begged Tot to rope them together, but he insisted that would only endanger them both. So they'd put the child on the tallest, steadiest pony, with Lawrence going first to test the rock bottom. Joanna wanted to cross next to Kamla, but Lawrence yelled back that the solid outcropping narrowed at the middle, with a sharp drop and uncertain footing over the edge, so she was behind Kamla when the girl stopped in midstream.

Tot yelled to keep moving. Joanna put up her hand. She could see something was wrong, the way Kamla twisted sideways in her saddle, searching the river with her eyes. Above them the Muslim woman had lost her pony. The rapids were sweeping the poor animal downstream, but the *begum* herself had been rescued.

'You can't stop!' Joanna shouted, and dug her heels into her pony to nudge Kamla's mount. Her right leg was pressed against the larger animal's flank, their combined weight tilting against the rapids, when suddenly Kamla lurched as if to throw herself into the water.

Instinctively Joanna reached to catch her, but the abrupt shift of balance and motion spooked her pony. He dodged sideways, and Joanna felt him yank out from under her as she pitched forward. Her arms closed around Kamla's waist.

In the next second the water slammed over them, dragging them under. Joanna's single thought was to hold on to the girl, but the cold was so intense and the battering of rocks against her arms and spine so incessant that she could not be sure of the location of her hands. The first time her head cleared the water she saw the ponies rear up, biting the foam. Then Kamla came up gasping and Joanna was pulled back under.

Whether they traveled ten feet or a thousand she had no idea, but when she next surfaced she heard Lawrence's voice thundering down the gorge: 'Catch!'

He was standing on an outcropping above them, twirling a loop of rope. Joanna found her feet, Kamla by some miracle still in her arms. They'd washed into a shallow, protected cove.

The girl's hair was in her mouth, and their clothes were pasted together, heavy as a double suit of armor. 'Are you all right?' she cried. Kamla glanced at her, white-faced, over her shoulder. She was shaking, but managed to nod.

Then Kamla put her hands in the air, and the rope sailed toward them. And Lawrence was hauling them to safety.

He threw a blanket over them, wrapping them tightly in his arms. Joanna looked up and saw tears in his eyes. She felt Kamla's heart thrashing against her own.

'I try,' the girl blurted out. 'The river is too strong!' She pulled back, looking past them up the shoreline to the Muslim merchant, who stood as if planted in the rock.

He was hammering a fist in their direction. Behind him his wife crouched, doubled over, the black mass of her *burqa* heaving. Even above the noise of the rapids, of her own retreating panic, Joanna could hear the wails pulsing through that black shroud, like the screams of a mortally wounded animal.

The caravan drivers discovered the baby's corpse on a gravel spit nearly a mile downstream. Muslim practice required that the body be wrapped and buried immediately, but they had to carry her for another hour before they found earth deep and soft enough to turn. As the baby's father chanted his prayer and the mother sat, mute now and rocking back and forth, the men placed a boulder over the shallow grave.

'It is so that wolves do not eat the body,' Tot explained so matter-of-factly that Joanna hated him for it.

They went on in a numb, exhausted procession. No one spoke directly of the Muslim child's death, but its shadow seemed to settle squarely on Kamla's shoulders. The fact that Kamla had touched the baby yet failed to save her made her responsible in the eyes not only of the father, but the caravan men as well. In a matter of minutes, the girl and her *firenghi* guardians, as well, had become a bad omen. The men scowled at Kamla as she passed and cursed behind her back. When Joanna asked Tot what they were saying, he answered, 'They do not trust her.'

The accident had not been Kamla's fault, any more than it was Joanna's or Lawrence's or Tot's. Less than it would have been her own fault, Joanna thought, if she and Kamla had drowned. If anyone was to blame for the infant's death, it was the father. What could he be thinking to keep his wife inside that death trap on a trek like this! Joanna searched for some means to convey her sorrow and sympathy for the woman. Offers of food, company, a clasp of hands. Even under these conditions, even across the language gap, such ritual tokens might have provided some comfort. But the merchant did not let his wife out of his sight, and if Joanna moved too close, he would stand glowering between them.

In the evenings two camps formed as Joanna and Lawrence and Tot closed ranks to protect Kamla. Lawrence quit drinking. Not even whiskey, though Joanna thought if ever there was a time for drink, this must surely be it. They had fuel for only a brief and single fire every night, and that barely sufficient to cook a meal; warmth was out of the question in any case, so the separate

126

groups would cook and eat quickly, then retire to their opposing zones. If it was not too cold, Tot would entertain the girl with games devised from pebbles and rope. Joanna spelled out words and sentences for her to read, and Lawrence would steer them into a four-hand round of gin rummy. Later, with the two men keeping watch outside, Joanna and Kamla would huddle in their tent and sing melodies dredged up from Simon's infancy. The girl, for her part, seemed to crave this attention. Outwardly she showed neither fear nor distress in the wake of the accident, but in the blue light of dawn Joanna often opened her eyes to find Kamla gravely studying her face as if fearful she might never wake. Then she would hold the girl close – or as close as their many layers of clothing permitted – and she would tell her about America, and Simon, and their house in Delhi, subjects that here seemed remote as fairy tales.

Even among themselves they did not discuss what had happened. Like the bullet in the pass and Joanna's decision to leave Simon behind, like their failure to find any meaningful clues to Aidan's fate, the drowned child became a point of danger that conversation and memory must circle from a distance. To obscure this danger, as they marched along, Lawrence made jokes and tried to teach them all cockney rhyming slang. *'China plate* means *mate,* see. *After darks* is *sharks. Comic cuts* is *guts.* Now, what do you think is a *loaf of bread?'*

Kamla smiled in polite bewilderment and answered the questions Joanna asked to rescue her. She said she was recognizing more landmarks now. Yes, she and her uncle had passed through this gorge and beneath that same stone archway. No, this pass had seemed no more frightening then, only harder and colder, as it had been near winter when she came through before. But very soon now, she told them, the earth would turn to red and gold. The fields of stone would give way to meadows, then dust. The rivers would narrow to trickling streams. This time of year the heat would be like the Punjab . . .

Joanna watched the girl's face change as she remembered. The color of her eyes seemed to deepen. Her gaze fixed on the luminous streaks of cloud that hung above the lower ridges to the north, and Joanna tried but could not imagine what scenes were threading through Kamla's mind. She was, as always, so poised, so contained, yet there was a new spark of hopefulness about her that not even the scowls of the caravan men could dispel. In a moment of complete stupidity, Joanna asked if Kamla was happy to be going back.

'Yes,' the girl replied, as if reciting a line from a primer, 'I am very happy.'

What a cruel word, Joanna thought. And who am I to use it?

4

The desolation of rock and bones lent a surreal quality to the single figure picking his way across the scree at the base of the Sanju, the fifth and last major pass of the route. It was midday, the glare of sun off the cliff wall intensifying the usual headache of altitude, and the image of an approaching human seemed so improbable that Lawrence half believed he was hallucinating. In the four weeks since their run-in with those Chinese soldiers, they had not encountered another living person.

He peered at the figure harder, shading his eyes with a hand. A man. Tall and thin. Alone, but for a single pack pony.

Joanna came up beside him. 'What do you think?' he said.

She didn't reply. Or move. But as they studied the man's approach, the answer became obvious. His gait was as smooth and mechanical as if his legs were fitted with pistons. He seemed to cover the intervening distance – perhaps half a mile – in a matter of seconds, and was already nearing the front of the caravan.

Kamla joined them. 'It is the *dak*,' she announced. As if a mailman in this lunar wasteland were no more surprising than a ten-year-old girl. Tot nodded, and Joanna quickly turned away. But not before Lawrence saw her face.

He lowered his voice. 'We'll *find* him, Jo.'

From the side, he could see the strain in her throat as she swallowed. She moved forward without answering.

The man was chatting with Muhammad when they reached him. He wore khaki, uniform boots, a visored hat with earflaps. A bulging shoulder sack hung across his chest, and his face shone a deep walnut brown. Above a dense black beard, his dark eyes shone out from a nest of weather-induced wrinkles. A short blue scar bisected his left brow.

He was an Indian courier, had been detained by Chinese authorities in Sinkiang for the past four months. Now heading back to Kashmir, he hoped never to see China again. But no, he said, he'd experienced no trouble along this trail. They should get through so long as they had the necessary papers and funds to pay off the Chinese customs extortionists. The caravan leader grunted and signaled his men to move forward.

Joanna handed the courier Aidan's photo. 'This is my husband. Have you seen him?'

He examined the picture then looked at her curiously. 'In Yarkand. Yes.'

Yes. The single syllable shimmered, elastic and dubious as a soap bubble. 'Are you sure?' Lawrence asked, for Joanna seemed unable to speak.

'Most definitely. He is American, I think. And Chinese. His eyes, they are green?'

Joanna nodded slowly. She was crushing the photograph in her right fist.

The man forked two fingers through his beard. 'He is looking for a car to take him to Kashgar, and I am telling him of a friend who possesses an old Russian lorry.'

'Kashgar?' Lawrence asked. Kashgar was over one hundred miles to the north of Yarkand.

The courier shrugged apologetically. 'I think so.' There was a long silence, then he bobbed his head and started to turn his pony onward. But Joanna grabbed the man's wrist.

'Did he give you any letters to carry?'

He cast his eyes down. She released him, looking stunned, and took a step backward.

'I am sorry, madam.'

This time her voice came out barely a whisper. 'Was he traveling alone?'

His head wiggled in an Indian nod. Maybe yes, maybe no. 'I am not seeing anyone with him. But truly, I cannot say.'

129

Lawrence sensed her marshaling her strength. Again the man started to leave.

'Wait!' She ran to her pack pony, which Tot was holding a few feet away. From one of the side pouches she pulled out the letters she'd written to Simon, one every night since leaving him.

'Will you take these to my son in Srinagar?' she asked the man.

He smiled and accepted the bundle.

'*Inshallah,*' he said. God willing.

'So you have him,' Lawrence said as they watched the courier's shrinking figure.

She glanced over to Tot and Kamla, just out of earshot, playing kick the stone. The rest of the caravan was ascending the first narrow switchback up the pass.

'You're relieved,' he persisted.

She put the heels of her hands against her eyes. 'I don't know what I am.'

'Here.' He stepped behind her and pushed her hands away, rubbed her temples with his thumbs. He felt her lean against him. 'You don't have to decide anything for the moment. We're well past the point of no return. No choice but to continue until we find a place to restock. Maybe by then we'll run into someone else who's seen him, give you more to go on.'

She touched his hands, stopping him. 'You don't have to do that.'

'I don't mind.'

She moved away. 'What do you think he's doing?'

'He's a correspondent, Jo. I imagine he's chasing a story, don't you?'

'Not anymore – ' Her voice faltered. 'What story could he conceivably be tracking that would merit this level of risk and time – and evasiveness?'

Aware that neither of them could speak Aidan's name, though for very different reasons, he tipped his hat back and squinted at the Sanju's gleaming face. She so badly wanted an answer, and he could not even tell her what he didn't know. Instead he stepped forward, swept the hair off her face and planted a hard, whiskered kiss on her cheekbone.

Then he strode up the trail after Kamla whistling 'God Save the King.'

5

The next day they left the cold. It was as Kamla had predicted, a new landscape of copper and rust tones and sun-drenched blue sky. With the Sanju Pass behind them they moved steadily downhill through aniline green meadows bobbing with small, brown marmots, past foaming streams and knife-straight waterfalls. The descent poured oxygen back into their lungs and brains. They peeled off layers of sheepskin and wool and washed away four weeks of sweat and dirt in swirling glacial pools. Even the drivers seemed cheerier, singing now as they swatted the few surviving ponies to stagger faster down the slopes. Only the *begum* appeared unchanged. No amount of heat or color could cause her to show her face, and every time Joanna caught sight of her she flinched. She couldn't shake the feeling now that this black apparition was a warning.

The second morning into the heat they came upon a Kirghiz settlement – three round felt dwellings clustered in an elbow of brick-colored earth. They had all shed their winter layers so recently that Joanna felt naked showing her bare head and hands as the herders circled around them. The few women in the camp showed their faces, but concealed their hair under tall white headdresses. Their children ran in brightly colored rags – except for one tyke clad in nothing but a pair of his father's leather boots and a round felt cap. Four bearded men came forward, eyes hooded with obvious suspicion, but when they saw the two women and Kamla and were reassured that none in the caravan were Chinese soldiers, the atmosphere warmed. While the caravan drivers and the Muslim merchant bartered for what fruit and meat the nomads had to sell, an elderly chieftain welcomed the foreigners into his yurt.

The large circular tent stank of sheep. They squatted around a low table while the chief's young wife and two small daughters poured cups of black tea and set out slabs of flat bread and butter.

Joanna could hardly see Lawrence's face in the dingy half-light, and only Kamla understood enough of the Kirghiz language to translate, though this may have been just as well since she was the one they were most curious about.

The chief, who shambled on footless stumps, grinned and nodded as Kamla (coached by Lawrence) described her kidnapping and journey to India. The old man asked if the kidnappers had been bandits and seemed disappointed when she said no. The bandits had taken his feet, he explained, then, absurdly, laughed. He warned more soberly of a Chinese garrison several hours on. The Chinese also were bandits, he said, but they had no sense of humor. Many Kirghiz taken prisoner by the Chinese had never returned.

Joanna covered her cup with one hand, felt the steam form a skin over her palm. What was Aidan *doing* in this nightmare world? What were they? She set the cup aside and produced the photograph. The chief's family passed it around, all talking at once. She couldn't tell whether it was the simple miracle of photography or the particular likeness that excited them.

And then Kamla spoke. 'They say, your husband was here.' The chief dug a hand inside his waistband and brought forth a fistful of American dimes. The girl continued with painstaking slowness. 'He is asking many questions.'

'But questions about *what*?' Joanna pleaded.

They conferred again. 'About a *memsahib*.'

For one blazing instant the tent was silent. Joanna found a pinpoint of light where a gap in the ceiling let in the sun. She could feel Lawrence's eyes on her throat, imagined she could hear Kamla and Tot exchanging telepathic laughter. Then the chief and his wife resumed their bombardment. How could human beings live like this?

When the jabbering stopped, Kamla translated into Hindi for Tot. Joanna forced her eyes down and around, skidding past Lawrence's ominous stare.

'Your husband is here maybe five days ago,' Tot said. 'The young lady maybe twenty days. She has yellow hair. She will travel to the northern capital, Tihwa. The chief tells this to your husband, and your husband pay him money.'

The stench of animal hides was making it impossible for Joanna to breathe. She got up, thanked the chief for his help, and stumbled out into the light. Half blind from the residual darkness, she groped her way down to the stand of alders where they'd tethered their ponies. She had no plan. Her mind was as blank as if the earth had opened beneath her feet, and she was falling, simply falling into wide open nothingness.

Then Lawrence caught up with her. 'You all right?'

'I don't think so.' She found her hand on one of the ponies' halters. The beast grazed on, ignoring her, and she stepped back in confusion.

'Joanna, there's probably a letter waiting in Delhi that explains everything.'

She glared at him. 'Where I'd be sitting twiddling my thumbs if I knew what was good for me!'

'I didn't say that.'

'You don't need to.' She shook her head. 'I feel like such a fool.'

'Why?' He took hold of her shoulders. 'You wouldn't feel that way if we'd found him lying in one of those ravines. Whatever this is about, *you're* not the one in the wrong.'

She looked up the grassy slope to the yurts, where Kamla and Tot stood talking with the chief. The rest of the caravan was moving on. She wished the earth *would* open – and she could disappear.

'Five days,' he said. 'That's pretty close.'

'Do you suppose I can get what I need in Yarkand for the trek back?'

He ignored her. 'If we catch him, what're you going to say?'

'We can't catch him. He doesn't want – ' She stopped herself. 'He doesn't *need* to be caught.' She started to shrug, then glanced down at his hands still resting on her shoulders.

'What matters,' he said, gently letting go, 'is what *you* want and need.'

They were silent for a minute or two. She pictured Alice James as a defiant Veronica Lake. In the same way, she used to torture herself with images of Aidan's Irish redhead as a renegade Maureen O'Hara. Two mistresses of seduction and adventure too stubborn to ask to be rescued. She squeezed her eyes shut, trying to push the faces from her mind, but in their place rose the image of Kamla falling forward, flailing about in the icy water for that drowning baby. And Simon's look of betrayal as she left him behind.

'What difference does it make what I need!' she said.

Lawrence took her hand. 'C'mon, Jo. There's no point wallowing in gloom.'

Her next words stung the air, as shrill and irretrievable as a gunshot. 'Is that what you thought when your son died?'

Lawrence's lips, cracked and blistered and nested in beard, parted briefly, then clamped shut. Before she could even extend her hand, he'd mounted his pony and was riding hard uphill. When he reached the top he swung Kamla like a Mongol's captive into the saddle behind him.

They did not speak again until the caravan arrived at the garrison, a bleak, windswept outpost of mud-walled huts where soldiers carrying fixed bayonets barked orders in Mandarin and exacted taxes – whole bales of hemp from the caravan and Chinese yuan from the Muslim pilgrims. The caravan leader had papers, but inspection looked like it could take hours, the soldiers repeatedly reminding them that the pass was officially closed. Even if she wanted to turn back, Joanna realized for the first time, there was no guarantee that she would be allowed to. For now, the soldiers motioned Lawrence to take her and Kamla and Tot to wait apart from the others.

While Kamla and Tot hunted for grass blades they could use as whistles, Lawrence stretched out on a patch of scrub outside the fort's stone barricade. Joanna knelt beside him. 'Never mind,' he said, not looking at her.

'I had no right.'

'You had every right in the world. You hit the nail bang on, if you want to know the truth. I just can't see any other way.' He seemed about to say more, but abruptly looked off toward a grove of blooming apple trees where the Muslim woman sat alone and silent, faceless as ever in her grief.

'Kamla had a nightmare last night,' Joanna said. 'I had to hold my hand over her mouth or she would have woken the entire camp. She shook so that I could feel her bones rattling, and after I released her I realized we both were drenched with sweat. Yet she never woke up through all of that.'

'That baby's drowning wasn't her fault.'

'Does that change how she feels about it?'

'It should,' he said.

'If wishes were horses . . .'

His eyes narrowed and he considered her for several seconds. Then he said softly, 'If wishes were horses they could trot us to the moon. Since they're not, we're on our own.'

6

Finally they were summoned to meet the garrison commander. Lawrence pushed himself up and offered Joanna his hand. As she took it he felt a light squeeze – whether of gratitude or apology he could not tell, but truce at the very least.

He beckoned to Tot and Kamla, who had been chatting some yards off with one of the Chinese soldiers – a sad-faced conscript who looked not much older than fourteen. The lad shrugged as they left him, and Lawrence recognized too well that look of resignation. 'We'd best adjust our story,' he warned. 'Rescuing native orphans might impress the Kirghiz, but it'll likely have the opposite effect on our Chinese hosts.'

The four of them conferred briefly, and proceeded to the commander's dirt-floored office. Guards armed with vintage US-issue Colt revolvers flanked the single door. The wood furnishings were crude and utilitarian, the room's only decorations a filthy mustard-colored felt carpet and a 1946 Standard Oil wall calendar picturing an ocean sunset. An elderly Kirghiz woman shuffled in bearing a tray of covered teacups, and the commander, who was short, chinless, and bizarrely dressed in tweed plus fours, signaled them to drink. They did so standing, as the commandant's was the only seat.

Eventually their host leaned back and asked their business in Sinkiang. With Tot translating, Lawrence produced their passports, Chinese 'visas' and travel passes, even a letter of safe conduct from before Independence with Mountbatten's vice-regal seal. Ignoring the discrepancy of names on the documents, which the commander evidently could not read, Lawrence referred to Joanna as his wife, Kamla their adopted daughter. He did not inquire about Aidan or the fabulous Miss James, but announced he was traveling to Kashgar as the newly appointed consul for Sinkiang – as if Australia had a consulate in Sinkiang. Inside the folded letter he had slipped fifty US dollars, worth ten times that on the black market. Farther east, where Chinese were actively fleeing the civil war, US currency was more valuable than gold.

The commander barked at the guards and Tot to leave the room. When they were gone he lifted the bills one by one to the dirty light angling through the barred window. Lawrence drew forth the twenty he'd kept in reserve. The man coughed and spat into the corner, then casually pocketed the lot. After a pause he reached under his desk and pulled out an old Lee-Enfield rifle. Smiling, he took aim at Joanna, then Kamla, intermittently glancing sideways at Lawrence, who swore under his breath for the other two not to move, though he sensed they weren't even breathing.

Without Tot to translate, Lawrence could only guess what the man was up to. It was not benign, but it was not a real threat either. The soldiers of this garrison wore the same Nationalist drill as the men who had attacked the caravan at Saser Pass.

Slowly Lawrence rose and moved toward the door. The commander was grinning at him now, nodding, rifle still in midair. Lawrence called to Tot, who was waiting outside. They spoke briefly, then Lawrence returned. The gun was still trained on Kamla, who stood with arms locked against her chest, eyes fixed on the one barred window. Joanna looked frantic, though she did not make a sound. Lawrence patted the air for her to stay calm. The Lee-Enfield swung back toward her.

'Just think of it as theater,' Lawrence said in a low voice. 'It's only an act.'

Her lips parted as if she might speak, but a knock on the door arrested her. The commander lowered his gun, laughing and slapping the desk with one palm, a whack that made them all jump. He replaced the weapon under his desk. The door opened, and Tot appeared in the entrance cradling a long thin object wrapped in jute. He handed the parcel to Lawrence, and withdrew again.

The commander remained seated as Lawrence slid back the sacking to reveal the MII, then laid it on the desk. Their captor muttered his satisfaction. He fingered the works of the Sten gun with admiration, even tenderness. Lawrence signaled Jo with his eyes. Her face was ashen, but she gripped Kamla's hand. The Chinese lifted the sight, and turning the barrel now on Lawrence, released another shock of laughter as his finger teased the trigger. His voice purred for them to go.

Lawrence brought up the rear, shutting the door softly behind him as Joanna and Kamla raced toward Tot, who stood waiting beside their pack ponies. The Sherpa met them with a tense grin. It was late afternoon. The rest of their caravan had vanished.

Moving as quickly as they could without breaking into an outright run, they cleared the garrison gate. Then Joanna stopped to check on Kamla. The girl's face was grave, and Lawrence could see something working behind the surface, but whether it was fear for herself, concern for Joanna, or something entirely different, he couldn't tell. Joanna folded her arms around her and smoothed her hair. Their bodies swayed in the copper light. Joanna's eyes closed as Kamla's face burrowed into her neck, and Lawrence looked away.

They continued on, following Tot past the garbage-strewn perimeter of the fort to a knoll where the rest of the caravan was assembling what remained of the cargo and animals. The commander's tariff had spared no one, and the mood of the men and the Muslim merchant was decidedly grim.

'It's not hard to see why the locals are up in arms against the Chinese,' Lawrence said.

Joanna released Kamla to Tot, who laid his palm fondly on top of her head and steered her off to help him saddle the ponies. Kamla smiled up at him, her fright in the garrison already behind her. Joanna, however, had not recovered. She sat on an old rock wall and wrapped her arms around her knees. She looked drained and confused, still deathly pale. She turned on Lawrence. 'If it was only an act, why'd you give him the gun?'

'Be glad we're rid of it. We've got our papers. Money. Our lily-white skins.'

'How reassuring.'

He sat beside her. 'Come on, Jo. Even here in the back of beyond, they know. There'd be hell to pay if that bastard touched a hair on your head.'

'So why surrender?'

'Kamla's skin's not as white as ours. Nor is Tot's.'

She flinched as if he'd raised his hand against her, but did not drop her eyes. 'Those were his men who shot Simon, weren't they? That's how he knew you had that gun.'

Lawrence swallowed. 'No.'

'Well, how, then?'

'Same way he knew not to shoot us,' he said. 'Lily-white's code for a lot.'

And partial truths were a coward's crutch. She let it go and was silent, but that didn't end it. 'What about Aidan? He's not lily-white either.'

He got up and turned away from her. 'Isn't that why you're going after him?'

The answering silence seemed to throb. When at last he looked back she was standing with her hands in her pockets, eyes on the sky. The horizon glowed hot mustard and pink. Below, the earth stretched, blue. Lawrence touched his forehead and felt the peel of sunburn and dried sweat. They'd been traveling together for thirty-eight days, and still he'd told her nothing.

'I wonder if he even knows,' he said. 'And if he does, whether he can begin to grasp what it's worth.'

'What?'

'To have someone care so very much whether you live or die.'

7

Strange how the mind opens and closes, casting memories over the present like shadows from a moving cloud. I did not recognize that garrison until it was nearly out of sight. By then the sun was low in the west, the light at once bright and dying. We passed a field of crude stone markers. That's when I remembered.

You see, when I had come through before with my uncle, there was still a great deal of fighting. The local tribes were burying their dead in this field, and as my uncle and I watched them from a distance, I felt as if I'd been lifted up and returned to my mother's funeral.

This memory now seized me again. I ran to Mem and told her,

but my words scattered. She could not understand. Was my mother buried *here*, she wanted to know.

No, I said. Not this place. But there, also, I had seen guns, soldiers. My mother was not yet under the earth when the uniformed Chinese took my father from the graveyard in a large black motorcar. For a moment I could see the day so clearly I tasted the soot in the air, felt the bite of the wind, the rumble beneath my feet as a convoy of lorries passed down the street outside the graveyard. But then, just as unpredictably as it had opened, my mind's eye snapped shut. I stared at the past, commanding it to present itself, but all I saw was darkness.

Mem's questions didn't help. My mind refused. I shook my head and continued walking. But that night as I lay pretending to sleep, I heard Lawrence say to Mem, 'Sounds like Tihwa.'

'What does?' she asked.

'The black cars. The secret police – the Chekka. Chinese death squads.'

It was too warm now for the tent. I lay in the open, just outside the circle of firelight. Mem and Lawrence sat alone. They took my words and turned them until I sensed that they were no longer talking about me or my father at all.

'Why Tihwa?' Mem asked.

'It's the capital. Up near the rebel territories – and the Soviet border.'

'Dr Akbar said the Americans were planning to build an air base in Tihwa.'

Lawrence nodded and spread his hands. 'Welcome to the Tournament of Shadows.'

'Perhaps that's why Alice James is heading there,' she said.

'Have you decided what you're going to do, Jo?'

'You know. You already said it.'

Oddly then, Mem paused. I felt her looking in my direction. She said, 'I've passed the point of no return.'

Yarkand was a large, gray, walled city three days on. We arrived just before the muezzin's call to afternoon prayer, and a crowd of kneeling worshippers filled the central square. Surrounding them, Chinese soldiers in ragged uniforms stood smoking at every corner.

Within five minutes a pair of these sentries stopped us. While Lawrence bribed them from funds concealed in his vest pocket, Tot slipped away to hire a jeep. Mem and Lawrence and Tot and I were to leave the caravan here.

Before we parted, however, the *begum* came silently beside me. Except for the songs she had crooned to her daughter, I never did hear her speak, but now I could feel her eyes touching me through their thick veil. She took my hand and gently wrapped my fingers around something small and dry, then released me and walked away. I lifted my palm and found there three golden desert raisins.

Over the years that followed, I would often wonder what significance the *begum* attached to that curious trinity. I had been one of three children when we began the march. I was one of three women who completed it. Or, had her gift represented the union of father, mother, and child – a well-intended wish for my future, or a grief-stricken token of her own loss? Perhaps these three raisins were simply all that she had to give? In any event, I sensed in this gift both forgiveness and thanks. It was my first instruction that the two go hand in hand.

We entered Kashgar well after dark, three blinding dust storms and two days beyond Yarkand. The night was clear, and the entire population appeared to be celebrating this relief from the desert wind. Donkeys, camels, sheep, and goats stumbled among the throngs. Oil lamps swung dizzily above the night bazaar. Towers of hats and melon pyramids leaned out into the road, and groups of boys squatted between the stalls playing games with sticks and stones.

Finally we came to a grand house outside the city walls. Torches burned above the gates and turbaned guards stood at attention. An Indian lady came out to greet us, older than Mem and clearly no servant. She wore her shiny black hair coiled fat behind her neck and a *bindi* the size and color of a cherry in the middle of her forehead. Diamonds sparkled from her earlobes, and black-rimmed glasses on a chain thumped against her peacock green sari. Her husband was away, but she welcomed us without hesitation, brought us inside to bathe and dine. She said that Mem's husband and Miss Alice James had been visitors here just one week earlier. Now they were gone.

I was glad. The very next morning we boarded a lorry full of Chinese soldiers bound for Tihwa.

CHAPTER 5

1

Every few hours for the next twelve days they would halt to refill the radiator or laboriously climb in and out of the dry watercourses that sliced the road like knife cuts. At night they camped or stopped in the rough communal inns that clustered about the oases. By day they drove beneath a bleaching sun or through curtains of flying sand. The lorry rattled, and the stink of petrol fused with the odor of too many bodies jammed into too few seats. Tot, accustomed to mountain climates, became sick with the heat, which was worse than summer in Delhi. Hands would blister at the touch of metal, and perspiration dried before it surfaced to skin.

As the lorry moved north, they passed through villages burned to the ground. Most were deserted, many half buried in sand. When Marco Polo was here, Lawrence said, he had recorded the danger of talking spirits, sirens who assumed the voices of loved ones in order to lead unwary travelers to their doom.

Joanna answered, 'I keep seeing the newsreel flash of atomic bombs.'

On the roof of the lorry, beneath their feet, and strapped outside the windows, canvas flapped around bundles of arms – bayonets, rifles, submachine guns, dynamite, plastique, fuses, and detonators – all being transported to the capital air base in preparation for action against the northern rebels who had allied themselves with the Communists. The war in the west was accelerating, it seemed, with the news that Shanghai had fallen last week to the Reds. This news had been passed on to Joanna and Lawrence in Kashgar by the Indian consul's wife, Mrs Desai, along with the information that Aidan had caught up with Alice James there at the consulate, then proceeded on with her to Tihwa. Alice apparently had arrived in Kashgar nearly two weeks earlier and had become quite the toast of the town. The Desais, both teetotalers, pretended not to notice, but the dark circles and blotchy skin on such a young girl's face, according to Mrs Desai, was a dead giveaway.

Such a young girl. The words spun through Joanna's head like marbles as she shifted Kamla against her arm, urging the child to sleep. Alice had apparently spent her evenings in Kashgar with a US State Department fellow named Douglas Freeman, a linguistics specialist sent to Sinkiang two years ago as a favor to Generalissimo Chiang. Freeman was stationed inside the Old City, and no one really knew what he did except that he'd become a champion at the local horseback sheep-tossing contest called *baiga* and was a renowned drinker, both of which seemed to interest Miss James most keenly.

'We thought perhaps they had taken up together,' Mrs Desai told Joanna in her clipped English-Indian accent. 'But then your husband arrived, and the very next day she set off with him for Tihwa!' She was pleating her sari between her fingers as she spoke, so that the fabric's golden paisley pattern broke into jagged spikes. When Joanna failed to answer, a flash of embarrassment crossed Mrs Desai's face. 'Your husband and this girl—' she groped. 'I am not sure they even liked each other, but journalists often seem to band together in competition. They are an odd breed, are they not?'

Joanna nodded equivocally. Then shrugged. Then rose and left the room.

On entering Kashgar she had noticed telegraph wires leading north over the desert like a string of empty clotheslines. That night, after putting Kamla to bed, she sat at the writing table in their room and composed a note to wire to Aidan, care of the American consulate in Tihwa: *Arrive Tihwa next week. I love you. Joanna.*

The irresistible desiderium incogniti. That was what Lawrence called it. He had hauled her into the Desais' library and presented her with a dog-eared volume by the Swedish explorer Sven Hedin. The book was open to a passage describing Hedin's obsession with Central Asia:

If ill luck prevailed, I might lose everything. But I did not hesitate for a moment. I had determined to conquer the desert. No matter how weary, I would not retrace a single step of my trail. I was swept away by the irresistible desiderium incogniti, which breaks down all obstacles, and refuses to recognize the impossible.

'Latin was never my strong suit,' she said, trying to keep her voice light. 'Is this "desire for the unknown," or "unknown desire"?'

'Or both.'

Lawrence's push-pull gaze hooked her. He placed his fingertips on the back of her wrist. It was nothing. A moment. The slightest of pressure. Yet the sensation coursed up her arm as if he'd never touched her before. It unfurled through her body in waves so strong that her breath caught at the base of her throat.

The book fell from her hand to the floor. The last time a man's touch had seized her this way, the man was Aidan. Now she drew back sharply, holding her wrist as if burned.

'Either way,' Lawrence said, regarding her quietly, 'this same spell seems to afflict us all.'

2

My father filled my dreams and thoughts through those long burning, rackety days, so clear at times that it seemed he must have been conjured up by the desert. I recalled the measure of his bones and flesh as he used to hold my hand. The backs of his hands were lined and brown like the skin of dried almonds, but his palms were pale and smooth and large enough to curl my whole fist inside.

My father, whose name I now decided had been Badam Chand, though it might have been Patu or Braroo instead, had always come and gone. He, too, had worn a uniform, but it was smarter than those of the Chinese soldiers, and was set off handsomely by a scarlet turban. He had a raven black beard and eyes that sparkled, high leather boots that he would polish until they shone like his eyes. I was his only child, and I could remember once or twice when my parents argued, my mother pulling her hair and wailing,

'If only this useless girl were a son, you would not speak to me this way.' But my father would look at me crouching in the corner, and say, 'She is my sun and moon. I would have no other.' My mother hated me even more for that. When my father went across the mountains she would weep, but if I attempted to comfort her she would scream for me to leave her.

My mother was a Tungan – a Chinese Mohammedan. She had told me proudly of her ancestry: As a people, the Tungans were warriors. A century ago they captured the capital of Sinkiang and killed many thousands of Han Chinese. Because of this, for a time the Chinese respected them. Tungans were landowners, even worked in the government. But my mother was illiterate. One day she burned the books my father brought from India, including the collection of stories he read to me. She said it was for our own good, and perhaps this was true. Perhaps there was danger for us to possess books printed in English. At that time, many men were being sent away to Russia. But I was too young to understand such things. I knew only that my mother had destroyed my father's gift to me, and in his absence this was as if she were destroying my father himself.

Uncle was my father's brother. Or so my mother told me the first time he came to visit. It was true he was tall like my father with the same almond-brown skin, but his voice was rough. He laughed with my mother and joked at me. He would stay with us at our home, our two bare-walled city rooms, for many days, but always left before my father's return.

Not long after one of these visits, my mother died, still big with a second child never born. I do not know what illness claimed her, only that it came over her suddenly, causing her to scream that she was on fire. My father would not allow me to go near her, and I believed this was because he did not want me to catch on fire as well. He told me not to worry, that I would be safe. He said he would take me over the mountains to his other home, and I must not be afraid. The night my mother died I woke in my father's arms. The house was silent. He took my hand and with his finger traced the lines of my palm. I remember, it felt as though he had his finger on my heart.

The next afternoon we buried my mother under a sky dark as

144

charcoal. Her sisters wailed. My father and I stood a distance apart. I wanted him to pick me up, but he told me I must be strong enough to stand alone. A few minutes later the soldiers came and ordered my father to leave me. I watched two of them grab his arms and drag him to the street. I watched them push him into that black car. I started to cry as the car pulled away, but my mother's sisters covered my mouth. They would beat me, they said, if I made a sound.

They took me to their village outside the city. I waited for my father to come for me, to take me to his other home, as he had promised. Instead, my uncle came. He put me on the back of a donkey and led me away at night. When I cried he told me my father would meet us in the mountains.

For the first weeks we traveled only in darkness or along trails out of sight from the main road. Uncle instructed me to call him Fotedar and said that the desert was full of bandits and policemen, who would be equally troublesome to a lone man and child. At first I told Fotedar when I was tired or hungry or sore, but he replied with the back of his hand. After that I understood the cost of weakness. I complained no more, and as my reward, he talked about the land beyond the mountains where my father and he had grown up. A land of lakes and trees and silvery waters, and snow and radiant meadows exploding with wildflowers. I pictured my father in this place, which he, too, had often described. I believed Fotedar. I imagined meeting my father within this crown of mountains that he called the Vale of Heaven. I thought this was my father's plan.

Gradually a truce settled between my uncle and me. Now when we rested he told of boats, the *shikara* he and my father had poled for British soldiers and officials and their wives. This was how my father had wangled his way into the British Army, Fotedar told me. 'He was always a good groveler, that one.' But when the big war started in Europe and the British began sending Indians to France and Italy and Burma, that's when my father finally came to his senses. He ran away following the *dak* trail over the mountains to Sinkiang, took up with my mother . . . and, Fotedar would always finish, 'now look at him.'

But when I 'looked at him' I saw my father in uniform, the shiny

145

colored ribbons fastened with polished brass pins, the horn buttons closing his pockets, the creases in his trousers, which he had my mother press with stones heated in the fire – even though he would not show these clothes outside our home. Or back even further I saw him as a boy, poling his way across the mirrored lake with reflections of snow-colored mountains and veils of pink and yellow blossoms. These visions carried me over the passes, past the heaps of bones and dying animals. They comforted me when our own donkey died, her knees buckling beneath her, and we had to walk the rest of the way. The weight of my pack bent me forward. I stuffed the splits in my shoes with dung to keep out the cold. Kashmir, my uncle told me. My father was a Kashmiri soldier. I was Kashmiri.

But then when I asked my uncle where and when my father would meet us, he turned and put his hands on his hips. He stared down at me as if I were a worm he meant to crush.

'Your father is dead,' he said. 'Forget him.'

I could not breathe. I did not believe him. My father had promised to meet me in the Vale of Heaven. But Fotedar forbade me to ask more questions, and whenever I mentioned my father now he twisted my arms so cruelly that I lost my voice.

Kashmir, I told myself, watching my feet, the moon, the snow and bones and ice and stone – anything but Fotedar. In Kashmir all would be well, somehow.

But my father did not meet me in Kashmir, and we stopped in the city of the lake only long enough to buy a yellow sari and a new pair of sandals for me, to spend a single night in a house full of men who put their hands on my head and shoulders and ran fingertips over my chest. And laughed just as Golba and his men would later laugh the night they raped me.

The lake shimmered in the distance as we boarded a bus bound away from the mountains. 'You need women,' my uncle Fotedar told me. 'What would I do with a girl child?'

'I was living with women,' I tried to protest, but I had not been sorry to leave my mother's sisters, so the words died in my throat.

After many days bumping through a country that I could hardly see for its brown clouds of dust, we arrived at a city larger and more modern and bustling than any I could have imagined. But

Fotedar took me directly to a lane of squat dung-colored buildings on a street not so different from the one I had left behind, except that cows and girls in brightly colored saris wandered everywhere. While my uncle talked with an older woman, I rinsed my hands and face at the public tap. I listened to strangers chattering in foreign tongues. Only the wall posters spoke to me. 'Callard & Bowser,' I recognized from the sweets my father would bring from his trips. 'Pears' Soap,' two words I could read apart, though I did not then see their connection to the glossy round cake in the picture. 'Bombay Gin,' I had read on the bottle of white fire my father sometimes drank. The posters gave me hope that when my father was released from prison he might find me here.

But the hand that grasped my shoulder and pulled me away from the water pump did not belong to my father or even to Fotedar. My uncle was gone, without a word. The old woman he had been talking to told me this was my home now. She asked for a name to call me.

'Ka– Ka–' I meant to say Kashmir. Kashmiri. I did not understand. But Indrani cut me off. 'All right, then. Kamla. Why not?'

By the time I learned to speak Hindi, I had buried the name my father once called me even as I buried the daughter he once knew. Kamla, my new sister Mira told me, means the lotus flower. A symbol of rebirth and survival, the blossom that grows in the stagnant pond, beauty that rises from filth. 'A most suitable name,' said Mira. 'A most suitable name.'

3

The lorry rattled into Tihwa on the tenth of June 1949. Late afternoon, the heat still brutal, the sun smeared across the horizon as if by a sooted thumb. Lawrence leaned out the window. The stink of flesh and gas, metal and sweat had become more familiar than the taste of water, but now the reek of coal from nearby mines choked all other smells. Outside the walls of the old city, the bazaar spread in a depressing patchwork of cardboard and corrugated tin stalls, ground displays of rusty nails and hinges, dried fruit and rotting vegetables shrouded in flies. The merchants wore porkpie hats or skullcaps and dingy robes. Women went without veils. Yellow-haired Russians with florid cheeks squatted next to Tatar traders, and Kazakh herdsmen led white stallions past kneeling camel trains. Chinese flyboys wearing leather jackets pointed camera lenses and gun barrels with equal hilarity.

Tihwa was a Chinese puzzle of Nationalist bureaucrats and secret police, Soviets masquerading as White Russians, and local Muslim functionaries with clandestine loyalties. According to Lawrence's researches, the Brits had been quietly shuttling back and forth among these factions for over a century, but the Americans with their wartime infusion of planes and guns and Yankee bravado had shifted the puzzle decidedly to the right. Before leaving Delhi Lawrence had equipped himself with briefing sheets on all the key players in Sinkiang, and the American consul, Daniel Weller, ranked at the top of the list. 'Just keep your head down if you get that far,' Jack had warned him during their final telephone conversation. 'No official identity. No affiliations beyond friendship. If this mate of yours is playing some game of his own, I want to know, but I have no intention of getting hung with it. And Weller could easily hang us if he discovers who you are.'

As they turned in past the Marines guarding the US consular compound, Lawrence watched Joanna peering forward. In this dusky, insistent light, with her windblown hair ringing her face, she looked terrified. Between them Kamla sat with her head lowered. Her hair had slipped from its accustomed plaits so he could not see her face, but the tension of her body betrayed her. She was coming home.

No affiliations beyond friendship, Lawrence thought bitterly. It was far too late for that.

'Do you have any idea what a fool thing you've done,' Weller demanded a half-hour later. 'Any idea what's going *on* here?'

'Thanks.' Lawrence accepted the tumbler of Scotch the consul held out to him.

They were waiting in the consulate drawing room while Weller's wife got Joanna and Kamla settled upstairs. Yet again, Aidan and Alice had eluded them. They left Tihwa almost as soon as they arrived, Weller had told Joanna. Over a week ago.

The American consul lifted his glass. He was well padded, of medium height, with salt-and-pepper hair. Clean-shaven. Blue button-down shirt and chinos. Ivy League, Lawrence thought. Yale, according to his briefing sheet. *'Gan bei.'* Bottoms up.

'I've heard rumors.' Lawrence skirted Weller's question.

'Well, you've no business coming here on rumors. We've just been ordered to evacuate all nonessential personnel. And I promise you, if my wife has to leave, so do you. We're just waiting for a plane to come available.'

'We heard the Reds took Shanghai.'

'Yeah.' Weller uttered a grunt of disgust. 'Without a shot.'

Lawrence glanced around the room. Chinese rosewood furniture and silk brocade. Porcelain vases. Cloisonné ashtrays. 'Gifts' from local Nationalist strongmen, no doubt. 'Is an evacuation this far west really warranted?'

'I don't make the orders.'

'But you're the expert here. Are things really that bleak?'

Weller leaned back in his chair. 'Far as I'm concerned, an air base here in the west is our only hope of stopping the Soviets from taking this whole goddamn continent. We should be beefing up, not clearing out. But tell that to Truman.' He gulped down his drink.

Lawrence thought of the shipment of arms that had traveled with them from Kashgar. He asked, however, only about Aidan and Alice James.

Weller snorted, 'I thought there was something off about those two. More than just the girl's snooping, I mean.'

'What *do* you mean, Mr Weller?'

'Dan.'

'Dan, then.'

'Well, he didn't exactly warn us his wife was on his heels.' He tapped his thumbs on the rim of his glass. 'I can't help but wonder if that cable she sent wasn't what prompted him to clear out.'

Lawrence didn't respond. Joanna hadn't mentioned sending a cable.

'Also, I ran a routine check – I always do on any foreigners who wander in unannounced. Nothing on the girl, but Washington wired back that China's the last place your pal Shaw ought to be hiding out. Is he or isn't he?'

'Is he or isn't he what?'

'Red.'

Lawrence frowned. 'He wrote a couple of articles criticizing Chiang Kai-shek, but far as I know the only card he carries is his press card.' He yawned broadly as if the whole subject bored him. Bloody American bullshit. 'Why do you say it's the girl who's snooping?'

'She's the one asking questions. But she's on the warpath over ancient history. Purges, secret jails, firing squads, all that's over and done with. Sheng got the boot in '44.'

'Sheng. The old warlord?'

'Right.' Weller lowered his large head, dislodging a hank of graying hair, which he shoved impatiently behind his ears as if reminding himself to get a haircut. 'Sheng Shih-ts'ai. Nasty piece of work.'

Indeed. According to Lawrence's information, Sinkiang's former governor had murdered more than two hundred thousand during his time in office. But he had an inkling that wasn't what Weller meant. 'How so?'

'Bastard kept changing sides. Played to the Bolsheviks one year, Chiang the next. Whoever seemed more likely to grease his palm. Hard for the locals to know where they stood.'

And for the likes of you to know how to play him, Lawrence thought. He asked, 'Where is he now?'

Weller jerked a thumb over his shoulder. 'After the Soviets beat Hitler back at Stalingrad, Sheng figured Stalin was the man to please, so he started rounding up Nationalist agents. That was one about-face too many for Chiang Kai-shek.' He played the name out in a drawl.

And Lawrence continued to play dumb. 'Chiang had him executed?'

'Executed! What good would that do?' Weller stood up, holding his empty glass. 'Sheng's worth too much alive. He made a healthy contribution to the Kuomintang coffers in exchange for early retirement.'

Yes, Generalissimo Chiang Kai-shek, the Yanks' prince of

humanitarian justice. Lawrence watched Weller stride across the room to the bar tray. As the consul said, Sheng was old news. Maybe tales of the warlord's atrocities had drawn Alice, but what could be in it for Aidan? There was doubtless a reason this local history never left Sinkiang – a reason that might not curry favor with Aidan's accusers if he wrote up the gory details. But perhaps this reason itself was the lure. Aidan had a perverse streak. When pushed to the wall he was as likely to break down the wall as he was to fight back.

Lawrence started at a sound by the door, thinking it was Joanna and Kamla, but only a houseboy glided past. He shifted his inquiry. If Kamla was now eleven – say, five when her mother died – then her father would have been seized in '43. During Sheng's last grasp. He said to Weller's back, 'I heard Sheng treated the Indians right shabbily . . .'

'The traders, yeah.' Weller spoke over his shoulder as he refilled his glass. 'Yellow and brown never wasted much love on each other, and in Sheng's clink the brown boys got the shaft. They used to hang in cages out in the bazaar, slowly strangling to death. And I mean slowly. Days. People here ate it up.'

Lawrence studied the spirals of lush design in the silk beneath his feet. He thought of Kamla's rigid back as they entered the city. 'Who's in charge now?' he asked.

As the consul turned, Lawrence thought he detected a stiffening of the man's sun-reddened neck. 'Nobody worth a damn. With Chiang Kai-shek running off to Formosa, we're gonna be left high and dry.'

'You mean the US intends to hang on here even after—'

'Don't be stupid.' Weller examined Lawrence with a look that said, who the hell are you, anyway? Clearly, he didn't know.

'All right.' Lawrence shrugged offhandedly. 'Alice James, cub reporter. What's her story? Or, what does she think her story is?'

Weller brought the decanter and topped off Lawrence's drink. 'Damned if I know. Hell of a looker, though.'

This last had the spin of a gambit. Lawrence elected to pass. 'Where did they go?'

'Back to India, if they know what's good for 'em.'

'You don't *know?*'

The consul melted back into his chair. 'I'm telling you, there was something off. They slipped out of here before dawn, for Christ's sake. No thank-you, nothing.'

Right. And Weller didn't have enough contacts or interest to track them down?

'No one's reported them since?' Lawrence asked.

'Well, there's always reports. Some of my tribesmen said they saw some foreigners heading up toward Ili Territory. But plenty of Russians in these parts look like foreigners.' He nursed his drink.

My tribesmen, Lawrence repeated to himself. Ili was an area to the northwest of Tihwa that straddled the Soviet border. A bastion for rebels backed by Stalin.

Weller turned at a clicking of heels in the hall. 'There you are, Lill. Thought our guests must have eaten you.'

Mrs Weller swept in with a businesslike nod in Lawrence's direction. She was a stout middle-aged woman with a chest like the prow of a well-built ship. This particular feature was shown off to full effect by a sleeveless yellow shirtdress, belted at the waist, and polished black high-heeled pumps, which both elevated and pitched her forward. Considering the two individuals before him, Lawrence was drawn back to one of Tracy's comments shortly before their divorce. 'You see, darling, people who are meant to be married resemble each other. They grow to resemble each other all the more the longer they're together, while you and I could not have grown more different.' The Wellers evidently were meant to be married. Lill even had the same cagey look about the eyes. Jack's warning was well taken. Lawrence didn't trust either of these two as far as he could throw them.

Christ, he thought, Weller's clichés are rubbing off.

The eagerness with which Lillian Weller drained her first martini told Lawrence that Joanna had been working on her upstairs the same way he'd been grilling the consul. As she lowered herself into a leather armchair beside her husband, Lawrence pretended equal interest in his own drink.

'So what's with the kid,' Weller said suddenly, and Lawrence suspected his host had been rewinding their conversation, clearing it, as it were, to the beginning. Now he noticed a flaw.

152

'Oh, honey, it's just awful,' answered his wife. 'She was kidnapped during the Sheng years, taken off to be sold in Delhi. Joanna's rescued her and brought her back.' She turned to Lawrence with a pinched expression. 'It's awfully good of you to help, but you can't honestly expect to find her family here in this place, after all that's happened.'

Good for Jo, Lawrence thought. Playing the lost child on a new set of heartstrings. 'That's just the point,' he said. 'We don't know what's happened.'

'Happened to what?' Joanna appeared in the doorway with Kamla close behind.

'To the two of you,' Weller said. 'Drink?'

But Joanna seemed unprepared for such a question. She started to shake her head, then stopped, glanced at Lawrence and quickly looked away. Her hair was wet and pulled back tight. She stood scrubbed and tan and skinny in a pale blue dress that Lillian must have given her. Gone was the aura of terror – trepidation, it must in fact have been as the countdown she'd started with that unmentioned cable drew to an end – but in its place now appeared a reluctant vulnerability that Lawrence had never seen in her before. She hardly looked older than Kamla. As he stared, she brought her gaze back to his.

'Thank you,' she said to Weller, but also, he sensed, to him. 'Please. I could use a drink.'

4

That night Joanna sat up in bed, roused by a dream that, though instantly vanished, left her skin feeling liquid. The room was thick with heat, and the mosquito netting hung in a blur above her head. Still half asleep, she reached for Aidan. Then she placed herself, and the chill that followed made her teeth chatter.

As her eyes adjusted to the dark, she could just make out Kamla coiled soundless on her cot. Familiar as she had become with the child's silent sleep, Joanna could never get used to it. Simon snored and rolled and flung his arms like a cub marking its territory. By contrast, Kamla seemed intent on disappearing, claiming as small a space, as little atmosphere as humanly possible. She could sleep anywhere, any time, under any conditions.

Not that these were hardship conditions. The silence here was opaque. No whining mosquitoes or rattling beetles. Nothing like Delhi, or even Kashgar. The nets were a fit of excess. Americans abroad. What Lillian had revealed to her when they were alone was Weller's 'keen' idea of establishing a 'third force' of tribal and Turki rebels – a US- and British-backed coalition that would remain in place even after Chiang's troops fled, to 'stand up against those Communists and defend the Free World.' Lillian thought Dan a hero for devising such a scheme, as it united three factions that heretofore had been ripping each other, as well as the Nationalists and Communists, to shreds. Literally, in fact, as some of the so-called freedom rebels were Kazakhs who fought on horseback with sabers as their preferred weapons – presumably before the US started furnishing grenades and machine guns. 'As we Americans well know,' intoned Lillian, 'a house divided against itself cannot stand.'

And in the very next breath she'd said, 'You know, that girl is trouble. Like Nancy Drew wandering into the middle of a gunfight. Dan tried to talk some sense into her, and when that didn't work he tried to tell your husband to steer clear of her...' The drift of her voice had completed the statement.

Joanna shuddered, threw off her covers, and climbed out from under her web. She and Lawrence had hardly spoken all evening. The Wellers didn't permit many words in edgewise, and on top of that they watched their guests so closely that it felt like surveillance. But Lawrence was the only one who could help her make sense of this.

Was Aidan, in fact, trying to escape her? Or was this disappearing act an attempt somehow to spare her?

She hugged herself, gripping the slate floor with her toes, her skin alive to the silk of the gown Lillian had urged on her. She traced a hand over Kamla's profile, registering the delicate contours of her face without penetrating the net. She envied the child's refusal to wake. Then she turned away.

She found a knob, stepped into the unlit hallway, and felt her way along the wall. But once outside Lawrence's room she stopped, and the chill of her waking came again. The door stood ajar. She could hear him breathing. Quiet. Alert.

She recalled Aidan's face smiling at her from a hundred directions. Dirty light and filtered amusement park music making the reflections vibrate. The muffled roar of the sea, and a flash, like the strobe from an unseen watchtower. *Please?* She'd begged, and he'd obliged her. Given her all that she'd asked.

She felt again the heat of Lawrence's touch in Kashgar, the power of his body surrounding her and Kamla after he'd pulled them from the rapids. She pictured his mismatched eyes in the dark, waiting for her to choose.

She put her hand to the wall to steady herself. Then fled.

5

You know, sometimes in the flash house I had seen men with the look that Lawrence now carried in his eyes. Mira in particular had that effect on her *babus*. They would make promises. They would beseech her. They would go to her bed in anguish and leave with an air of tragedy. I thought Mira had such power! But she insisted that all power is illusion and none more illusory than this power of the flesh. Sure enough, the *babus* would come for weeks, sometimes months, and then we would not see them again. You see? she would say if I asked after them, and snap her fingers. Illusion. But she did not seem to mind this so much. Better them, she told me, than the ones who cannot distinguish between love and rage. She would show me the scars on her neck and wrists, the bruises on her back to illustrate. Or the ones who mistake us for banks, she would say, laughing now. You know, show me the slot. The trouble is, they never put in more than five rupees at a time! Sometimes the moon-eyed *babus*, they would pay one hundred.

The moon had entered Lawrence's eyes in the mountains and grown to fullness by the time we reached Tihwa. The first morning after our arrival at the American consulate I left Mem sleeping and stole downstairs to find him alone in the garden. Over the weeks we had spent together Lawrence and I often met each other sleepless and wandering in the dawn. We did not talk a great deal at these times, but he might take my hand. We would watch the sun rise. Sometimes he told me about his son's antics or the jungles and oceans where he had traveled. We did not talk of Mem, but I could sense in him the tangle of emotions that she aroused. That morning as I came out of the house the high, pulsing wail of the muezzin's call to prayer began, and the sound seemed to echo what I knew Lawrence was feeling within his breast.

He stood with his hands clasped behind his wide back, facing away from the house. The great sky above him was striped with saffron clouds, the air soft and still. The garden, unlike the city we had passed through the day before, was dense with greenery and flowers that masked the smell of coal dust. I called out softly, and he started, turning with that full-moon look of hope, which changed as soon as he saw me. But I was accustomed to this shadow of disappointment, as well as the quick shift to a welcoming smile. 'Couldn't sleep, eh?'

I shook my head. 'It is different.'

'Tihwa, you mean?'

I nodded.

'Could be the Americans.'

'I do not remember them.'

'No, that's what I'm telling you. There were none. Americans are new in this part of the world.' We had been walking away from the house along a gravel path. Now he looked back at the consulate.

'Will you take me to my father today?'

Lawrence stopped. He turned to me with a kind of care that was at once alert and tender. He touched my cheek with his fingertips, and just then a commotion of dropping pots and yells broke from the servants' quarters, but he did not remove his eyes from me. The moon was still in them, but it had retreated almost out of sight. I had driven it away.

I do not know if that was what I intended, if this was why I had chosen this moment to ask for my father. But my words stung the soft morning air.

'Ah, Kammy,' he said finally. 'We're going to try.'

Then he squatted in front of me, clamping his big hands over my shoulders. 'But whatever happens,' he said, 'Mem and I'll see you're safe. *Whatever* happens, you hear?'

156

I was not accustomed to promises, and my life had taught me not to believe those that did come my way. Yet I knew at once this promise was different. The two colors of Lawrence's eyes seemed to lock me in an embrace, and I felt the fervor of his vow run through me like a current. *Whatever happens.* This was not merely an offer of protection. He was begging me to hold him to it.

6

May 2, 1949

Dear Mem,
Dr Milne is taking good care of Ralph and me. My leg is almost all better. Dr Akbar shows us how to do rope tricks. He let me use one of his swords to cut a paper box in half. Dr Akbar has lots of friends. They come around and smoke from a hookah and talk all night. I'm learning a little Kashmiri. Dr Milne says they're all Communists but he likes them too. They bring me candy and I let Ralph have some. I teached them all to say A-OK.

I hope you and Lawrence and Kamla are A-OK. Dr Milne says this letter will take five weeks to reach you. He showed me on the calendar. He says it will be longer for your letters to reach me because first you have to find a dak.

I can pray to Allah. You go lower than in church. You put your hands and knees on the ground. Your forehead, too.

I hope you find Daddy soon.
Love you,
Simon

Joanna stood alone in the consulate sunroom with tears streaming down her cheeks. Simon's letter had been relayed from Kashgar. It was accompanied by a note from Milne assuring her that Simon was indeed safe and well – *thriving* was the word he used.

'Thriving,' she said out loud and sat down hard on an upholstered ottoman that let out a gasp in reply.

She wiped her eyes with the back of her wrist and licked the tears from the corners of her mouth. Outside the window Lawrence and Kamla were walking hand in hand, their faces obscured by the salmon-gold brilliance of sky behind them. They couldn't see her seated here below eye level, and this fact intensified the effect, not of spying exactly, but of observing with heightened appreciation and a kind of full attention possible only when undetected. Lawrence leaned toward Kamla as he walked so that their arms both swung at full extension, without him pulling her up. Joanna wondered if she did the same when she swung arms with Simon. She thought so. She knew Aidan didn't. She had a clear picture of Aidan sauntering down the road with Simon's hand yanked up past his ear. It used to touch her to watch her dashing, worldly husband making time for their young son. She'd never considered the *way* they walked. Whether Lawrence was conscious of his solicitousness or not, his whole body reflected the attention and concern he was directing toward Kamla.

Simon was *thriving*, she told herself again. It seemed nothing short of a miracle.

She breathed in softly and drew her gaze down Kamla's silhouette. The top of the girl's head came nearly to Lawrence's shoulder. She was taller than Joanna had realized. Was it possible she had grown just in the time they'd been together? She computed the weeks. Two months at ten, eleven years of age. Yes, more than possible. And then another thought seized her. Last night after supper Mr Weller had promised to review what files he had, see if anyone answering the description of Kamla's father was listed. He promised to check with the British consul as well. He'd warned them not to get their hopes up, but Joanna saw now that hope was exactly what they had to keep up – no matter what the cost.

She rose and pushed open the French doors to the terrace just as the two reached the house. She smiled.

'Hullo!' Lawrence's eyes took her in. 'What do you have there?'

'It's from Simon.' She showed him the letter. 'He sounds fine. Though by the time we get back, Akbar may have turned him into a Communist, a brigand, *and* a Mohammedan.'

'Please?' Kamla took the page from Lawrence and studied it intently. She had a natural aptitude for reading, seemingly memorizing each new word as it was pointed out to her, but she had not

158

yet mastered writing, and Simon's ability impressed her no end. She grinned when she came to her name, but the smile faltered as she reached the end. *I hope you find Daddy soon.*

'Come,' Joanna said abruptly. 'Let's see about getting some breakfast, shall we?'

As they emerged from the sunroom, Mrs Weller appeared down the hall, smoothing the collar of her polka dot dress and setting her scarlet lipstick with rabbity pinches of her mouth. 'There you are!' She beckoned them forward. 'You're all so quiet and sneaky, I thought you'd stolen away in the night.'

A stricken look crossed her face as she must have realized Joanna was mentally completing her comment, 'just like that woman and your husband.'

'Not at all,' Lawrence jumped in. 'We woke early and didn't want to disturb anyone.'

'Oh, for heaven's sake. What could you possibly disturb! Dan was up at the crack of dawn. He went over to the British consulate on that matter he promised you.' Lillian threw a meaningful glance toward Kamla, who hung back in the sunroom doorway.

'And?' Joanna asked.

'He's still there.' The consul's wife slid her tongue along her front teeth, checking for lipstick smears. 'By the time we finish breakfast he should be back.'

As they proceeded to the breakfast room she rattled on about the capital's sights – temples, mosques, bazaars, camels, modern shops. Having flown into Tihwa from central China, Mrs Weller apparently had no conception of the miles they had covered or the conditions under which they had traveled. She seemed equally casual about the political landscape, Tihwa's reputation for danger and intrigue, the pending evacuation, and the two errands that had brought her guests, though when her husband strode in some minutes later, she did turn to him expectantly. 'Learn something, dear?'

Weller ignored her, addressing Lawrence alone. 'Could I have a word with you?'

Joanna opened her mouth to protest, but Lawrence beat her to it. 'If there's news, it's more Jo's business than mine.'

The consul's woolly eyebrows shot up. He was probably

handsome in his youth, Joanna thought. A quarterback or class president. The thought prompted a twinge of hostility, and she realized simultaneously that she didn't trust this man and that she identified him with the same forces in Washington that, in Lawrence's words, had pegged Aidan for the Red Menace. 'There's news, and there's news,' he said. 'Suit yourselves.'

Joanna felt Kamla's stillness beside her. This business, in point of fact, was the child's if it was anyone's, yet Weller's gruffness was not a good omen, and he was hardly one to cushion the blow. 'It won't be long,' she promised Kamla.

'Come, dear,' Lillian Weller barreled through. 'Do you know how to play gin rummy?'

7

As they entered the office, Lawrence looked past Weller to a sallow man of indeterminate age seated in front of the consul's black lacquer desk. He had floppy brown hair, large, red-veined ears, and wore his tailored tan linen suit as if it rubbed him the wrong way. From the single recessed window behind the desk, a diagonal strip of sunlit dust motes split the high-ceilinged room in half. The man squinted over it through wire-rimmed glasses, rising as the three of them approached.

'John Henderson,' Weller introduced him. 'My counterpart over at the British consulate.' He shut the door behind them, and Henderson shook hands first with Joanna, then Lawrence. His handshake was dry and tepid, noncommittal rather than weak. The arrogance of this withholding irked Lawrence enough that he returned it with a bone-crushing squeeze. Henderson's thin lips tightened, and he retrieved his hand.

Joanna and Lawrence seated themselves in two oval chairs on one side of the sunbeam, Henderson on the other. As in the rest of the house, most of the furnishings were distinctly Chinese rather than Sinkiangese, and of suspiciously high quality.

Weller took his place behind the desk with the window at his back. 'John's come up with a name that matches.' He slid across his desk a plain sheet of notepaper on which was scrawled 'Patu

Chand. Former lieutenant, Jat Regiment, H.M. Indian Army.'

Joanna turned the sheet over, but there was no other information. Lawrence looked at Henderson. 'From Kashmir?'

The British consul nodded. 'Sikh, married to a Tungan woman.'

'And he was arrested five years ago?' Joanna leaned forward, sounding breathless.

'I can't tell you exactly – I only arrived here last year and the records are spotty, but thereabouts, yes. Accused of being a reactionary.'

Weller set his elbows on his desk and kneaded his hands together. 'That much the kid had right. But she was wrong on one major detail.'

Henderson said, 'Chand never deserted.'

'I knew it,' Lawrence thought out loud. Then he read Joanna's confusion. 'Kamla's father was a British agent.' And to Henderson, 'A news writer. Am I right?'

'The early 1940s were a horror here,' Henderson continued as if Lawrence hadn't spoken. 'Of course, most of the English had left by then, but there were still quite a few British Indian traders, and they bore the brunt of it. Chand was a good soldier.'

'What happened to him?' Lawrence asked.

The British consul nibbled his upper lip. 'I'm afraid he's dead.'

'You know this for a fact?'

'Yes.' But his tone was evasive.

'*How* do you know?' Joanna demanded.

'Honey – ' Weller began, but at this Joanna shot him a look of admirable venom, and he retrained his statement. 'Mrs Shaw, the war may be over in other parts of the world, but here in Sinkiang' – he pronounced it Sink-yang – 'it's at full tilt. You've got your Turkestan rebels up in the hills with Joe Stalin's guns and advisors. You've got your Chinese Reds padding around the underground right here in the capital. You've got Chiang's boys looking to fly the coop, and a bunch of native tribesmen with more brawn than brains, but at least the natives are a tough lot and terrific guerrilla fighters – ' He had evidently forgotten the question and was rehearsing his position statement.

'Mr Weller,' Joanna broke in. 'I appreciate the politics, but my concern right now is this child, who according to you is an orphan.

If I'm going to tell her that her father is dead, I want to be damn sure it's true. If there's proof, I want to see it.'

A series of horizontal lines appeared in Weller's forehead. He seemed on the verge of laughing. 'I like a woman who cusses,' he said to Henderson, who frowned distractedly and checked his watch.

'That's just it,' Henderson answered Joanna. 'Proof. We have no record that Chand had a daughter.'

She stared at him.

Lawrence said, 'You mean there was no birth certificate.'

'No document of any kind.'

'But surely that's not unusual here – especially for a girl child.'

'No, it's not. Nevertheless—'

'When you hear how he died you may decide she's better off not knowing,' Weller interrupted.

No one spoke.

'All right, then,' Henderson said. 'After Hiroshima, there was a brief honeymoon period here when the Nationalists and Communists pretended to shake hands. The jails were emptied as a gesture of goodwill. Most of the former prisoners scuttled off to join the Reds in Yenan. Your boy Chand headed in the other direction.'

'He didn't die in prison?' Joanna lifted a hand and folded it absently around her throat.

'No,' said Henderson. 'He was headed for India, but somehow wandered into Tibet. The Tibetans have never been fond of outsiders. We think it was a misunderstanding – wrong place, wrong time, or perhaps just a communications gap: Chand couldn't speak the local dialect, so the tribesmen took him for an intruder.'

'Tibet's not exactly on the main route back,' Lawrence observed.

'It's an alternate route,' Weller said smoothly.

Alternate for an expendable brown 'boy' running a king's errand, Lawrence thought. He'd seen similar scenarios played out countless times during his years with Special Operations. The loyal spy who knew too much cunningly played out of the game.

'How do you know he's dead?' Joanna persisted.

The slash of light had moved with the sun and now pressed against her face. She neither squinted nor blinked. Lawrence resisted the impulse to shield her with his own body.

The British consul picked up a manila folder from the desk in front of him. 'If you must, you may look at this, Mrs Shaw. I think you'll regret it.'

She opened the file. Lawrence got up and came behind her. A round-faced man with light skin and amiable black eyes stared out from a constabulary photograph dated 1941. He wore a turban and a thick black beard and army fatigues. His face and lips were as delicately shaped as Kamla's, though his nose was larger and coarser. Strangely, the eyebrows resembled her most. Just as hers did, they started far apart and slanted evenly upward, dropping short at the outer corners. It was a strong face, and not unkind, but like Kamla's it seemed to conceal more than it revealed.

The paperwork in the folder substantiated what the consuls had told them. It bore various official British signatures and stamps. The certificate of death was dated June 1946. No next of kin was listed.

Joanna flipped to the photographs at the back of the folder. She uttered a low moan, and Lawrence placed his hands on her shoulders. The pictures were straightforward and graphic. The shoulders and boots pointed in opposite directions. Only the face was recognizable. It appeared Kamla's father had been hacked to death.

Joanna wordlessly passed the folder back to Henderson. 'You understand,' he said, 'all of this is strictly confidential. I've shared this with you purely as a courtesy.'

Lawrence spoke. 'What about Kamla? Surely she's entitled to some compensation.'

Henderson again looked at his watch. 'I'm afraid I must go. As I told you, we have no record that Chand had a child. And evidently neither do you.'

'Just like that?' Lawrence said. 'You admit the man died serving British interests. You admit that all the evidence we've laid in front of you suggests this child is his daughter, and you know bloody well why there was no birth certificate – precisely *because* he was your spy!'

Henderson stood up. 'It's not my policy, Mr Malcolm. Chand never reported a daughter to his superiors. It was his choice.' He looked significantly at Lawrence. 'If this is the only reason you've come to Sinkiang, I'm afraid you may have made the trip for nothing.'

A question mark teetered at the end of this statement. Joanna frowned, and Lawrence fully expected her to declare her larger mission. He couldn't tell if Henderson was fishing for this, or for some more subtle revelation from Lawrence himself. Either way, the consul had destroyed his own leverage. His disavowal of Kamla granted them full license to remain silent.

But Joanna held her tongue only until Henderson was out the door. 'Mr Weller,' she said leaning forward.

Weller's wooden chair creaked loudly as he drew back. She had her hands on the desk. Her cheeks flamed.

'Can you arrange for me to adopt Kamla?'

8

While we waited, Mrs Weller and I played gin rummy – she was quite surprised that I knew how to play, but I told her Lawrence had taught me, and she nodded and said that made sense. She herself was so familiar with the game that she could shuffle and deal and make her plays without paying the least attention. All the while she talked on and on, seeming to feel it necessary to fill the air with words. She spoke with a great deal of energy, and at one point her eyes brimmed with tears. She was childless, she said. This was her 'sorrow.' I thought how odd it was that she had no children and I no mother, yet there was not the least desire for affection between us. I thought of the many children we had met along the road who had also lost parents and were left to beg or scavenge for scraps as I had in Delhi. I thought if Mrs Weller truly wanted children, there must be countless ones she could claim as Mem and Lawrence had claimed me.

I had talked with some of those children, asked them where were their mothers and fathers. Many did not know. But others could describe their fathers' jails as if they themselves had been imprisoned – windowless cells without water or air into which they were herded like animals. The children said men were beaten on the palms and soles with bamboo until their flesh was pulp. They were strung up by the wrists with razor wire, with their feet just touching a pile of coal dust so that any movement would lower the pile and cause the pressure on the bindings to cut their hands off, and when they were thirsty they would be given drink with sugar or salt, this to multiply their thirst until they were mad with it, and then they were given nothing. Some were put into petrol drums half filled with water that was slowly heated until they confessed to crimes dictated by their jailers. Or had their feet covered with boiling oil or branded with burning wood. Even after confessing, many still did not know what they were accused of.

Though I tried not to, I saw my own father in many of these stories. But even as I worried that a similar fate had befallen him, I also took comfort because the tales proved that some of the men had survived. Therefore my father, too, might still be waiting to tell me his stories, if only I could find him.

From the terrace where we were sitting, I could see when Mem and Lawrence stepped back into the hall, and I tipped the table in my haste to meet them. Mem took me by the hand. She was not smiling. I waited, hoping that her expression meant only more of the same no-news that we both had been enduring throughout these long weeks. But then I looked at Lawrence and his face, too, seemed cut from iron. Except that his one green-brown eye quivered behind a wall of tears.

Mem led me alone out into the garden. We sat in the shade of a willow tree. A light breeze caused the fronds of the willow to sway, stirring the veil of coal dust so that it seemed as if spirits moved around us, warming us with their breath, even making fun of us sitting there so serious. Mem held on to my hand, and I thought this was all I wanted. All I had ever wanted.

She told me my father had not died when and how I imagined, but later, after I was already sold to the flash house and had given up hope of seeing him again. She told me he died in the mountains. She did not tell me the circumstances, and she said she did not know why, though she thought it was an accident. He did not die in the death car. He did not die in prison. Perhaps he was coming to find his brother. Perhaps he was coming for me. All these things blew through my mind as she talked and held my hand. I knew they mattered more than life itself. At the same time, nothing mattered but the comfort of Mem's skin, not as pale as it once had been but the color of roasted grain from our long hours together under the mountain and desert suns. Our travels together had made our skins almost indistinguishable. She no longer wore gloves. She had changed, and I had changed. When she said she wondered if I would like to become as her daughter now, I shook my head not understanding.

'I am as your daughter now.'

She let go my hand and wrapped me in her arms. I felt her cheek wet against my forehead, her lips soft at my temple. She surrounded me like a gathering net, pulling me inward, shaping herself against me. And then we began to rock in this bundle of darkness and sorrow and warmth, and I shut my eyes and imagined the spirits lifting the two of us as we shrank to a single flame upon the stream.

CHAPTER 6

1

While Mem and Lawrence were learning what had happened to my father, Tot went into the bazaar to ask questions about Mr Shaw. That afternoon he took us to visit a Russian mechanic who said that he had rented a jeep to a foreign man and woman who intended to drive up toward the Soviet border. The couple claimed to be Western journalists and said they wanted to interview Osman, one of the rebel chiefs whose camp lay in the mountains above Heaven's Pool. They were supposed to return with the Russian's jeep in three days, but that was over a week ago.

'Aidan thought they'd be back before we got here,' Mem said to Lawrence. 'That's why he didn't leave word.'

Lawrence did not answer.

When they told Mr Weller, he said they shouldn't believe anything they heard in the bazaar, but the next morning at breakfast he said that maybe the Russian was right. 'Some of my tribesmen found a jeep in the foothills, about four hours from here.'

Mem pulled her shirt collar around her neck, as if she were suddenly cold.

They did not want me to come. They would be gone only overnight, Lawrence said, a quick, rough trip into the foothills north of the city with Mr Weller and some of his men. I could stay at the consulate with Mrs Weller, where I would be safe and comfortable until they returned. But the length of a night is measured not only by the hands of a clock, and experience had taught me that even the shortest of separations too often turned out

167

to be permanent. My father was dead, and Mem and Lawrence's hurried talk and nervous gestures betrayed their fear.

So I pleaded. I used tears and silence and protests of need. I wedged myself between them, holding on to both their hands, and said I did not believe, if they left, that they would ever return.

'Let her come,' Mem said finally.

Because of me, no space remained for Tot to accompany us. No one realized this until the very last moment when Mem and Lawrence and I squeezed into the back of the consulate jeep and Mr Weller got in beside Chen, his driver and translator. Mr Weller said Tot could ride with the Chinese soldiers in the escort jeep. But the soldiers only laughed at him. 'How do we know you're not a Communist?' they barked. Tot glared at them, then stomped back across the motor court on his short thick legs. I had never seen him so angry. He told Lawrence that it was his duty to make sure we were safe. Had he not guided and protected us all the way from Leh? He felt responsible for us even here, he said. Lawrence asked again if I would stay at the consulate, but I stubbornly shook my head.

As we drove out through the hot crowded streets no one spoke a word. Mem kept her head turned toward the lowered window. Lawrence wound and rewound his watch and tapped his thumb on his knee. Mr Weller bent over his map up front, pulling on the brim of his cap. (The cap was dark blue with a *Y* stitched in white, and Lawrence whispered that in Weller's world that *Y* was like the caste mark of a high Brahmin.) Every few minutes the driver would lean on his horn as we swerved around a flock of goats, an overloaded truck, or a mangy dog.

Once we left the city and its haze of coal dust, the heat of the northern desert intensified. The sun pounded down from a cloud-less sky, and we had to stop barely an hour out of the city when one of the jeep's radiators boiled over. My father had died, but I had Mem to one side of me, Lawrence to the other, and though they each were locked in their separate thoughts, if I moved my arms just slightly I could feel their skin against my own. I could finger the folds of their shirts. They had tried to leave me, and I had not let them. A small victory, you might say, but I marked my victories, whatever their size, like gems to be hoarded and cherished.

Not even the roadblocks alarmed me. The Han Chinese soldiers that manned them looked too lazy to give us trouble. They stood or squatted in circles and smoked. Some fingered their rifles like flutes. One caught his breath, lifted his gun, and squeezed the trigger. Mem jumped in her seat, but the soldier was only shooting at a flock of wild ducks, and when the bird he had killed dropped to the road, the other men shouted, slapped him on the back. Then they waved us on.

'No need to look so stricken,' Mr Weller said over his shoulder to Mem. 'Remember, they're on our side.'

'Exactly what side is that?' she asked. But the engine roared as we turned uphill, and Mr Weller touched a finger to his ear as if he couldn't hear her.

We stopped at an oasis for water, passed one last checkpoint, then turned off the main road for a wide dirt track that led up toward the Tien Shan. Any farther, Mr Weller said, and 'we'd be playing chicken with the Reds.' Lawrence explained that Communist rebels controlled the rest of Sinkiang between here and the Soviet border, but the Kazakhs who controlled this territory were 'friends of Mr Weller.'

As soon as we began to climb, the air cleared of dust and heat. Green meadows appeared. We passed fields of sunflowers tipping their crowded faces to the sky, and sheep and cattle and horses grazed beside waterfalls that fell like white braids. Apple orchards and pastures covered the foothills, and I thought I had not seen such beautiful land since our brief flight over Kashmir.

As we entered the forest that grew above the pastureland, however, I noticed that our soldier escorts seemed to sit higher in their seats. They clutched their rifles and peered at the road. Lawrence asked Mr Weller what they were looking for. 'Mines,' he said. Then he grinned and jerked his head toward the other jeep. 'That's why they go first.'

I asked Lawrence what the word *mines* meant. He brought his fingertips together to form a ball, then flung his hands apart.

'Don't,' Mem said. 'You'll scare her.' I was startled by the fierceness of her voice, for this was the first she had spoken since we left the city, and she'd hardly looked at me all day. Now her eyes were glassy. She lifted an arm around my shoulders, but I had the feeling as she turned toward me that she was really comforting herself.

'She needs to understand not to go wandering off,' Lawrence said. 'Sometimes it's wise to be a bit scared.'

'In that case, I'm wise enough for all of us. Leave her to me.' Her mouth stretched back, as if she were trying to smile but had forgotten how. I opened my own to speak, thinking that might break the terrible spell that seemed to have settled between us, but suddenly the jeep rocked sharply to one side. Mem fell hard against me. I tasted her hair, her skin and shirt. Her panic. I saw again Lawrence's hands flying into the air, and I suppose some part of me was afraid as well, but that's not what I remember. I remember wanting the fear to last.

The jeep righted itself. We had simply tipped into a deep rut. Mr Weller made a joke about it and clapped the driver on the back. Mem pulled away from me and took a breath. She tucked her shirt into her belt. Then she smoothed my hair back from my face and asked if I was all right. I said yes. I smiled. She bit her lip and nodded.

I turned and saw Lawrence frowning across at her, but she ignored him and he leaned forward, steadying himself on the back of Mr Weller's seat, to ask how much farther we had to go. Mr Weller spoke to the driver, then yelled back that the next stretch of road was clear. The Kazakh camp was just over the rise, he said. We were almost there.

A few minutes later we reached a crest with black spruce forest off to our left and a view to a long, glittering lake far below us to the right. 'Heaven's Pool,' Mr Weller called.

The sight brought a knot to my throat. I stopped breathing and felt my pulse race. Ever since we'd left India I had experienced these moments. A taste of wind, a scent of smoke, the precise color of water or stone would awaken me to the fact that I had stood in that exact place before, that I was revisiting another life. It had happened in Leh and along the trek, outside the Chinese garrison, and again upon entering Tihwa. Each time it was as if the past were reaching out to touch me, but not without some disbelief. After all, I'd left no trace of my former self behind. No home, no belongings, no one to welcome me back. So how could I be certain I'd been here before? This time there was no doubt.

I had come here with my father. We had ridden from the city on horseback. I remembered the quiet, the lake's reflection so untroubled, like a vast spill of liquid silver. I recognized the smells of deodar and hemlock, dry earth and this same chill breeze, the echoes of donkey and goat bells settling like garlands on the high, thin air. We had picnicked on the shore of the pool. My father lifted me onto his shoulders and ran with me toward the sun. I believed with all my heart that day in the illusion of safety and freedom.

The road twisted back into the forest. By the time the lake returned to view the sun had fallen behind the peaks. The sky was engorged with peach and gold, but the earth beneath it lay in shadow. As we drew closer, I saw that a large Kazakh encampment now stretched along the lakeshore – several dozen yurts in rows like white parcels tied with string. From the center of the camp rose a greasy black twist of smoke. I smelled sheep droppings and damp wool from the flocks being herded to either side of us. I saw children and women wearing long red and blue skirts and bright folded headdresses. They stood still as we approached. They studied our Chinese escorts warily and pointed without expression toward the headman's tent.

Everything had changed. The past might touch but it could not hold me. My father is dead, I told myself. It was a mistake to believe in illusions.

2

The driver, Joanna noticed, was nervous again. Each snapping twig beneath the wheels caused his head to twitch. Weller, too, breathed sharply, leaning into the windshield to scan the shadows in front of them. Mines, he'd said dramatically. We're on the edge of rebel country. He wants us to be terrified, she thought. The man in charge, with that ridiculous Yale cap and suede hunting jacket. He thinks if we get frightened enough we'll agree to turn back. Only the Kazakh chief seemed unconcerned. He carried no flashlight or lantern and rode with his eyes straight ahead, his white stallion seeming to pull the jeep's lurching headlights like tethers.

Nurga, Weller called him. Under other circumstances Joanna would have found the man 'colorful,' with his long black curls and heavy beard, scarlet jacket and high leather boots. In another life, she'd actually fantasized traveling with Aidan to places like Heaven's Pool, encountering characters like Nurga and inhaling 'native culture' while Aidan got his story. What a fool she'd been!

The chief refused to address anyone but Weller. Back at the lake they'd stood awkwardly outside his tent, clearly expected but uninvited. Yes, the driver translated, a boy tending sheep had come upon the debris of a small explosion over the next ridge. Yes, a jeep. No, no bodies.

How far? Weller had asked, looking up into the draining sky.

But Joanna didn't care how far. 'Take us now,' she said with a command in her voice that she'd never known she possessed.

So here they were, grinding up a path meant for horses and sheep. Lawrence had suggested they, too, ride, but the loathing with which Nurga regarded the Chinese warned that he'd never allow them on any of his ponies, and Weller wouldn't hear of continuing without the escort.

The jeep pitched to one side. Joanna saw Kamla brace herself against Lawrence's knee. The girl's presence flickered like a question on the tip of her tongue, but she could not hold on to the thought. Up front, Weller grimaced, and a spurt of voices intercut the grinding of gears. Lawrence to Kamla. The driver to Weller. The exchanges disintegrated before they reached Joanna. She gripped the frame above the door and kept her eyes on the ghostly twitch and step of the Kazakh's enormous steed.

Then the undercarriage hit something hard, and the driver, Chen, cursed as the headlamp beams swept the wall of trees. Joanna heard a loud metallic squeal. The vehicle shuddered to a stop, and behind them the escort driver jammed on his brakes.

Lawrence reached across Kamla, addressing them both. 'Steady now. Right?'

Joanna looked down at his hand in the darkness, clasping her arm. After a moment she nodded.

They'd stopped on an incline strewn with boulders and stones. The trail had vanished. At the top of the rise, washed by the headlights, the white horse turned in a circle. Nurga lifted one hand against the glare and with the other motioned them out of the cars.

'The jeep's all right,' she heard Weller say. Chen and the other driver had the hood open. 'But this is the end of the road. We go the rest of the way on foot.'

Lawrence pressed a flashlight into her hand. He'd brought three and gave the third to Kamla. Joanna couldn't bring herself to turn hers on. The night was cold and clear with a newly risen three-quarter moon and stars like broken glass. The divided silhouette of treetops ahead of them indicated a clearing. From the same direction she heard running water and was suddenly intensely thirsty, but she'd left her canteen in the jeep and didn't dare take even those few steps backward.

'Doesn't it work?' Lawrence asked, spotting her in his beam. She couldn't see him behind it. The slam of the hood went through her like an electric shock.

The clearing on the other side of the rise had originally been formed by a river. The bed was now mostly dry, and two tracks in the pale silt suggested it was used at least occasionally as a road. The slope down to it from their approach was so steep that the Kazakh's horse had to nose sideways, and the rest of them scrambled just to stay upright in the crumbling earth, but the clearing itself when they reached it was flat and smooth – unbroken. Joanna dried her palms on her pants leg.

Then Weller called out, 'Nurga says it's just around the bend.' He and the others had gone ahead. The beams of their flashlights and the broader glow of an electric lantern glittered through the trees. Joanna noticed the sound of water again, off to the right. At first she couldn't see the actual stream, but as they approached the bend of a few yards on, what remained of the river curled close enough to the road that she could touch it with her light. The water looked icy and clear. Her mouth was so dry she could hardly swallow, but as she started toward the embankment, Lawrence placed his hand on the small of her back.

'I wouldn't,' he warned. 'If the place is mined . . .'

He handed her his canteen and she rinsed her mouth. The water was warm and tasted of iodine, but she forced herself to swallow and kept walking.

Kamla moved beside her. Joanna took her hand. 'Look what we've gotten you into.'

The girl brought her other hand over Joanna's. 'Mem is afraid?' she said.

But at this Joanna balked. Kindness right now could devour her. 'I'm sorry,' she said, squeezing Kamla's palm tighter even as she pulled away.

'Jesus Christ.' Weller's voice drilled through the trees. Its hard saw-toothed edges launched Joanna into a run.

As she rounded the corner she saw the light beams tracing a hole the size of a small fishpond. She smelled pine and mud and honeysuckle shot through with burnt metal and motor oil. The jeep lay by the side of the road, its undercarriage facing her. She stopped just short of it.

Then everything seemed to stop.

The blast must have caught the front left tire, which, along with the engine and windshield, no longer existed. The gas tank would have burst into flame, incinerating what was left of the vehicle after the initial concussion. Here and there, scraps of scorched canopy fluttered like dead leaves, several of them caught in a spider's web spun from the metal frame.

Weller stood turning a piece of shrapnel between his fingers while his men peered and poked at the wreckage. One of the Chinese nervously laughed and held up the electric lantern. Another ran his finger along the twisted door handle. As Joanna came within range she saw the finger come up black with soot. The man wiped it on his trousers. Her flashlight wavered as she passed it over the shell of the jeep's interior.

The seats had burned down to the springs, the windshield and rearview mirrors shattered to a fine gravel of blackened crystals. Because the jeep had been hurled sideways, these glass pebbles coated the ground. The crunching they made under Joanna's boots turned her stomach. She lifted her head. A white strip of cloth maybe two inches long fluttered from a birch branch several feet above her.

'Where are they?' She whipped around to confront Weller.

'Nobody could survive this. Where are the bodies?'

The consul stretched his neck, glanced at the scrap of cloth. 'I just got here, Joanna. Same as you.'

'Ask him, then.' She pointed to the Kazakh, who sat on his horse watching them from the far side of the blast crater.

Weller grimaced, but he summoned Chen, and they made their way around the depression.

Nurga's eyes traveled from Joanna to Weller as he answered their questions. The two boys who had found this place touched nothing. They had seen no bodies, no bones, no indication who the driver might have been. No cargo in the vehicle.

He pointed. Even if there had been cargo, he said, it would be of no use to anyone after the fire. His boys had touched nothing, he repeated.

Joanna's mind filled with the memory of Ben Eldon's knuckles rapping against his prosthetic knee as he described Aidan standing on the rim of that other minefield, futilely shooting off rounds of film as if the record mattered. Witnesses. He wanted to capture the witnesses. But what if there were no witnesses? Now she was the one with her eye at the lens, and the only images that came into view were a succession of charred twists of metal, a mangled steering wheel. A tire melted above the earth. And that scrap of white.

She saw Lawrence step down into the crater while Kamla stood watching from the edge. High above them the wind shuffled through the treetops. Weller and the Kazakh continued talking, but they would tell her nothing. The Chinese soldiers were now combing the dirt with birch branches they'd picked up from the knoll behind them. Kamla found a branch for herself and began to follow suit.

'Jo?' Lawrence beckoned her closer.

'He's not here,' she said. 'Nothing about him is here.'

Lawrence lowered his voice. 'I heard what they told you. One or both of them are lying. Someone's been here before us and picked this place clean.'

'What are they looking for, then?' She motioned with her chin at the soldiers.

'Maybe it's for our benefit. Maybe they're making sure nothing was left behind. Or maybe they're hoping to find an intact screw or bolt they can sell back to our Russian friend. I don't think they're having much luck.'

Out of the corner of her eye Joanna saw Kamla bending over the far edge of the crater, poking at something with her stick. The child's flashlight was turned on a small square flap, which looked to Joanna like skin. She glanced around to make sure no one else was watching. Then she touched Lawrence's wrist and switched off her light. They reached Kamla just as she dislodged her find from the soil.

'Easy,' Lawrence said to the girl. 'This is our secret.'

What had appeared to Joanna as skin turned out to be a small glassine envelope caked in dirt. Lawrence put his arm around Kamla's shoulders, and the three of them faced away from the others as if to comfort the girl. Lawrence aimed the flashlight. Joanna had already rubbed the envelope clean with her fingertips. Now she opened the flap and removed its contents: a photograph about three inches square, with the lower left corner torn off.

The white scalloped margin was fraying, the image in the center so badly soiled that Joanna at first did not recognize it. Or perhaps she couldn't bear to recognize it. She focused first on the rounded hat with a brim like an American cowboy's. This rode flatly on large, splayed ears. But the ears belonged to a five-year-old child wearing a checkered shirt. His cheeks were wide and high, chin pointed, eyes round and wary. A tooth was missing between lips that were almost, but not quite smiling.

Joanna remembered like yesterday the hot, muggy evening in July when Aidan took this picture. Simon's fifth birthday in the yard of their house in Rockville. Aidan's present had been a set of three finely tooled leather collars and name tags for Simon's beloved cats, so after dinner they'd gone out into the yard, and Simon had posed with each cat in turn wearing its new finery. Something had gone wrong with the camera. Only one of the pictures had turned out, the one with Simon holding his favorite, a cross-eyed tabby named Willy. They'd left Willy with their friends the Bermans before moving to New Delhi. The cat's head had appeared in the lower left corner that now was missing from the photograph.

Lawrence brought his palm up underneath her hand. At first she thought he was afraid she would drop the picture. Then she realized he wanted her to turn it over.

Aidan's neatest print was smudged across the back. *What matters most,* he'd written, then, along the bottom in smaller letters, *If lost, please return to Joanna Shaw, 39 Ratendone Road, New Delhi.*

A sound emerged from Joanna's throat as if someone inside her were drowning. She wanted it to stop, but her teeth were chattering so hard she had to open her mouth to silence them, and when she did that, the drowning sound only grew louder.

She felt Lawrence's arms around her rigid body, rocking her back against him as Kamla extinguished the light. He guided her hand to her jacket pocket and pried open her fingers, patting the photo into safekeeping. He was trying to help. She knew that, but the sensation of his breath on the back of her neck was like acid. Her lungs and ribs hurt. She lurched away from him, doubled over by that recurring thirst, now compounded by a wave of nausea. She heard the croon of the stream to her left and pushed toward it through the moonlit undergrowth.

She slid down the sandy bank and crouched over the water, dipped her hands in it, splashed it into her mouth and over her eyes and cheeks and neck. The cold was like a slap in the face, the taste unspeakably foul. She spit it out, gagging.

'Jo?' Lawrence called down to her.

Her hand went to her pocket. She could feel the photo's scalloped edge. The torn corner. She gathered her wits.

'Weller's rounding up his troops. He wants to head back.'

'No!' She scrambled back up the bank. 'There's more here. Aidan dropped this on purpose. I know it.'

Her eyes fell on Kamla crouched a few feet away. The girl was using her hands to sift through the dark, damp earth. Joanna looked again at the crater, the distance and angle at which the vehicle had been thrown. The flutter of white in the birch tree. She pictured a body flung through the air, the trajectory arching up and outward. The stream twisted around the point just beyond the birch, and the bank widened.

Weller and the Kazakh knew this place. Others had been here before them.

'You're right,' she said. 'Give me back my flashlight.'

'About what?'

She took it from him. 'Stay here with Kamla. Don't let her follow me.'

'Joanna, you can't—'

She ignored his protests and shook his hand from her elbow. 'Just keep Weller and the others occupied for a few more minutes.' She returned to the water's edge and made her way as quickly as she could over the tumbled rocks and branches that littered the narrows. Her boots were soon drenched, her feet numb with cold, and her teeth again began to clatter uncontrollably as she rounded the turn to the stretch below the site.

Looking up over the top of the bank now, she could just make out that ghostly flag from which she drew a mental line to the stream, and played her flashlight over the surface of the water. It ran swiftly but was nowhere more than a foot deep, and contained nothing more noteworthy than a dead badger tucked under a tree root on the opposite shore. She brought the light back to the wide berth of sand on which she was standing. Chunks of moss and black earth and pine needles made a patchwork, as if the ground had been dug up and haphazardly reassembled.

She found a long, firm stick and prodded the first stretch of ground. The light in her hand was shaking, but she soon determined that only the surface of the earth had been disturbed. She moved on to the next patch, and the next, keeping her eye on the white cloth and her ear open to the sounds of the men on the other side of the rise. Nurga's voice, low and impatient, now rumbled under Weller's. Lawrence announced that Joanna was answering a 'call of nature.'

The wide beachlike shore ended abruptly at a massive boulder. She had almost reached this natural obstacle when the breeze shifted into her face. She gasped and covered her nose, took an involuntary step backward and stumbled over a buried log, dropping her flashlight. It came to rest at an angle, so that the light seemed to glaze the earth.

The glaze shimmered, undulating.

Joanna screamed. She grabbed the flashlight back and got to her feet as two rats sprang from the moving ground and darted under the boulder. The seething motion, though, was caused not by rats, but by a mass of maggots working their way up and over the leaves.

She turned and vomited into the water. The first of the Chinese soldiers were stomping down the bank with Weller close behind. She forced her eyes back to the ground, holding the flashlight with both hands in order to steady it.

A hasty, single grave. The spread of sand and leaves made a flimsy coverlet in which the escaping rats had torn a hole several inches wide. Joanna pressed her mouth and nose into the shoulder of her jacket and crept as close as she could bear. She trained the light on the head of the grave. From under the blanket, freed by the breeze, rose a spray of pale yellow hair.

3

Lawrence and Kamla were standing beside Weller when Joanna screamed.

'Shit,' Weller said under his breath. Even in the moment, it struck Lawrence as a curious reaction. The consul seemed less alarmed than annoyed and, almost before the others could register what was happening, started off in Jo's direction.

Kamla had frozen like a startled animal. 'You okay?' he said. She nodded, but took his hand.

From the top of the embankment they could make out Joanna crouched at the edge of the stream, her back heaving as the Chinese soldiers stepped past her. Farther on, Weller pulled a bandanna from his pocket and tied it into a mask over his nose and mouth.

'Go to Mem,' Lawrence instructed Kamla. 'Maybe you can help her.' The child gave another solemn nod and fingered the end of her braid. Together they slid down the bank, and only when he saw her touch Joanna's shoulder and Joanna's arm slide around Kamla's waist did Lawrence move ahead.

One soldier held the electric lantern while the others raked at the earth with sticks because no one had bothered to equip them with gloves or shovels. Weller stood with his hands on his hips. He glared at the corpse his men were uncovering. He's pissed off, Lawrence thought again. This wasn't in his bloody game plan.

Then he looked down and saw the exposed head. Shiver of flies crawling over the tongue, necklace of shiny black beetles, the mass of maggots solid as spectacles under the brow. He couldn't even see where the eyes had been – gone now, in any case, to judge by the hole in the cheek. He'd seen enough decomposing bodies in the war to know that this one had been dead just about as long as that jeep had been lying on its side. In this climate, one, maybe two weeks. Moisture and easy access had given the blowies their way with her.

Her. Not Aidan. It came to him late, the hair. Long hanks of it pale as straw where it wasn't crusted in mud.

Weller barked at one of the Chinese soldiers to check the pockets. The lad did his best, but his hands were trembling, and the consul pushed him aside. 'Want a job done, do it yourself. Give me your knife.'

The Chinese stood back beside Lawrence as Weller kneeled over the body and skillfully slit first the outer pockets, then plucked off the buttons and flipped the jacket open to rifle the interior compartments. Every one was empty, and the movement of insects inside the chest cavity made the body appear to be panting. For all his disdain of the young soldier's squeamishness, Weller was careful to keep his own hands a dagger's length clear at all times, and he made no attempt to turn the corpse over before declaring the hunt a lost cause. 'There's nothing. Cover her up.' He stood, ripping the cloth from his face, and stepped back into Lawrence.

'It's Alice James, isn't it?'

'Your guess is as good as mine.' Weller shouldered past him.

'Like I said, it's Alice James.'

'The question is, who's responsible?'

'Who buried her?' Lawrence said to his back. 'Or who killed her?'

But Weller spat into the darkness and kept going. 'I need to get somewhere I can breathe.'

Lawrence watched the American consul stop at the base of the incline, yank his Yale cap from his head and whack it against his thigh as he took in several long drafts of air. Then Weller turned and made his way back up to the Kazakh, who remained through all of this on his white mount like some kind of mascot. Lawrence

180

had the distinct sense that the consul was less concerned about Alice's death than he was about their finding her body.

'Let's get out of here,' Weller yelled down to his men. 'We've reached the end of the line.'

'What about Aidan?' Joanna's voice rang out. She aimed her light up at Weller's face, so he looked like a child's jack-o'-lantern. Lawrence hadn't realized she was standing so close.

'It's dark, Mrs Shaw. It's late. We've all had a shock. We're exhausted.' He reminded Lawrence of a kindergarten teacher trying to put his charge down for a nap. 'We'll go back with Nurga, get some rest, and return in the morning.'

'You go,' she said. 'I'll wait here.'

'Get that light out of my face,' Weller said. 'We've been over every inch of this ground. There's nothing else here.'

'How do you know that?' Joanna's voice shook. 'You would have said the same thing an hour ago.'

Weller didn't answer, but Lawrence could tell he was reaching his limit. Joanna had called his bluff, and the consul was not a good loser.

The soldiers had finished tidying the grave and were trudging up to the road, coughing and spitting as they went. Joanna moved up the embankment, hugging Kamla to her side.

'How much farther is it to the rebel camp?' she demanded.

'Larry,' Weller said as Lawrence came up behind them. 'Talk some sense into her, would you?'

'Sorry, Consul. There's nothing about this situation that makes any sense to me. The lady's come a long way to find her husband.'

'Jesus.' Weller took off his cap again and clawed his fingers straight back through his hair.

Lawrence checked his watch. 'Look,' he said. 'It's nearly midnight. What do you say we make camp by the jeeps?' He pointed at the sky for Joanna's benefit. 'The moon's about gone. It's going to be darker than pitch in another half-hour. We can walk back come sunup. Consul?'

A phlegmatic sigh was all Weller would give them, but it was enough to satisfy Lawrence. 'Come on, Jo. There's blankets and food in the jeeps. We can't sleep here.'

'Can't sleep, period,' Joanna said. But she laid her hand on

Kamla's head, and the two of them began walking.

That night, in spite of the circumstances, Lawrence was glad that Kamla had come along. Her presence soothed Joanna as he could not, for as hard as the evening's discoveries had been, Kamla seemed merely tired, and this uncomplicated fatigue was in itself calming. When they got to the jeep they both managed to get down a handful of saltines and a few swigs of tinned juice from the packs they'd brought from Tihwa. Joanna refused to sleep in the vehicle, as Weller was doing, for fear he'd drive off in the night. So she and Kamla rolled up together on a bed of pine needles. Protestations aside, within minutes Joanna was snoring softly right along with the girl.

The Kazakh went back alone to Heaven's Pool.

In the morning the three of them were back at the blast site before the others woke up. Dawn stripped the scene of its macabre glitter. The carcass of the jeep with its skirt of metal and glass debris appeared hardly more sinister than trash in a junkyard. Lawrence thought of a New Guinea village he'd passed during the war, where two hundred civilians had been slaughtered. Days after the killings their bones were still visible in some charred doorways, but already grass grew up through the ashes. Butterflies lighted on the corpses of animals, and the stink of death was absorbed by the sponge of warm moist earth. Nature's oblivion could be callous. It was also a real impediment to any search for the missing. Here several layers of cedar and pine needles, slicks of mud and matted leaves had already obliterated the tracks that might have provided clues to Aidan's fate. Joanna's hope was that these same layers had concealed other vital evidence as well – notebooks, a camera, film, or letters.

'If they killed him or kidnapped him,' Joanna wondered aloud, 'would they take his clothes and pencils? He probably went off looking for help – ' A dogged light flashed in her eyes, and Lawrence was torn between admiration and a hard desire to shake her to her senses. But she didn't say anything more about confronting the rebels, so he left her and Kamla to comb the earth on their hands and knees while he investigated the surrounding forest.

Though blue sky twinkled between the trees and sunshine gilded the ground, the likelihood of buried explosives took some of the fun out of this walk in the woods, and he was not inclined to search far. His reasoning, in any case, ran counter to Jo's: If Aidan had gone off in search of help he'd have left more obvious evidence than that one cryptic picture. After half an hour he returned empty-handed.

Joanna confronted him. 'Why are we the enemy?' She had swollen circles under her eyes, and her hair fell in an unruly mass from the clip at the nape of her neck. She looked almost savage in her intensity.

He glanced away and caught Kamla watching them. She was squatting on her haunches a few feet behind Joanna, elbows on her knees.

'What do you mean?' he asked.

'Weller didn't want us to find that body. He doesn't want us to find Aidan.'

'I'm not sure what his hand is in all this,' Lawrence admitted. 'Maybe he just doesn't want to be bothered – now he'll have to notify her relatives and the State Department. But it's also possible his rebel friends are involved. He could be protecting this Osman character.'

'You don't think Weller *ordered*. . . '

He saw her bite back on the thought. 'No,' he said. 'I don't think he'll lose much sleep over her, but Alice James can't be important enough to warrant an execution. More likely she and Aidan came here uninvited, and this was the rebel strongman's way of turning them back at the gate.'

'Then where's Aidan?'

'I don't know, but this place has been so sanitized I can't believe that picture of Simon was simply overlooked.'

'What are you saying?' She put a hand to her forehead to block the rising sun.

'I think he survived the explosion.'

'And buried Alice?'

'Possibly.'

He could hear her swallow. 'Then what?'

'Logically, he'd make his way back to Tihwa. But Alice has been dead for over a week. It wouldn't take that long to get back to the capital, even if he walked all the way.' Lawrence glanced up the road. Weller and his men were arriving like the cavalry, in a cloud of sun-spangled dust.

'Look,' he said. 'I know you want to keep searching, but if we go any farther without Weller's sanction we're more likely to blow ourselves up than find Aidan.'

Before she could answer, the consul was on them.

Sleep had restored him: His cap was on straight, his face wiped, shirt tucked, and suede jacket open at a jaunty angle. He waved a yellow cable envelope. 'Messenger just brought this from the city. Plane's coming in tomorrow for the evacuation. We've got to get back to the consulate.'

So. Weller had his trump.

Lawrence expected Joanna to say she wouldn't leave without her husband. He expected her shoulders to straighten, her chin to lift. He expected her to browbeat the American consul with cries of duty and obligation. Instead her arms came up, crossing over her breasts, fingers gripping her shoulders. She opened her mouth. For the first time Lawrence read futility in her eyes.

She said softly, 'Alice deserves a proper burial.'

Weller's left eyebrow lifted as if he thought she might be joking.

'There must be a church in Tihwa where she could decently be put to rest.' Those were her exact words: *decently be put to rest.*

'Now, hold on,' Weller said. 'You saw that body. You smelled it. Once the worms have finished their work we could move it. Not now.'

'Here then.'

'You want a service, is that it?'

'I want us to recognize' – she groped for the word, looking tortured as her eyes found the tree where a scrap of white fabric had wrung itself around a branch – 'her *humanity.*'

Weller glanced at Lawrence as if expecting him to back him up, but Lawrence held up his hands.

Joanna tore her gaze from the tree. 'I'll stay here alone if I have to.'

'Oh, for Pete's sake.' Weller chewed on the corner of his mouth. Lawrence could almost hear him thinking: *Just humor the bitch.* But not without his quid pro quo. 'If we help you do this, you'll come along?' *Like a good girl,* Lawrence mentally finished for him.

Joanna hesitated but nodded.

Weller summoned the squad. The men grumbled and wrinkled their noses, but this time Chen had had the forethought to bring the shovels he and the other drivers kept in the back of their jeeps.

Joanna settled for a deeper grave next to the existing one. That way they could simply roll the body into it. She offered to help dig, but Weller wouldn't hear of it, so she and Kamla went off to fashion a marker from twigs and vines while Lawrence and the soldiers dug the new hole. When the time came to transfer the corpse, however, Joanna insisted. Under Weller's scrutiny, she placed one shovel under the shoulders while Lawrence applied the other to what was left of the pelvis. All three of them, he knew, wanted one more careful look as the blanket of earth momentarily peeled away. The body lifted and rotated. Lawrence noted again the hole in the cheek, the yellow of the hair. No rings on the fingers or ornaments of any kind. In the dapple of light that fell through the trees they could see the delicate shape of her skull and now the empty orbits of her eyes. He held his breath and gave a heave. They all stepped back at the redoubled stench. Lawrence turned his head and caught Joanna staring at the bits of hair and fabric and clots of indescribable matter that clung to the original grave. He gently pushed her back toward Kamla, who was sitting on a log far enough away that she could neither see nor smell the corpse. Then he handed their shovels to the soldiers, who quickly filled in both holes.

Weller, the only one among them who had ever exchanged words with Alice, gave a generic and hurried eulogy to 'this young life, ended so tragically in the wrong place and the wrong time. May she rest in peace.' Then Joanna approached the grave alone.

She planted the crude cross she and Kamla had made. For several minutes she continued standing there, fists clenched at her sides. She moved her mouth, but no sound escaped. As she turned from the grave she looked past Lawrence and Kamla, past Weller and the circle of Chinese watching from the embankment. She searched the edge of the forest, downstream, upstream, then glared at the crystal blue sky. She truly seemed to believe that Aidan was going to step

185

from the wilderness, that this act of generosity would bring her husband home.

Lawrence knew better than to warn her, but he didn't have to watch. 'Come on, Kammy,' he said and, slinging an arm around the child's shoulders, led her back the way they had come.

CHAPTER 7

1

A heat wave had gripped the capital in their absence, and as they drove back into town that evening past shuttered shops and families pushing wagons piled with household goods, it became clear that the latest news from the war was making the locals restless. The line of visa applicants, which four days earlier had consisted of a few White Russian landladies and wealthy Chinese merchants, now stretched around the consular compound. And it bristled with Kazakh and Kirghiz warriors who might have been Nurga's cousins.

Lillian Weller came barreling out the door as they crossed the inner courtyard. 'The Desais left Kashgar two days ago! And everybody from the British consulate flew out last night.' She flailed a hand in the direction of the gate where two armed guards were struggling to hold at bay the local traders and officials who demanded a private audience with the consul. 'My God, Dan, I'm so glad you're back, you cannot imagine!'

Clearly, where her husband had been or why did not concern her, and she scarcely looked at the rest of them. But as the consul extended a hand to her shoulder and gave her a clumsy pat, she stepped away, nostrils flaring. 'You're *filthy!*'

'You're absolutely right, my dear. I'd say a good cleanup is the first order of business. Then we'll just take this one step at a time.' Weller threw Lawrence an equivocal smile: Let's keep what happened up there between us.

But he didn't dare look at Joanna.

'My hands are tied,' he insisted an hour later when they cornered him in the hallway outside his office. 'I've got the Chinese mayor and a full retinue of local yes-men waiting inside there. If I don't find a way to get them out of here—'

'Aidan's a US citizen,' Joanna interrupted. 'Isn't your first responsibility to him?'

'He and that girl were traveling without sanction or permission.' Weller shifted the leather binder he was carrying, tucked it officiously under one arm. 'Bucolic as those mountains might look, they're a war zone.'

Lawrence thought of the blast crater, the charred shell of the jeep. Alice James's decaying face. Bucolic.

'They broke the rules and therefore deserved what they got, is that it?' Joanna asked bitterly.

'I don't know all the rules they broke,' Weller retorted. Then ominously, 'Or why.'

The flicker of the electric torches that lined the corridor exaggerated Weller's jowls and the pouches under his eyes. He reminded Lawrence of a vexed bulldog. 'Wouldn't you like to?' Lawrence asked.

'I'm sure I would. But Aidan Shaw's not the only missing person in Sinkiang, and I'd say the odds of any of us finding him under current conditions are slim and none. Now, I'm going to get the two of you out of here. That's a favor, Larry. As you well know, whatever my responsibility may be toward missing Americans, I have no official obligation to Australians.'

'Is that a threat?'

'No.' Weller repeated, 'It's a favor. And if I were you I'd accept graciously, because if you don't, I've got an officeful of guys who'd be pleased as punch to take your seat on that plane.'

'What about you?' Lawrence asked.

'What *about* me?'

'Are you getting out?'

Weller's mouth twisted into a smile. 'Sure,' he said. 'When I'm told to.'

'What about Kamla?' Joanna asked.

He blinked.

'You said you're getting me and Lawrence out. I'm not leaving without Kamla.'

The momentary wrinkle of confusion receded. 'Look, Joanna, I know we talked about this, but there's just not time. She's got no papers. The Brits won't claim her, and the Chinese have their hands full saving their own skins. I don't have jurisdiction here.'

'Consider it a trade,' she interrupted. 'You get my husband. I save a child.'

Weller glanced at Lawrence. 'A trade.'

She nodded, wincing as if he'd just flashed a light into her eyes. A mutter of voices rose behind the thick wood of his office door. 'All right,' he said impatiently. 'I'll try.'

Lawrence caught a glimpse of swirling cigarette smoke and a trio of pinched Chinese faces as the door opened and shut. Then one of the houseboys hurried past, arms full of overstuffed suitcases.

Lawrence took Joanna by the elbow and steered her back toward the staircase. 'It's a dangerous game,' he said. 'Trading one life for another.'

'It was just a ploy.'

'I understand. And it looks like it worked. But it's a hell of a burden to put on Kamla if you even start to believe it.'

The horn of a lorry sounded through an open window at the end of the hall. Joanna put her hand on the banister and turned away from him. 'Don't worry,' she said.

Fifteen hours later, as Tot stood out in the withering sun loading their bags into the consular Chevrolet that would take them to the aerodrome, Weller handed Joanna a brown paper packet tied with twine and sealed with scarlet wax. The documents inside were marked with the Chinese governor's official chops and Consul Weller's signature.

'That's that, then,' Weller said, sweeping his arm from Jo to Kamla with an air of forced showmanship.

Joanna looked down at Kamla. The girl's gaze questioned her.

'Mother and daughter,' she said.

The aquamarine of those eyes surrounded her, pure and grave and uncompromising. She knelt down quickly and embraced the child. 'You will come with me and I will take care of you. We really *are* family now.'

But even as she spoke the words, she knew just how false they

189

must sound. Lawrence had it exactly right. This was an impossible game.

2

An hour after Mr Weller gave Mem the papers authorizing my adoption we boarded a Chinese transport plane. A large C-47 was painted on the nose, and Lawrence told us the Nationalist government owned the aircraft, though the pilot was a big American with brown hair and freckles who looked as I imagined Simon would someday. I squeezed in beside Mem, and Mrs Weller and Lawrence took the seats behind us.

The plane was stifling and the noise of the engines roared in my ears, but I was too busy thinking to care. *We really* are *family now.* What did Mem mean with these words? Was Simon to be my brother? Was I to accept Mem's missing husband as replacement for my missing father? And what of Lawrence? Would he leave us, now that the trek was over? I did not dare to ask these questions, but one thing needed no asking. After all the time we had spent together, all the distance we had traveled, it had come to this: Without Mem and Lawrence, I had nothing.

The soldiers who escorted us had tied Mrs Weller's valises and parcels down the center of the cabin. The other seats were occupied by a French woman and her Chinese husband and child and two Chinese officials with their families.

Outside, Mr Weller and Tot stood waving, their figures like moving water in the heat waves rising from the airstrip. Mr Weller, the night before, had told us he intended to stay in Tihwa until he 'could see the whites of those Red eyes.' Tot did not intend to stay. As soon as we were gone he would start back overland to Kashmir with a fellow Sherpa he had met in the Tihwa bazaar, but he would not turn away before us, and looking down on him as he stood out under the parching desert sunlight, I felt my throat fill with sadness. That frank, gentle face, his ready laughter and familiar phrases, did much to help me in this difficult journey. He had promised that someday he would find us again, but that prospect seemed to vanish with him as we taxied down the runway, and he shrank to a small dark grain.

190

We stopped only for refueling, flew two days to Hong Kong. The windows were no bigger than *chappatis,* but when the clouds cleared at night sometimes I could see the lick of fighting below, like fireflies.

We arrived in the monsoon. Hong Kong was piled high with refugees, everyone shoving and crying, carrying their households on their backs and huddling in what doorways they could find to shelter from the rain. I remembered equal crowds of refugees during India's Partition, two years earlier. I wondered if these people, too, would set each other on fire, or rampage through the streets at night, or cut each other's hearts out. Lawrence told us there were not enough beds at any price, so we would all have to share one room. I was grateful for the chance to stay close to Mem and Lawrence for at least one more night.

3

In Hong Kong the downpour made a screen, and the darkness was glossy with pink and green from the neon ideographs blinking outside the window. Moths had destroyed the curtains and carpet, and the room smelled of mildew and rancid oil. Kamla slept curled on an old loveseat. Joanna lay beside Lawrence.

He had offered to sleep on the floor. Don't be ridiculous, she told him. They had danced this stupid dance until they both were worn to the quick. They had taken turns leading and following each other to the end of the earth, and for what? The Hong Kong airport had been electric with the screams of hysterical women and desperate men forced to leave loved ones behind – husbands, wives, children lost at the crucial moment. How many of those were not lost at all, but in fact had run away?

Aidan had abandoned her. If she didn't believe this she would become one of those hysterical women – or worse. She had to blame him. She needed to hate him. She thought of the photo they'd found at the site and felt her heart in shreds.

Through a wartime 'mate' at the telegraph office, Lawrence had succeeded in getting a cable off to Reggie Milne that afternoon. Six hours later they'd received their reply. Simon was mended.

Kashmir stable. The welcome mat was out.

Simon loved Lawrence. Kamla, too. They loved being with him. They loved his stories, his bawdy songs, the way he held their hands and laughed. They loved his playfulness and his longing.

Joanna closed her eyes. She moved her arm. Her hand sank into the thicket of hair that covered Lawrence's chest. She felt him waiting, motionless, and when she did not pull away, he rolled onto his side to face her.

'I don't know what to say to him,' she whispered. 'I don't know what to say to my own son.'

'The words aren't important. *You* are what counts. Having you back.'

'I've failed.'

'Not everyone can be rescued,' he said.

After a moment she asked, 'When your son died, how long did it take before you stopped seeing his face every time you closed your eyes?'

She was afraid he would pull away and close against her, but it was an honest question that she needed to ask. He replied by drawing her to him. For several minutes they lay perfectly still. His hands clutched the thin cotton of her shift. Her cheek grazed his neck. She could feel the muffled thump of his heart, smelled the oils of his body seeping through the shower-clean surface of his skin.

He did not smell like Aidan. This simple reality hit her with a visceral punch, and she froze, her stomach clenched.

Then Kamla sighed in her sleep. The girl's breath lilted melodically.

When Joanna moved her eyes to the opposite wall she could see Aidan watching them, his black hair combed neatly to one side, his mouth tipped up in a smile. Go ahead, he seemed to say. I dare you. And in the next instant she kissed Lawrence. Out of desire to punish Aidan. Out of raw physical hunger. She couldn't tell the difference.

Lawrence yielded, cradling the back of her head, and their mouths met with a jarring of teeth and tongues. She wound her legs around his hips, ground her palms against his bones. But as the truth of this contact came home to her, Aidan's presence vanished. Now with a violence of abandonment she clasped Lawrence, rocking, sobbing without sound. He stopped her sobs with kisses.

She touched his eyes and felt her own tears. Soon she could not distinguish between his anguish and her own.

His jaws opened and closed on her shoulder, and the silent concussion of his breath penetrated her skin. The hollow of her throat filled with sweat that he lapped up with his tongue. When his mouth continued down the ladder of breastbone she shuddered and arched her back, and he moved his hands and held her like a bridge on the verge of collapse.

4

In public, Lawrence and Mem did not so much as brush elbows. Through our week in Hong Kong, as we waited for hours in one line or another to arrange passage back to India, they hardly dared to look at each other, and when they did, as often as not, they quickly looked away. Perhaps I had fooled them into believing that the pace of my nighttime breathing was a measure of my mind. But I saw that the moon had returned to Lawrence's eyes, and I knew the act between man and woman. I knew from my days at the flash house. I knew by the force of Golba and his men. I knew also that what transpired between Mem and Lawrence must be the same yet vitally different. I willed this difference as I lay watching the pulse of lights outside, as I absorbed the sighs of skin and breath within. In this way I became their accomplice.

After four days, we boarded the first of many planes that would take us back to Simon. We flew west from Hong Kong to Rangoon, Burma, then to Calcutta, touched down in Delhi, and continued directly north to Srinagar. Lawrence showed me each stop on his big map, which he smoothed across my knees. The line that he drew to mark our travels resembled the head of a dog with a long pointed snout. Srinagar lay at about the spot where this dog might prick up his ear.

I wondered what Simon had been doing all these weeks since we parted. I wondered if he would blame me for returning instead of his father. I wondered if he would notice the moon in Lawrence's eyes, and I worried above all else that this might break the fragile thread that had bound us in Simon's absence.

It would be months before I pieced together the answers to these questions, before Simon knew me well enough to confess that he had not missed his father.

He was too busy, he told me. Even as those first weeks turned into months, he and Ralph Milne had filled each day with their play as junior Kims, dressing up like Pathans, haunting the bazaars and addressing each other by code names, or swimming underwater breathing through straws. He never stopped long enough to wonder if his father was coming back. He missed his mother, of course, felt her absence like a stomachache that was sometimes stabbing and sometimes dull but always just embarrassing enough that he did not dare complain about it. And maybe that was the problem: If he'd let himself miss his father, too, he couldn't have concealed all the missing. But as it was, Dr Milne made a kindly substitute father, Dr Akbar a stupendous uncle, and, after all, he was used to his real father being gone. So he lived as if content on the Milnes' spacious but not too fancy houseboat.

It was summer, and the rumors of war that continued to ripple through Kashmir had little effect on Simon as he soaked up the attentions of men and boys, learned to wield a sword and shave a birch branch, dive like a cormorant and whistle out the side of his mouth. Sometimes, as they lay awake at night with the windows open to the lake and moonlight like talcum filling the room, Ralph would wonder aloud what it was like to have a mother. His own had died days after he was born, and his father had never remarried. Simon, lying for the sake of the other boy's feelings, told him that if he had to choose, he would rather have a father.

'But your mum's lovely,' Ralph protested. 'She even wears men's trousers!'

Simon nodded. He had thought at first that he could never forgive Mem for sending him back with the Milnes. But he discovered in spite of his anger that these, his first weeks ever away from her, were also his own. And neither being away from her nor being on his own, apparently, was fatal. He reminded himself that some of his classmates in Delhi, mostly children of diplomats, were left from the age of five or six in summer camps or boarding schools for months at a time, and these weeks with the Milnes were better than any summer camp. There were also days when he recalled the awful dizziness and headaches he'd experienced in the high mountain passes and was almost grateful for the bullet that had sent him back. It would be a good story to take to school, the scar great show-and-tell. Mem was lovely, and brave, and good. He pretended to let Ralph persuade him. But what troubled him now was that he hadn't entirely been lying after all. Not that he would rather have a father than a mother, but that he'd rather have a different father than his own.

His dad loved him. Simon knew that. He used to give him bone-crushing hugs. He used to muss his hair. He would let Simon sit on his lap and spread the jam on his toast. Simon knew that his father had gone away for nearly a whole year when he was really little, but Simon couldn't remember those days. What he remembered was packing for India alone with Mem while his father was busy in his office with papers or off at meetings or work. It was around that time when his father began to push him away, when he never seemed to hear what Simon said, when he always had a line between his eyebrows or eyes filled with argument. Mem said his father would be different when they got to India, but he wasn't.

Simon remembered their last family holiday together. A Christmas car trip up to the hill town, Mussoorie. Simon recalled how endless the drive had seemed, especially toward the end with his mother's fingernails digging into his shoulder as they rounded the hairpin bends, his own eyes fixed on the back of his father's head as he sat up front beside the Sikh driver they had hired for the trip. A large, neat head it was, with tucked ears and freshly barbered black hair lying flat beneath a brown felt hat. His father sat erect, never slouching, and watched the road as if he were driving. A sharp groove divided the back of his long neck from his starched collar to the trimmed base of his scalp. If his father were a puzzle, Simon thought, a special piece would go in there. He touched the back of his own neck, but felt only soft flat skin and the top knob of his spine. Finally his curiosity got the best of him, and he leaned forward and pressed his finger against the hollow, and it was indeed like fitting a peg into a hole. But to his surprise, though the day was cold, his father's flesh was hot. It twitched and jerked at the unbidden contact, and Simon snatched his hand away. He expected – wanted? – his dad to turn and scold him, ask what in hell he thought he was doing, and then, perhaps, to laugh. But his father kept his eyes on the road and never said a word. Mem pulled Simon back against her, combed his hair with her fingers, and promised they were nearly there. Moments later they reached the town, where snow lay like wedding cake frosting and the bells of Christ Church were tolling.

Simon's father spent that holiday reading and working on one of his newspaper articles while Simon and Mem went off on long hikes – explores, Mem called them. At night, from the alcove in the hotel room where they set up his cot, he could hear the smooth rumble of his father's worry like thunder rolling over his mother's lighter, quicker reassurance.

Simon could not remember his father once reading him a bedtime story. Dr Milne read the boys a different story every night. Ivanhoe, Robin Hood, Ali Baba and his forty thieves. And *Kim,* the book Lawrence said was based on real-life explorers and spies. Simon's stomachaches only sharpened when he received his mother's letters saying that she and Lawrence had very nearly caught up with Simon's father.

Then, one afternoon at the end of June, he and Ralph came back from a swim off a neighboring houseboat to find his mother and Lawrence waiting in Dr Milne's parlor. It was such a surprise he burst into tears. So did Mem. She hugged him so hard he saw stars. She kissed and kissed him. Lawrence mussed his hair and grinned. They shook hands like grown-ups, then Lawrence, too, pulled him into a hug that lifted him off his feet. Finally he wiped the wet out of his eyes and noticed Kamla standing back beside Dr Milne. He wondered out loud why she was there, and Mem said, 'She's going to stay with us.' Kamla smiled, and Simon didn't know what to do next or what Mem was talking about, and partly that's because all the while he was thinking his first words ought to have been, 'Where's Daddy?' But he never did ask about his father.

He didn't want to. He didn't dare. He saw now how his mother had changed – how thin she'd become, how deep shadows had grown around her eyes, how sharply her cheekbones stood out. She stood there rubbing her lips together. She kept crying without

196

making any sound, touching his cheeks and shoulders and arms, and swallowing as if something were caught in her throat.

It was Lawrence who had to tell Simon that his father was still in China. Probably he was okay, but they'd been ordered to leave the country before they could find him. The politics had changed things. They couldn't continue the hunt, so they must go back to Delhi to wait for word. Maybe Simon's father was already there. Maybe he'd come out of China through another route. Anyway, his dad was sure to get out soon.

'No worries, mate,' Lawrence said, grinning too hard.

Even seeing Mem's strange behavior, Simon had *not* been worrying until Lawrence said that. Why did grown-ups always tell children not to worry, when children knew this could only mean the grown-ups were lost and scared?

5

As Joanna studied the reconnaissance map on Akbar's desk, she could smell the weedy warmth of Lawrence's hair. He leaned beside her, kneading the back of his neck with one hand as he traced the map's pale, veined colors with the other. Through the carved cedar doorway, she could see Simon and Kamla tying gaily colored ribbons on the tail of a cat that young Ralph Milne held captive. The children were laughing.

Akbar jabbed the map with one nicotine-yellow finger. 'I think you were less than two miles from Osman's camp.'

Joanna used the glass loupe he handed her. To the northwest of the sardine-shaped Heaven's Pool, a small cross-hatched area was keyed 'Osman, the Terrible.'

'Is this your writing?' Lawrence asked.

Akbar came around his desk and handed a bound manuscript to Joanna. 'The map was sent to me with this book by my good friend Lloyd Harkness.' He seated himself in a large red velvet armchair across the room. 'Lloyd was a fellow Central Asia scholar. We met at Oxford. Later he chose the political arena, while I gravitated to ethnography. But we stayed in touch.'

Harkness, Joanna read from the frontispiece, was the Asian

correspondent for the *Chicago Daily News* and consultant to the State Department. She sat down, holding the manuscript so that Lawrence could read over her shoulder.

'Only last year,' Akbar continued, 'Lloyd made the same trip your husband was attempting. Please look where I have marked.'

A red leather bookmark directed Joanna's finger to the page.

Osman, in his yurt headquarters high in the Tien Shan ... a tremendous Kazakh with hamlike hands and beetling eyebrows, forty-nine years old ... His steel gray eyes and black beard reminded me of the Mongols who terrorized and conquered Eurasia centuries ago, yet at the same time his stature seemed heroic, as if he'd just stepped from some mythic tale.

Osman first organized his nomadic bandits against that same Chinese despot Sheng Shih-ts'ai who had imprisoned Kamla's father. He allied himself with rebels in Mongolia and the Ili region, but when those rebels later sided with Stalin, Osman turned against them and joined Sheng's Nationalists. He defended these shifts as proof of his anti-Communist zeal.

According to Harkness, this man was a monster. He had burned down villages, pillaged farms, press-ganged conscripts, and murdered several hundred of his fellow Sinkiangese. When his own nephew was sent as a peace emissary by his former Mongol allies, he responded by executing the child.

Yet the United States was grooming this sterling fellow. *Osman cuts a rakish figure at dinner parties at the US consulate in Tihwa, and enthusiastically champions the strategic importance of Sinkiang as a base for American operations against the Red Peril to both East and West.*

Consul Weller, it seemed, not only had supplied Osman with funding, arms, and military expertise, but in his zeal to unite Sinkiang's 'divided house,' he had teamed him with the 'Butcher of Turfan,' a young warlord who had risen to power by leading an army under the green Muslim banner against an insurrection of lightly armed civilians. The people were protesting Chinese Nationalist brutality and corruption. When they saw their fellow Mohammedan's banner they rushed to welcome him as a brother. He replied with machine gunfire, killing thousands.

Joanna thought of all the burned-out villages they'd passed in the desert. She could just see the beetle-browed Kazakh in conference with this ruthless brute, both of them gulping whiskey in Weller's drawing room as he instructed them in the fine points of land mines.

A sphere of influence in Central Asia, wrote Harkness, *could prove critical in a future anti-Soviet war. However, at the time of this writing, all details of any strategic alliances between the US and forces in and around Sinkiang are considered classified.*

Yes, Akbar confirmed, like Joanna's husband, Harkness had been investigated by the House Un-American Activities Committee. Under pressure from certain elements of the US government, he had elected to postpone the book's publication.

'Yet he sends a copy to you,' Lawrence observed.

'The privilege of friendship.' Akbar shook his head. 'Sadly, he suffered a heart attack this past winter. He is no longer.'

'Weller knew,' Joanna said. 'He knew they were looking for Osman. Probably he told them exactly how to find him. And then he warned Osman—'

'You've no proof,' Lawrence cautioned her. 'And if you start making claims like that to US officials about one of their own, they'll tell you there's a war on. Casualties happen. They've dealt with crazy wives before.'

'Crazy wives.' She looked at him. 'Is that what I am?'

Before he could answer, a screech erupted beyond the doorway, and the children burst in carrying Akbar's mewling cat trussed up like a Tibetan prayer doll. Their faces were flushed and laughing. Joanna turned and saw Lawrence's green eye watching her, darkened to the color of moss.

'Did Aidan ever tell you his story about the broken mirror?'

She was whispering into the dark as he lay beside her, face to the stars. His arm cradled her bare shoulders. The waves lapped against the hull of the houseboat with the others sleeping inside. Lawrence didn't answer.

'He learned it from an amah who took care of him and his brother in Shanghai. A romantic, Aidan called her . . .' Her voice faded, then resumed. 'The story had to do with a couple who were separated when the husband went off to war. Before he left he took his wife's favorite mirror and broke it in two. He gave her one half and took the other himself. Thirty years she waited. Finally one day an old man wearing rags and a long white beard appeared at her gate. He asked if she owned any broken mirrors. She held out the piece her husband had left her. The old man pulled its mate from his sleeve and fit the two pieces together. "When the broken mirror is round again," he said, "you know that your husband is home."

'Aidan told me there are hundreds of versions of the story,' she went on. 'In some the man dies and a friend takes the mirror, posing as the missing husband. In some the man loses the mirror, and his wife refuses to recognize him. But sometimes the story turns inside out, and the husband sends his broken half to warn his wife that he's never coming home.'

Lawrence said, 'You're thinking of that picture of Simon, aren't you?'

'What matters most?' she asked. 'Do *you* know what he means?'

'I know what you want it to mean.' He took her hand and kissed the inside of her wrist. 'I hope for everyone's sake but mine that you're right.'

Book Two
July 1949 to December 1950

CHAPTER 8

1

All things changed for me after we returned to Delhi – or so I wanted to believe. This time when I entered the district of radiant lawns I did not slip in like a thief but rode like a princess down the tree-lined street in Mem's green motorcar. It had just rained, and the leaves and grass and rooftops sparkled. I smelled jasmine. A damp breeze blew. A black bear stood with his trainer by the roadside, paws up as if paying respect.

As I stared out at the compound walls I could hear *firenghi* children behind them laughing and shouting in play. The very houses seemed confident, with their gleaming yards and tall iron gates. Yet even as I thrilled to the notion that this was to be my new home, I felt a dark squeeze of uncertainty. It was like watching an enactment of the gods, knowing that soon the performance would end and the actors will remove their masks and show themselves mere mortals.

When last we had been in Delhi together I knew Mem as Mrs Shaw. I claimed her then, it is true, but what I claimed was desire and faith rather than understanding. Now, returned to this place where I had been of one life and she of such another, my claim on her was seasoned by our mutual experience. I had memorized her smells and voices, the rhythms of her breathing. I had studied the pattern of lines on her face, the sounds of her struggle and surrender in the night when Lawrence held her. I knew her fear, her kindness, her stubborn will – her secret frailty.

Yet as it turned out, I still did not know her. For when we returned to Delhi I discovered in Mem a whole new stranger. A wife. The wife of a man who was not there.

You will say, surely, she had been a wife from the very beginning. Yes, but I had not seen this in her. Of course, I knew she was worried about her missing husband, and that was why we traveled so long and so hard. I even knew, without understanding, that our failure to locate her husband had caused her to become Lawrence's lover. But in all our weeks together, I had seen only one photograph of this husband, and that was small and worn – a black-and-white portrait that she carried of a dark-haired man with pale cheeks and straight brows and long eyes set in an upward tilt. A handsome man, to be sure, but an image only. I could not picture her with this man, for I'd seen her daily instead with Lawrence. Or striding up the mountain alone.

Mem's husband had seemed to occupy the same place in her heart that my father occupied in mine. He was a memory, perhaps. A dream. A desire, certainly, but a desire linked so precisely with another place and time that his recovery was impossible. Foolishly I believed when I heard those sounds of flesh in the night that she had chosen Lawrence as a new husband of the heart. I wished for this union to continue, to grow, to embrace me and Simon, as well. I imagined that this was to be my new family.

The first thing I noticed when I entered the white house on Ratendone Road was the shadow Mem's husband seemed to have cast there. Photographs of him stared from every shelf and table. In most he posed in the company of strangers, though one showed him holding Simon as a baby, and in another he and Lawrence sat grinning down from a howdah on the back of an elephant. One showed Mem together with her husband on their wedding day. She wore a white hat with a feather stuck in the brim. He was bareheaded and smiling. She squinted, gazing up at him, as if leaning toward him with her lips and eyes. Whatever she was asking appeared to amuse him.

There were other objects around the house which I noticed that first day – an ivory chess set laid out for play in the downstairs sitting room, an iron letter opener with a twisted shaft, a gray felt man's hat dangling from the rack inside the entry door. On a teak desk in Mem's bedroom upstairs sat a tall black typewriter that Simon said was his father's. And opposite the desk stretched a wide bed with a cotton print coverlet – and two shallow indentations. As I stood in the hallway peering in, I tried to imagine Lawrence crossing that polished marble floor and settling himself in the place of Mem's missing husband. Instead I found myself staring at yet another photograph of this man called Aidan Shaw, this time seated in front of that same typewriter, with a river flowing behind him.

'Come, Kamla.' Mem pressed my arm. 'Your room is down here, with Simon.'

I did not move. For three months I had shared Mem's room, Mem's tent, often as not Mem's bed. Now she was thrusting me away.

'What is it?' She lowered her hands.

I looked past her to that photograph of Mr Shaw and knew that somehow this was his doing.

But I said nothing. Poor Simon was waiting at the end of the hall, his small square face split in a smile. I followed Mem toward him as if being marched into exile. I remember, as we walked, the stiff swishing sound of her skirt, like the brush of a devout Jain flicking out of harm's way all incidental life-forms.

2

Back in Delhi, Lawrence asked if he should leave her. She answered him with a kiss.

With the monsoon beating on the flat roof above them, they made love in Aidan's house. They made love in Aidan's bed, with Aidan's child sleeping down the hall.

'I feel like I'm standing in the doorway,' she told him.

'Stand there as long as you need, Joanna.' He was conscious of her name sliding over his tongue. 'If I pull you against your will, you'll hold it against me forever.'

Each night as he crept away he imagined a constellation of ears and eyes recording his movements. In the photographs that she insisted on leaving around the house, he began to see himself in his old friend's self-conscious poses. With the passage of days he took to combing his fingers through his hair, sitting with hands locked behind his neck, squinting ever so slightly as he studied Joanna's face.

Only Kamla seemed to notice. 'Why are you different here?' she demanded, coming upon him one morning in the living room. He and Joanna were to make their daily pilgrimage to the Red Cross office to scan the lists of refugees pouring out of China. Afterward, they would visit the American, Chinese, and British embassies, futilely inquiring, demanding investigations only to be told yet again that all Western and Nationalist 'personnel' were being evacuated from China. They would go to the bank, where Joanna would withdraw yet another chunk of her dwindling savings – and promise to accept Lawrence's offer of a loan just as soon as she really needed it. They would go to the post office and mail her latest pleas for help to friends back in the States. They would visit the office of Aidan's newspaper only to be told that he had entered China on his own authority ('chasing his own tale,' one asinine typist had the nerve to joke), and that while the 'powers that be' in Washington were doing what they could, Joanna would have to deal directly with the State Department. In the meantime, Bill Fisk, the prep school dropout who'd replaced Aidan, had slipped her the princely sum of five hundred dollars from the publisher to assuage whatever conscience he possessed. And the State Department already had informed her that since the US had no diplomatic relations with the mainland Communists, Aidan was effectively on his own.

Lawrence would accompany Joanna on all these rounds soon enough. But right now, he sat on Aidan's black leather sofa, one leg thrown casually over the opposite knee, the newspaper neatly folded back into a trim column. He was wearing a starched white cotton short-sleeved shirt and, in spite of the heat, long khaki trousers with a leather belt. Kamla studied him like a stranger.

Suddenly his scalp itched. Perspiration trickled down his back. He cleared his throat, meaning to ask what she meant. But those relentless eyes bored into him as if she could read his veins. He thought that Kamla and Davey were the only two people in the world who had ever looked at him that way. *You are different here.*

He tossed the paper aside and got up, grabbed the girl by the waist. She was so light he could lift her almost to the ceiling. He danced her up and down so that her full skirt billowed. 'How am I different?' he demanded back, dropping and catching her until she squealed, causing Simon to come running. 'What do you mean, Kammy? Different? *Different?* Who's so different now?'

Simon clapped his hands and cried, 'Me, too!'

Kamla's black braid was flying. One sandal had fallen to the floor. Her hands clutched at his shoulders, bare legs wrapping around his hips. He growled and she laughed. Simon shouted for more.

Lawrence turned and saw Joanna standing in the doorway, one hand over her mouth, in her eyes an expression of longing so true he felt his heart stand still.

He retreated to his flat, on the third floor of an unremarkable building near Connaught Place. He had taken the room originally because it was close enough but not too close to Aidan and Joanna's. Its outside balcony overlooked a continuous tumult of commerce during the day and after dark was filled with the mutters of sidewalk sleepers and passing rickshaws ferrying their night trade. His Goan landlady, Mrs D'Costa, had let the room to him 'furnished,' which meant that he had a single *charpoy*, a disintegrating rattan arm chair, and a low Indian-style writing desk at which he sat on the floor beneath a naked bulb screwed into the ceiling. Aside from his stacks of notes and books, the place was as impersonal as a safe house, which it might have been but for the nosiness of Mrs D'Costa. Before tearing off after Aidan in April, Lawrence had paid the year's rent in advance (just as he had on Aidan's behalf paid off the Ratendone Road rent and, through the trustworthy Nagu, Joanna's servants' wages), and Mrs D' had kept the room swept and as clean as could be expected.

Unaccustomed to finding himself here before midnight, Lawrence poured himself a long finger of whiskey and sat turning the pages of odd editions he'd found among sidewalk stalls from Kabul to Mandalay. Memoirs of spies and cartologists, accounts of treachery and escapes from native despots. He was surprised by the size of the collection he'd amassed, and by the volume of notes he'd made on his own wanderings along the frontier. He actually had enough to write this book. More than.

In one of the flats below, a woman began to scream. The sound was raw and ragged, with intermittent pauses like hiccups as she caught her breath. It was a noise of agony, grief perhaps, or betrayal – if there was a difference. He had first heard women cry like this during the war when they were told their husbands had been killed. Later, when Davey died, he'd thought back to those wracking, explosive wails – strangely akin to ecstasy and mysteriously beautiful – and he'd envied those women their ability to discharge so much emotion in a single howl. He wondered cynically if there was a trick to it, some muscle one twitched or nerve one stroked, like tickling the back of the throat to induce vomiting or tensing jaw muscles to wiggle the ears.

Lawrence closed his eyes. The noise died down. Now only the blather of the street, the throb of voices from the sidewalk, filtered up to him. He went onto the balcony and stood looking out into the steamy, rumpled darkness.

Burying Alice James hadn't worked. Nor had adopting Kamla. So it was his turn: If through him Joanna could arouse enough jealousy, Aidan might just come raging back from the back of beyond.

Hadn't Lawrence engaged in far more devious deals with the gods after Davey's death? Once he nearly killed a man in a brawl, only afterward realizing he'd meant to trade the poor sot's life for his son's. He'd divorced Tracy in a similar ploy. Then told Jack Battersby to fuck himself one afternoon and left Australia the next. If he disappeared, he thought, perhaps Davey would replace him. Physical suicide was the only tack he hadn't tried, but perhaps serving as Joanna's bait for her husband was the next best thing. Or perhaps what Kamla had detected was his desire to finally shed himself by becoming Aidan.

Lawrence lay on his bed watching squadrons of moths and mosquitoes collide around the bare overhead light bulb. *You are different here.* He'd walked away without explanation, saying he would be back, but not when. A question had risen in Joanna's eyes as she watched him turn toward the door, and he'd met it with one of his own. For several seconds they stared at each other in a draw. It occurred to him that they'd never been more honest with each other than in those few seconds of stalemate. Neither of them possessed the answer.

Worse, he was no closer to an answer than he'd been three months ago.

He returned to his desk and the titles and papers that lay like pieces of a puzzle. The cloak-and-dagger antics of the Brits and Russians during the Great Game had laid a fine groundwork for the Wellers of today to play at their own hapless skullduggery in Central Asia, but was Aidan a casualty of this new round? Or would he, like the immortal British spymaster F. M. Bailey, mysteriously resurface months from now unscathed? Bailey, then an officer in the British Indian Political and Secret Department, spent seventeen months trudging around Central Asia playing cat-and-mouse with the Bolsheviks in 1919, acting the part of a double agent and traveling the thousand miles from Kashgar to Persia under a variety of disguises and pseudonyms. His superiors and family had long since given him up for dead when he came pounding back from the back of beyond. He pulled off the coup of survival while tweaking the nose of the enemy and was duly lionized as an adventurer – even though his exploits accomplished little of either political or secret advantage to the Brits. The superiors who heretofore had been demoted for sending him into no-man's-land were miraculously redeemed, and Bailey and his wife spent the next twenty years comfortably hobnobbing with ministers and maharajahs until their retirement back to England in 1938.

Happily ever after.

If he could separate his own cloak from dagger, he'd surely root for an equally cheery outcome for Aidan. Or would he?

The irresistible desiderium incogniti breaks down all obstacles and refuses to recognize the impossible.

Lawrence wanted Aidan alive *and* gone. Alas, he couldn't help but recognize the impossible.

3

Nighttime. Two children. The rote, hesitant comfort of a bedtime routine. There were baths to give, a fairy tale to read, kisses to dole out like candies. Nagu in his spotless white waistcoat brought ritual glasses of warm milk. As Joanna checked the clock the bearer kindly averted his eyes, as he had ever since their return.

She could do this, she told herself. Hadn't she always? The months when Aidan was traveling. The nights when he stayed out late. She had years of practice, and surely Kamla didn't tip the scales. So silent and careful, the girl demanded nothing, was no more trouble than a shadow. At the same time, Simon clearly adored her. Just that afternoon Joanna had heard them outside laughing as Simon taught her to ride his bicycle. He had always wanted a sister or brother. Joanna had always wanted another child. No, Kamla was not the trouble.

'Where's Lawrence?' Simon asked suddenly.

Joanna let down one side of his mosquito net. The room was sticky hot, dark around the edges, the chaos of toys on the floor like a Lilliputian battleground. 'At his flat.' She tried to sound matter-of-fact.

'*Still?*' Simon counted on his fingers. One. Two. Nights and days. 'Why?'

'I don't know.' Joanna studied the narrow wedge of light streaming down over Kamla's hands, clasped on the turn of sheet at her waist. If Kamla were praying she would hold her hands so, but Kamla was not praying. Her eyes, like a Siamese cat's, reflected the light. She watched Joanna intently.

'I don't know,' she repeated, meeting the girl's unflinching gaze.

'He said he'd be back,' Simon said.

'Yes.' She sat on the edge of Kamla's bed and stroked the girl's fingers. They unfurled like leaves and held her. Joanna closed her eyes, remembering that morning in Kashgar, looking up from Simon's letter to see Kamla and Lawrence silhouetted against the sky. Then, again, the day before yesterday morning, the two of them whirling and laughing with Simon.

As she leaned forward and kissed Kamla's cheek the mingled scents of coconut oil and Pepsodent engulfed her. She drew back to find Kamla smiling past her.

Lawrence stood in the hallway.

He asked, 'Am I too late to say g'night?'

'I thought you'd decided to stay away,' she said when they were alone.

'Thought, or wished?' He sat at the chess table fingering a black knight. Joanna handed him a glass of Scotch.

'Why didn't you?' she asked.

He shrugged and drank. 'If I wanted to escape you, Jo, I'd have done it long before this.'

'I know, but . . .' She didn't know what she was asking. Aidan seemed to be watching from a dozen directions. She wished she could muster the nerve to clear out all these photographs, but she kept imagining him walking through the door and finding himself erased.

'I don't see how you stand it,' she said. 'Me. This. Him.' She pointed at the picture of Aidan and Lawrence grinning down from that Burmese elephant. 'Don't you wish you'd never met him!'

'Are you talking to me, or yourself?' he persisted.

She sat down hard on the sofa and passed a hand over her face. The muscles around her eyes throbbed as she felt Lawrence's attention tighten.

'The children,' she said. 'If I hadn't adopted Kamla, you would have done it yourself. Wouldn't you?'

'Why does it matter?'

'And if anything happened to me now, you'd take Simon in a flash.'

'Joanna—'

'Aidan wouldn't.'

'What?' Lawrence dropped his hand, sending the chess piece skittering across the stone floor.

'I always thought if I died, Aidan would either pack Simon off to boarding school or find some woman to look after him. A nanny or governess or a quick wife. You wouldn't do that, would you?'

'But, Jo, neither would he, unless—'

'Yes, unless he was so preoccupied with the more important business of his life, which he would be, of course, because he always has been.'

'Wasn't that why you married him?' His eyes drilled into her. 'Because he's so damned impressive?'

She looked down and saw the darkness of tears spattering her gray skirt. Then she felt Lawrence's hands on her shoulders.

'I'm sorry,' he said. 'I'm not here to take you away from him.'

If only you could, she thought.

I t was August before they were able to secure an appointment with the US Ambassador. Robert Minton had been on home leave. 'Twelve weeks gone, and I'm buried,' he remarked, continuing to sort through a pile of correspondence as they seated themselves in front of his desk.

Joanna glanced at Lawrence. He gave her an encouraging nod. 'I'd actually appreciate your full attention,' she said.

The Ambassador, a balding, middle-aged man with fleshy lips and a large square jaw, hesitated without looking up, then slowly, deliberately pushed the pile of papers aside and folded his hands in front of him. The tip of his tongue appeared, snakelike, and circled his mouth. At last he lifted his eyes, two chips of slate embedded in the lenses of his spectacles. 'It's good to see you again, Mrs Shaw. I was relieved to hear you got back safely.'

'Unfortunately, my husband did not.'

'No. I realize that. And I wish I had something reassuring to tell you.'

'I'm beyond reassurance, Ambassador. I just want to know what's being done to find him.'

'Everything we *can* do, but as you know, that's not a lot.' Minton rolled his jaw from side to side before he spoke. 'The border posts in India, Pakistan, Afghanistan, and Nepal all have been issued a description of your husband. We're hoping he makes his own way out. If he does, you'll know it as soon as we do.'

She curled her fingers around the arms of her chair. 'Did you see Mr Hoover when you were back in the States? Pay your respects to the Un-American Activities Committee?'

Minton pushed his glasses up the bulge of his nose, letting her outburst drift between them like a noxious fume. At length he cleared his throat and spoke calmly. 'I'm going to tell you something that is not yet common knowledge, but it will be in a matter of days. Moreover, it's likely to hang over our foreign policy for the foreseeable future. I'm telling you this, Mrs Shaw, because it is our belief that your husband knew full well the risks he was running, and that he chose to remain in China even as the borders were closing. I'm telling you this so you understand just how dangerous the game has become, so you understand that any further attempt at a rescue mission is now out of the question.'

He paused, settling a reproachful gaze on each of them in turn. 'This is all, of course, strictly confidential.'

Joanna heard Lawrence shift in his seat, but she couldn't bring herself to look at him.

'Last week the Soviets detonated an atomic test at Semipalatinsk, roughly five hundred miles from Tihwa.' Minton moistened his lips again, squinting slightly, eyes on Lawrence. 'I don't have to tell you what this does to the politics of the region. Mao's troops are at the eastern border of Sinkiang right now, and virtually every outpost in China is surrendering without a shot. There are no longer any safe air routes out of the country. Yours, in fact, was one of the last flights out. Mr Weller, who I understand entertained you when you were in Tihwa, has been forced to travel out using the same route you took in – over the Karakorams. He's been incommunicado for nearly a month.'

Joanna felt a deliberate pressure against her ankle. Don't, Lawrence was warning her. Don't let him get to you. But she couldn't help it. 'What about Weller's scheme to preserve America's "sphere of influence" through a "third force" of rebels?'

'I'm hardly an expert on Sinkiangese politics,' Minton said crisply. 'And I wouldn't presume to speak for Dan Weller.'

She said, 'Why don't you just tell me what they're saying about Aidan in Washington?'

At that Minton actually smiled. 'Look, I'm sympathetic, honestly, but your husband is not the only American trapped in China. And nobody, including his own employers – including *you*, unless I'm mistaken – has the slightest idea what he was doing there.'

'He's a journalist. It doesn't take a brain surgeon to figure out what he was doing.'

'Is that why you went chasing over the mountains after him? To support his journalistic zeal?' There it was. The petulant thrust of the jaw. She'd defied him. Worse, she'd ignored his authority.

Lawrence leaned forward. 'The lady and her husband are American citizens. She came to you for help.'

Minton pulled off his glasses with a motion so premeditated that whatever he said next would have been galling. But his new deflection knocked Joanna completely off guard. 'I understand you came out of China with a native child in your custody.'

'Kamla – ?' She looked at Lawrence, who gave her back a slow, grim nod, and she thought of their showdown with that Chinese garrison commander before Lawrence handed over his Sten gun. Again she sensed the undercurrents of a game she couldn't quite grasp. 'I've adopted her,' she told the ambassador. 'If that's what you mean.'

'There's no indication of that in your State Department file,' Minton said.

'But Weller drew up the papers himself! He gave us emergency visas . . .'

'I checked your file this morning, Mrs Shaw. Consul Weller's report doesn't mention any adoption. And now that China's closed—'

'I'll wager she'd let you have a look at those papers,' Lawrence said.

Minton breathed on the lenses of his spectacles and wiped them with a white monogrammed handkerchief. He conspicuously ignored Lawrence's interruption. 'You must be aware, Mrs Shaw, that India's border is a great deal more porous than America's – which is potentially good news for your husband – but right now there are hundreds of thousands of Chinese applying for asylum in the States. Even among those who have American sponsors, there are no guarantees.'

'Are you saying Weller's signature is no good?' Lawrence asked.

'I'm merely making Mrs Shaw aware of the circumstances,' Minton replied, still not looking at him.

'Considering that Weller himself is incommunicado and you wouldn't presume to speak for him' – Lawrence wasn't bothering to conceal his anger now – 'you seem remarkably certain of these particular circumstances.'

Joanna reached for his arm. Her hand trembled, but her voice held steady. 'No, Lawrence,' she said. 'You don't understand. This is nothing personal, is it Mr Ambassador? It's just policy. Like the State Department's attitude toward refugees. Did you ever read my husband's articles about the ships full of European Jews that came within spitting distance of Miami during the war, but were refused permission to dock? Quotas, you see, and, of course, some of those refugees might have been Communist! Most of them wound up dying in Hitler's camps, but I'm sure they understood. Nothing personal.'

'I don't make the rules, Mrs Shaw.'

'I'm so relieved to hear that. For your sake. Otherwise, someone might just blame you.' She stood, still gripping Lawrence's arm. Though she didn't dare catch his eye she could feel him silently warning her, this is your show, your country. Your bleeding husband.

In the car the steering wheel felt molten under her bare hands. Perspiration blurred her vision and streamed between her shoulder blades. Lawrence sat quietly in the passenger seat as they drove out of the embassy compound past the Marines in their stifling white uniforms, the limp folds of an enormous American flag. Everything here looked bleached and shrunken, as if it had been irradiated, yet outside the embassy gates the world remained unchanged. Bicycles and *tongas* plowed the parched avenue; families squatted with parcels and children in whatever shade they could find; three policemen pushed a manacled boy into the back of a lorry. Joanna wondered what had possessed her to think Minton would help.

Finally Lawrence spoke. 'He's either covering up for Weller or he's afraid he'll be accused of aiding a Communist himself. Kamla's just a bargaining chip, Jo. He wants you to stop asking questions.'

'What does it matter?' She refused to look at him. 'He said it himself. The only way I get Aidan back is if he finds his own way out. If he does, this is where he'll expect to find me. And nobody's going to take Kamla away from me as long as we stay here.'

'In India, you mean?'

They entered a roundabout. A truck decked in political banners pulled in front of them. Bawdy music blared from its loudspeakers, and a multicolored icon of the goddess Durga rode her tiger on the cab's roof. Durga, the beautiful goddess of destruction, mascot for the Hindu nationalists. 'Look at this place,' she said. 'Think what this country's gone through since Partition. Yet through it all, and

215

in this infernal climate, these people keep on trudging, smiling, working, believing . . .' She veered onto Ratendone Road. 'It makes Minton's game-playing seem so infantile it shames me.'

Lawrence's voice came at her sideways. 'You have nothing to be ashamed of, Jo.'

'I have everything to be ashamed of. And you, of all people—'

'I said *you* have nothing to be ashamed of.'

She stared straight ahead, unwilling to accept his emphasis. Halfway down the street sat a modest rectangular house encircled by whitewashed walls and rendered even more anonymous than usual by the midday dust and glare. Aidan had signed a three-year lease on this house. Lawrence had paid out the first year. Musical chairs, change partners and dance. By default, this was home. During the war Joanna had met any number of women whose husbands were missing in action. These women, too, got up every morning and washed their faces, made their beds, put their shoes on. They worked. They raised their children, took lovers. They marched in place, and some remarried, even while they waited. It happened.

She pulled into the drive and parked in a wedge of shade. Across the garden the children sat cross-legged on the grass. They were playing a board game, and Simon, intent on his move, didn't even look up. But Kamla did. Her gaze was slow and long, inquisitive. It was not, ever, the gaze of a child.

'I talked to Hari yesterday.' Joanna pulled the keys from the ignition but made no move to get out of the car. 'All's forgiven. He wants me to come back to run Safe Haven. Says he's gotten approval to pay me if I'll agree to a year.'

After a pause, Lawrence said, 'What did you tell him?'

'I'm thinking about it.'

'You're serious.'

'I don't see Minton's given me much choice.'

'But if it weren't for that – ?'

'You mean if it weren't for him, for Aidan, for Kamla – for *you?*' She looked at him, the dusty light illuminating his gray eye, softening the green. *The irresistible desiderium incogniti.*

She started to get out of the car, then stopped. Meeting Kamla's unswerving gaze she said, 'I've got to keep going.'

E xile. Perhaps it seems odd that I should view the world of the nursery in such a way, but I had never known, could never have begun to imagine the kind of childhood that I was now expected to embrace. Toys, games, the simple liberty of play were foreign luxuries. Even the architecture of a house in which children were given a room apart banged on my heart like an insult. I was not a child. Not like Simon. I might lie beside him. I might hold his hand and listen to his pattering talk with curiosity, growing affection. I might even follow him through the labyrinth of tunnels he loved to build from towels and pillows and blankets and chairs, winding through the false darkness of play to a nest of imagined safety. But I knew what he still was fending off – the truth that we builders, we players, we children, are ourselves mere playthings of the gods.

As far as Simon was concerned, I was his new sister and disciple in the laws and pleasures of childhood. 'Hide-and-seek!' he would cry, dashing around a corner. 'You're it!'

It. The term baffled me. I would sit, waiting, immobile as a thing, an object, not human, an 'it.' Simon at last would emerge from hiding, his face twitching with hurt and anger.

'Why didn't you come after me?'

'You say I am it.'

'That means you have to find me. I hide, you *seek*. That's the game.'

'Why?'

'It's a game, Kammy. What do you mean, why? For fun!'

It took Simon a long time to explain the word *fun* to me. My lessons consisted of more hide-and-seek, tag, and catch, and blindman's bluff. *Fun*, I learned, meant chasing lizards with Nagu's sons in the wild lands behind the compound, fashioning slingshots out of twigs and rubber bands, shooting pebbles at termite mounds, or sending paper boats down the flooded avenue after the rains. *Fun* was pretending to fall asleep after Mem and Lawrence put us to bed, then huddling together with flashlight and comic book under the tented sheet while the monsoon raged outside.

Fun, Simon taught me, was what we must do to protect and keep ourselves separate from the grown-ups. It was our defense. As I was now Simon's ally in childhood, *fun* was my responsibility. Mem and Lawrence were not.

But sometimes we played in the grown-ups' territory. Especially, by Simon's choice, in his father's domain. When Mem and Lawrence were out, as they were many hours each day, and we were left at home with Nagu and the cook, which is to say we were left to our own devices, Simon would insist we play with his father's chess pieces, or set the phonograph spinning with his father's recordings of American band music – Tommy Dorsey, Glenn Miller, Benny Goodman were names I came to know from the album covers. We played at dancing. We typed declarations about gods and monsters (*Krishna is great! Kali kills. Mickey Mouse is mighty!*) on the tall Underwood typewriter his father had left in Mem's bedroom. And we played what Simon called 'dress-up' with clothes from his parents' closets.

I would twist my hair up in combs and put on my favorite dress of Mem's – a long red silk evening gown with a high collar and deep throat, sleeveless and slinky. Simon said she used to wear it when she and his father attended formal dinners. I had never seen her wear it, but it carried her carnation scent from the other clothes in her closet, which I was careful not to disturb.

Simon took no such care. He entered his father's closet like a rummaging goat, pushing coats and jackets aside, pulling sweaters over his head, stepping grandly in shoes that he said were made of the skins of 'crocodiles, snakes, and lizards from all over Asia.' His father had told him so. When Simon put on the white dinner jacket and black trousers that his father had worn to accompany Mem in her red dress, the jacket came to his knees, and the legs of the trousers puddled at his feet, but the shoulders and waist were not enormous. His father must have been even taller and slimmer, I thought, than he appeared in photographs.

One day Simon decided he wanted to try his father's hats. These sat in boxes on a shelf across the top of the closet. They were in the state the rest of the closet had been before Simon's first visit: neat and orderly, even precise, ranging from small to large.

Simon fetched a chair and stood on the seat, just able to reach the shelf. He handed down each box in turn. The hats were of felt or

218

straw and stylish as those I had seen in the film magazines on newsstands in Connaught Place. The larger boxes were heavier. One contained a solar topee such as Lawrence sometimes wore. The second to last contained a green helmet. This was the one Simon had been looking for. He eagerly put it on his head, pulling the strap beneath his chin. 'My dad's during the war,' he said. 'He wasn't a soldier, but he was out with them lots, and this is the same as the ones they wore. He told me that a long time ago.' We looked an odd pair staring in the mirror, me in Mem's blood-red evening gown and Simon in his father's dinner jacket and green army helmet. Even Simon must have thought so, for he soon was climbing back on his chair to return the helmet to its place on the shelf.

'Ooph!' he said, lowering the last and heaviest box to me.

But it contained no hat. Instead we found two brown paper parcels tied with string. Simon did not hesitate. We sat on the floor as he untied the first. He was most disappointed, for the parcel contained two notepads and some documents, nothing more. He tossed them aside impatiently, and I put the wrapping back around them while he wrestled with the other package, which was more solidly tied.

As first the paper and then the flannel underneath came undone, I heard his breath come out of him like a leaking tire. I looked down and gave a gasp myself, for in his lap lay a gun. I thought it must be a toy, it looked so much like Simon's own cap pistol, which he called a cowboy gun and often turned on me when he decided that I was the 'Indian.' But Simon's face had drained of color and he was pulling his hands back and away. I reached over and took the gun myself. It was of very heavy metal, with a long stem like a pipe and a smooth black handle. I was surprised at how cool the metal felt in spite of the heat in Mem's bedroom. I could not resist putting it against my cheek, my forehead. I smiled at Simon to reassure him. I waggled my fingers to show that they were nowhere near the trigger.

'Put it back,' he snapped at me. 'It's my father's.'

Then he got up and left the room.

I wiped my hands on my skirt and replaced the gun in its flannel pouch and paper wrappings. I returned both parcels to the box, and the box to its place on the shelf. I spent the next hour setting the closet in order, just as I imagined Simon's father would want it. We did not play dress-up again.

6

A idan once asked, as incredulous as he was direct, how Lawrence could stand to whore. Lawrence replied that whores were simply women who knew their priorities. They understood what they needed, and what they had lost forever. In that, he considered them wiser than the vast majority of their so-called respectable counterparts. Certainly than himself. Aidan told him he was glamorizing poverty – 'typical bleeding-heart blather' – that wasn't what he was asking and Lawrence knew it. 'How could you expose yourself like that?'

Lawrence said exposure was precisely the point. With a whore he could expose everything – or nothing. His anonymity remained the same.

He let Aidan think he'd frequented brothels from Bangkok to Bokhara. He chose not to deny that he'd slept with streetwalkers, cage girls, barmaids, and courtesans. He knew there was little point in denials because he once boasted such conquests, even stooping to categorize them as just that: conquests. In fact, these women had conquered him with their wheedling hands and predatory smiles, their casual air of destruction. He had let himself be talked into bottles of whiskey, undrinkable wine, swill masquerading as champers. He had let himself be talked to on bar stools and dance floors, in public gardens and vestibules of tenements, always paying and trying to listen, so that he, too, might understand what he'd lost and learn to live with that. But all he'd learned was magic and how to wiggle his ears, how to make other people laugh and forget themselves.

They had names like Bijoux, Fifi, Queenie, Joy, Arabella, or Liberty. Names that were stolen, grand, and interchangeable. Names that, like the establishments where Lawrence met them, could be abandoned in an instant. Even after he arrived in Delhi and exchanged Aidan's family and Joanna's relentlessness for his own listless roamings, he would occasionally wander up G. B. Road with its shoddy, ill-lit 'hotels' and pervasive bleat of jazzy film music or late at night to the New Delhi roundabouts where street girls gathered by relic statues of Curzon and Victoria, and he would feel a sorrow so overwhelming that he mistook it for nostalgia.

Perhaps this was why, when Jack Battersby inevitably turned up in Delhi and asked him to choose a safe meeting place, Lawrence selected the rear car park at the Jai Mahal – a dark, anonymous fucking ground where the street girls sated their *babus* in the back seats of big sedans. The hotel winked in one direction, the police in another while waiters discreetly slid among the vehicles bearing trays of whiskey and cigarettes in exchange for the understood *baksheesh*. The park was unlit, identification prohibited, and the mutter and squeak of surrounding sexual activity sufficient to mask any private conversation.

Jack picked him up outside his flat at eleven o'clock on a weeknight in early September. He was driving himself, in a black Ambassador, one of the chancery's unmarked fleet. The night was cool, rinsed by a rogue shower that afternoon, and a quarter-moon shone down. As Lawrence settled into the passenger seat he could just make out Jack's trademark silver sideburns and mustache, that squashed toadstool of a nose. Fifty was Battersby's natural age, though he was only yet in his forties. He'd looked fifty for more than ten years, and doubtless would look it still at eighty.

Jack had been Lawrence's superior in Special Operations early in the war, his peer when they both joined MacArthur's Allied Intelligence Bureau toward the end. Then Jack married, fathered two sons, and rose like a windup toy through the Department of External Affairs. His desire to launch an Australian Intelligence Agency bordered on the obsessive, and he was not amused that Lawrence's test operation had run aground. 'You fucked up' were Jack's first direct words to Lawrence in fourteen months.

'Go straight through to the next corner, and turn left,' Lawrence replied evenly. 'You'll like this spot. It'll remind you of Shanghai. Remember the Kissing Alley?' The pitch-black street lined with trucks and cars seething with groping lovers on hot Chinese nights. Homosexuals and underaged whores, couples violating parental prohibitions, spies passing messages under cover of sex. One of Jack's favorite ploys, sending Special Operations agents into this cauldron to find each other and trade secrets coded into sweet nothings. The joke of a voyeur, a vicarious thrill for a man who had all the true grit of warm milk.

'Not personally, no,' Jack shot back as a mangy pariah dog scuttled across the road. It glared into the headlights, and Jack braked with a sharp intake of breath.

'You're allowed to hit anything here except the cows,' Lawrence reminded him. 'Turn in at those pillars . . . but turn out the lights first. Otherwise you're likely to catch some high minister in a compromising position.'

'Cripes,' Jack said as the drive went dark. The canopy of leaves overhead shut out even the moonlight. 'Am I allowed to hit the other cars, too?'

'Just pull over there. Can you make out the waiter's white jacket? Slip a twenty-rupee note out the window. He'll bring us some whiskey and leave us alone.'

The waiter glided forward. Jack handed him the note and barked, 'Whiskey soda.' The man vanished back into the shadows. 'No police with little torches?'

'They'd be breaking their rice bowl if they tried it. I'll wager half of that twenty finds its way to the local inspector's pocket.'

'What about the girls?'

'Street girls mostly. There's a roundabout down the road where they show their merchandise, then the *babus* bring 'em here for delivery.'

'So this is what you're doing with your hard-earned American dollars.'

'You know me, Jack. I never pay for the privilege.'

'What do you pay for, then, Larry?' The voice in the dark turned on him. 'More importantly, what do I pay you for?'

'Look. You asked me to recruit Aidan. That's what I did. Wasn't thrilled that he spilled the story to Joanna – his wife—'

'I know.'

'But she knows nothing of our involvement. She thinks Aidan got wind of that Czech saboteur through journalistic instinct. Thought he was going up to Kashmir in search of an anti-Soviet news scoop to repair his image back in Washington.'

'As opposed to an intelligence scoop.'

Lawrence sighed. 'The thing is—'

He heard a footstep outside the car. The glint of a tray and glassware. Jack rolled down the window letting in a welcome flash of cool air and took the tray. The waiter vanished. Jack set the glasses on the seat between them and poured. 'Go on.'

'That plane crash. The one those idiots wired Joanna about. I've been doing a little digging along Embassy Row. It turns out the Czech was supposed to be on that flight.'

'Along with your man.'

'Yes. But the Czech canceled at the last minute.'

'And your man bailed out midway.'

They drank in silence for several minutes.

'Sounds like your mate was up to something a touch more sinister than news gathering.'

'Aidan's no fool. It might be as simple as the last-minute cancellation tipping him off. He could have been the mark himself.'

'So he saves his own skin and sends those other poor blokes to their maker?'

'It would have destroyed his cover to tip them, and if he wasn't certain, maybe he didn't want to take that chance. Or maybe it *was* just an accident.'

Jack's glass made a cracking sound against the steering wheel. 'Pretty ruthless fellow.'

'I've never seen that side of him, but it wouldn't surprise me if it's there. His mother went mad and the rest of his family were wiped out by the Japs.'

'That why you've felt free to help yourself to his wife?'

Lawrence's hand squeezed around his glass.

'You've fucked up,' Jack repeated. 'About ten times over. This was a little nothing assignment. Bump into an old mate, feed him a juicy story, offer him a sweet if he'd catch this Czech with his knickers down.' Jack shifted in the dark. 'Just a bit of simple spying to grease Austral-American relations. Figured I was doing *you* a favor while we were at it. Get you back in the game, distract you from your bloody melancholia. You realize you've single-handedly convinced the home team *and* the Yanks that we're a bunch of bludgers.'

Lawrence still didn't answer. The car was hot and close and smelled of cheap whiskey, warm skin and sweat, Jack's old-man cologne.

'Talk to me about Sinkiang,' Jack said coolly, ignoring his silence. 'Who's recruited your Yank? That's what I want to know.'

Lawrence said finally, 'What makes you think somebody's recruited him? Maybe he's dead.'

'Nice way to talk about an old mate. Is that really what you think? Or only what you hope?'

'I saw what was left of the girl.'

'Alice in Wonderland.'

'If he was in that jeep with her, he wasn't likely to have been in much better shape.'

'But there was no sign of him.'

Lawrence thought of the picture of Simon. 'No.'

'And what if he wasn't in the jeep with her? What if he went ahead on foot, or wandered off to take a piss . . . ?'

'Right. If he can blow up a plane with six UN peacekeepers, he can certainly blow up a jeep with one overzealous young blonde. But why would he?'

The fizz of soda. Then silence. Shadows of two cars rolled past them through the grainy darkness.

'I was hoping you could tell me that,' Jack said finally.

'Well, I'm sorry I can't oblige. You want your money back?'

'What's the little girl about?'

Lawrence felt Jack's eyes even if he couldn't see them. He corrected his tone. 'My ticket to Sinkiang, you mean. Figured I needed my own mission, in case Joanna lost her nerve and tried to haul me back.'

'Bit thin, wasn't it?'

'Kamla plugged nicely into Joanna's social ethic. I could see there was a bond – she couldn't fault me for trying to save the kid. And there was a historical precedent, which appealed to me. Robert Shaw took along a Chinese orphan as a mascot for his expedition.'

'If I recall, *he* didn't bring his kiddie back out with him.'

Lawrence drank. 'That was Joanna's doing, not mine.'

'Tough guy.' He could hear Jack's smirk. Then, 'Look. You owe me, Larry. I gave you an assignment. You turned it into a fiasco.

And now you're sleeping with Shaw's wife. Playing dad to her kids. You'll excuse me for questioning just how hard you're really working to locate your old mate.'

Lawrence stared at the flare of a match in a car on the other side of the yard. A man's black eyes, a red turban. The edge of a girl's unsmiling face. Then the light shrank back to a spot of orange.

'I'm working,' Lawrence said.

'The Americans want to know what happened. They want us, as they say, to name names.'

'They still don't know it was Aidan?'

'You think I *want* us to look like a horse's ass? No, and so far I don't think they've pinpointed you, either. But they're circling. The Soviets are actively supplying the rebels up in Kashmir, and the Yanks think your botched operation made that possible.'

'That's absurd.'

'Of course it is. But we're going to remain the scapegoats until we can tell them what the hell actually happened. Which is why, as I say, your motivation concerns me.'

'Joanna is our best hope of finding him. She'll never give up.'

'What makes you so sure?'

'Believe me.'

'Ah. Well, I'm sorry to hear that. But I hope you're doing a little of the digging yourself.'

Lawrence sipped his drink.

'You actually working on this book about the Game?'

'In my spare time.'

Jack chuckled. 'Good. I met an old classmate of yours the other day. Rodney Tynsdale. Said you played football together. He's a publisher with Morrow and Hoag. Specializes in historical odds and ends. I told him a bit about your book, and he said it was just up his alley. I think you should drop him a note.'

'Why?'

'Legitimacy, mate. The wandering historian. Solidify your cover.'

'What do you *want*, Jack?'

'You know me. I want to know which way the wind blows. I want trinkets for our American friends and a trophy to woo the Prime Minister. I want you to find out what the fuck happened to your old mate, Aidan Shaw.'

'So do I,' Lawrence said quietly.

'Then we're fair and square.' Jack started to turn the ignition, but Lawrence stopped him. He collected the tray and glasses, the bottle of soda, and set them on a rise of lawn beside their parking space. 'The waiter'll be docked,' he explained, 'if these don't get back to the kitchen.'

'What about the whiskey?' Jack asked, holding up the bottle, sloshing its remaining contents. Half full.

'That's yours for your trip home,' said Lawrence. 'Something to remember me by.'

7

When Mem told Simon and me that we would soon be starting school, I was quite beside myself. I had never so much as set foot in a school! When my uncle took me from Tihwa, I was still too young. In the flash house, whenever I mentioned the word, Indrani would tell me not to be stupid. Why would I need schooling? Of my sisters there, only Bharati had passed her lower levels. She had been a middling student, she told me, but she'd loved her crisp navy and white school uniform, and the other girls in her class had been more of a family to her than her own. I used to picture school as a kind of party, so many girls together laughing and gossiping, poring over books and scribbling out lessons. I thought this sounded very heavenly, and I could scarcely believe my fortune when Mem said that I should go.

But fortunes may prove good or bad, and the selection of a school was more complicated than I realized. We could not return to the American school Simon had attended in the past, Mem said, because of 'the situation.' Lawrence said that we ought to try the Delhi public school, where the children were mostly Indian, because there no one would know or care whether Aidan was accused of being a Communist. 'But,' Mem answered, 'everyone *would* know and care that Kamla is a half-breed – not even an Anglo-Indian, at that, but some combination so obscure that, by Indian reckoning, she'll automatically be viewed as Untouchable. If her complete background became known, she could be in real danger.' They tried to hold these discussions privately, but there were few conversations in Mem's house that I didn't manage to hear, so I knew even before Simon when Mem made her choice. 'Prejudice is a reality they'll both have to face, but at least at the All-Nations School they stand an even chance.'

The next morning Mem told me we were going shopping, just the two of us. Not even Simon would come along. Lawrence would take him to the cinema.

'Mothers and daughters do this,' she explained as she steered her green Austin between a line of camels and a bullock cart piled high with sugarcane. 'I used to love shopping with my mother. We went every year before school started. My mother did mean well...' Her voice trailed off, and I toyed with my braid, uncertain what she wished me to say. All I knew of her parents was that they had died before Simon was born.

A knot of grown boys stared through the dust as we pulled into the car park at Khan Market. Typical crony layabouts, they were not serious *goondas,* but their eyes were sinister, nevertheless, and there were half a dozen of them, some chewing *paan,* some squatting on the steps, others leaning against the passageway through to the central court of shops. From the looseness of their arms, the tilted jut of their chins, and the sneering set of their mouths I recognized them as high-caste Hindus of no account, probably the sons of village landowners come to make trouble in the city. It was boys like these, I recalled, who had poured through Delhi during Partition, setting fire to the homes and businesses of Muslims and gang-raping any girl they chose to call Muslim. My flash house sister Mira had explained that these *zamindar* were raised from infancy to know one thing only, and that was their absolute right to take whatever they pleased.

I did not believe these boys could be so stupid as to trouble an American lady, yet the way their eyes flicked back and forth between Mem's face and mine as we started toward them told me they did not wish us well. Mem only made the situation worse when she took my hand. They spat and stood, a current of disdain passing among them at the sight of a white woman touching a low half-breed.

Khan Market was a square arrangement of stores set around an inner court. To reach Hormasji's Tog Shoppe we needed to pass in front of these men and through a long dark hallway to the colonnade on the other side. 'Dignity,' Mem said under her breath, tightening her grip on me. 'Just look straight ahead. Ignore them, that puts you in control.'

I felt her eyes press forward to the light at the end of that hallway. I sensed the protection this light promised her, like the white moon she wore on her upper arm. I now wore a similar moon since she'd taken me to Simon's doctor, but even standing beside her, with her hand wrapped securely around my own, I had experience enough to know that not all of Mem's immunizations would work for me. Ignorance for girls like me was a source of weakness, never power. So I did not look ahead. I looked to one side, then the other, staring my accusers down.

One had orange teeth and a mole shaped like a rabbit above his left eyebrow. Another was missing part of an earlobe – it looked to be a birth defect. Two more were exceedingly short, perhaps brothers, whose hooded eyes seemed to bear their affliction. It was a trick of the flash house, one Bharati had passed on to me as a survival tool. Even the most powerful of men, she told me, will possess something you can pity, and the sooner you locate that weakness, the sooner you can claim their power for yourself.

One boy after another flinched. Then the current shifted, and with another few steps we had passed them and were through the murky tunnel to the inside square of stores.

Mem hugged me to her. 'Remember that. Never let them get to you.'

There was light in her voice, and her step bounced a little. I did not dispute her. If it pleased her to think that our victory over the layabouts was due to a shared strategy, then why should I disagree? What pleased me was her hand lingering on my shoulder, the sway of her body against my own as we proceeded down the colonnade. My fingers curled in the folds of her skirt, and I remembered how I had dreamed of such a moment when first I claimed Mrs Shaw.

But, of course, we could not hold on forever. We had business to do. We entered Hormasji's Tog Shoppe, with its racks of Western-style clothing packed so closely under the swinging light bulb that the colors seemed to run together. Behind the counter two elderly men glanced up from a game of checkers. They did not offer assistance but nodded for us to look ourselves among the blouses and skirts.

'Which do you like?' Mem asked, easing two blouses from the rack and holding them to my chin.

One had a square collar and pearl buttons and was the color of the night cream on Mem's dressing table. The other was dead white trimmed with scratchy lace and puffed-up frills. Unable to decipher which she favored, I nodded.

'What does that mean? You want both?'

My head slid back and forth in the gesture, like an Indian shrug, that I had acquired in the flash house. For some reason it irritated Mem. I knew this and during our trek I had all but cured myself of the habit, but in Delhi it came back to me like a native accent. By the time I stopped myself she had already put down the blouses and cupped her hands over my ears to still my head. 'You can have both blouses if you want them. You can have different ones. You will need some skirts and sandals as well. You will wear Western clothes to school, Kamla, but I want you to choose them for yourself. I want you to know your own mind. I want you to *decide.*'

The ferocity of her words came down hard between us, but her emphasis perplexed me. 'I choose this one,' I said, laying my hand across the pearl buttons. In fact I knew my preferences perfectly well. If anything, decision came too easily to me – dangerously easily on occasion. In quick succession, I selected a pleated blue skirt, a pair of buckled English-style sandals, and a package of white bobby socks. If she wants me to be decisive, I thought, then that is what I will be.

In any case, the clothing meant little to me. All that mattered was that hug outside, the lightness of her smile. But now she seemed to distrust my decisiveness. Her lips pursed as she watched me, so that I stopped and began to put things back. I thought of the revolving door at the entrance of the big hotel where Lawrence and Mem had recently taken us swimming.

She told me not to move anything else. The clerks had halted their game. At Mem's signal they busied themselves scribbling in

229

their account books, making the second and third and fourth copies of receipts that every transaction in India seems to require, to this day. While Mem signed the four receipts I drifted toward a display of barrettes. Yellow, pink, purple, red enamel ornaments in the shapes of birds and butterflies. I was only looking. At this point I would not have dared to ask for anything else.

Without warning Mem plucked one of the pink butterflies from the tray and tossed it in with the garments the second clerk was wrapping. My confusion must have been written on my face, for she leaned over and brushed her cheek against mine. 'It's not a crime to want more than you think is allowed,' she whispered.

The shopkeeper finished his tallying, and Mem paid the total. We were standing in the doorway when two foreign women passed down the colonnade in front of us. They wore pink and yellow shirt dresses and flat white hats, white gloves that buttoned at the wrist. They did not show that they recognized Mem, but I knew from the way they glanced at her and the way she in turn fixed her gaze on their backs that the women and Mem were not strangers.

'If it were my husband,' the words of one floated back to us, 'I'd have gone home the first day and be camped out in Congress demanding a proper investigation. What can she be thinking to stay on *here*?'

'But her husband's a Communist.' The other one halted, checking her reflection in the next shop window as she straightened her hat. Her voice boomed. 'Why would anybody in Congress lift a finger to bring him back? No, I can see why she might hide out here, but someone told me she's actually trying to *adopt* that native girl. Imagine!'

Mem stepped forward. I thought of her earlier advice, to 'never let them get to you,' but she spoke in a tone that dared these two to turn around. 'Of course *your* husbands' politics are pure as the driven snow. And you can hardly bring yourselves to speak to the natives, God forbid loving one of them. So exactly what right do you have to pass judgment on me?'

The two foreign ladies looked back, breathing out in little gasps. Mem bent down and stabbed my forehead with a kiss. Then without waiting for them to answer, she took my arm and led me away.

God forbid loving one. I would repeat this phrase over and over to myself in the years to come, turning the syllables in my mind like leaves of a book that defied me.

The next morning I scrubbed myself head to toe, dressed in the new navy skirt and white blouse, tied my braids in two round loops, and was ready long before Simon. While he spilled his milk and ran upstairs to change and then came back and complained his toast was cold and too brown to eat, I sat arranging and rearranging my pencil box and paper in the book bag Lawrence had bought for me. I had a clear vision of my new life at school, and I was impatient to get there.

Within minutes of our arrival, however, I saw that this All-Nations School was not what I had expected. Oh, there was plenty of laughter and scribbling, but the other children used odd terms such as 'milk money' and 'roll call' and 'recess.' Boys sat together with girls, and I had to learn to raise my hand and follow the rules and restrictions of countless new games. The very colors and sizes of my schoolmates awed me. They came in pink and chocolate brown and white, some stick thin, others round as coconuts. They wore clothes of all styles and colors as well. The language of the school was English, but knots of boys and girls would form to speak in foreign tongues. Our teacher, Miss Le Doux, told me that the children in our school came from sixteen different countries.

Miss Le Doux wore a Western-style dress tailored from a scarlet sari. Golden bangles draped her arms, but she had the soft cheeks and rounded chin of a comfortable, protected life. She informed us this was her last year of teaching, as she was soon to be married to a young *gendarme* back in Lyons, which she pointed out for us on a large map of France, her home country. I tried to picture Miss Le Doux bedded and pinned beneath her new husband. I thought of my sisters in the flash house. I thought of Mem and Lawrence. I recalled that square of black bars, blue night, Golba and his men, and I wanted so badly to ask Miss Le Doux if she had ever known what it is to feel a man's skin inside her, if she should not ask *me* to teach her a thing or two.

I tried to explain that I, too, had come to India from another country, but Miss Le Doux plainly saw no comparison. Nor did the other children, whose laughter and gossip and notes were often slanted at me. Boys with hair like cornsilk would call me Blackie and Jap. Girls who giggled behind cupped palms would turn from my approach. It was not merely that I was 'native' – there were several Indian students at the school, but they, too, kept their distance from me. No, the children knew, as children do, that I was different in another way. 'She's from the streets,' I heard them whisper.

Miss Le Doux was content to let Simon and me sit off by ourselves in one corner of the open-walled tent that served as our hot-weather classroom. This pleased Simon, for he was new to this school, too, and here she rarely called on him. She never called on me. In fact, I thought she must look on us in much the same way Simon and I watched the monkey *wallah* who came down Ratendone Road every morning. How else to explain the marvel on her face when she returned this monkey's first reading quiz with a grade of one hundred percent!

'It appears I have underestimated you, *cherie,*' she said to me in a voice like gushing water.

Simon beamed. He had had to explain three times before I understood what was meant by this word, 'quiz.'

But now she was saying that if I continued to perform this well she would recommend my promotion to a class of children closer to my age. I felt Simon grip my hand. A look of confusion passed over his face. He had just realized that the object of the game we were playing was not to win, but to lose, for Miss Le Doux was not suggesting that Simon should be promoted with me. I stroked Simon's fingers to reassure him. I would continue the charade as long as I could. For his sake, I would play at being a child. But the falseness of the game was in front of us now.

That night for the first of many times I woke to find Simon under my covers. He had crept in under the mosquito net without waking me and now was sound asleep. The closeness of his sticky hands and warm boy smell aroused such tenderness that I was tempted to keep him with me. But soon the antics of his sleep changed my mind, as he flung an arm across my throat, twisted the sheet into knots.

Simon rolled over, his cheek against my bare shoulder, his sleeping palm on my stomach. His knee pushed the hem of my nightdress up my thigh. His closeness was innocent, harmless – but I knew that I myself was neither.

I whispered in his ear, stroked a fingertip inside the collar of his pajamas, found the shallow softness there behind the bone. When he was half awake I took his hand and gently stood him up, guided him in a kind of trance back to his own bed. In the morning I opened my eyes to find him staring down at me through the netting. His expression was half accusing, half meek. I let him think he had been dreaming.

8

Lawrence leaned against the balcony railing outside Joanna's bedroom. Scarlet clouds stippled the sky, and the plane trees along Ratendone Road cast umbrella shadows over the afternoon bicycle traffic. Inside the high white compound walls Joanna's garden was lush, thanks to the old *mali* Musai, who loved and tended the foliage as dotingly as if it were his own. He was down there now with Kamla, the only member of the household who seemed to understand his thick northern dialect. Lawrence couldn't hear what Kamla was saying, but he could see her smile. As she and Musai moved across the lawn she caught back her long black hair with her hands and twisted it on top of her head. She wore a celery green blouse and brick red skirt. At the edge of the grass she squatted beside the old man. Simon came crawling out from under the hedge and excitedly held up his palm, and soon the three of them were engaged in what appeared from Lawrence's vantage to be an animated conversation with a snail. He could have stayed there happily spying all evening. When Joanna entered the room behind him, he turned and beckoned her to join him.

She waved down at the children, then stood very still looking into the sky. 'It's so beautiful. I forget.'

'That's a bad thing to forget,' he said.

She caught her lower lip between her teeth, worked it for several seconds. Her eyes still distant, she asked, 'Will you help me do something?'

233

'I suppose that depends.'

She nodded and came back to him then, taking his hand and leading him inside. They stopped in front of Aidan's closet.

'Are you sure?' he asked. They had gone through Aidan's desk weeks ago, finding nothing of relevance, but she'd been unable to face his clothes.

She yanked open the folding door. Her eyes traveled the jackets hanging inside, the trousers and rows of expensive shoes. 'Nagu tells me the children come in here. Simon plays dress-up in his father's clothes. Maybe it would be better if he borrowed yours instead.'

Lawrence had been careful never to leave his belongings here. 'Is that an invitation?'

There was a long silence.

He sighed. 'Well, one step at a time. What shall we do with these?'

'Up there.' She pointed to a compartment above the closet, reached by standing on a chair. 'We can put them back in the suitcases he used coming over.'

They worked together, packing Aidan's clothes into the luggage and restowing it up top. They didn't speak, and Joanna hardly glanced at the garments she was folding. Half an hour later the closet stood empty except for some boxes on the upper shelf. 'His hats,' she said.

Lawrence began to move these up with the suitcases, but the last two boxes weighed more than the others. 'These are no hats, Jo.'

She took the first from him and lifted the lid. 'It's his helmet from the war.' She frowned. 'We argued over his bringing this. I said, the war's over, and anyway, what would a bureau chief need with a helmet. He said, war's never over – and in this part of the world the military would hardly share their precious equipment with journalists.'

Lawrence said nothing. Aidan might reasonably have taken this helmet to Kashmir, but it would have been a dubious burden on the trek to China. Was this evidence that he'd planned the trek going in?

She held the helmet between her hands. 'Once, back in Maryland, we took a whole roll of pictures of Simon wearing this thing, strutting like a little soldier, but Simon accidentally opened the camera, exposing the film, and we never thought to do it again.'

Unable to look at her, Lawrence took the helmet. US Army issue. Definitely war vintage, with two pronounced dents at the back and one nick just above the left strap. 'Do you know when he got it?'

'It came back with him from China. For a while he ran a listening post in the foothills near Burma. Sometimes, he said, there were skirmishes. I always assumed he meant with the Japanese. But . . . he never talked about it.' She turned abruptly and paced the length of the room.

'He didn't talk because I didn't ask,' she said. 'He had an affair in Chungking. Serious. Maybe you know this . . . ?' She glanced back at him. He shook his head. She returned her gaze to the ceiling. 'It ended – or I believed it ended when he came home. We got past it. Through it. But now I wonder – maybe the affair was the least of it. Why do you think he brought that thing here?'

'If it were me—'

'Aidan's nothing like you,' she said gently. Then she came back to him. 'Tell me what you really think.'

He watched her clench her hands. This morning those same tapered fingers had caressed his face.

'He never talked to me about Chungking, Jo.'

Without speaking she put the helmet away and opened the other box. She pulled out a pad of paper. One of the three that Lawrence had given him, of the two Aidan apparently had left here.

He hesitated, then said quietly, 'These are one-time pads. It's a system of encryption we used during the war. Each pad belongs to a pair, each pair having its own code. At least in theory, a message written on a one-time pad can be deciphered only by someone who possesses the corresponding pad and code.'

'Why would Aidan have these?'

Lawrence shook his head. 'They were standard issue in the Office of War Information. Still are, throughout the foreign service.'

'Aidan's not in the foreign service, Lawrence.'

He felt her look at him, heard the accusing undertone. He reached into the box. An unmarked manila envelope lay at the bottom. He opened it and removed the document inside.

The policy was dated September 1948, naming Aidan as the insured, Joanna as beneficiary of $10,000 in the event of his death.

She stared at the date. The amount. 'He took this out before we left Washington.' She spoke so softly he could hardly hear her. 'And never told me.'

Lawrence scanned the legalese. It was, on the face of it, straightforward. Only one statement caught his eye. It had been typed in as an addendum.

If the insured is found to have been missing for nine months, and all good-faith attempts to locate the insured have failed, then at the survivor's request the Company will deliberate whether it is reasonable to conclude that the insured is dead and if so decided, full benefits will be payable. Such request should be directed to the Bethesda address listed below.

Lawrence heard a splash outside the window as Musai emptied his pail in the yard. The evening chatter of bicycle bells was reaching a fever pitch, and from the kitchen came Nagu's voice softly berating the cook for some marginal offense. At the other end of the hallway Simon cajoled Kamla to sing with him 'Three Blind Mice.'

'Nine months.' Joanna looked at him sharply. 'He knew before he ever came to India that something like this—'

'Jo, you know as well as I, Aidan never wanted a desk job. He came here expecting to go out on assignment. Up into the war zone in Kashmir. To the Khyber Pass. Dangerous territory. No-man's-land.'

She pulled away from him. 'But what if he *knew* he was going to disappear? What if he *planned* this?'

'Insurance is only a precaution. It shows he loves you. It shows he's responsible.'

But he couldn't keep the doubt from his voice, and one look told him she heard it.

9

In late September an unseasonal heat wave swept over Delhi. The entire city slept outdoors, and the household on Ratendone Road was no exception. The servants arranged their *charpoys* in the driveway outside their quarters. The family took theirs to the roof. These nights Lawrence would stay through to morning. The children loved this, of course. As Joanna came up the stairwell, arms stretched around extra pillows, she could hear them crying out, 'Scorpio!' 'Cancer!' 'Virgo!' 'Orion!' It was a game that Lawrence had spun in the mountains, back at the start of the trek, when Kamla, in spite of her fledgling English, had bested Simon every night. Now, after a summer of practice with Ralph Milne, Simon was intent on reversing the score.

But the third night, as Joanna was about to step out onto the rooftop, she heard Lawrence counsel her son, 'Waste of breath to compete with a woman smarter than you. Smart thing is to bring yourself up to snuff and climb along onto her team.' Then he sighed and clapped Simon on the back. 'Enough now. Lie yourselves down, the both of you, get to sleep.'

The *charpoys'* wooden frames creaked obediently. The children lapsed into silence. But Joanna hung back inside the stairwell. Lawrence's words taunted her. *Smart thing is to bring yourself up to snuff and climb along onto her team.*

Could this have been what he himself was doing when he hightailed up to Kashmir to help her search for Aidan? Had he used Kamla as his foil? Was it all some sort of scheme? What was Lawrence doing here . . . really?

The unexpected force of her suspicion hit her like a blow. A most unwelcome blow. The mystery of that insurance policy was making her paranoid! The real question wasn't what Lawrence was doing, but what was she?

With vicious clarity she remembered another night – early March, more than six months ago now. *Only* six months ago. The temperature had shot up wildly through that late afternoon and evening. Of course, it was nothing like the coming heat of May or June, but this had been Joanna's first taste of India's summer. She'd been bewitched by the idea of sleeping on the roof ever since their October arrival in Delhi. In fact, this private enclosure with its waist-high parapet and pitched tile flooring was the main reason she and Aidan chose this house. She'd had Nagu move up the wood-frame *charpoys* as soon as the dry chill of winter eased off. Then she'd waited for the first onset of true warmth with a sense of anticipation she knew would wilt the instant summer descended in earnest. But that March night she put Simon to sleep in his room and dismissed the servants early. Then she made Aidan close his eyes and led him up this same dark stairway.

'Now we're really here,' she said tugging him across the roof terrace and down onto the big double *charpoy.*

'What makes you so sure?' He'd played his fingers up the back of her neck, refusing to open his eyes. 'It feels the same to me.'

'No.' She leaned into him impatiently. 'Look! Look at this sky, this moon. It's a mango. And listen. You can hear the wheels of the bullock carts, *tonga* horns, bicycle bells, and there – hear that jackal? No other sky has stars like these. They're the color of marigolds. You just won't admit it, you cynic. This is India. And it's wonderful and awful and I love it, and I'll make you love it, too, if it's the last thing I do.'

'I love you,' he said, stunning her. Then he turned her head in a single movement and pulled her into a kiss, which lasted, it seemed in retrospect, the full length of the night. Later, when she ran her hands over his back and buttocks, she could feel the marks the *charpoy* webbing had made in his otherwise sleek skin. 'You have them, too,' he'd said and traced the grid of indentations along her arms and hip, the side of her left breast. It was as though they were bound together by a contraction of longitude and latitude.

What had become of that loving young wife, and where had her capacity for happiness – and trust – disappeared? *Climb along onto her team.* What team was that, she wondered, and what game were they playing? That night with Aidan she had not yet met Lawrence, and so much had happened since. Comparisons were futile and cruel. But she stopped short of assuring herself that if Aidan reappeared right now he would find her blameless.

He is not going to appear right now. The words banged inside her skull. Years are passing each day that goes by. He's not going to reappear. Ever.

Those words drove her from her hiding place. They propelled her past Lawrence as he stood beside the low block parapet. They burned her lips as she kissed Simon, her fingertips as she stroked Kamla's hair. They stung her eyes as she lay down on that same double *charpoy.* They were words she needed to tell herself, the

238

way a tightrope walker needs to know the exact play of swing and tension that would plunge her to her death. But she could still *smell* Aidan as he'd smelled that night, every night. A smell like warm sage.

The wood frame and jute strings creaked as Lawrence lay down beside her. He turned onto his side, placed a hand on her belly. She could feel the effort with which he held his arm so the full weight of the limb would not fall on her. The way Aidan had touched her when she first told him she was pregnant with Simon. Aidan had run his hand over her abdomen as if to check the truth of her claim, and when he was finally convinced, he hardly spoke to her for two weeks. When he did, his tone was as distant as she'd ever heard him. After those two weeks were past, he admitted he was worried – money, the war, her health, the idea of parenthood – but now he became extraordinarily attentive, even surprising her with impromptu purchases of baby clothes, a cradle, and antique high chair. When Simon was born, Aidan exulted – filling her hospital room with massive bouquets of daffodils and white roses.

Lawrence smelled like dark, loamy earth.

At length he removed his arm.

Ten minutes or four hours later – who knew? – he was whispering in her ear. 'You awake?'

'No.' She opened her eyes. He was standing over her, lifting her hand.

'Come here.'

'What is it?' Against the moonless night Lawrence's pale shirt seemed to float above the black of his trousers. Her own loose white *kurta* made her feel equally ghostly. She wished he would slap her to prove they both were real.

Instead he drew her to the parapet and pointed across the desert. Where they stood the air was hot and still, the sky variegated as onyx, but in the distance that same sky turned opaque, starless, and, though she could only sense this dimly, it seemed to be roiling.

'Listen,' he said.

'It's too late for dust storms,' she protested vaguely, but she could hear the signal pulsing like a long lamenting sigh.

'It's a raga.' He placed his hand on the small of her back. 'With each repetition you can hear it building, coming closer and gathering strength.'

'Sounds like it'll be on top of us soon.'

'Sometimes it changes course.' He released her. 'Or weakens unexpectedly.'

'Or simply stops,' she said.

'I don't think that's going to happen tonight.' She was conscious of his voice inside her own head.

'What should we do?' she asked.

He bent down and kissed her roughly. 'Enjoy it.'

Then he strode over to Simon and shook him by the shoulder. 'Wake up!' he scolded, laughing. 'Kammy, you, too! Dust storm's coming.'

The children bolted upright and in the next seconds, in a frenzy of enthusiastic alarm, the four of them whipped off their bedding and pillows and tossed them down the stairs. Nagu and the sweeper came racing from the servants' quarters. They helped Joanna and Lawrence flip the *charpoys* so they wouldn't blow away. Then they all followed the children into the house, bolting the door to the roof behind them, and ran from room to room slamming shutters, wedging rags into cracks beneath the windows.

Ten minutes later the storm was upon them, wailing and whirling sand and debris and knocking out the power. In the nursery Lawrence led the children through several raucous choruses of 'Inky-Dinky Parlez-vous,' 'Waltzing Matilda,' and 'It's a Long Way to Tipperary' until they sank back in happy exhaustion.

Then he and Joanna crept down the hall, the storm's raga their camouflage.

The next day she officially returned to Safe Haven.

Vijay spotted her as she entered the courtyard and immediately sent up a cry. 'Mem has returned! Our beloved Mem is back!' He hurried forth beaming, fingertips to forehead. '*Namaste!*' he cried. 'Welcome home!'

She was surprised that he looked the same – weak-shouldered, young, eager, black hair shaggy about the ears, arms spindly where they emerged from short sleeves, belt cinched to hold up too-big trousers. It seemed inconceivable that he hadn't changed.

But the old sweeper, Banda, appeared the same, too. He promptly threw himself at Joanna's feet so that she had to lift him by the shoulders, scolding and reassuring that yes, she was still the same *memsahib* who would not tolerate such humiliating customs. To Banda's credit, he gave her a wink. Just testing, he seemed to say.

Hari had warned her the place was disheveled and under-populated. Vijay and the elderly ayah, Suman, had done their best, but five girls had run away since May, and unlike the staff, those who remained looked to have aged more than just a few months. Their faces were etched with resignation and boredom. Their hair and clothes were unkempt, and they regarded Joanna as if they had never seen her before, though all had been here when she left.

She found liquor bottles now hidden among the girls' piles of screen magazines. The books Joanna had ordered from the States moldered in the hall. The four donated sewing machines were rusting inside their housings, and the buildup of grease was so thick in the kitchen that tatters of flyaway newspaper stuck to the walls. Vijay, tagging behind her like a puppy, seemed unaware of the shambles this place had become under his governance.

'Any visits from the police in my absence?' she asked as they entered the dumping ground of papers and files that her office had become.

'Only once,' Vijay said, 'a few days after you left. They roughed things up a bit, claimed to be searching for a thief who had disguised herself as a prostitute. They took two girls away saying we lacked proper paperwork to keep them here. It was most terrible, Mem. All they wanted was a bribe, but I had no money to pay them. And who knows, perhaps that was just as well. If I had paid them off they might have returned, but they have not been back since.'

'And how are your studies coming?' Joanna asked to change the subject.

'Oh, most excellently,' he replied, grinning broadly. 'I am passing the first round of exams, and Mr Kaushal has informed me that he will recommend me to the Social Welfare Committee for an advocacy position as soon as I pass my finals. In this case, I would continue working directly with you, Mem. This would be my greatest pleasure. I am assuming, of course, that you have returned to us for good.'

Joanna sighed. 'I hope not.' But at this, Vijay's face crumpled with such guileless dismay that she was forced to take his hand. She rubbed it briskly between her own. 'I only meant that I hope far greater pleasures await you in your life. Of course I look forward to working with you, Vijay. And I thank you for taking good care of Salamat Jannat in my absence.'

His dark eyes widened suddenly, as if he had just remembered. 'Your journey was successful, then?'

Joanna looked over his shoulder at the array of jaded, only mildly curious faces peering in from the veranda. She caught the ayah's covert glance, watched the sweeper busily whistling across the courtyard as he crouched over his half-length broom. It dawned on her that not one person here had even a remote idea where she had been these past five months or why she had gone away. All they knew was that she'd returned to pick up where she left off.

'Yes,' she lied to Vijay with an abandon that felt dangerously uplifting. 'My journey was a big success.'

CHAPTER 9

1

The winter months that first year came and went in a blur. We were all so busy, so happy together. At Christmas Simon and I decorated a potted fir tree with tinsel and tissue paper snowflakes, and Lawrence bought us each a brand-new Raleigh bicycle. I performed in the school pageant as an angel and Simon as a shepherd, and later we caroled under a round desert moon. I thought, this is what it must mean to actually be *firenghi*.

On regular days Mem drove us to school, then went on to work at Salamat Jannat. In the afternoons usually Lawrence picked us up in a cycle rickshaw. We would go for a picnic in Lodi Gardens or visit Humayun's Tomb, or we would explore the shops of Connaught Place, listen to records, or stop for a sweet. Sometimes Lawrence would bring us along when he interviewed someone for his book.

I was impressed by how many interviews his book seemed to require and that his subjects seemed as varied as the children at our school. Though most were men, they were rich and poor, brown and yellow and white. But Simon and I never actually heard what was discussed because Lawrence usually held the meetings at one of the big hotels, and while the men talked, we were sent off to explore the lobby shops and grounds.

My favorite stop was Govinda's Bookstore in the Imperial Hotel. We would lose ourselves there for hours, and the young clerk never bothered us. With the money Lawrence gave us, we bought so many stories. Later, after Mem came home from work and we all had supper together, she would sit us down on the big sofa, Simon to one side of her, I to the other, with Lawrence across as our audience, and together we would read these stories aloud. Mary Poppins, Robin Hood, Robinson Crusoe. Line by line I discovered the streets of London, the forests of Sherwood, how it might feel to stand on the deck of a ship and gaze out across a glittering sea.

I thought at first that these stories were magical, like the tales of the gods my sister Mira once told me. But no, Mem promised, these places were real. Yes, Simon agreed, he and Mem had crossed just such seas on their way to India. Only, their ship had its own library, tennis court, game rooms, even a swimming pool that floated *above* the ocean. 'And,' he said, 'when we go home you'll see for your very own self.'

I looked up at Mem to see if Simon was telling the truth, but she leaned forward so abruptly that her hair swung down blocking her face. And then before I could ask her, Lawrence suggested we sing a song.

'Waltzing Matilda!' Simon cried, and that was the end of that.

When Mem used the word *home* these days she most often was talking about Safe Haven. Each night over supper she would tell us what changes she'd made there. How proud she was of her 'new girls.' What progress she'd made just in the few months since her return. It seemed that her first act had been to hire a husband-and-wife cook-and-ayah team who slept on the premises. Then, through the Catholic charities, she found two lower-caste teachers who were willing to come part-time. By February four girls had qualified for something she called 'elevation.'

Now, Simon had never been to the rescue home, and I had not been back since Lawrence stole me away, but Mem decided we all should come to witness this special occasion.

'You sure that's a good idea?' Lawrence asked.

'Of course it is,' Mem replied. 'The girls are always asking about Simon. And Kamla, aren't you curious to see the old place?'

'They'll wonder why you don't adopt them all,' Lawrence said before I could answer.

'I *have* adopted them all, in a way. And I think Kamla will inspire them.'

Simon's eye rolling only made her more determined, and

although Lawrence still didn't like the idea, he said nothing more. As for me, I was not particularly curious, but I didn't mind Mem showing me off. I didn't mind that at all.

My first surprise was the uniforms. Soft pink *salwar kameez* with navy trim.

'There was a fight over some clothing,' Mem explained. She touched the shoulder of a girl several years older than I and adjusted the navy *dupatta* over her shoulder. The girl frowned at me. 'Pretty, don't you think? I keep their other clothes and all jewelry in the safe as long as they're here. That way there's no reason to fight.'

She also had taught the inmates to vote. In this way, she said, the majority ruled what games were played each evening, and which girl would serve as house leader each month. 'Some rules, of course, are not open to debate. No makeup. No liquor or cigarettes, and *bhang* – or any drug – puts you back on the street.'

'You run a hard bargain,' Lawrence said.

'It's for their own good!'

'I'm not saying it's not. Must take some adjustment, that's all.'

'They need limits. They like them. This way they know exactly where they stand. Simon, stop that.'

A box radio sat on a table in the common room. Simon was twirling the dial. He turned the volume down so low that Mem no longer heard it, but he did not turn it off. The girls covered their mouths and whispered to one another, looking from Simon to me.

Not one of these girls had been at Safe Haven when I was last here. They did not act as those girls had, either. They did not call out or clutch at Lawrence. They did not tease him with their eyes. Without their collyrium and rouge and bright, clinging saris, they did not look like prostitutes. Instead they resembled schoolgirls, which in a way they had become.

A row of typewriters lined one wall of the common room, a bank of sewing machines the other. A large chalkboard stood in one corner, and several bookcases held not just the books that had been sitting in boxes eight months earlier but also colored files representing each girl's work. Their crayon drawings of birds and mountains and winding rivers decorated the walls. It was very different from the sprawling campus of the All-Nations School, and yet it was not so different from the school Bharati had described to me long ago.

Suddenly I understood why Lawrence objected to my coming here. I understood why these girls all stared, and I wished that I might disappear – or else change from my Western skirt and blouse into one of their *salwar kameez* and take my place in their line.

But Mem was calling us outside for the ceremony. Chairs had been placed on the veranda. The two teachers and the husband-and-wife cook-and-ayah were waiting. Simon and Lawrence and I were seated in front with Vijay, who had recently completed his examinations and now served as the rescue home's advocate and general translator. The rest of the girls sat behind us except for the four honorees who stood before Mem at the podium.

These four ranged in age from fourteen to sixteen. Two had completed grammar school before going into the red-light district. One had been taught to read Hindi by her parents and the fourth by a *babu* who had taken a liking to her in the brothel. Here at the rescue home they had an advantage over their illiterate sisters much like the advantage my father had given me. And now Mem was to reward them.

'You should be very proud,' she started off. 'You have done well. You have learned to read. Reading will allow you to educate yourselves and eventually to take good jobs. I would like you to start by working with the other girls here at Salamat Jannat. You will be teachers' helpers. In the evenings you are to read to the other girls, assist them with their lessons. And the teachers will give you special study assignments to improve your skills even more.'

The girls stood in a row, like a quartet of ruffled finches. Their eyes were dark and round, lips pinched. Two clasped their hands. The other two hugged their elbows.

Vijay caught Mem's eye and rubbed his fingertips together.

'Of course, you'll be paid for your work!' Mem took from the podium four small red purses, which she distributed among the girls. 'Three rupees per day to begin, more depending on the effort you make. But this is just the beginning. There are many positions in shops and offices around Delhi for which you may qualify. You must look for notices each day in the newspaper. If you find an appropriate position, you will be allowed to pursue it.' She turned to address all the inmates. 'As I see it, we are partners in a mission. That mission is to equip you with the skills and support each of you needs to achieve an independent life.'

Bimla, the girl whose *babu* had taught her to read, shyly raised her hand. She had glistening hair, which hung in two pigtails over her shoulders. As she voiced her question in Hindi to Vijay she kept her eyes on Mem's feet.

'She wants to know if you will allow her to leave the home in order to find her boyfriend, as she has not been in contact with him since her arrest.'

Mem sighed. 'That is *just* what I'm talking about! No, you may not go out looking for boyfriends. You must not look to marriage as the answer to your problems.' She stopped. A muscle moved in her cheek. Then she turned again to the others. 'As I've told you before, if I catch any of you flirting with men, either on or off the premises, you will be given a single warning. If it happens again, I will consider this grounds for dismissal.'

'But, Mem – ' Vijay tugged on his ear as if sending her a stage cue. Lawrence squinted at his fingernails.

'No, I mean it. There are hundreds of girls who will gladly take their place if they don't like my rules.'

A murmur ran through those girls behind us, and the four up front stared straight ahead. India was a country where most girls were married off by age twelve, where widows were expected to throw themselves on their husbands' funeral pyres, and parents who could not afford dowry killed their daughters at birth. Only prostitutes remained unmarried. Was Mem lying, then, when she said they were prostitutes no longer?

The girls' fingers closed over their new red purses, confusion straining their faces. I shrank in my seat, trying not to look at them, but I was not to get away so easily.

'I want you all to meet Kamla,' Mem said, crooking her finger for me to stand.

Simon jabbed me in the ribs. He thought it was funny. I stumbled forward.

'Kamla is an example for you all.' Mem placed a book in my hands. 'Just a few months ago she could barely speak English. Now

I would like you to listen as she reads this passage from the great Indian poet Rabindranath Tagore.'

As I stared at the page she had opened for me, the words seemed to swim. I heard Lawrence clear his throat, Simon shift his feet. All eyes were on me. I felt them like a hundred pinpricks.

' "Where the Mind is Without Fear",' I read finally.

I swallowed. I had read aloud at school. I read aloud with Mem and Simon every night. This was the first time I felt my heart pounding through my chest, the first time my voice lodged in my throat.

Mem's hand squeezed my shoulder.

I read on, not hearing, not thinking the words, only reading the sound from the page.

And was met with dead silence.

Then Mem stepped away from me. 'Beautiful,' she said. 'That was beautiful, Kamla.'

She began to clap. Lawrence and Vijay and the staff smiled stiffly. Then Simon clapped and whistled out the side of his mouth. Finally the others joined in.

Mem told me I should be proud of myself. Why, then, did I feel so ashamed?

I would never go back to Salamat Jannat. If I had to feign illness or run away, I would never see this place again.

But the very next week Mem called me into her bedroom and sat me down at her dressing table. She removed my pink butterfly barrette and began to brush and braid my hair the way she used to during our trek. 'Your performance the other day gave me a wonderful idea,' she said. 'I've invited a lady named Mrs Solomon to have tea with us. She's going to write an article for the *New Delhi Gazette*.'

I watched her in the mirror as she tugged at my head, squinting and frowning and turning me this way and that. She seemed nervous for me to make a good impression on this Mrs Solomon. 'If people read our story, they might be moved to donate money to Salamat Jannat.'

Our story, I repeated silently.

Mem continued, 'Bertie's been to the home a few times, and

she's talked to Hari, so she knows its limitations. She's American, Jewish, from New York I think. Friendly. The *Gazette*'s not much – mostly social puff pieces. But the women who read it are the same ones who've been gossiping about us, so maybe this will crimp some of their rumors. It could also help over at the embassy next time we try for your visa. Especially since she's agreed not to mention Aidan. There.' She finished tying my hair into two thick bunches with black velvet ribbons and refastened the pink butterfly above my left ear. Then she stood back to admire her handiwork.

Outside, the day was overcast, and the rest of the room – including Mem – wore a violet shadow. But I wore a new black-and-white checked dress and sparkling black patent leather shoes, and the lamplight reflected in my eyes and hair. 'You look wonderful,' she said, and leaned to kiss me. I watched the kiss in the mirror as if I were outside myself.

Soon Mrs Solomon arrived, and we sat down around the tea tray. Nagu and the cook had outdone themselves, so excited were they to be entertaining. There were soft yellow cakes and salty crisps, crustless tea sandwiches and biscuits in frilly paper nests. Lawrence had dragged Simon off to the cinema to keep him from attacking the tray. Mem had consoled them with promises of leftovers, but watching Mrs Solomon help herself to a large pile of sweets, I was not so sure there would be any leftovers.

'I do love these Indian teas,' she said, settling her plate on her knee and lifting a butter cookie toward her mouth. Then she laughed a hearty, ha-ha laugh. 'But you can certainly see that!'

It was true. Mrs Solomon was a padded lady with round gray eyes, her pink face encircled by springy brown curls. She proceeded to tell us that although she had only arrived a few months ago, she had always wanted to come to India. Her British uncle, Colonel William Solomon, had lived for years in Madras and sent the most exotic presents when she was growing up. Strange musical instruments and birdcages, wooden cosmetics boxes and bells that one wore on the hands and feet. Only when she was older did she learn that her uncle had been active in the Vigilance Movement, and most of these objects had been given to him as gifts by *nautch* girls he had rescued.

'Perhaps you can see now why I was particularly interested in your story, Joanna,' she said.

'It's Kamla's story more than mine,' Mem said.

Mrs Solomon licked a crust of sugar from her lips and beamed at me. 'Isn't she an angel!'

Mrs Solomon meant no harm. She was like a grown-up baby, all full of pinkness and flesh and innocence. But her words made me uncomfortable. Did she not see me? Did she not know where I had come from and what had been done to me? I thought that was why she was here, to write my story. I thought she must at least be able to glimpse what the girls at Safe Haven could see so plainly – that I was no angel.

'Yes,' Mem was saying. 'I knew at once that Kamla was different. In part that's her heritage – she's half Sikh and half Tungan Chinese. At first we thought she was a hill child – from the Himalayas – but then we learned she was born in Sinkiang. And when we determined she was an orphan, I just knew I had to adopt her.'

Mem turned her eyes on me – they appeared golder than usual under the yellow lamplight. I had never heard her speak of me in such a way. I did not recognize this half Sikh, half Tungan Chinese orphan who might have been an ornamental pot, or an exotic pet.

'But, you know,' she raced on, 'every one of the girls at Salamat Jannat has a unique story of her own. I'm happy to tell you ours, but you must understand, Bertie, *all* these girls deserve the chance I'm giving Kamla, to be educated and lead normal, productive lives. Sadly, adoption is a realistic solution in only the rarest cases. That's why I prefer to describe the home as a "school of opportunity" rather than a rescue mission. But we're just beginning this new approach, and it's not cheap. If your readers are moved to help, we need books, clothing, vocational training and equipment, funds for more teachers and facilities . . .'

Mrs Solomon finally set aside her plate and took up pencil and pad. I became conscious of her lead scratching the paper. It sounded like a lizard trying to escape from a cardboard carton. *Tsk, tsk, tsk.*

As Mem talked on about conditions at Salamat Jannat, her words seemed to blend together. It struck me as the talk, not of Mrs Shaw, but of those radish-nosed, cloud-haired *firenghi* Indrani once warned me about. Those *memsahibs* who pretended to save the souls of lost girls, when all they truly cared about were their palaces and ball gowns.

'Kamla,' Mrs Solomon said, for the first time addressing me directly. 'Tell me about meeting Mrs Shaw.'

I looked to Mem. She held her cup to her lips, then slowly set it down. I watched the muscles of her long throat tighten as she swallowed. Two silver dewdrops dangled from her mango-shaped ears. I tried to remember. She was slimmer than she had been then, her body even more hard-edged. Her older eyes and hair now made me think of the whiskey she and Lawrence drank, rather than imagined honey. 'Well,' I said, 'the first time she comes to G. B. Road, even before she reaches my house I am watching her. She is *firenghi*, but, you know, I do not feel she is a stranger.'

Mem smiled at her hands. I could see she was pleased.

'And the day she rescued you . . . ?'

I hesitated. In all our time together Mem had never asked, and I had not told her that it was her inquiries which had caused Indrani to turn me over to Golba. Mem merely thought she had failed to save me.

Smiling at the good-hearted Mrs Solomon, I said merely, 'Yes.'

'Actually,' Mem said, 'you mustn't make it sound so heroic. Kamla rescued herself. You see, for me to take her from the house where she was living, I would, in effect, have had to arrest her. But because she gave herself up to us, we were able to take her directly under our protection. She's the one who took the risks, escaping from her keeper and finding her way alone and penniless out of Old Delhi. Can you imagine, a girl that young?'

Mrs Solomon looked at me. She lifted her pencil from its pad and rubbed her nose with the back of her hand. 'How young are you?' she asked.

It sounded across the chill of the room like such a simple question. But I did not know what to say. A look at Mem's face told me she, too, was confounded by the reversal. Not how old, but how young. Mrs Solomon waited, turning her gray eyes from one to the other of us. Sounds of washing up clattered from the kitchen. I felt Mem's husband watching from his photographs and was drawn back to the scene of the explosion in Sinkiang. I recalled

Mem's face that night, the false light of the flashlights yellowing her skin. And something else. A feeling of relief within my own breast. A feeling, even, of gladness that now in the contest of sorrow Mrs Shaw and I were even.

Mem was explaining that because my birth date was unknown, she could only guess at my age, but according to the doctor I must now be about twelve. Mrs Solomon wrote that down. Then she pulled a camera from her large handbag to take our picture. Mem slid an arm around me, cheek against my forehead.

We smiled.

2

'Say cheese!' Lawrence heard Bertie Solomon bray as he opened the front door. Fortunately, the entry was not visible from the living room. He could slip right back out and rejoin Simon in the servants' quarters with Dilip and Bhanu. Simon's blow-by-blow of the Marx Brothers movie they'd just seen was bound to be more entertaining than the ladies' tea party, which he'd assumed would be over by now. Lawrence had met the effervescent Mrs Solomon on her arrival. He was pleased Joanna had found a champion and that her get-together seemed to be succeeding. That was about as much as he wished to do with it.

But as he was backing out, his eye fell on the day's incoming mail stacked on the hall table. A pale blue aerogram with US stamps crowned the pile. Automatically Lawrence scanned the return address. Milwaukee, Wisconsin.

He knew – or believed he knew – everyone in the States to whom Joanna had written for help. Most of these supposed friends had replied with condolence cards, clearly presuming Aidan to be dead and saying they hoped she would ring them up when she returned home. None of these friends lived in Wisconsin. But Lawrence knew from his own investigation that Alice James's mother and sister did.

'Oh, one more!' Bertie Solomon cried in the other room. 'I'm just never sure I know what I'm doing, and we'd better be safe than sorry.'

Lawrence leaned over the table. The name above the Milwaukee address was small and pinched. It looked like a woman's hand. G. Darling, he deciphered finally, and whisked the envelope into his pocket.

Out back he told Simon he was off to a meeting, then took a cycle rickshaw to his flat. He steamed open the seal. What Joanna didn't know wouldn't hurt her, and a day's delay would make no difference. This was simply a precaution, he told himself. He was protecting her.

February 1, 1950
  Milwaukee, Wisconsin
  Dear Mrs Shaw,
    My name is Grace Darling. You don't know me, but Alice James was my sister. After months of runaround and misinformation from the State Department, my mother and I received a call last week from your friend Ben Eldon, who informed us that you were responsible for finding my sister's body and seeing her properly buried. Ben said he was contacting us on your behalf and asked if my family had any information that might help you in your search for your husband. I was sorry to have to tell him how little we knew, but I was grateful to him for offering a way to get in touch with you.
    However belatedly, I want to thank you, Mrs Shaw, for your generosity under circumstances that must have been unbearable. I wish I had more to tell you, but I am older than Alice by eighteen years, and we were never close. I am a housewife and the mother of two. Our parents were both schoolteachers, pillars of the community. We were none of us much for adventure, except Alice. In fact, I can no more imagine running off to China in the face of that Communist invasion than I can imagine going on vacation among a bunch of headhunters. Alice was always a puzzle to us. She was a girl of high spirits, all right, but so stubborn that no one could tell her what was right or safe or smart. I have no idea what she even thought she was doing in China.
    The State Department said they had to rely on Chinese

253

Nationalist reports for information about the explosion that killed Alice. Those reports blame the bomb on rebel tribesmen – Communists, I think they mean – though they call the explosion 'accidental.' I would like to know whether you agree with this explanation . . .

You see, America is a kind of peculiar place right now. Maybe you can't see it from all the way over there in India, or maybe that's why you're still there. Considering what Mr Eldon told us, I wouldn't blame you. The other day Senator McCarthy released a list of more than two hundred men and women with the State Department who he claims are Communists. Then yesterday I got a call from some news reporters asking was it true that my sister was a Communist agent? Was it true she and your husband were on their way to meet with other Reds in a secret camp near the Soviet border? Was it true they were having an affair?

What can I say when people ask me things like that, Mrs Shaw? I don't mean or want to hurt you. Please believe that these are not my own questions, but as they are being thrown about, many of them in the press, I thought you should know. I thought you might even know the answers. Alice was my sister. Can you tell me what's true?

Lawrence reread the letter twice. Eldon was one of the first friends back in the States Joanna had contacted upon her return to Delhi, and the only one who had urged her to keep her hopes up. He'd also warned her she was better off out of the country, given the climate in Washington, but promised to keep quietly digging for any information that might help locate Aidan. According to Joanna, Eldon had as many contacts in Washington as Aidan did. 'If anyone knows anything, Ben will find out.' Since then, Eldon had sent a Christmas card saying he was still digging. He hadn't mentioned Grace Darling.

What's true? Lawrence had no idea. But one thing was certain. Joanna's precarious equilibrium would shatter if she saw this letter.

Was it true she and your husband were on their way to meet with other Reds in a secret camp near the Soviet border? Was it true they were having an affair?

254

He folded the pale blue sheet and hid it under a pile of his own correspondence.

For a month it was that simple.

Then one morning, after he'd returned from his rounds and was about to bullshit his way through yet another 'update' to Jack, he heard footsteps coming up the stairs. Not the heavy thump of Mrs D'Costa or the light drag of the sweeper, but a quiet, tentative tread that stopped and started. And stopped directly in front of his door.

Lawrence didn't entertain visitors. There was too much potentially compromising material in the flat, and even if much of it was encrypted, even if most of it served no purpose, he was responsible for protecting the identities of the drivers and hotel clerks, travel agents and relief workers who had become his key informants. So, from the first, he'd warned Joanna that the flat would insult her feminine sensibilities. She'd replied that she would feel 'sordid' meeting him there, in any case, and because this suited his own constraints, he'd let her nonsensical reasoning slide. The children had begged more emphatically to see his 'secret hideaway' but he held his ground even with them, claiming that no room was as stuffy, messy, and boring as an office where a writer sat all day. Eventually they, too, quit asking.

'Lawrence?' Joanna sounded as if she were leaning her face against the door. 'You'd better let me in.'

He quickly shoved his paperwork out of sight. Stacks of books teetered in the corners. The *charpoy* was covered with maps, and dust motes shimmered in the sunlight between the blinds. The place was hot and close and every bit as uninviting as advertised.

He opened the door. She held a paper parcel in one hand, her straw hat in the other. Her face was drawn, eyes wet. The parcel he recognized as a bottle from the government liquor store.

'What is it? What's happened?'

'April fools,' she said tonelessly and kicked the door shut behind her. She dropped her hat on the floor. She tore off the newsprint and held up the bottle. Indian whiskey. 'It's been nine months!'

Her hand trembled as she passed him the bottle, then reached into her shoulder bag and pulled out the insurance policy they'd found in Aidan's closet.

255

Lawrence set the bottle down and folded her in his arms. Her whole body was shaking. Suddenly she lifted her face and kissed him so hard he tasted blood. He felt her nails dig into his scalp, then her hands fumbling with his belt.

'Joanna!'

But she would not stop. She was out of her shoes, yanked her hair from its clasp, with one sweep cleared the bed. She pulled her shift off over her head. He smelled carnations as she buried her face and fists in his skin. He loved her because and in spite of those fists.

Afterward, she lay with her back to him. The corrugations of her ribs expanded and contracted as he curled himself around her, and he sensed that her eyes were open as he skated his palm over her shoulder, but she would not look at him.

'What happens,' she asked finally, 'if I declare him dead, and he's alive?'

Lawrence rolled away from her. A horn blared in the street. Soon the children would need to be fetched from school. It was more than hot enough for a swim. Then there would be supper, reading, the evening routine. He stared at the unopened bottle of whiskey on the floor.

'No one's forcing you to declare him dead. If it's the money—'

'I love you, Lawrence. But that doesn't mean I've stopped loving him.'

'I know that.'

She sat up. 'I shouldn't have come here. I shouldn't have looked at the calendar. I shouldn't *think.*' She got up, collected her clothes, and disappeared into his squalid toilet. He pulled on his shirt and trousers.

When she emerged, she was dressed, her face composed.

'I warned you,' he said. 'It's not the Ritz.'

'You warned me,' she said, and came to him where he sat on the edge of the bed. She kissed his forehead. 'I'm sorry. Time . . . I saw the date, and I just felt blindsided.'

'I know.'

'I wouldn't blame you if—'

'I'm not going anywhere, Joanna.'

Hands on his shoulders, she sighed. Then a catch in her throat made him look up. Her eyes were fixed on his desk. At first he

256

thought he'd left out the letter from Alice James's sister. But no, the desk held only a shambles of books and, pushed to the corner, his photograph of Davey.

Lawrence knew the picture by heart. Tracy had taken it. Davey at the beach, ocean at his back, age six with arms outstretched for the ball that Lawrence, out of frame, had just thrown. The boy wore a white short-sleeve shirt with the collar wings askew. His mouth was open, head tipped back, the sun full on his wafer-round face. He was so skinny, with jet-black hair and high, wide cheekbones. Light danced in his eyes, and he had written his name in red grease pencil on a diagonal over his chest. A child's hand.

Joanna moved toward the desk as if drawn by a wire. She picked up the picture, placed a fingertip against the glass. 'He's beautiful,' she said gently. 'Such bright black eyes.'

'That's his mother's doing.'

'Ah.' She rubbed her lips together. Then, finally, 'What happened, Lawrence?'

'You don't need to know that.'

'You know everything about me.'

'Do I?'

'Please. I think I do need to know.'

He sat forward, hands between his knees. 'It'll take some of that.' He pointed at the whiskey. She placed the picture in his hands and returned to the bathroom. Through the open door he watched her rinse out the single glass he kept there. She came back, filled the glass with the thick amber liquid, and sat down beside him. He drank deeply, then handed her the glass. She did the same.

'My parents were country people,' he began. 'My father was born in the outback, and my mother grew up there. They hated city life, needed space to think, to function. That's one thing you need to know, I guess. Another is that my father, Charlie, was cheap. It didn't matter that we had one of the biggest ranches in New South Wales. Or maybe that's what made him so frugal, always saving against the next drought. The war only made it worse. The rationing, the loss of me and my brother as hands when we went off to serve – the loss of me permanently, as it turned out. Even after the war ended he continued to skimp, especially on petrol. Tracy and Davey and I lived in Sydney, about six hundred miles from the ranch. When my parents came to visit they drove an old Morris touring car that they'd bought when I was about five. A huge thing, high off the ground, and difficult to maneuver. You could hardly see out the rear window, the glass was so scratched, and it burned fuel like the devil, but my father refused to pay out the money for a new, more efficient model. Instead, he had this inventive trick of turning off the motor on every downhill slope. They only came to visit us once a year, and the only reason they did that was because my father had figured out he could coast halfway.'

Joanna refilled the glass. She didn't say anything, but Lawrence could see her brow knitting. 'You need to know all of this,' he said. 'Otherwise it won't make sense.'

She nodded and handed him the glass. He rolled it between his hands. 'Like I said, my parents didn't belong in the city. Though they hardly spoke, let alone argue at home, they bickered constantly when they came to visit. Part of the problem was that our house, a quaint little cottage in Pennant Hills, really wasn't big enough for guests. Another was that Tracy had her hands full with Davey and, truth be told, she thought my father overbearing and my mother broken-spirited, which was about right, although living in the outback seemed to have that effect on most couples I knew. Tracy was a nurse from Melbourne and couldn't live without her friends and parties, so she and my parents had little in common, and I wasn't much help, being at the office all day. My father was too cheap to consider staying elsewhere, but my mother especially hated the crowding, the sense that they were imposing, and so every morning she would urge him to take her out for a drive. Of course, he didn't want to spend the petrol.'

He emptied the glass feeling the whiskey like a lick of flame. 'All right. Now you need to picture the setting. Our house sat on a knoll with a long driveway to one side that sloped at about a twenty-degree angle down to the street. A privet hedge tall as our house ran alongside. It was a good neighborhood, lots of families, kids out morning and night, especially during warm weather, everyone looking out for each other, you know?'

Joanna nodded.

'I had to be at the office at nine, but Davey was an early riser, so I liked to play with him a bit before heading off. And my parents, being farmers, were up at dawn, too.

'At breakfast that morning I remember my father was on a tear over the price of coffee and tea, insisting that Tracy and I threw money away, and he could live like a prince on half what we spent in a month, and perhaps what he and my mother should do *this* day was prove to us that our neighborhood grocer, a nice Greek fellow, was stealing us blind. My mother said, actually, what they should do was shop for a new car, since the Morris had been making strange noises ever since they left the ranch. Davey and I escaped to the sidewalk. He'd seen some older boys playing American baseball and wanted to learn how to pitch, and I'd played a bit with some of the soldiers I met in the war, so the day before, I'd bought him a Spalding baseball and mitt. Now out front I showed him how to pull back his arm, then snap it forward.'

He winced, remembering Davey's laughter as he let the ball fly, his own pride at the power of his son's right arm. Joanna's hand rested on his knee, but he couldn't feel the weight of it. He couldn't physically feel anything.

'A dog was barking. Blackie, the neighbor's German shepherd. And the trolley went by, packed with morning commuters. Down the block I saw Davey's friend, Paul Grant, who was a little older but looked up to Davey because he was so much more athletic than Paul. Maybe I heard our screen door. I think I did. It was a hot morning, and the sun was in my eyes as I threw the ball back. It fell short, and Davey ran forward to catch it. Henry Colson, an engineer who lived across the street, stopped and called out, "You want to be a Yankee when you grow up, son?" But Davey paid no attention. He had such power of concentration, when he put his mind to something, the rest of the world disappeared.'

He refilled the glass for himself this time. The whiskey blurred the image in his head, as if he were looking at it through heat waves. 'Davey was only seven years old, but he was throwing long, and I kept backing up, and he kept coming forward. I was on the wrong side of that privet hedge. I could barely see our roof up there over the top of it, and it stretched all the way down to end just short of the sidewalk.'

'Oh!' Joanna's voice curled in her throat. 'I know—'

'You see it, do you? How we were both so caught up in our game? As Davey pulled back his arm again, I saw Paul racing forward, hands in the air, screaming. I thought it was a ploy to distract Davey, kid stuff. Dimly, in the back of my mind, I knew that wasn't like Paul. He was a galoshes sort of lad – earnest, kind. But he was too far down the street, and I couldn't hear him, couldn't see his expression, and Davey had his back to him. Davey was facing me.'

He felt his voice floating away from him. 'Suddenly, just before he let go of the ball, I realized he was standing in the middle of the driveway. I had my mouth open, my hand pushing the air for him to back up, just in case. The angle of the drive made it impossible to see a child standing at the bottom when you were driving in reverse. I'd had a fright with Paul once when he was little, so I knew. I *knew.*' He shut his eyes but could not escape. 'The warning never got past my lips. I saw a flash of sun on steel, and then the Morris's gray rear fender slammed into Davey's shoulder, knocking him to the pavement.

'My father was letting the car coast to the street before starting the engine. That's why we didn't hear it. And sitting so high, with that useless rear window and the angle of the drive, he never saw—'

Joanna's face was a mess of tears. She pleaded with her eyes for him to stop. He said, 'The left rear tire of that heavy old car crushed my boy's pelvis and spine. Charlie stepped on the brake while the weight was still on him. He said later he thought he'd hit a cat or a squirrel.' Lawrence stared at one of the many cracks in the wall. 'Davey was conscious, but we didn't dare move him, and it took nearly an hour for the ambulance to come. By then it was too late.'

There was a long silence. He could feel her eyes on him, but refused to look at her. 'Now your curiosity is satisfied.'

The coldness of his rebuke curled between them, refusing comfort from any quarter, but Joanna chose this time to reach past it. She pulled him into her arms, and for several minutes they held each other, rocking back and forth until finally they came to rest in the belly of his bed. After that they lay without moving or speaking. Together they let the clamor and heat of New Delhi roll over them.

With the arrival of summer and school holidays, Lawrence took Simon and me to the Cecil or Jai Mahal hotel to swim almost every morning. The groups seated around these pools included rich *firenghi* and high-caste Indians alike, but usually the two did not mingle, and as the only white family with a native child, we drew stares and whispers from both sides.

Sometimes the comments carried over the water: 'A touch of the tar brush,' or 'Charity case.' Unlike Mem, Lawrence did not ignore these remarks. Instead, he would address me loudly, in his most proud voice. 'Princess Kamla of Kashgaria, would you and young Simon care for a swim?' Then everyone on the pool terrace would look as I stared gravely back at them.

The game did not fool me. Were it not for Lawrence, I would have been shown the gate regardless of my regal bearing. From this point on, however, the test was between Simon and me. For we had to cross the blistering concrete on our bare feet without a whimper. We were to step gracefully into the pool, looking neither to right nor left, and only when the cold blue water closed above our heads were we allowed to scream.

Simon took full advantage of this self-granted permission. I would hear his yells underneath the surface muted as the mumblings of a flea, but when I opened my eyes his mad dancing made him look more like a scrawny underwater Shiva. Simon loved the game of playacting, first appearing so solemn and controlled, then erupting into this clownish performance. He'd puff out his cheeks and cock his arms, put his finger to his head like a gun. Once he yanked down his swim trunks and waggled his naked bottom at me, just barely getting the suit back up before he ran out of breath.

I played along with these antics at first, but it didn't seem wise to encourage him and so, soon, I began to pull back into myself. While he pranced on his underwater stage, I would go into hiding. Even before I learned to swim, I could lie flat on the shallow bottom and watch the scattered patterns of light break along the pool's surface.

'You must be half fish to stay under so long,' Lawrence said more than once. His frown told me he disapproved, that my time underwater alarmed him, but then, stepping to the side of the pool, he would correct himself, saluting me: 'Half *royal* fish.' And he would swing out his arms, sunshine catching in the hairs that covered his shoulders and chest. Bouncing on his knees, every muscle tensed, he would propel himself into a dive that carried him clear to the other end.

And then I would join with Simon in a chorus of pleas for Lawrence to give us our daily lesson. That summer I mastered the front crawl, and Simon and I both learned to perform a passable racing dive. And I pretended to believe Lawrence, that the raised eyebrows and whispers that followed me each time we crossed the hotel lawn indicated awe and admiration rather than disgust.

'Your beauty and grace, Your Majesty, drives ordinary mortals mad with envy. 'Ave pity on 'em for they'll never know the 'alf of you.'

I can still see him, one large white towel wrapped around his waist, another turbaned around his head, as he clasped his hands and fell to his knees, gazing up at me with his push-pull eyes as if *I* had the world to offer *him*.

By July Delhi had cracked open, baking before the monsoon's deluge, which week after week refused to come. Mem and Lawrence decided we all needed 'a change of pace,' so we climbed into Mem's green Austin one morning before dawn and drove north all day across the searing plains and up into the foothills to the hill town Kausali. Lawrence called it a birthday trip, as Simon was just turning ten and Mem had suggested we celebrate my birthday at the same time. Of course, we did not know my true birthday. Only my father had ever made an occasion of this event, but he had done this with gifts brought home from afar, weeks or months after the actual date, and my years in the flash house had erased any notion I might once have had of the season of my birth. In any case, Simon's generous soul exulted in sharing his special day with me, and Lawrence joked that it was a good thing; if they'd had to foot the bill for two separate parties, he and Mem couldn't have afforded this trip to the mountains.

'You see?' Mem said. 'Every sacrifice has its reward.'

Her eyes were on the road, so I couldn't tell whether she was answering Lawrence or speaking to us all. She was steering around an uphill turn so sharp that the car shuddered. The hillside dropped away long and steep, and there was no barricade. I wondered for the first time why it was always Mem who drove.

But Lawrence seemed unconcerned. 'I don't believe in sacrifice,' he said. 'But I'll take all the rewards I can get.' Then he threw his arm across the back of the front seat and half turned to Simon and me. He winked so that he was looking at us only through his silver eye, then he winked again, so that only his green eye was watching. He seemed to be two people behind a single skin.

Kasauli was cool and green. Terraced fields stepped down either side of the narrow ridge on which the village perched. There were patches of forest, with views of snowcapped mountains to the north. To the south stretched the bleached yellow plain we'd just crossed, with the Yamuna River like a silver snake. Simon and I put our heads out the windows and breathed in the cool pine-soaked air. We were greeted with yawns by rows of brown monkeys sunning themselves on the roadside walls, more solemnly by the families of black-faced langurs keeping watch from the trees. It was not as grand as Kashmir, not as bleak as the Karakorams or as wild as the Tien Shan, but it seemed familiar nonetheless.

The road ended in a square car park filled with the vehicles of other *firenghi* escaping the heat of the plains. Before we could open the doors we were surrounded by porters and rickshaw pullers offering their services. These were hill men, some locals with orange hair and green eyes, others Nepali and Tibetans whose broad faces reminded me of Tot. Lawrence passed our luggage to two of the local porters, who loaded up quickly and trotted ahead. We followed on foot along a narrow path past native shophouses, hotels and bungalows built by the British, and a steepled church made of gray stone. Soon we were out of the town. Footpaths slid sharply from the main trail to houses tucked below. The breezes carried the fragrance of wood smoke, and the last of the daylight fell like lace across the dirt tracks. As we walked, Mem breathed deeply and swung her arms. Lawrence took her hand.

The path to our guesthouse plunged down an incline between rows of pipal and deodar trees. The house itself, which sat out of view from the main trail, faced north into the mountains. It had two stories, a tin roof painted red, and a small surrounding yard and rose garden. A radio crackled from one of the upstairs windows.

Mrs Swetenberg, the elderly lady who owned the house, answered our knock herself. She wore a long black skirt and a starched white blouse, and welcomed us warmly. We were her only guests. Her husband had been a major in the British Indian Army, though he had gone to heaven many years ago, and she was born in Denmark. She told all this in a single sweep of words, as if it was important we know her story before entering her home.

Simon leaned over and asked, didn't she remind me of the little old lady in his Babar books? We agreed, she seemed very nice. So nice, in fact, that by lunchtime the next day, she and Mem had baked us a birthday cake.

It was iced in chocolate with yellow frosting roses around its base. Simon, who craved sweets, was quite beside himself at the sight of it and gulped down his meal in anticipation. I did not share the intensity of his craving, but I was amused by the excitement he always brought to such moments. Finally Mem and Lawrence began lighting the candles – twelve on one side for me and ten for Simon on the other, with two in the middle, Mem explained, for good luck. 'Children, say thank you to Mrs Swetenberg.'

'Thank you,' we cried.

Mrs Swetenberg's face lit up. 'You are most very welcome, but it is I who should thank you for having me to your party. If only I'd been blessed with children. I do so love having young people in my Kasauli home.'

She said it just like that, as if she had fifteen or sixteen other homes. It seemed quite natural, then, for Simon to ask, 'Where are your other homes?' But this brought tears to her eyes. She pressed at them with a white handkerchief.

'No,' she said, 'you misunderstand. They're all gone now. I have no other home anymore.'

Mem touched the old lady's hand, and a look passed between them that seemed briefly to exclude everyone else in the room. Mrs Swetenberg sighed and closed her eyes.

Lawrence finished lighting the candles. Then he loudly hummed a note, and everyone sang 'Happy Birthday to You.' That broke the sadness. Lawrence shouted, 'Who can blow out the most candles! On your marks, get set . . . Go!'

Simon and I leaned over the cake. Our heads banged together as we blew. Three breaths later the flames were out.

Mem insisted that Mrs Swetenberg judge. The old lady took her time. She tapped one long finger against her chin, staring hard through the field of smoke. She inspected one set of candles, then the other, frowned at each of us in turn. At last she said, 'Simon, you certainly blew out more than your ten, and Kamla, you fell a bit short of your twelve, but that boils down to a tie. I suggest you receive equal slices of cake.' She placed a hand on each of our heads, and smiled at Mem. 'All right?'

'All right.' Mem smiled back. She liked the old lady. I could see that. And she liked this place. She seemed more at ease here than she ever seemed in Delhi. She had fixed her hair in a pretty fashion, clipping it back with a sprig of jasmine behind one ear. Even her lipstick seemed softer, the color of a fresh peach instead of the geranium red she normally wore.

I looked to Lawrence, saw the way his eyes played over her bent head, the slope of her arm as she helped Mrs Swetenberg remove the candles. He smiled and swallowed at the same time.

We ate our cake. Simon and Mrs Swetenberg both had second helpings. Then Lawrence brought out our birthday presents. Simon's consisted of a wooden cricket bat ('For playing with Nagu's boys,' Mem explained) and, from Lawrence, a spyglass in a leather case. Mine were a copy of *Jane Eyre* ('At the rate you're progressing in school,' Mem assured me, 'you'll be ready for the Brontë sisters before you know it') and, from Lawrence, a black-banded Timex watch, ordered from the States.

I kissed Mem and Lawrence each on the cheek to thank them. Lawrence returned the kiss with a hug so strong my shoulders ached afterward. Then Mrs Swetenberg excused herself to take her nap, and Simon asked if he and I could go outside. It was a fine day, warm and clear, and he wanted to test his new spyglass.

'Be back before dark,' Mem said. It was not even two in the afternoon.

The guesthouse was surrounded by paths that led up and down

the mountain. Even the immediate grounds stretched over several levels, with old servant quarters and sheds and other outbuildings to each side. But Simon wanted to stay close to the main house. 'Let's spy on 'em,' he said, training the glass back across the ribbon of lawn as Mem and Lawrence came through the dining room door to the terrace. Lawrence waved. Simon lowered the glass. 'We need to go somewhere they can't see us,' he whispered. 'I want to see if I can read their lips.'

I was willing to play Simon's games because he was my brother, because I was expected to behave like a child, and because I had no other friends. In truth, while I enjoyed his enthusiasm for play, and marveled at it, I did not often share it. This game, however, appealed to me.

We went behind the servant quarters, up the hillside behind the house, and back down on the far side of an overgrown rose garden that bordered the terrace. We squatted under a veil of petals that, when Simon passed me the spyglass, appeared as enormous pink blurs in the lens. When I aimed between them, however, Mem's and Lawrence's faces leapt into focus, seeming as close to me as Simon. Lawrence sat sideways on a lawn chair with his hands knotted between his knees. Mem lay on the chaise beside him, one arm up against the sun. She had removed her shoes, and her bare toes pointed skyward, ankles crossed, her skirt fanning out around her like a great blue blossom.

In fact, we hardly needed to read their lips. Except for the occasional trill of a bird, the rustle of langurs in the tall pines, and the faint scrape as Mrs Swetenberg's *mali* raked the front walk, the mountain was quiet. The breeze carried Mem's and Lawrence's voices as effectively as a telephone. I offered Simon the glass, but he was so pleased at my interest in his game that he motioned for me to keep it.

'You realize,' Lawrence was saying, 'a year ago we were in Kashgar.'

'Seems more like twelve,' Mem said. She cupped her hands over her eyes to watch a formation of geese flap across the sky.

'Not all twelve equally unbearable, I hope.'

'Not equally.' She smiled at him. 'No.'

Her arm came down so that her elbow lay crooked above her

head. The sun beat on her face. She closed her eyes, and the smile ended.

He placed a hand on her ankle. 'You've done all you can, Jo.'

Suddenly Mrs Swetenberg's radio came on, pouring static from her upstairs window. A man's voice sounded, loud and stern, then quieted to a murmur.

Mem sat up and rubbed her forehead. 'I don't know.'

'At a certain point, it's not about him anymore. You realize that.'

'But what is that point?' She shook her head. 'The worst of it is, I don't know whether I love him or hate him.'

'Maybe the answer is both.' He leaned toward her. 'It usually is, you know.'

'There's nothing *usual*—'

He cut her off. 'The thing is, what if he really is dead? You need proof, I know. But what if there *is* no proof, or no way to find it? What if I asked you to—'

Simon ripped the glass from my hands. I'd forgotten he was there. Still, I didn't see why he had to grab. But then I realized he was not merely taking the spyglass. He was growling – whining. He yanked me by the arm. 'Come away!' He began to scream, dragging me now, his face like a fright mask. I had no idea he was so strong. His shrieking seemed that of a mouse, but a mouse with the energy of an elephant.

'Simon – !'

I watched the spyglass fall behind us, the lens cracking on a rock, but Simon paid no heed. He had me by the sleeve and was running. We rounded the servant quarters and nearly tripped over Mrs Swetenberg's *mali*.

'*Ek dam jao!*' Simon screamed at the man. '*Saap!*'

'Snake?' I asked. 'What snake?'

'It was in the grass, right by your foot.'

As the gardener grabbed up his hand scythe and motioned for Simon to show the way, I realized I was trembling. We hurried back, the *mali* sending up a shout of alarm that brought the entire household to attention. Mrs Swetenberg was roused from her nap. The cook and bearer came running. Mem and Lawrence stood at the edge of the terrace looking stunned and anxious. They had Simon and me come stand beside them as the servants proceeded to beat the ground around the roses to drive off any remaining snakes, then searched more closely, poking sticks underneath a pile of loose rocks.

A short distance from where we had been squatting, they found a pocket of leaves containing thirty small egg sacs. It seemed we had taken cover in front of a cobra's nest.

'You saved my life,' I told Simon that night. We were sharing a corner attic room under the eaves. There was no light, but our beds, as in Delhi, stood close enough together that I could see him in the darkness. I reached across the gap and touched his shoulder. He turned his small sweet face.

'I'd do it again,' he said. 'I love you.'

The words sprang from him like pebbles from a slingshot, and I sensed an urgency in his voice that I had never heard before. He curled his hand over mine. Our palms were the same size. Outside, it began to rain.

I thought of our dress-up days. Simon in his father's white dinner jacket and I in Mem's red evening dress, the low collar slipping off one shoulder and my hair twisted up on top of my head. How, stepping in, stepping out through the long leg slit, I would pose for him, chin up and saucy as a film star. And his eyes would grow large, his voice hushed. 'Princess Kamla.'

At the time I thought he was merely playing back to me. Now I was not so sure.

I didn't move, didn't push him away. He slipped out of his bed and into mine. I sat up, brought my knees against my chest, pulled my nightgown down over them. He lay behind me, hugging my back. His chin pressed too sharply into my hip, but still I didn't object.

The next morning Mem and Lawrence told us that war had broken out in a place called Korea. American soldiers would be fighting against Korean and Chinese Communists. Simon asked if we knew any American soldiers, and I thought of the green helmet in his father's closet, but Mem hugged him and said, no, no soldiers. If we were lucky no one we knew would be hurt by this war.

Lawrence poured himself a glass of whiskey and stared off into the mountains.

4

'In 1868,' he spoke into her ear, 'two British adventurers spent three months in the middle of winter crossing the Karakorams, the very same route you and I traveled. One of them was Robert Shaw. The other was George Hayward. Both of them were determined to be the first Brits into Chinese Turkestan, and they often camped no more than a mile from each other, but in all that time they met face-to-face just once, for about an hour. Months later they were taken prisoner separately by the King of Kashgaria. After weeks of confinement Shaw was released and told he could return to India. He was also told that Hayward would be kept on as a hostage. Shaw refused. He said he wouldn't leave unless the King released Hayward, too.'

'Don't tell me Aidan's related to this noble spirit.'

'No.' He lifted his voice above the rain slamming like artillery fire against the tin roof. 'That's just coincidence.'

'Then why are you telling me this?'

'Shaw loathed Hayward. He called him "the thorn in my flesh," yet he risked his life to save him.' Still holding her fast with one arm, Lawrence ran his other hand flatly down her side, grazing the slope of her naked breast, the channeled ribs, finding the valley at her waist and sinking the hard edge of his palm into her softest flesh.

'We're at *war* now,' she said. 'And Aidan's trapped inside enemy lines—'

'A year after Shaw got him out of Turkestan, Hayward was back trotting over the Pamir Steppe, tempting fate all over again. He sent out news dispatches about the local Maharajah slicing up babies from some rebel tribe. Guess what? The Maharajah had Hayward killed – in his camp, along with his loyal servants. A single stroke of the sword. Shaw'd saved his life for nothing.'

'What more do you want from me?'

She attempted to roll away from him, but he snaked an arm around her shoulder, brought his hand across her chest, and pinned himself against her back. 'What are we doing?' He moved his hips, unlocking her legs. 'Is it only the thrill of betraying him? The dare?'

She struggled against the power of his thigh now curling over her, the intrusion of heat and desire. He could feel it. The affliction of her own lust.

'Yes.' She was crying. 'Yes! Are you happy? You win. It's all about Aidan. And maybe he's not worth it, but he's not *dead*. Not for me!'

He felt the air go out of him as cleanly as if she had driven a hatpin through his lungs.

CHAPTER 10

1

He escaped to Calcutta. Preposterous thought. Calcutta, the fabled Black Hole. Mecca for refugees, headquarters for the Goddess of Death and Destruction. Well, maybe not so preposterous after all, he considered, settling down for a late morning drink in the lobby of the Grand Hotel.

There were the usual palms in shiny brass pots, twirling ceiling fans, and mahogany paneling. It was coming down outside, and the morning light from the veranda slanted pale green and viscous. Most of the desk staff stood lethargically staring through the open doors at the downpour. Occasionally put-upon guests would straggle in shaking off beads of rain from their slickers, stamping sodden feet, and snapping umbrellas in the bellboys' faces. The energy with which Europeans battled the monsoon struck Lawrence as one more example of the gulf between Asia and the West. Asians, who waited most of the year for the rains and then, often as not, were flooded or even drowned by them, threw monsoon parties to welcome them. They would run out in their finest suits and saris with arms spread wide and mouths open to catch the first drops. Europeans, by contrast, treated the monsoons as a personal affront, wearing their rain gear like armor and ranting over India's lack of storm drains, gutters, protected cisterns, popping malaria pills like candies and ordering their gin and whiskey neat because they dared not trust the ice – even in the best hotels. Like this one, he thought, jiggling the cubes in his own sweating glass and drinking deeply.

He was alone in the bar except for the Assamese waiter and a shirt-sleeved man tuning the piano. The instrument seemed to be

271

resisting the tuner's efforts – doubtless the effect of humidity. The thudding repetition of notes was like a faltering heartbeat. *Tung, tung, tung.*

He thought of Davey splayed on the ground, the roar of his own pulse as he turned his face so the child wouldn't see the terror in his father's eyes. He thought of Joanna down on her knees, clutching Simon and Kamla – safe. Did she have any idea how lucky she was? Was she even capable of appreciating just how much more she had to lose?

He dug a hand into the silver bowl of cashews on the table in front of him and popped the whole fistful into his mouth, then washed it down with gin and tonic. Breakfast.

'Mr Malcolm?'

A thin man, tall for an Indian, with a long graying beard and penetrating gaze, stood over him. 'Krishna Gosh.'

Lawrence rearranged his head. 'Yes. Of course.' They shook hands and Gosh sat down. He was here for the same reunion of Indian news writers that ostensibly had brought Lawrence to Calcutta. Like Kamla's father, these former agents had posed as merchants, servants, traders, and pilgrims – Britain's eyes and ears throughout Central Asia before 1947. They'd had a rough time of it, between the Nationalist warlords and Soviet 'liberators.' Some had returned only recently, and it was these men Lawrence had spent the past week interviewing – asking questions about their view of the Great Game while casting fruitlessly for clues to Aidan's fate. Gosh was neither more nor less promising than the others. But he was the last.

'I spent eleven years in prison in Tihwa,' he announced in a perfect Sandhurst accent, 'accused of stealing vegetables.'

He recalled smuggling out weekly cipher notes on the political rumors floating between prisoners and guards. His reports were relayed back to Simla, Calcutta, and ultimately London. No attempt was ever made to free him, yet his loyalty to British India remained unshaken. He was proud, he said, that several shipments of Soviet arms had been intercepted on the Afghan border as a result of his intelligence, and he fervently believed that India's Independence had been a ghastly mistake.

'What better proof of folly than the slaughter of all those

272

innocent women and children – all Indians by Indians – during Partition?' Gosh shook his head and sipped his tea. He'd missed Independence, sitting in his distant jail cell.

The piano tuner hammered away. The British had sucked India dry, Lawrence thought. They'd imprinted their language, their system of justice and government, even their network of railroads and trade on a country that never looked on them as anything but outsiders – *firenghi*. A country most of them openly despised. Yet they had forced a unity, a sense of common identity and purpose that could inspire men like Gosh to risk their lives and feel good about it. And when the Brits left, all hell broke loose. Was that the legacy of their commitment, or a reaction to their abandonment?

The British had left a similar stamp on Aidan. The Shanghai schools of his youth, his predilection for Burberry's trench coats and fair-skinned women. However Aidan might struggle against it, he'd been colonized every bit as thoroughly as these news writers. And, arguably, he'd turned around and occupied Joanna in exactly the same way.

'Did you ever go up to the border territory around Ili?' he asked Gosh.

'The rebel territory in Sinkiang, you mean?' Gosh shook his head.

'Anything on a fellow named Osman?'

'Hunh! I met him once in passing. Like a Turki pirate that one. Do you know, he killed his own nephew – a twelve-year-old boy. No, he's madder than a hatter, in my opinion. Madder, I dare say, than Stalin.' He lifted an eyebrow. 'Just don't let Henderson know I said so.'

Yes, they all knew the British consul Henderson, who must have been even more in cahoots with Weller and Osman than Lawrence had suspected. Having evacuated everyone else in his consulate, Henderson had stayed on in Tihwa long enough to be arrested by the newly arrived Liberation Army. Lo and behold, the Reds found the consul sitting on a sizable cache of arms and explosives. Eventually he was expelled from the country, saved by his diplomatic skin, and was now taking extended gardener's leave in Surrey while Whitehall decided whether to excommunicate or commend him.

273

'On your way out of Sinkiang, did you run across any Americans who might have been left behind?'

'Personally? No. But I heard of a few.'

'Such as . . . ?'

'Well, the American consul, for one. Mr Weller was still in Tihwa when I left.'

'Yes. Well, we know he got out. Anyone else?'

Gosh stroked his beard. 'Not in Sinkiang, but there was one story I heard – I came out through Afghanistan. I met another fellow there – he'd had a most terrible journey. The Soviets imprisoned him in Kazakhstan. He remained there for nearly two years. His only luck was in his size – he was just this big.' He held his hands up, inches apart. 'Every night in the dark he worked to loosen one of the bars in his jail cell. Finally he succeeded. Only a man so very small could have made it out, and only a man so very strong could have made it alive to Kabul.'

'An American?' Lawrence asked.

'I believe he was Nepalese.'

'But . . . you said there *was* an American?'

'Ah, yes. This fellow saw a foreigner in the prison in Alma-Ata just a few days before he himself escaped.'

'He actually saw him with his own eyes?'

'I believe so, though he did not know the man's name.'

Ting, ting – the piano tuner was still at it. Lawrence frowned. 'Dark-haired?'

'Mmm. I don't think so. I remember he said the man resembled the young Lord Mountbatten – like you, one who reddens instead of browns with the sun. But he spoke – and swore – like an American. I believe he was heard being tortured.' Gosh stared at the piano tuner.

'Is this Nepalese fellow findable now?'

Gosh shook his head. 'He was dying with tuberculosis when I met him.' Then he asked, 'Are you looking for someone in particular?'

Lawrence considered the question. 'No,' he said. 'No, just chasing shadows.' He brought his hand to his forehead in a salute. 'The King should knight every one of you mates.'

Gosh stood up. 'I appreciate that, sir. But I have a pension. I have my health, God willing, and a new young wife and a child on the

274

way. I am one of the lucky ones. That is enough.'

'The lucky ones,' Lawrence repeated to himself as he watched Gosh stride into the rain. 'Yes, you bastard, I suppose you are.'

He stood up and went over to the piano. The tuner was a wiry young fellow with the sharp features of a Eurasian. 'Mind giving that a break?'

The man squinted back at him appraisingly. 'If you buy me a drink.'

'A'right.' He held out his hand. 'Lawrence Malcolm.'

The piano tuner grinned. His handshake was strong and game. 'Lazarus Figredo.'

'You Goan?'

'Nah.' Lazarus seated himself at Lawrence's table. 'Father was Portuguese, mother Malay. Grew up in the Philippines.'

'You're not in the Philippines now.'

He shrugged. 'Parents were killed in the first Jap offensive. Missionaries tossed me into a boatload of refugees headed for Bengal, and I wound up at Dr Graham's school for Eurasians in Kalimpore. I was twelve. Been here ever since.'

Yet another colonized soul, Lawrence thought. 'How'd you come to be tuning pianos?'

'Apprenticeship. Here in Calcutta, a Mr Jamison. Bloody racist, called me Blackie, but he taught me the trade. I can build a goddamn piano from scratch. Or the better part of a house, for that matter.'

Lawrence smiled. 'Good ear, good hands, eh?'

Lazarus shrugged, asked what he was drinking, and told the waiter he'd have the same.

Lawrence liked the man's scrappiness. He took full possession of that black leather club chair. Appearances meant little, he seemed to say, but to let an opportunity pass unexplored was a fool's mistake. With his snapping black eyes and long bony beak of a nose, the young man reminded Lawrence of a crow. He had that interested but disengaged look that birds do have. Lawrence found it easy to talk to him.

By the time he'd finished his fourth gin and tonic that talk had come around to Joanna – and Aidan. It was the confidence of strangers. An exhilarating release. 'The thing is,' Lawrence

275

concluded, 'I'm not convinced she ever really knew this husband of hers. She loves the idea of him, and it's that idea she can't give up. But ideas don't keep you warm at night, do they? My God, you've never met such a stubborn woman—'

'What *is* the idea?'

'Ah, you know. The dashing adventurer who'd sweep her off her feet and show her the world, turn her into something she never thought she could be.'

Lazarus squeezed his face back, showing large yellowed teeth. 'Not a bloody bad idea.'

'No.' Lawrence sighed, abruptly sober. 'Quite irresistible, in fact.'

The noise of the monsoon hammered across the wide veranda and through the open windows, but he could still hear the cries of peddlers and dying children, the city's staccato of bicycle bells and honking horns. For all the hotel's spit and polish, it was a fragile fortress.

'You want to know what I think?' Lazarus asked.

'What?'

'I think you're out of your bloody noggin over this *memsahib*, but maybe she's as much an idea to you as you say her husband is to her.'

2

The rains turned the streets to rivers, the gardens to sludge. They flattened the tarpaulin tenements of the poor and forced the lizards to swim. Two of the girls at Salamat Jannat were hospitalized with typhus, and encephalitis and cholera lurked in every pitcher of unboiled water. Dozens drowned in the swollen Yamuna, hundreds more in the Ganges. Every day the *Hindu Times* trumpeted another monsoon disaster. Bridge collapse. Mud slide. Train derailment. Family of ten crushed in their sleep when a lorry skidded off the road and through their bedroom wall. There were shortages of clean water all over the city and daily electrical outages. A leak in the roof caused Salamat Jannat to flood with the final downpour. Joanna welcomed the distraction if not the ordeal of mopping up and patching, interminable consultations with workmen and even more interminable phone calls and petitions to the Committee for money to do the repairs properly. She threw herself into this minor crisis with such fervor that Vijay (product of a Catholic grammar school) jokingly called her Noah. 'We should be renaming this place the Ark and bringing in animals two by two. But what, then, must we be doing with all these unwed girls?'

Joanna looked past him to the veranda where the new teacher Mrs Sen was upbraiding said girls for failing to distinguish between prepositions and pronouns. 'I suppose,' she said quietly, 'it's not that kind of ark.'

She didn't blame Lawrence. That, perhaps, was the hardest part. She'd pushed him and pulled him in so many directions, it was a wonder he wasn't hamstrung. Still, he'd remained, so constant, so patient. He'd gone with her to the end of the earth.

But what he was asking in return she simply could not do.

Two weeks after he'd left for Calcutta, he sent a note along with a package of books for the children. The note read, 'Visiting Ambala, Kipling's locale. Thought it only fitting to send Simon a copy of *Kim* from the very place, but it turned out the bookstore had a few other irresistibles as well.'

The note contained no more information than that. No suggestion how long he'd be gone or where else he intended to travel. The tone, Joanna thought, seemed forced, as if he were covering his tracks. She actually turned the parcel over to check, but it had indeed been posted from Ambala.

Inside, the children found the announced edition of *Kim*, plus *Gulliver's Travels* and a beautiful volume of Hans Christian Andersen's *Fairy Tales* containing the story 'The Moon Maiden,' which Kamla said her father once read to her. There was also a book of magic, *The Stolen Secrets of Harry Houdini*, with an inscription from Lawrence to Simon, 'You can accomplish the impossible through mirrors and sleight of hand. You can tumble whole mountains. You can make a pig fly. Just remember, it's all in the timing. I hope you'll do better than I.'

Joanna, reading over Simon's shoulder, wondered if this message wasn't really meant for her. All in the timing, indeed. It was just like Lawrence to send the truer, more heartfelt and painful farewell coded to her son. Simon, fortunately, didn't read it that way. He immediately flipped to the middle of the book and began studying the illustrations of Houdini handcuffed and hanging upside down off the side of a skyscraper or bound and chained in a box at the bottom of a river. 'Escape artist extraordinaire!' trumpeted the caption for one drawing. 'He wants me to learn these,' Simon explained importantly, 'to show him when he comes back.'

Kamla looked up from her fairy tales. She and Simon were sitting on the living room sofa with the *tats* lowered against the midday sun, so that as her eyes widened the pupils expanded, turning her gaze half black. She seemed about to say something. Indeed her lips moved as though the words were already forming. But she remained silent. The page open in front of her showed an Indian girl crouched beside a moonlit river. A burning lamp floated in front of her. The caption read, 'He lives!'

Joanna rested her hands on the back of the sofa. She could feel the heat rise from Simon's body. The temperature in the room was well over ninety degrees, yet her arms were covered with goose flesh.

In August the children returned to school, where, to Simon's chagrin, Kamla was placed another year ahead of him. But otherwise they seemed steady enough, and a second postcard arrived from Lawrence, now in Dehra Dun, where he said he was 'plowing through archives of the Game.' In his absence Joanna felt more helpless than ever. She was tempted to fire off yet another round of letters about Aidan, but the news from Korea stayed her hand. MacArthur was using Taiwan as a staging ground, and Chiang Kai-shek's influence in Washington had never been greater. Meanwhile, fanatics like that Senator Joseph McCarthy were using the war as an excuse to turn the witch-hunt for Communists into a national obsession. By criticizing Chiang, Aidan had virtually ordered up his own persecution – and now complete abandonment by the US government. Without Lawrence, Joanna was on her own, and on her own she'd run out of ideas. Unable to think where else to turn, she cabled Ben Eldon. Had he found *anyone* who was willing to stand up for Aidan?

About three weeks later, as she was concluding a meeting at Safe Haven with Vijay and Hari, she looked up and saw a short, slight, towheaded man hovering out on the veranda. He seemed familiar, but it wasn't until she saw the ungainly way he moved that she permitted herself to believe it. She quickly excused herself and went out to him.

'Ben!'

He gave her an emotional hug. He still looked boyish, his face and arms heavily freckled, his straight hair falling into brown eyes. He wore a white shirt with the sleeves rolled up, blue jeans, and the shoes Americans were calling loafers. Even before he opened his mouth it would be impossible to mistake his nationality.

'I don't want to interrupt,' he said in his molasses-thick drawl.

'Don't be silly. We were just finishing.' She made the introductions, and Hari looked as though he might linger, always prospecting for useful connections, but when she said Ben was a personal friend of her husband's the meeting disbanded.

Joanna clicked the ceiling fan to top speed and poured two glasses of limewater. The girls' chanting recitation of poetry in the outer room made it possible for them to talk without fear of being overheard.

'How are you?' Joanna asked, with a nod to his left leg. 'It looks good.'

'Yeah, the technology of prosthetics is right up there with A-bombs, y' know? 'Specially now they're getting ready for a whole new crop of blasted boys coming back from Korea.'

'It's going to be bad, isn't it?'

'Bad enough.'

'You're not heading out there, are you?'

'Nah. I quit the news. Working for Kodak now. I'm a camera salesman.' He grinned, his big straight white teeth like a farm boy's. 'Least it's got me traveling again. Asia and the Middle East are my beats. A day here, a day there. Chop chop.'

'So you're just passing through Delhi on work.'

Ben rolled his glass between his hands. His voice dropped. 'Not entirely.'

She felt her fingers and feet start to tingle.

'Joanna, you asked me to dig up what I could back home. I got a couple old buddies at State. One of them called me last week, as I was packing for this trip. He said some news about Aidan had just come in. Heavily classified, and he risked his job getting it to me.' He passed her a manila envelope. 'I can tell when shots have been doctored. It's become one of my specialties. This hasn't. Been doctored, that is.'

Joanna took the envelope. She could no longer feel her fingertips, and had to concentrate to undo the clasp. A photograph fluttered into her lap, face up.

It was Aidan.

Alive.

Perceptibly older.

Doctored. The word pounded in her ear. There were flashes of gray in his hair. This was impossible. The man in this photograph smiled, relaxed. He wore a laborer's jacket and had his hands clasped in a gesture of friendship with another man. A Chinese man who looked familiar, though in her shock Joanna didn't recognize him. Instead another, clearer image of Aidan raced through her mind. A dream image so vivid she knew it must be part of a recurring nightmare. Aidan's face was superimposed on those pictures Weller had shown them of Kamla's father. Hacked to death. Martyred. Without thinking why, she knew the picture in her hands was worse.

Ben read her confusion. 'It's Chou En-lai, Joanna. Aidan's shaking hands with the Communist Premier. This was taken early this summer, just before the Reds pushed south in Korea.'

She realized he was watching her intently, expecting her to fall apart. She wasn't sure when she'd breathed last. She inhaled. Exhaled. The fan whirled precariously overhead. The background in the photograph was anonymous, a wall, a window, blurred. Outside anywhere. Neither man looked at the lens, and the image was grainy. They were not posing, she realized. This had been taken covertly. 'Where is he?' she asked.

Ben took a drink and set his glass down. He ignored her question. 'I'd be careful what I said, if I were you. You know me, Jo. Aidan saved my life, and I stand by my friends, but it don't look good. You'd best watch out for yourself and your boy.' He licked his lips and brushed his fair hair back from his eyes, glancing briefly at the ceiling. 'May God strike me dead if I'm wrong, but the absolute worst thing would be if any of this rubbed off on you, and it could, what with the war and feelings running so high back home. I've tried and tried to think what I would do if I were in your shoes, after all you've been through. You're a brave woman, Joanna, and a good one, too. But there's got to be a limit, you know?'

'What are you telling me?' Her voice seemed to creep out of her. But she would make him say it.

'They think he's gone over. I mean, they *all* think he's gone over, not just J. Edgar and his merry band.'

'On the basis of a single photograph?'

'I sincerely doubt that.' His jaw worked, and she thought he would continue. Instead, he gripped the wooden arms of his chair, preparing to stand. 'I'm really sorry to do this, but if I'm not at the airport in an hour, my head's gonna roll.'

She watched him get up.

'I don't know any more than I've told you,' he said, 'and it could severely compromise my friend – and me – if you let on that you've seen this. But I know how hard you've been searching for Aidan. Though I don't expect you to thank me, I couldn't not tell you after all we've been through. You understand?'

Steady on his feet now, he opened his arms to her. She accepted the hug without feeling it, though she was dimly aware of his smells, of Brylcreem and Ivory Soap and Old Spice – scents from another life.

He kissed her cheek and eased the photo out of her grip, trading it for his card. 'If you need anything . . .'

She dug her teeth into her lower lip and shook her head.

'You will survive this, Joanna.' And then, 'I'm sorry. He fooled us all.'

3

After the monsoons ended the cool months arrived. Still Lawrence did not return. Mem did not say that she missed him, but it was clear in her silence, the absence of her smile, the sadness of her touch. I dared not even speak his name. And Simon pretended nothing had changed, but in fact, he was changed most of all. At school he had taken up with the naughty boys, enticing them with his Houdini tricks, which he practiced by the hour. One day I caught him showing off the scar where the bullet had grazed his leg. He told the boys he had nearly died. Another bullet nicked his ear, he said – and he showed the cleft in his left earlobe from which Lawrence used to pull magic coins to amuse us those first nights in Leh. Another day he and his new friends were kept in after school for placing toads in teachers' cupboards and writing dirty limericks on the blackboard during lunch.

Mem paid little attention. Lately, when not at work, she was lost in her papers, her telephone calls, her staring into space. Even when she read the notes the headmistress sent home, she would merely kiss the back of Simon's neck. 'Keep an eye on him, Kamla, would you? He wears me out.' Then Simon would grin at me as if I were his accomplice.

But I preferred to follow Mem's example, escaping into my books, my schoolwork and private thoughts. So it was that on the last Sunday in September, when Simon went off with his friends to fly kites over the desert, I stayed home with Mem.

Nagu and the new cook had gone off to market, and Mem was in her room with the *tats* down as she had been for days, working, reading. She needed to be alone, she said. I had heard her in the middle of the night pacing her bedroom floor, and I should have known better, but I was trying to read the book she had given me in Kasauli – *Jane Eyre*. I was enjoying it a great deal, as it told the story of an orphan like myself, a most resourceful girl, but the language was difficult. I needed help, and I dared to knock and then open Mem's door. She was lying on her bed under the mosquito net, surrounded by newspapers. I asked her to explain the meaning of the word *precocious*. I had thought she might take me onto her bed, and we might read together. Instead, Mem sighed and said, '*You* are precocious.' Then she pointed to a shelf beside the desk and told me to take the dictionary there, and close the door behind me.

I was disappointed but not unhappy. To me that little leather-bound volume was a treasure chest. I curled up on the living room sofa with the dictionary in one hand and my book in the other and would have been content to remain there all day, only minutes later I heard a familiar cry outside.

'*Aina!* Best-quality looking glass!'

You see, among the parade of vendors who streamed down Ratendone Road each day was a boy who rode a bicycle laden frontward and backward with mirrors. Round mirrors, framed mirrors, small flashing mirror stars and long rectangles the size of a door. He tied them on with jute twine so that his bicycle resembled the pictures I had seen in some of Simon's books, of an American circus calliope. And he would ride through the neighborhood singing out, '*Aina!* Best-quality looking glass!' He was a sweet boy, the son of the glasscutter who manufactured these mirrors. I seem to recall he wore spectacles like Mahatma Gandhi, and he also had Gandhiji's large ears. And Nagu had befriended him, I think, or perhaps he knew his father because I would often see the two of them chatting by the front gate.

Ordinarily, if Mem wished to buy a mirror, she would send Nagu down to negotiate. This had not happened in some time, as Mem lately seemed to avoid reflections of herself. But a few days earlier Simon had his friend Brian Wilcox over, and Simon was showing off the cricket bat Mem had given him for his birthday. There had been a sandstorm, so they were playing indoors. Brian tossed him a low ball in the hallway, and Simon hit it too hard. He shattered the living room mirror. 'I cannot *deal* with this,' Mem said when she saw the damage. So on this Saturday morning, when I heard the familiar cry, '*Aina!*' at the gate while Nagu was gone, I thought I might please Mem by replacing the mirror myself. I had a little money tucked away, and I knew that Nagu would repay me from his household allowance. I took my wad of rupees and hurried to the gate.

At first I thought that some trick of the heat had caused my vision to waver, but when I came closer I saw that indeed this was not the usual boy. This mirror *wallah* wore no glasses and his ears were like those of a mouse, but what I noticed most about him were the terrible scars on his legs from the hem of his shorts to the top of his feet. They were old scars, white and brown, that had shriveled the skin like crepe paper. He gave me a hard and curious

283

look as I asked where the usual boy had gone. He said there had been an accident, that Dabbu had dropped one of the mirrors and broken it, severing two of his toes, and so this boy was taking the route until Dabbu was well again. I said please to pass on our respects and wishes for a swift recovery, then I selected a mirror and bargained a little over the price. All this time the *wallah* continued to stare at me until I felt that I must have a piece of spinach between my teeth or some pickle in my hair. Still he said nothing but accepted my payment, examining the wad of rupees in my hand with a look of disbelief that again mystified me. The old *mali*, Musai, came to carry the mirror back to the house. But as I was about to close the gate, the *aina wallah* put out his hand.

'Is it really you?' he asked. 'The girl who ran away?'

In that instant it was as though my past appeared in demon form and breathed fire into my eyes. I shook my head violently and said, 'No, you are mistaken,' and shoved the gate closed as quickly and forcefully as I was able. But as I leaned my full weight back and locked it I could hear him still outside, laughing. It was the laugh of the alley, a laugh borrowed from *goondas* and lecherous men. Then I knew him, too. This was the boy Surie whose burned legs Mem herself had tended, who had grown almost into a man in the months since I last saw him in the lane behind the flash house.

I tried to convince myself that Surie meant me no harm. Perhaps he no longer lived near the flash house. With luck, Indrani might be dead. One and a half years had passed, after all. To me it seemed like thirty, and because my existence had altered so radically, I thought surely those I had known before must also have moved along. You will say this is nonsense. I was living still in India. The streets teemed with people whose lives had been laid out for them generations ago, for whom the notion of change was as threatening as war. I knew this. I had witnessed the convulsions when Partition gripped the city. I had seen the residents of Old Delhi chop off the heads of their neighbors and burn their own daughters alive rather than agree to change. But illusion had gripped me in much the same way as the madness of those days. It had cast me under a kind of spell that seemed to change all rules. I was thinking like a *firenghi* even though I was not one of them.

I was thinking this boy is nothing. What could he do to me now?

It is not even worth troubling Mem. Better just leave it alone. But I knew in my heart that this boy Surie held the power to destroy me.

I buried my nose in my book all afternoon and kept my alarm to myself. That night Simon wanted to know what was wrong, but I took a tip from Mem and simply muttered, 'Headache.' I was glad Simon had made other friends. I was glad to be free of his questions, his need. But I directed my anger at Lawrence. Though I had no reason to believe this, I thought, if Lawrence had not gone away, Surie would never have found me. If Lawrence had been there, I might have told him, and if I had told him, he might have comforted me. But Lawrence was not there, and so I blamed him for my own fear.

4

In India it is possible to drown without touching water. 'You travel this place long enough,' Lawrence told an Austrian he met one noon near the Hindu mountain shrine of Yamunotri, 'and you realize nothing's more trivial than human desire. Just look – ' He swept his arm back to indicate the gorge they'd just ascended, with its clusters of pine and vertical shale walls, the switchback trail blooming color and skin, the sheen of oiled black hair. Families rode four to a pony or were carried by up to five porters on flat-bedded wooden dandies. Some wore gold-laced turquoise and magenta, others saffron tatters. Old men struggled with the support of acolytes. Old women bent over hand-hewn staffs. Veiled girls plucked edelweiss and buttercups, while their brothers threw stones to tempt avalanches. Lawrence continued, 'They'll reach the temple, dab their foreheads with the headwaters of the Yamuna, mumble some hackneyed prayer, then hightail it back to their milk tea and whiskey before the sun goes down.'

'But it is magnificent, no?' The Austrian's eyes fixed on the snowcaps ranged above the gorge. He was a mountaineer and intended to spend the next six months exploring the Himalayas.

'Magnificent. No.' Lawrence squinted at the parade of human ants until they blurred. 'It is simply . . . motion.'

So he marched from one staggeringly beautiful landscape to

another. By the end of September, he had trekked the width of Uttar Pradesh, skirted the base of Nanda Devi, and hiked through the Valley of Flowers. He slept in the open, in pilgrim rest houses, in old caravan *serai* and Buddhist hostels. He wandered through camel auctions and Hindu *melas*, worshipped at altars for the blue-skinned Krishna. He spun prayer wheels at abandoned lama-series and consigned his own prayers to the turning drum. In roadside *dhabas* he watched tubercular porters gamble for cigarettes. He caught rides on the backs of wagons loaded with the skins of freshly slaughtered lambs. He listened to the drug-induced ravings of a *sadhu* in an ashram in Badrinath, witnessed the stabbing death of a midget who'd been caught stealing a packet of sugar. He drank and danced until he passed out in the fleshpots of Rishikesh.

In three months he chalked up a baker's dozen recruits for Jack, including the Austrian mountaineer, and posted watchdogs of his own from Nepal to the Pakistan border. He tripped across equal numbers of agents on the American and British payrolls, all competitively scouting for Communists, but he still was no closer to a reading on Aidan than he'd been in Calcutta.

Then, in Simla as he walked into the Cricket Club one evening, he spotted Reggie Milne.

'By God!' Milne grabbed his hand. His bluster did not conceal the fact that he'd misplaced Lawrence's name.

Lawrence had no such difficulty. The Karakoram beard was gone, the hair was cut, thinner and grayer than it had been last year, and he was wearing tweeds instead of khaki, but Milne's blue eyes retained their practical ease, receptive yet noncommittal and deceptively placid.

Lawrence reintroduced himself and offered to buy a round of drinks. Milne went him one better and offered supper.

'Started a practice here in Simla,' he said, tucking into a large bowl of mulligatawny. 'Been in Asia too long to go home.' He threw Lawrence a shrewd glance. 'From the look of you, I'd say you're in the same boat.'

'Probably right. Hadn't given it much thought.'

'Not something you do think about. One day, it's just a fact.'

Lawrence had a sudden memory of Milne reading *Ivanhoe* to the boys on his houseboat in Srinagar, one arm around each of them while they steadied the book on his lap. Afloat.

'How's that boy of yours?' he asked.

Milne replied with a broad grin. 'Stellar, thanks. He's in school in Mussoorie. Still asks about Simon. I'm sorry we haven't kept in touch.'

'Simon's all right. Kamla and Joanna, too.'

The doctor's voice altered to a clinical timbre. 'That's good. I hesitate to ask, but did anyone ever find her husband?'

'Not yet. Joanna's still hoping he'll surface one of these days.'

Milne watched him across the table. 'What's your guess?'

'I'm not sure what you're asking,' Lawrence said.

The doctor absently tapped his left ring finger on the damask cloth. 'I'm not entirely sure myself. But when that Sherpa came back to fetch me on the trail—'

'Tot.'

'Yes. He told me a bit about Joanna's situation. Led me to believe her husband was in danger. I can't say why, and I never dared put the question to Joanna, but I got the impression he might be a danger to himself.'

Lawrence stirred his soup and let the clamor of the dining room settle around them. 'Suicidal?'

Milne nodded. 'As I say, I didn't see the point of raising the question when you returned to Srinagar. It was none of my business, in any case.'

Lawrence said, 'I think you must have misunderstood.' Though this did explain why Milne had been so willing to take Simon back with him to Srinagar – and why he hadn't opposed Joanna's continuing the search. 'Aidan's no more suicidal than your average foreign correspondent. If he were, he'd never have made it to Sinkiang, and we know he got as far as Tihwa.'

'Right. Wouldn't take much to off yourself in the Karakorams, would it?' Milne smiled grimly. 'I suppose it's politics, then. Probably poked his nose into one Chinese corner too many. Same thing happened to a couple of the Swedes I worked with in Yarkand.'

'Did you figure out who was responsible?'

'My bet's the Nationalists.' Milne wiped his mouth. 'Bloody butchers, half of them.'

'Even with foreigners?'

'Not in the beginning. But after the Western powers started climbing into bed with Chiang Kai-shek, everybody became fair game.'

'What do you mean, fair game?'

'Well, I tried to stay out of the politics as much as possible, but you couldn't plug your ears. It was the Americans made the biggest mistakes. Bloke named Freeman didn't know his arse from his armpit, running around playing pat-a-cake with every bandit in the province. Hard to play with one without making an enemy of the others, but he thought if he dealt them all in they'd learn to love each other *and* him. Instead he put everybody at risk.'

'Freeman.'

'Douglas Freeman. Called himself a linguistics specialist, but I have it on some authority he was really one of those Central Intelligence agents.'

Lawrence dimly recalled Mrs Desai mentioning a linguistics specialist who had taken Alice James drinking. 'Was he based in Kashgar?'

'Spent time there, no doubt. But I think he did most of his business up north, with the British and American consuls. Weller and Henderson drew down the funds, Freeman distributed the wealth.'

'What happened to him after the takeover?'

'Disappeared.'

'Did he get out?'

'If he's lucky.' Milne drank his beer.

'He didn't come out with Weller?'

'I was in Srinagar when Weller's motley crew straggled in. A more pathetic bunch of Chinese and Kazakh robber barons you can't imagine. But Freeman wasn't among them.'

Lawrence buttered a piece of bread, trying to appear offhand. 'I met a news writer a few weeks back who told me an American had been reported in a prison in Alma-Ata. Fair-haired, fair-skinned. Don't suppose that could have been Freeman?'

'Possible.' Milne leaned back with a thoughtful expression. 'You know who might know about that, though. Akbar.'

'Akbar. Joanna's friend?'

'Right. He always joked about being apolitical, which meant a third of his friends were Soviet sympathizers, a third Congress Indians, and a third Muslim Leaguers. There was, of course, considerable overlap. If anybody *would* know, he's the one.'

'He still in Srinagar?' Lawrence asked.

'Was when we left two months ago, but he's not well. My guess is stomach cancer, though he absolutely refuses to get a proper diagnosis and treatment. For all his Western training the old boy's a fatalist at heart.'

'Have you kept your houseboat?' Lawrence asked.

'Why? Need a place to stay?' Milne cast him another shrewd smile. 'You're welcome to use the boat anytime you like. I'll let Waza and Mistri know to look out for you.' Then, with regrets, he excused himself. 'Going down to see Ralphie for the weekend,' he said. 'I'll give him your regards.'

5

Day after day Joanna scoured the press. The US papers, of course, were filled with news of the war in Korea and anti-Communist hysteria. Joanna imagined Aidan's detractors would be delighted to learn that he was the traitor they had always claimed, and she fully expected to see his defection announced in banner headlines. But there was nothing, not even a footnote confirming Ben's leak. Wishful thinking, she knew, but she couldn't help wondering if Ben might conceivably be wrong. She had looked at the photograph so fleetingly before he whisked it away that inevitably now she started to question whether it was really Aidan, whether there might be some other explanation . . .

She was tempted to write to Lawrence. He had sent the address of a Thomas Cooke office where he was collecting mail. But what would she say? The bad news is, Aidan's alive. The good news is, he's the enemy.

And what would she then expect Lawrence to do? Come racing back to help her fill out the divorce papers?

No, she was better off on her own. At least until she was *sure*.

Through a young Communist friend of Vijay's she located a

newsstand in Old Delhi that carried the official *People's Daily* only a month past date. Even if the US refused to acknowledge a traitor, surely the Chinese would parade this news. She found an old card in Aidan's desk with the characters for his name and also memorized the ideograms for 'rescue,' 'American,' 'defector.' She spent hours each night scrutinizing the smudged, cramped columns of this impenetrable language, and with each paper's failure to mention her husband, she became firmer and firmer in her belief that Ben had made a terrible mistake. Yet the revived conviction that Aidan was alive refused to let her rest. If she could find independent proof of that alone, she could take it to the embassy and demand their help.

She had talked herself into such a corner that when she finally saw what she was looking for she almost glossed right over it. A photograph of high-level Communist cadres at a banquet in Beijing. What could this have to do with Aidan? If his head had been turned, if another figure had even partially blocked him from the lens, if he had stood just a foot or two farther into the background, she never would have looked twice. But he was standing in the front row. Smiling, lifting his glass. He wore that same spare Maoist jacket, and his hair was cut short. His eyes stared straight at her.

The US embassy reception area was festooned with orange and black crepe paper garlands. A mobile of Pilgrim and American Indian cutouts dangled from the fly fan. On the glass coffee table, surrounded by bureaucratic black leather chairs, squatted an enormous papier-mâché jack-o'-lantern. All of India was poised for the Festival of Light, Divali, but evidently the children of the American School preferred the fall rituals of home.

Joanna had barely sat down when a young thin-lipped Indian woman wearing a magenta sweater set approached. Though Joanna had called that morning to confirm, the Ambassador had been detained. But, the secretary said blandly, consular attaché Bob Cross would see her.

Joanna followed the girl out one door and through another. She was being shunted. She knew it, resented it, and yet was almost glad she didn't have to deal with Minton. Maybe Bob Cross would at least try to act human.

290

Her reflection in a wall mirror rose before her. She had on a green serge suit and heels, makeup. She'd done up her hair. She looked a hundred and ten. She felt a hundred and ten. And twelve. At breakfast she'd caught Kamla watching her and wondered which of them was the grown-up.

'Mrs Shaw.' The secretary had been replaced by a tall, brawny collegian. Ash blond hair with a ruler part on one side, blue eyes crisp as larkspur, mildly crossed, and that white starched shirt and diagonally striped Ivy League tie that was almost as out of place in New Delhi as his Boston accent. When he shook her hand she could feel every muscle.

'Won't you come in here?' *He-ah*. He was twenty-five, tops.

She stopped. Down the hall a tinny rendition of 'Over the Meadow and Through the Woods' poured from a transistor radio. She could smell the stone floor, secretarial perfume, antiseptic American scrub. She longed for the familiar must and charcoal stink of her own Safe Haven. But she had taken the morning off to come here instead. To show her hand.

She turned to find Cross watching her. 'Are you all right?'

'Fine,' she lied.

They entered an office the size of a closet, one window banded with half-closed blinds that sliced the floor into strips of light like tissue paper. Stacks of files and briefing papers covered the battle green metal cabinets and desk. A framed diploma from Brown University hung on the wall beside the chair Cross indicated. A tourist poster of the Grand Canyon hung behind his own chair.

'How can I help you?' he asked, pulling his pen from its holder on the desk.

'I don't know if you can. I came here to see Ambassador Minton.'

The young man's lips pressed into a pout. 'The Ambassador sends his apologies. He was called to the Prime Minister's residence this morning. He had to cancel all his appointments.'

'I don't know,' she said again and settled her handbag in her lap.

Cross took up the chrome pitcher on his desk and poured some water into a Dixie cup. Both pitcher and cup, American issue. He offered her a drink, and when she shook her head he emptied the cup in a single gulp and crushed it in one hand. 'I assure you, I'm well briefed before taking the Ambassador's appointments,' he said. 'I assume you're here about your husband. You want to know if there's any news.'

His eyes were like windows at night, thinly curtained but brightly lit so that she could see the shadow of someone walking back and forth across them. Someone pacing. Uncertain whether to throw open the drapes and show himself.

'That's right,' she said. 'It's been well over a year and in all that time—'

He opened a folder and ran his finger down the top sheet inside. 'You've remained here in India the whole while?'

'Yes.' She frowned down at her purse. 'This is where my husband would expect to find me.'

He cleared his throat, not looking at her. The broad shoulders pulled back and he stretched his neck. Wrestling, she thought. That's his sport. Without the physical contact, he's lost. Aidan used to say American men craved that skin-to-skin struggle because they were still trying to figure out who they were. Also, they thought with their muscles and not their minds. Unlike the Chinese, whose ancestry went back so far that they never questioned their identity – or the supremacy of their intellect.

'I admire your faith, Mrs Shaw,' he said. 'I wish I could offer some news or evidence to support it.'

'That's why I wanted to talk to the Ambassador,' she said pointedly.

'I assure you, we went over your husband's file together. There is nothing – ' He stopped. 'That is, *we* know nothing. I'm making a terrible presumption here. Perhaps you've learned something we haven't?' He leaned toward her, smiling.

She swallowed. And suddenly, she was so enraged she could not look at him. He was baldly lying, assuming her to be some nitwit wife who would lie down and invite him to step on her. Well, if that's how they wanted to play . . . She sighed to conceal her anger, brought her voice into line, and shot back at him, 'I've been to the Chinese embassy, if that's what you're asking.'

'The *Communist* embassy?' You'd have thought she'd talked to the devil himself.

'I was terrified, of course,' she said. 'But what did I have to lose?'

'And ... ?'

'Oh, they don't know anything. Or won't tell me anything. I might as well have been talking to a bunch of stone statues.'

'Yes,' he said sympathetically. 'I understand they're like that. You were very brave.'

She opened her handbag, pushed the photograph of Aidan into the depths, and pulled out a white handkerchief. She blew her nose and dabbed at her eyes. Cross busily scribbled notes.

'There was one thing the Ambassador asked me to discuss with you,' he said, 'that may come as good news. Though it's not about your husband.'

He flipped through some papers on his desk. 'You have a little girl, I think. You've adopted her.'

'Kamla?'

The shadow marched back and forth again, larger. Closer. 'Yes. Well, restrictions have eased a bit, what with our involvement in Korea. And when the Ambassador saw Mrs Solomon's article about you and your daughter in the *Gazette,* he remembered how much you wanted to take her home with you to the States. He thinks he can get you a visa for her as early as New Year's. Of course, you'll have to formalize the adoption back in the States.'

She looked at the visa application he was thrusting toward her. Pre-stamped with today's date and Minton's signature. Trading one life for another. She'd behaved, and this was her reward. She took the form and stood up.

Cross stood as well. 'It must be so hard,' he said. 'I admire you tremendously. We all do.'

You lying bastard, she thought. But she had to get out of here. Her teeth were clenched so tightly that her whole face felt numb.

'Thank you, Mr Cross,' she managed. 'I appreciate your concern.'

She waited four days, deliberating. Watching. Noticing for the first time the driver of the white Ambassador parked outside the rescue home. And the clean-shaven, turbaned man who appeared to be dozing under the plane tree across from the house. And what about those two policemen chatting with the *tonga* driver up the street? Or the green Mercedes stopped at the corner?

She told the children nothing of her visit to the embassy, even about the visa. It would be too cruel to get Kamla's hopes up – to get both their hopes up about going to the States – when the fact was, her only hope of seeing Aidan – confronting him – now lay with the Chinese here in Delhi. And, she realized, that had to be handled with such secrecy that she didn't dare breathe word of it to anyone.

Finally, she was satisfied. Her act as the idiot wife must have worked. She wasn't worth following. Besides, she thought, pleased with herself, she'd already *been* to the Chinese, hadn't she? So why should she go back again?

She drove to Lytton Road late in the afternoon, telling the children she had a meeting. In the twilight she could barely see the red stars that marked the guards' navy caps. The iron gates stood closed, and beyond the compound walls strains of martial music spilled from the old British colonial mansion. Even across the street the air smelled faintly of garlic and peanut oil, an aroma distinct from the sweeter, more complex spice of Indian cooking.

She turned the corner, parked two blocks away on a side street filled with vendors and beggars, and sat for several minutes fingering her wedding band. She hadn't worn it since she started sleeping with Lawrence. Now it felt loose and heavy. Through the windshield the full moon shone like a mirror fractured by the leafless branches of the plane trees.

She pulled a black shawl up over her head and climbed out. She locked the door after her and placed her keys inside her pocketbook, which she tucked up under her arm. The beggars stretched out their palms. She steeled herself and walked quickly past them. At the intersection she waited for a break in the six-lane river of bicycles. Finally she darted across and up the opposite curb.

She approached the embassy gate. 'Excuse me,' she said to the guard. 'I have business inside.'

He had a thin face, wary eyes. He looked her up and down, then pressed a buzzer. In a minute a door opened at the side of the embassy, and a man wearing the formless blue suit of a civilian came out.

'May I help you?' His English was good. He was older than the guard, and he smiled.

'I've come about my husband,' she said. 'Aidan Shaw.' She lowered her voice. 'I can't talk here.'

He barked something at the guard, and the gate swung back to admit her.

'I am Comrade Chou,' the man said.

He led her inside to a barren green reception area with a dozen or so identical hard-backed chairs and low occasional tables lining the walls. The regimentation made her think of firing squads, but Chou's tone was polite, even engaging. He pulled two of the chairs out to face each other and urged her to sit down.

Although she hadn't seen him alert anyone to their arrival, a young Chinese woman appeared almost as soon as they were seated, bearing covered pots of tea. She set these down within their reach and went away. Chou offered Joanna a cigarette. When she declined, he lit one for himself.

He had thickly lidded eyes, a wide face, and closely cropped gray hair. His mouth was soft and expressive. So this is the great Red Menace, she thought. He might have been Aidan's father.

She opened her purse and pulled out the clipping from the *People's Daily*. 'My husband disappeared a year and a half ago,' she said. 'My government tells me nothing. But I am certain this is Aidan.'

Chou glanced at the picture. He nodded. 'Actually, I am familiar with your husband, Mrs Shaw. He has been in Beijing for some time now.'

She felt as if the floor were dropping out from under her. She had braced herself for more lies. Denial. Not this.

Chou puffed on his cigarette and asked calmly, 'He has not been in contact with you himself, then?'

She shook her head.

'And does your government know that you are here?'

'No.'

He leaned forward and tapped his ash into a porcelain dish. 'I was told that you might come here at some point. It is my understanding that your husband intends to remain in China.'

He looked at her. 'Please,' he said gently. 'Drink your tea. It will warm you.'

She cradled the pot in her hands.

'A year and a half is a long time, Mrs Shaw. I believe it has been suggested that you and your son join your husband in Beijing.'

She felt the pot slipping and barely managed to set it down without breaking it.

Chou nodded. 'But your husband refuses.'

She thought of the picture they'd found of Simon. *What matters most.* She could still feel where Aidan had touched her cheek the last time he said goodbye.

This was wrong. All wrong. Aidan had not left her and Simon by choice. And he was not pushing them away by his own choice now.

Careful, she warned herself. Be very careful.

'Mr Chou?' she asked. 'Could you deliver a letter to my husband?'

'That depends . . .'

'I understand it will be censored.'

His mouth stretched apologetically.

She drew the envelope from her purse. The foolscap inside was almost weightless. She'd written and rewritten the message so many times that it was etched on her brain. *Why, Aidan? In spite of everything, I love you. I believe in you. But I must see you.* Please.

A loyal wife's plea. Nothing more, nothing less. She handed Chou the envelope.

'Do you think, Mr Chou, that if Aidan were willing . . . ?'

He smiled and stubbed out his cigarette. 'Anything is possible,' he said.

'And when . . . if it is allowed through, when might it reach him?'

'That is difficult to say. Perhaps one week. Perhaps one month. I wish I could promise.' He lifted his palms.

'No one can promise anything. Thank you for your time.'

6

My encounter with Surie, I decided as the weeks passed, was less a threat than an omen. He did not come again, and though I woke often in the middle of the night to the sensation of Golba's fat hands at my throat or Indrani's gold teeth winking in the darkness, though I scoured the streets with my eyes and grilled old Musai to know if he had seen unsavory characters hovering about the compound gates, I found no further evidence to support my fears. But Surie forecast doom nonetheless.

The longer Lawrence was gone, the more unhappy Mem seemed to become. She never laughed anymore. She hardly spoke to Simon and me. And her rules at our house on Ratendone Road were now as strict as her rules at Safe Haven. She fired the new cook, a sweet man from Madras with a velvet voice and a gift for making fragrant rice, because he once forgot to boil the drinking water. She snapped at Musai for leaving his gardening tools in the driveway, and she was even short with our beloved Nagu for allowing his sons to play their radio at night in the servants' quarters. Simon and I were to go to sleep promptly at eight o'clock with no more talk or song or even reading, and once, when she caught me cutting photographs for a class project from one of her American magazines, she grabbed them away from me and said I must never, ever, touch her books or papers without asking permission.

I blamed Lawrence for leaving us. I told myself everything would return to normal if he would just come back. But week after week, he did not come.

On the last night of Ram Lila, much to my surprise, Mem suggested that we should go out to the *maidan* by Delhi Gate to watch the fireworks. Ram Lila, you see, celebrates the god Rama's victory over the demon Ravana. Every year on the final night Delhi turned out in throngs to cheer the triumph of goodness, and many of our wealthy neighbors along Ratendone Road had private fireworks parties. Last year with Lawrence we had simply watched from our rooftop and agreed it was quite a show. At the time Simon begged to go to the old city, having heard of the spectacle from Nagu's sons, but Mem refused, saying the noise would be deafening, and the crowds too rowdy, and we might get too close to some of the fireworks and be burned by falling cinders. This year, I think, she was trying to please Simon.

Every so often she would seem to realize that days had passed since she last heard a word we said, or even truly looked at us. Then, as if waking from a dream, she would sweep us into the car and off for ice cream or a trip to the bookstore or cinema, and for an hour or maybe two she would lean close and stroke our hands.

And Simon would kick me under the table and make a joke of it, but I understood that this was Mem's way of showing her good intentions. So, on this last night of Ram Lila, I did not upset those intentions by mentioning my own concerns about making an outing to the old city. In any case, Nagu and his boys came with us. Nagu would not allow us to go alone.

The broad lawns of the *maidan* were indeed mobbed with families when we arrived, and Delhi Gate twinkled with a thousand flickering wicks. It was a cool night, dry and clear and moonless but pulsing with artificial light. We had to park near the river and walk a long way. As we walked the smoke burned my throat. Already the ground was treacherous with burning ash and dropped sparklers, and as a result the crowd had a fluid quality, moving this way and that like rings of water backing away from each newly ignited firecracker or roman candle. Vendors continuously jostled past us selling sweets and soda pop. Trained bears and monkeys did their dances to drums, and snake charmers waved their flutes. Up ahead, enormous effigies of Ravana and his cohorts sailed forty feet up in the sky.

To either side of the *maidan* outdoor stages had been erected under strings of glowing bulbs, and actors with painted faces were portraying scenes from the Ramayana. Nagu's sons stopped to buy sparklers, and Simon edged closer to watch the enactment of Sita's rescue from Ravana's palace. He joined in energetically when the audience yelled for Hanuman, the monkey king who flew like a bird. Equally, he booed along when Ravana's guards came forward to meet Hanuman's monkeys in battle. I envied Simon for his ability to hurl himself into such distractions. I myself was too busy keeping an eye out to enjoy the play.

The crowd and noise were overwhelming. The movement of bodies tugged like a current. Already several dozen people had edged in between us, and not all in the surrounding mob were innocent, merrymaking families. So many young men here swaggered and smoked and grinned with the cockiness of *goondas*. There were a few leering policemen also, and some older women with iron eyes who reminded me too much of Indrani. But, I reassured myself, nowhere did I see Surie or anyone truly from my past life.

I had followed Simon forward. Nagu had gone off after his sons. Several dozen people now separated me from Mem, but I could still see her over and between the faces transfixed by the actors. She was talking to two men and a woman – *firenghi*. The woman I recognized as Mrs Solomon. One of the men had an arm hooked around her waist. The other was very thin, with pale hair under a straw hat. Mrs Solomon, as always, seemed to do all the talking. By the light of a fire fountain I saw Mem's eyelids close, her brows squeeze together. Mrs Solomon put a hand to Mem's shoulder. The two men backed away, looking embarrassed.

Suddenly Mem opened her eyes and caught me staring. At that moment a plume of white brilliance divided the sky. A loud boom followed, and I watched her mouth a sound that I could not hear. I thought she was angry with me for spying on her, so I looked up into the sky. Then the noise of the rocket subsided and I heard her cry over the bodies between us, 'Simon!' I turned back toward the stage. The performance had ended. Simon was no longer in front of me, nor to the right or the left. I glanced up and saw Mem pushing people aside as if she were flailing through water.

'Where is he!' As she reached me I spotted Nagu and his sons, searching with their eyes.

I shook my head, unable to pull any sound from my throat.

'You were standing right next to him!' Mem's fingers dug into my arm.

Mrs Solomon and the two men tipped this way and that, their faces like white balloons. At the end of the *maidan* a low whooshing sound erupted, and the crowd surged forward to view the illumination. I felt myself being pulled from Mem, and the noise around us increased so that she was forced to scream at me. 'You must have seen where he went, Kamla! For God's sake, what's the matter with you?'

It was the light, I told myself. Yellow and harsh, it seemed to tighten the skin around Mem's skull and hollow out her eyes and mouth. I didn't know what was the matter with me. I didn't know where Simon had gone. But most of all, I didn't know this screaming *firenghi*. Could this be the same Mem who had fed and clothed me and kept me warm, who had stripped herself naked before me and comforted me in her arms? No. No, this was a stranger.

She was still shouting, but I did not hear her. Why was she accusing *me*? I had done nothing. I had not vanished, had not run away. If Simon were indeed lost, then he had lost himself. No one would dare steal an American boy.

Her eyes shivered with tears, and the sky exploded in ribbons and spirals of rocketing light. I gazed upward, not noticing when Mem released her grip on me. I didn't see her arm rise or her hand, but in the next instant I felt the full force of her rage and terror strike me across the face.

'Answer me!'

'Mem!' Simon cried from the stage. I looked up expecting him to shout out that she had made a terrible mistake, that none of what happened was my fault. But he hadn't seen her slap me. 'I'm here!'

Nagu rose behind him, nudging him forward. 'He went backstage to see the drums,' he yelled.

'Oh, my God.' Mem stepped back and hugged herself. She closed her eyes, and the explosion of Ravana reflected in the streaming surface of her face.

I saw Mrs Solomon closer now, one hand covering her mouth. The two men also had seen Mem slap me. They had been moving toward us. Now all three drifted away.

Mem reached her fingertips to my cheek. She shook her head. 'Kamla—'

I must have flinched, for she stopped before touching me and started to pull back, but I now saw the sorrow and fear in her eyes, and so quickly I put up my hand and clapped it over hers, pressing her palm against my skin.

'I'm sorry,' she said. 'I'm so sorry.' And even in the darkness I could feel her looking into me, searching for something I did not possess, though I would do all in my power to find it. If only I knew how.

That night I let Simon into my bed. Within an hour he had kicked all the covers onto the floor. I left him and went to sleep in his bed. When I woke he was standing over me with his hands on his hips.

I yawned and sat up. 'Simon, I can't help it. You're too big.'

He gave me his hurt boy expression. 'I'll be good.'

'It's not your fault,' I said, then, borrowing Mem's expression, 'You wear me out! Besides, we're too old to share a bed.'

His eyelids flickered strangely. Without a word he bent down and picked up his pillow from the floor. Holding it out in front of him he charged me, knocking me to the ground. He burst into a false, high-pitched laugh and, pillow to my chest, sat astride me, clasping his hands above his head like the pictures he'd been clipping lately of Joe Louis, the American prizefighter.

I wriggled out from under him, pushing him away. Still he would not let go, and this time instead of using a pillow he hit my shoulder with his fist. It left a large bruise shaped like a dog's snout that stayed with me for weeks.

CHAPTER 11

1

The streets leading from Srinagar's airport were muddy and barely paved. As Lawrence rode to Milne's houseboat at the southern end of the city, his trishaw slithered on patches of ice. The twilight smelled of burning coal from the *kangri* – small pots of embers covered with matting that Kashmiris carried to warm their hands – and encampments of refugees still clung to the edges of the city as they had the last time he was here, though now, if Lawrence read the brown beards and colorful headdresses correctly, as many of the refugees appeared from Sinkiang as from the border fighting with Pakistan. Clusters of felt yurts rose among the tin-roofed shacks, and some of the displaced Kazakhs tended straggling herds of sheep. Children roamed with ragged hair and eyes like blue ice, and through it all laced the stench of garbage in the canals.

Still, for all the tatters and filth, the beauty tore at your heart. The way the ancient mud brick walls reflected in the violet lake. The patterns of frost like talc on the floating gardens of lily pads. The silhouette of the old hill fortress Hari Parbat pressed against the white slabs of the Pir Panjals, and the way the muezzin's call to prayer lingered in the cold thick silence. It was as easy to see why nations would fight over this paradise as it was to see that such fighting was both unconscionable and futile.

After nearly an hour of skidding and straining, the trishaw pulled up by the inlet where Milne's boat was moored for the winter. The two houseboys Waza and Mistri were delighted to have a new tenant; almost immediately a flotilla of merchants with names like Marvelous the flower seller, Cheap John, and Suffering Moses

302

began circling the good ship *Triumph*. All turned on Lawrence their brightest charms and most earnest wiles, lifting lanterns to show off their wares, but – to the dismay of Waza and Mistri, who were counting on their take – the new foreigner was not much of a shopper. He was here, he instructed them sternly, 'on important business.' To prove it he set off early each morning and did not return until dark.

For days he explored the bazaars and waterfront. He bought knickknacks for Simon and Kamla, toured the refugee camps, and chatted with aid workers. He interviewed the soldiers, including General Farr's replacement, using a press pass from the *Sydney Telegraph* as his cover. He recruited a Turki doctor and a local Kashmiri official. No one could tell him anything new about Aidan, but these last two had their own networks of informants and thus would pacify Jack.

Periodically he would drop Akbar's name like a pebble into the pool and count the rings of reaction. Whose brow lifted, whose hands tightened, who pretended indifference or ignorance of the aging ethnographer. Milne was right; there was no pattern to Akbar's acquaintances. They crossed both political and religious spectra, including separatist Muslims and loyal Sikhs and Hindus alike. And the good doctor's image varied depending on the acquaintance, from eccentric to wise man, from nonpartisan to political agent. Even those who suspected him of being an agent, however, could not agree on *whose* agent he might be. Some pointed to his education in England as proof that he worked for the Brits. One Hindu jeweler insisted that Dr Akbar 'had proven above and beyond all doubt that his allegiance lies with India,' though he could not – or would not – say how he had proven this. And the manager at the Shalimar restaurant – a native Kashmiri Muslim – maintained that Akbar was staunchly in favor of Kashmiri independence from both India and Pakistan. After all, the man pointed out, Akbar was a Muslim himself. No one raised the possibility that his sympathies might lie with Stalin. But then, if he was good at his game, that's the one possibility that would *not* spring to mind.

Finally, one afternoon, Lawrence made his way to the northern end of the city. It had snowed that morning, then the sun had come out warm and moist, giving the ancient streets a scrubbed shimmer.

They were largely empty here in this residential area, except for the reverberations of prayer that poured over the walls of the Hazrat Bal mosque. Akbar's religious devotions might have him at Friday worship with his fellow Muslims, but Lawrence doubted it. According to all reports, Akbar rarely left his house.

Lawrence recognized the ornately carved, time-stained facade as soon as it loomed into view. Like most of the homes in Srinagar, Akbar's was designed to present a closed front against prying eyes and the harshness of the Kashmiri winter, but today the hatchwork screen on the upper balcony and the wooden shutters were all thrown open like mouths to catch the sun. From several of the windows dangled bright red tongues – rugs and blankets out for an airing. And through the window directly above the front door floated a man's voice singing 'Blue Skies' in a wide, clipped, and faintly familiar accent.

Lawrence knocked loudly. The singing stopped and was followed by the stutter of footsteps inside. A minute later the door opened and Lawrence, to his astonishment, found himself face-to-face with Tot.

The Sherpa, dressed in a bright red, green, and blue pullover sweater and baggy maroon trousers, looked otherwise much as he had done when Lawrence last saw him waving goodbye at the Tihwa aerodrome. His straight black hair was chopped unevenly as if he had cut it himself with toenail scissors. He looked neither fatter nor thinner, only a bit more wizened around the eyes. After a moment of obvious disorientation at the sight of Lawrence, he grinned and stuck out his hand. 'Mr Malcolm!'

They thumped each other on the shoulder. 'I don't believe it,' Lawrence said. 'You made it out!'

'Yes! With Mr Weller and his caravan. I am their guide.'

'With Weller, eh? What'd you do, wait around Tihwa till the bitter end?'

Tot lifted his palms. 'I hear that no more planes will fly. The Communists are coming. I think Mr Weller must leave soon, I can wait. But this time we are too many. Chinese governor, Prime Minister, wife, children. There is much sickness, much complaining.'

'You earned every annah. That what you're saying?'

Tot grinned, then seemed to remember himself and urged Lawrence to enter.

'And what are you doing *here*?' Lawrence asked, though he had a fair notion. Tot was no houseboy.

'Dr Akbar has a big house. He asked me to stay here.'

Lawrence looked down the dark hallway with its embroidered hangings and displays of masks and antiquated weapons. 'How is he?' he asked.

Tot pulled in his lips. He dropped his eyes. Lawrence heard the wooden stairway creak at the end of the hall.

'Dr Akbar!' Tot shot Lawrence a warning nod, and moved to the bottom of the stairs. 'Look who comes to see you. Mr Malcolm. Can you believe?'

It was difficult to see clearly in the dim passageway, but it seemed to Lawrence that Akbar had shrunk. His frame as he descended the last steps appeared spry enough, not stooped or slow or visibly suffering. But the body that little more than a year ago had seemed fit and trim now was dwarfed by a small gray cardigan that mushroomed around his waist. The light that filtered from the landing behind him pressed through the white *kurta-pyjama* bottoms to silhouette two pencil-thin legs. And his previously thick, brilliantined crown of black hair had thinned to a patchwork of black and gray tufts that were noticeably softer in texture than the wide brush mustache Akbar still sported across his upper lip.

'La-awre-ence!' Akbar stretched his arms, sweater sleeves flapping like the wings of a kimono. As they clasped hands Lawrence smelled cigarettes and sour breath and the cold, clammy odor of decay.

Akbar stood back, pushed his spectacles up his nose. 'You are looking very well, sir.'

'Thanks.' Lawrence flailed for a rejoinder. 'It's good to see you . . . Good to be back in Srinagar.'

Akbar ushered him into the sitting room. 'I understand already you have been here several days, and yet only now you come to me. Tot, would you please ask Bassu to prepare some refreshments for our friend?'

Lawrence toyed with the idea of lying to Akbar, but he knew this would be a mistake. However diverse, the good 'doctor's' sources were evidently still loyal. Doubtless, everything he had said or asked in the past days had been relayed in full.

He settled into a rattan chair opposite the wormwood throne on which Akbar was working himself into a nest of bright silk cushions. The room was cluttered with books and papers and more decorative artifacts, and two bolts of effulgent yellow sunlight slanted in through the windows at the end of the room.

'I ran into Reggie Milne in Simla,' Lawrence said. 'He told me you were ill.'

Akbar pulled his feet up under him. A Siamese cat leapt into his lap. 'Reggie Milne is a decent enough chap,' he said, 'and he knows how to set a leg, but a simple stomachache is beyond him. Cancer, he said! Can you imagine? When in fact it was just a superficial ulcer!'

'He said you didn't care for his opinion.'

'I do not care *about* his opinion. I simply desired some of the medications that he so ably dispenses.'

'Painkillers.'

Akbar yawned, blowing out that same scent of decay. He stroked the cat. 'This subject does not interest me. I do not believe you returned to Srinagar out of concern for my health.'

'Not entirely.' Lawrence paused. 'I suppose you could say I'm here on a fact-finding mission.'

'I see.' Akbar closed his eyes briefly. 'You know, Lawrence, I believe that there exist in the world two types of people. One type resists facts at all cost, preferring to cling to illusion and faith. The other just as determinedly believes that facts alone hold the answer. You and I belong to this second group, I think. Our entire lives consist of one long fact-finding mission, as you call it.' He yawned again. 'The problem is that truth, in the end, requires all three. Fact, illusion, faith – alone, each is equally incomplete. Ah! Here we are.'

Tot had entered the room carrying a tray of coffee and small baked crescents that gave off an aroma of curry and lamb and cinnamon. He set the food on the leather trunk that served as a table, then turned his attention to the large stone hearth, where a fire was laid but unlit.

'Thank you, dear Tot,' Akbar said. The Sherpa looked over his shoulder and smiled.

306

Lawrence poured the coffee. 'Joanna and Simon Shaw are still in Delhi,' he said. 'Did you know that?'

'I did not. Are they well?'

'As well as can be expected.' Lawrence addressed both men, but only Tot showed any reaction.

'What of the girl . . . Kamla?' he asked.

'She's with them. Going to school with Simon – thriving – while Joanna runs her rescue home. It's almost like real life, except for Jo's missing husband.'

Tot lit a match and started the fire, then squatted before it, elbows on his knees. How many nights had he manned their campfires in just this pose, Lawrence thought, quietly watching him and Joanna and Kamla across the flames. How had it never dawned on him? All those weeks trekking over the mountains and around the desert – no wonder Tot had been so put out when Kamla took his place on that final jaunt to Heaven's Lake. No wonder he had hung on in Tihwa, making himself available to serve as Weller's guide. Tot was Akbar's personal news writer. Source of the facts that were Akbar's lifeblood.

Akbar calmly sipped his coffee, thickened to a syrup with milk and sugar. 'I believe you have an appointment, Tot.'

The Sherpa ducked his head. Yes, he said, he was to meet with a German mountaineer who believed that in Ladakh's Chang Chenmo Range there lay a peak taller than Everest. 'Who knows?' He smiled at Lawrence. 'With foreigners, anything is possible.'

'So,' Akbar said when Tot had gone. 'How have you occupied yourself since last we met?'

He was not going to take the bait about Aidan, so Lawrence decided to bide his time. 'Been working on a book, actually. Cross between a history and biography of the Great Game.'

'A noble enterprise,' Akbar said with more than a hint of sarcasm. 'I, too, have a book in progress. I like to think of it as an ethnic portrait of the Karakorams. You know, I suppose, that the cultural traffic across these mountains dates back hundreds of thousands of years. This is the true melting pot of the world. Chinese, Persians, Greeks, and Romans. Some say that Jesus Christ himself passed through Kashmir more than once. And each new wave leaves its trace in the local populations. Even your British, who were latecomers, spread their seed here. Though they are the least willing to admit it.'

'I'm aware of that,' Lawrence said dryly. 'They've a rather inflated – and immaculate – view of themselves when it comes to Australia, as well, you know.'

'I have never been to Australia.' Akbar leaned forward and helped himself to one of the lamb pasties. He used his tongue to retrieve the pale crumbs of crust that caught in his mustache and let the cat lick his fingertips.

Akbar not only had never been to Australia but evidently had never considered that the land down under might have a political identity apart from Britain's. Lawrence let the idea percolate as they ate, then said, 'I think what fascinates me most about the Game is the role of men like Andrew Dalgleish and Alexander Gardiner, who took the other approach—'

'Who went native,' Akbar said.

'Yes.'

'You find that romantic, do you? When one's identity merges into these cultural borders?'

'I'm not sure whether it's a matter of identity or affinity.'

'You must find Joanna's girl Kamla most romantic, then,' Akbar said. 'I do not disagree. In fact, I began working on this thesis soon after you all came to see me. Imagine, a Tungan Sikh with blue eyes! Perhaps she is my muse!'

'I have a feeling that one day Kamla's going to put us all to shame,' Lawrence said.

'And why is that?'

'In my opinion these border crossings result in a kind of strength – wisdom, if you will – that the rest of us can't comprehend. I'm inclined to think purity is vastly overrated.'

'And yet you are in love with Joanna, are you not? You do not choose for yourself to cross this fundamental frontier. And this, I think, is why men such as Gardiner and Dalgleish must fascinate you.' Akbar gently turned the cat out of his lap.

Lawrence put his hand to his neck, felt the heat of his skin. In a flood of shame, he remembered making love to Joanna in the same room with Kamla, and later on Milne's houseboat, later still within earshot of Simon singing the songs Lawrence and Aidan had sung as they marched through the war. Aidan, who was himself born straddling this frontier.

'I feel the need for something a bit stronger,' Akbar announced. He went to a cupboard in the corner and came back brandishing a bottle of Russian vodka.

'I thought Muslims were teetotalers,' said Lawrence. 'Especially Muslims with ulcers.'

'I thought Aussies were drunken louts.' Akbar poured into their empty coffee cups and drank to both their health. He winced as he swallowed.

Lawrence said, 'Joanna told me the first ayah she hired in Delhi poured gin into Simon's water glass thinking it was her own.'

Akbar turned his wire-rimmed lenses appraisingly. 'Did Joanna fire her?'

'Mmm. I believe that was the first and last ayah for Simon.' Lawrence examined the bottle's label. Stalingrad. 'I prefer gin, myself.'

'A bit too British for my blood.'

'I thought you and the Brits were boon companions. Didn't you study in England?'

'I did indeed.' Akbar smoothed his palm down the front of his sweater, lingering on the thin swell of his stomach.

'Vodka's rather an acquired taste as well,' Lawrence said. 'Especially firewater like this stuff.'

'Travel encourages such acquisitions.'

'Along with curios and antiquities.'

'And friends.' Akbar raised his cup again, and this time waited for Lawrence to join him. 'To friends.'

After a lengthy silence Lawrence asked, 'Did you consider Alice James a friend?'

His host chewed on his mustache. 'Of course,' he said at last, and lit a cigarette.

'A useful one?'

Akbar blew a smoke ring. 'Watch this.' He took another puff and added a trail of dots so it looked as if a comic strip balloon was rising from his mouth. 'You like tricks. You can do wonderful things with smoke.'

'I don't smoke.'

'I detect a note of disapproval.'

'American Indians used smoke signals to send messages over long distances.'

'Ah, yes,' said Akbar. 'Smoke and mirrors.'

'Alice James was your Indian. And Tot as well, I think.'

Two fans of short distinct lines appeared at the outer corners of Akbar's black eyes. He leaned forward, suppressing a cough. 'Amusing.'

'You acquired your taste for vodka in Moscow?' asked Lawrence.

'I would say, more likely Leningrad. I spent some months there before the war. The collection of Central Asian antiquities at the Hermitage is exceptional.'

'So I've heard.' Lawrence waited for Akbar to regain his breath. 'Why'd you send Joanna in?'

' "Send" is a bit emphatic, don't you think?'

'You planted the thought. You showed her the map. You all but gave her the same marching orders you gave Alice James.' He watched his voice. Words aside, this was not an accusation. 'You told her about Alice James.'

'I merely told Joanna the truth as I knew it. I did not read her mind. I only guessed at it. To be told that a husband has died . . . She was understandably distraught, but that error was not mine.'

'Whose was it?'

'Ask your American friends.'

'Why would they tell her Aidan was dead if they *knew* he wasn't on the plane?'

'They will say, I am quite certain, that it was an honest mistake. Perhaps it was.'

'An inexcusable blunder, you mean.' Lawrence felt the heat again climbing the back of his neck. 'I can hardly believe they were so stupid.'

'Not many women are as tenacious as Joanna.'

'The evidence suggests that Alice was equally tenacious, yet you were afraid Aidan would stop her before she got through.'

The firelight deepened the hollows in Akbar's face. He watched Lawrence without replying.

'Who did stop her?' Lawrence asked.

'We didn't think they would dare to harm an American,' Akbar said. 'Especially not someone like Alice.'

Lawrence heard the subtle shift in Akbar's voice, like a gate sliding open. He asked quietly, 'What does that mean?'

Akbar gazed into the flames. 'Alice was a special case. A man's woman, if you understand. Perhaps they would have tried to abduct her, but never to kill her. This was my thinking. I was wrong.'

'They.'

'You are the master of the Game, are you not, my friend?'

'You think Weller and his Kazakh goons targeted her?'

Silence.

'Was she your recruit?'

Akbar emptied his cup in a single swallow and hurled it into the hearth. The shattering of clay on stone reverberated up the wide chimney. 'It didn't matter which of us she was working for,' he said finally. 'She was exceptional. She should not have died.'

So Alice was Akbar's border-crossing. Or would have been. Lawrence decided to adjust the subject.

'What do you know about Douglas Freeman?'

Akbar looked at him sharply. 'The American.'

'I heard a rumor he was captured in Kazakhstan.'

'He was well trained.'

'He didn't talk?'

'He escaped.'

'I don't imagine you know where he is now?'

A log split, the two halves spraying embers up the chimney. 'Is it really Douglas Freeman you wish to discuss?' Akbar asked.

Lawrence smiled. 'All right, then. What happened to Aidan Shaw?'

'We rescued him.'

The two men's eyes met. 'Go on,' Lawrence said.

'You understand, I use the word *we* in the most general sense.'

'I understand.'

'I did not know this when you and Joanna came to Srinagar for Simon. I did not mislead you.' Akbar removed his glasses and rubbed the bulge of his nose. 'It was several months before I learned that there was an American in Ili Territory. He'd been wounded in the explosion. Some of our rebels were in the area.'

'Following Aidan and Alice.'

'No.' Akbar stretched his hands to the waning fire. 'They were doing reconnaissance on Osman. Of course, had they all crossed paths earlier, everything might have been different. It is difficult to be certain . . . However, I do not believe that land mine was intended for Alice and Joanna's husband. This was Mr Weller's mistake.'

'Your side buried Alice and took Aidan with them,' Lawrence said. And in the process Aidan dropped that photo of Simon – a message to Joanna that he was alive.

'This is my understanding.'

'Then what?'

'He was taken to hospital in Alma-Ata.'

'Why over the border?'

'He was badly injured. It was the closest hospital – that is, for our side.'

Lawrence smiled ironically, recalling Aidan's presumptive motive for accepting the mission. To prove his loyalty. 'So Aidan fell into the trap meant for your Reds, and they in turn saved his life.'

Akbar didn't answer.

'What were his injuries?'

'I know only that it was some months before he could walk.'

Lawrence took a deep breath. 'Where is he now?'

'Now I have told you everything I know. And none of it is official.' Akbar got to his feet and stood looking down on Lawrence by the dying firelight.

'Why *are* you telling me?'

'Because you asked. Because my information is too stale to be any longer relevant or reliable. Because I am now out of the Game.' Akbar pressed a hand against his stomach. 'My days, as they say in the West, are numbered. Anyway, it is clear to me that you are as disappointed in the outcome of all of this as I am. So much time chasing facts, my friend, and still so little truth.'

2

Joanna, he wrote. *I'm a chastened man. It was wrong of me to press you. I realize that now. I'll be back in Delhi by week's end. Not sure how long I'll stay, but I must see you . . .*

Joanna frowned, folded the letter, and returned it to her skirt pocket. She nursed her drink and stared across the sunswept lawn. With its white-clothed tables and glittering service, the Imperial still reeked of the Raj. The gentry queuing up for the luncheon buffet would have felt right at home in the time of Victoria. Yellow-haired women in long white dresses. Balding men with ruddy complexions and pocket handkerchiefs. Laughing. Embracing. Tendering plates to brown-faced men done up like birds in fluted red turbans and fitted white waistcoats. On which side of that table would each of them stand? Aidan? Lawrence? Herself? Was it possible that, in the end, this whole nightmare would come down to this one fundamental question?

More than a month had passed since her visit to the Chinese embassy. When she telephoned last week, Chou had warned her to be patient. He said he would contact her as soon as he heard anything. But she should be circumspect. Aidan was under Chinese protection. He – Chou – was acting out of sympathy, but neither he nor the Party leaders wished this to become a diplomatic incident. There must be no intrusion from her government. Did she understand? She must not call again. And she must tell no one.

No one.

She closed her eyes. Where was Bertie Solomon? They were supposed to meet at noon, and it was already half past.

Not that she was one to judge. Three days ago she had left a girl sitting in jail overnight because she forgot to send Vijay to sign for her. Hari finally insisted she take a week off. So here she was, free for lunch in the middle of a clear, sunny Tuesday, the children busy at school, and Nagu and Vijay covering her other so-called responsibilities. Not even the distraction of work could disguise the fact of her powerlessness now.

Bertie stepped through the lobby doors and out onto the terrace. Black-lensed sunglasses, white straw hat ringed with fake strawberries, and fleshy brown arms jiggling braceleted charms. Bertie was easily twenty pounds overweight and gloried in every one of them.

'Joanna!' she cried, charging across the lawn. 'Why are you hiding way over here?'

She dropped into the other lawn chair, fanning her face, and immediately slipped her feet from their black patent pumps. Deep

313

marks scored the skin along her instep. She flexed her naked toes. 'At least you've found some shade. I will never adjust to this climate. Forty degrees at night, and ninety at noon! Some December. Waiter! Tonic water, please. Do you know if the ice is made with boiled water? Are you *positive?* All right, then. Yes, with ice. Thanks . . . Joanna, are you all right?'

Joanna hesitated. This was a friend. 'Just a little tired.' She picked up her drink. Her own tonic was laced with gin. 'Thanks for coming.'

Bertie smiled. Relaxed. 'I'm glad you called.'

'I've been meaning to for weeks. I wanted to thank you for getting your article published in the States. We've received over five hundred dollars since summer.'

'Good old Temple Isaiah. My congregation back in Great Neck. I knew they'd come through.'

'Well, it's making a real difference. Last week we installed a new stove in the kitchen, and next month three girls are heading off to boarding school. All because of you.'

'Don't be silly. I'm only the reporter, Joanna. You're the miracle worker.' She smiled a little too emphatically. 'How's Kamla?'

'Oh. Perfect. Straight As. She hardly stops reading long enough to sleep.'

'You should be very proud,' Bertie said, again pressing down on the corners of the words as if Joanna needed convincing. The black lenses concealed her eyes, but Joanna could feel her inspection.

'Actually, that's the other reason I called. I want to explain about that night at the *maidan*—'

'You don't have to explain.'

'I do, though. I know you saw what happened, and I'm so ashamed of snapping like that. I thought I'd lost Simon. For a second I went out of my mind, and Kamla was . . . well, she was just there.'

'You don't need to apologize to *me*,' Bertie said pointedly.

'I know. I've tried to explain to Kamla. I've asked her forgiveness. But if anything, she's too quick to forgive.'

Bertie wagged her finger. 'You want me to scold you. Is that it?'

'I just need a friend.'

'Whatever you need, honey.' Bertie got up out of her chair and clumsily wound an arm around Joanna's shoulders. She smelled of gardenia eau de cologne. The waiter arrived with her tonic. The women disentangled themselves and tapped their glasses together. Joanna wondered why she didn't feel better.

'Here I am living in the most crowded country on the planet,' she said, trying to backpedal into lightheartedness. 'You'd think I'd crave solitude.'

'We all feel alone, sometimes.' Behind the dark glasses Bertie's expression shifted. She nibbled on the corner of her mouth, then said, 'Joanna, we've never really talked about your – your circumstances. I didn't think it was my place. But Bill's filled me in a little.'

Bill. Bertie's husband. A press officer with the US Information Agency.

Bertie placed a cigarette in her mouth and struck a match. The glint of her wedding band caught Joanna's eye. It dug into the soft skin of her finger as if rooted there. Joanna pushed her own ring back off her knuckle.

'Then you probably know as much as I do,' she said.

'A circular went around last week. Officially, there are more than four hundred Americans trapped inside China. Twenty-three in jail. The Chinese say they're all spies, of course, but the State Department is keeping this a deep dark secret.'

'Why?'

'Well, probably because some *are* spies.'

'What about the rest?'

'Missionaries, mostly, I think, some academic types who were so far out in the middle of nowhere they couldn't get to the border in time. And maybe a few old naive lefties who thought Mao Tse-tung was the Second Coming.' Bertie sighed. 'What I'm trying to tell you in my usual roundabout way is, I know what folks in Washington have been saying about your husband, and maybe that's kind of a smoke screen. I mean, it's easier to blame the victim than for them to admit they haven't the foggiest idea how to rescue him. Right?'

If only you knew, Joanna thought. 'You'd probably better not speak too loudly, or they'll put a black mark next to your name as well. But I appreciate the thought. By the way, who was that man with you at the *maidan* that night? There was so much noise I

315

couldn't hear when you introduced us.'

Bertie wriggled in her seat. 'Oh, he's a wonderful guy. Doug Freeman. He's new to Delhi, works for one of the agencies. International Vision. Literacy programs mostly. Right up your alley. You know, actually, I wasn't sure if it would be appropriate, but I was sort of thinking you two might hit it off . . .'

'Oh, Bertie.' Joanna groaned. 'I don't think so.'

Bertie put her cigarette down and fished in her pocketbook. 'Well, far be it from me to push it, but I just happen to have his card. And that's the end of it.'

Joanna took the card to appease her. The waiter stopped to see if they wanted another round. Joanna's drink was almost empty, and she longed for another, but that would mean sitting here another half-hour. She shook her head. 'I'm terribly sorry, Bertie. But the heat seems to have killed my appetite and given me a splitting headache. I think I'm going to go.'

Bertie removed her glasses, settled her round brown eyes on Joanna, and held them there. Too gently. 'I don't suppose this is any of my business either, but what's become of your friend, Lawrence Malcolm?'

'He left Delhi months ago.' Her hand dropped over her pocket. 'Why?'

'Are you still in touch with him?' Bertie's attempt at circumspection was pathetic.

'*Why?*'

'Oh, this is probably nothing, but there's apparently a file on him.'

'*Lawrence?*' Joanna stared at her, then burst out laughing. 'Who *isn't* there a file on!'

'You told me he worked with British SO during the war,' Bertie pressed. 'Maybe you know, there were a lot of Communists connected with Special Operations.'

'Lawrence also worked with MacArthur. Was *he* a Communist?'

Bertie blew out a stream of smoke. 'Doesn't it strike you as odd, this man wandering around India, ostensibly doing research, but without a job or a family, checks coming in at regular intervals—'

'And what about you, Bertie! What's your job?'

That threw her. She smoothed the blue crepe lap of her dress and

316

crossed her legs. Her round little toes wagged up and down, barely missing the edge of the low table as she reached to stub out her cigarette. After a long silence she said, 'I heard Bill on the phone the other night. He mentioned your husband's name, so I stopped to listen. He was talking about your husband. Something about it being a setup. Then he brought up Lawrence Malcolm – "This Malcolm guy really cultivated Shaw." That's what he said. He asked if it was true Lawrence recruited your husband and sent him up to Kashmir.'

Joanna squinted at the shimmering tops of the palm trees that ringed the hotel grounds. She took a final swallow of her drink, then asked, 'Was it Bob Cross?'

'Who?' Bertie picked up her purse and rummaged through it for a mirror and lipstick, which she chose this moment to apply.

'On the other end of the phone. Cross. He's in the embassy. Consular attaché.'

The resulting kiss of red was crooked. 'I've never heard *that* name. No. I don't know who it was.'

Joanna backed up a beat. *Smart thing is to bring yourself up to snuff and climb along onto her team.* 'What exactly do they think Lawrence is doing?'

'I don't know,' Bertie repeated. 'Spying, I guess. But not for us, from the sound of it.'

'I wouldn't think so. He's Australian.'

'You know what I mean.'

Joanna didn't say anything.

Bertie shook out another cigarette from her pack of Lucky Strikes. But she didn't light it. 'Whether you believe me or not is up to you. I like you, Joanna. Which is more than I can say for most of the other Americans here. I just thought you'd want to know.'

3

He had barely set down his bags when Mrs D'Costa appeared at his door waving a fistful of mail. 'You are too trusting, Mr Malcolm, going away for months at a stretch. Here I come this very morning to find a young rascal nosing about. Shooh! I say, what are you doing, and he says, I am just leaving a chit for Mr Malcolm. Then why are you lingering? I ask him. Oh, he says, I just want to make sure it doesn't get lost. Well, you leave it to me, I say and push him straight out the door. Can you believe it? Who knows what he might have done had I not come along? I am telling you, I would be happy to have a locked mailbox installed for you, Mr Malcolm. Just a few annahs for peace of mind.'

'Thanks, Mrs D', but you've made this kind offer on many occasions, and I assure you, there's nothing in my mail a thief would want. I'd much rather give you an extra annah for my peace of mind than waste it on a bit of tin.' To her delight he pulled a coin from her ear and traded it for the mail. In point of fact, the old woman was more reliable than any lock box. But he pitied her, which complicated their relationship. Age had worked on Mrs D'Costa like a landslide, and her eyes and bones and teeth were lost beneath multiple pleats of flesh. She smelled like gently rotting fruit, and because she was Goan, with mostly Portuguese blood, she presumed a special affinity with Lawrence (as opposed to the other, Indian, tenants), had twice appeared at his door after midnight bearing a bottle of Jameson's as a token of mutual understanding.

He shuddered at the recollection as he shut the door on her ruined features, her mouth still moving. If he went away again, he must install someone here in his flat – someone he trusted – to hold her at bay.

To distance himself now, he took his mail out onto the balcony, where the cold gray morning light and babble of the street curled over him like a breaking wave. It was not yet eight o'clock, and already the owner of the hardware shop next door was screaming at one of his clerks. Another version of Mrs D's diatribe. 'What do you think, you can come and go as you please, any time, any day, you are welcome, so dazzling your smile, so devoted your custom-ers, I am hiring you out of the goodness of my heart because you come to me weeping with despair, your father has died and your studies cut short, all the weight of your family falls on your poor young shoulders, and this is how you repay me! Strolling in after two days gone, demanding your pay a day early, you must think suddenly I am working for you . . .'

'I lift you up, you put me down,' Lawrence muttered to himself. The outrage of the savior over the ingratitude of the saved. It was a scene the British had played to perfection – until the ingrates finally kicked them out. Now the newly minted local *sahibs* had usurped the script, performing the lines with a zest and vengeance all their own. This borrowed arrogance used to infuriate Aidan more than the colonial attitudes that had spawned it. As if tyrannizing someone of another race was somehow more palatable than lording it over one's own. That was his British schooling again, Lawrence supposed. As was his whole notion of a Greater Good. The image of a puppet master pulling the strings of shadow figures across a stage. During the original Game the two puppet masters had been Britain and Russia. Now they were Communism and Democracy, with Aidan himself the shadow. But which master pulled his strings?

He turned from the ongoing squabble below and flipped through the bundles of mail Mrs D' had collected. Anything of formal importance was funneled through the High Commission. Here was a note from Rodney Tynsdale in Sydney asking when he planned to finish his manuscript. Announcements of sale days in Connaught Place. A birthday card from Tracy wishing him well and informing him that she and her new husband had moved to England. He dropped these into the small oil drum that served as his fireplace. But one envelope bore no stamp or return address, only Lawrence's name, typewritten. This was clearly Mrs D's mystery delivery.

He ripped open the envelope. *Enjoying the reports of your walkabout. Hope to catch up in person during your stop home en route to the States. Jack.*

Permission granted.

Lawrence stared over the roof blocks at the sun's reddish blur burning through the mist. Then he dropped this paper into the drum with the others and followed it with a lit match.

Half an hour later at Ratendone Road Kamla opened the door.

'Princess!' Lawrence bowed from the waist.

She must have been dressing for school, he thought while awaiting permission to rise. Her blouse was out of her navy skirt, on her feet only bobby socks. She must have heard his knock and run downstairs. Nagu would have answered, but he was in the kitchen scolding the cook. A new cook, judging by the clatter of pots and the weariness in Nagu's voice. *Two* eggs for *memsahib*'s breakfast. Joanna would be in her bedroom, and Simon either out with Nagu's boys or making faces in the mirror as he brushed his teeth. Lawrence felt the household's morning rituals take hold of him like a warm glove. Then he remembered: Aidan was alive.

Kamla didn't move. She didn't speak. At length he stood up feeling foolish and guilty. It had been three months. The girl had grown inches taller. Just look how her shoulders strained at the seams of her blouse. She was losing the childlike roundness of her face and throat. Her cheekbones seemed higher, her chin and nose more tapered. And those lake blue eyes, always arresting, now reproached him.

He grinned sheepishly and held up a paper bag containing two stuffed elephants that he saw would not do at all. 'For you and Simon.'

She gestured vaguely toward the stairs. 'Mem is dressing.'

'Kammy – ' He reached out but she pulled away from him, an emotion that he could not read darting across her face.

'I will tell her you've come.' She let go of the door, her look warning him to stay where he was. She lifted her chin and straightened her back and smoothed her palms on her skirt as she marched up the stairs.

It's the cold-shoulder treatment, he thought, both dismayed and impressed at her polish. She's furious I've been gone so long, and this is how she shows it.

But if Kamla had mastered the art of sangfroid, Simon was raw nerve. 'Where have you been!' the boy screamed, tearing past her down the stairs and hurling himself into Lawrence's arms. They hugged, violently, crazily. Simon was still wearing his red pajamas and he smelled just as he should – of dirt and grass and sticky sweets. Even his accusation was welcoming. 'We didn't think you were ever coming back!'

'Of course, I was. Didn't you get my postcards?' He had not, like Aidan, simply disappeared.

'But you never said you were coming *back*!'

'I just didn't know when, that's all.' He tousled the boy's hair and put him down. 'Here.' He passed him the bag, which now had a long rip down one side.

Simon pulled out the elephants, went deadpan, then whacked them against each other by their trunks, so hard their embroidered howdahs fell off. 'Wham, wham, wham.' Simon contributed the sound effects, then just as suddenly stopped and grinned. 'Thanks.'

'I guess you're back in school.'

Simon shifted both elephants to one hand and reached into the breast pocket of his pajama top. 'Want some Bazooka? My friend Brian brought it from home.'

'Thanks,' Lawrence said. 'You mean the States?'

'Yeah. He just moved here. We're friends.' He wrinkled his nose, and Lawrence detected a note of defiance in his voice. 'Kammy's not in my class again this year.'

'No?'

'She's *two* classes ahead now. All she does is read. She wears Mem out.'

'I'm sorry to hear that.'

'All Mem does is work.' Simon lifted his brown eyes with a look of surprise, as if only this minute realizing that two plus three is five. 'Why did you have to go away?'

'Simon.' Joanna stood at the top of the stairs. 'Time for school. Better get dressed.' Her voice was tight. She wore a long gray skirt and chalk-colored blouse. Her hair was pulled into a knot, her face unnaturally pale. The effect, Lawrence thought, was of a handsome but overworked schoolteacher.

Simon sighed and looked down at the paper bag by his feet. He kicked it aside but did not pick it up as he started back upstairs. The two elephants dangled from his hands like vanquished dinosaurs.

She led him into the living room, refusing to meet his eyes. Every detail was as he'd last seen it – the arrangement of furniture in an open square, the game table with Aidan's chess set, the stacks of big band phonograph albums. And the photographs of Aidan still smiling down. Every single one.

'I got your note.' She remained standing.

Lawrence sat on the sofa. 'Fair warning.'

'I'm not sure where to begin.'

His eyes fell to her hands. She was wringing them, but that's not what caught his attention. She was wearing her wedding band again.

'Has something happened?'

'Ben Eldon came to Delhi last month,' she said.

The teakettle whistled in the kitchen, and Nagu appeared through the open panels to the dining room. He welcomed Lawrence with his usual warm but noncommittal smile and asked if he should bring coffee. Joanna shook her head. 'Nothing, thank you. But could you get the children breakfasted and off in a rickshaw to school? I won't be able to take them this morning.'

'But of course, Mem.' The bearer dropped his eyes and closed the panels after him.

'And?' Lawrence asked.

She leaned her head against the wall. The cool morning light flushed the shadows from her eyes but illuminated the new, fine lines that had etched her skin in his absence. When she spoke her voice broke. 'Aidan's alive.'

Lawrence fisted one hand and wrapped it in the other. 'Go on.'

'Ben thinks he's defected.'

'What's the evidence?'

Outside in the hall Simon shouted to Kamla. A clamor of feet and dishes sounded in the dining room. Joanna signaled Lawrence to follow her.

Upstairs she shut the bedroom door behind them. The *tats* were up, the French doors open to the balcony so that the room seemed thick with orange sunlight. The familiar paisley spread lay in a crumpled twist over the unmade bed, and the clutter of books and magazines, pads of paper and pencils and empty drinking glasses on the bedside tables suggested more than one restless night. The only photographs on display here were of Simon and Kamla.

She had her back to him, was unlocking the desk drawer. When she turned she held a piece of newsprint.

A car backfired out in the street. Lawrence felt the concussion in his chest. Then a wave of nausea as he took hold of the clipping.

'Eldon gave you this?' he asked.

'No . . .' She leaned back against the desk, bracing herself with

322

her hands. 'Ben showed me a different picture. I found this one on my own.'

As Lawrence stared down at Aidan's image, Weller's smirking voice came back to him: *I don't know all the rules they broke . . . or why.*

He had only to tell her, yes, this makes sense. We were duped, betrayed, should have seen it coming. It's all Aidan's fault. But that gold ring warned against it. He could feel her question without her speaking it.

'Have you gone to the embassy?' he asked.

She nodded. 'They still pretend complete ignorance. Minton wouldn't even see me. He passed me down to this idiot, Bob Cross, who was so obviously trying to find out whether I knew that I left without telling him anything.'

He examined the clipping more closely. 'How can you be so certain *they* know? American intelligence is not necessarily fail-safe. You and Eldon may be combing the Chinese press with a more particular purpose than our mates at State. You know what they say about all Chinese looking alike. And Aidan looks remarkably Chinese here.' And remarkably sympathetic to the cadres around him.

'The photograph Ben showed me was similar to this one, but it wasn't a news clipping.' She walked past him to the window. 'It was blown up, grainy. It looked as if it had been taken covertly. And Ben wasn't supposed to have it. He took it back almost as soon as he showed it to me, said a friend at the State Department had smuggled it out to him. They know, Lawrence. They definitely know.'

'Eldon came all the way to India to show you?'

'He was on his way to Hong Kong, I think. On business. I'd been writing him while you were gone. I didn't know who else to turn to.'

'Christ, Jo, I'm sorry. Why didn't you contact me in Simla?'

She had her back to him. 'You've known all along he's alive. Haven't you?'

Downstairs the front door slammed, and through the open window Lawrence heard Nagu's gentle murmurs walking the children down the driveway, Simon humming 'Waltzing Matilda.'

Joanna stepped out to the balcony, and waved them goodbye.

He came up behind her, put his hands on her shoulders. She didn't move.

'You're wrong.' He withdrew his hands. 'But you're right to suspect me. There's something I should have told you a long time ago.'

She turned her head. Strands of hair fell into her eyes, and one thin blue vein pulsed against the paler surface of her temple.

'Come and sit down,' he said. 'This needs a bit of explaining.' He took the wooden chair against the wall. She shut the glass doors and sat on the bed, again averting her eyes.

'I'm responsible for Aidan going to Kashmir,' he said. 'That tip about the Czech trying to sabotage the UN mission. I fed it to Aidan, thought I was doing him a favor – though that's only part of it.'

'What kind of a favor?' Her voice sounded hollow.

'I need to back up. After the war, when I joined the External Affairs Department, I started sliding into intelligence work. Mostly at home or at conferences, I'd monitor visiting diplomats who might be Soviet sympathizers. It wasn't official exactly. More like a favor I was doing on the side for certain powers that be. But after Davey died and I announced my intention to leave Australia – to leave everything, really – my superior offered to send me here as a kind of experiment.'

'Experiment?'

'There's a push on to launch a bona fide Australian Intelligence Agency – like your CIA. But there's also political opposition. Not all the ministers are as keen as mine on the value of cloak-and-dagger games against the Communists. So my job was to prove our worth, set up a preliminary network, conduct a trial operation . . .'

A small brown lizard darted across the ceiling. Running upside down. Joanna watched it.

'I received some information,' he went on, 'that this Czech official was bent on destroying the peace plan up in Kashmir. My higher-ups passed this on to their counterparts in Washington, and it was decided that the best strategy would be to expose the man publicly through the press. Show the Reds as enemies of the United Nations as well as of the Free World. We needed a journalist, but the Yanks didn't want it to be an American.'

'Aidan *is* an American.'

'No, Joanna. He had clearly been labeled as *un*-American by your own FBI. My department knew about my acquaintance with Aidan. And they knew he was here. Sydney, not Washington, gave me my orders.'

'So you didn't just run into each other up there on the Khyber Pass.'

'Not exactly.'

'You recruited him, in other words.' Her calm chilled him.

'It never occurred to me he'd be gone more than a couple of weeks. I swear to you, Jo.'

'Why didn't you tell me?'

'Because you believed in Aidan, you loved him. I knew you'd turn against me. And it was just too dangerous for you to know.'

'It would have compromised you,' she said acidly.

'That's irrelevant now.' He rubbed his eyes, wished they could leave this room. 'Look, I didn't know anything about this.' He tapped the clipping. 'But I've turned up a few things that may help to explain it. Your friend Akbar, apparently, was more influential than you realized.'

'Akbar?' A flicker of confusion softened her face.

'I've just come from Srinagar,' he said. And for the next half hour he related Akbar's so-called facts. That Aidan had been captured, then hospitalized in the Soviet Union. That the mine which had killed Alice had most likely been intended for the same Communist rebels that captured – or rescued – Aidan. He omitted only Akbar's personal remarks about Alice James.

'He didn't know what happened to Aidan after his recovery. But it makes sense the Chinese would ask for him back. It also makes sense that Aidan would play along with them for the sake of his own survival.'

'You're defending him,' she said. 'Why?'

'Because whatever he may be, he's not a defector.'

'Last summer you could hardly wait to declare him dead.'

'I *believed* he was dead. I was wrong.'

She got up and paced the length of the room before turning on him. 'I don't know what to believe. Ever since Ben dropped this on

325

me, I've been going back and forth like a seesaw. I can't even bring myself to tell Simon his father's alive!'

'Maybe that's just as well,' he said quietly. 'For now.'

He took a closer look at the photograph. In one hand Aidan held his glass in a toast. In the other he held a small book, face out, the Chinese characters scrolled down its cover. Fully visible to the camera.

'What am I supposed to do?' she asked.

He turned the clipping face down on his knee. 'Have you been to the Chinese?'

'Why would I?'

'If you wanted to get a message to him . . .'

She returned to the bed and sat down, her back rigid. 'If Ben's right, Aidan's had every opportunity to contact me, but he chooses not to.'

'There could be any number of reasons why he hasn't.'

'If I divorced him for abandonment I wouldn't need to contact him. They'd probably let me take Kamla back to the States then. I'd still be disgraced, but pitied instead of reviled.'

'Is that what you want?'

'I should.'

'But you don't,' he said.

'I keep thinking of that story you told me about George Hayward and Robert Shaw. How some people don't deserve to be rescued.'

'And others can't help but try to save them anyway.' He got up and placed the clipping on the desk, then came to sit beside her. 'There's a fine line, sometimes, that separates heroes from fools. I was being selfish – and cruel – when I told you that story.'

'What if you were right?'

'Joanna. Aidan's too smart ever to be a fool.'

'That doesn't necessarily make him a hero.'

'Do you know what he was really doing in China during the war?' He knew she didn't. 'He planted false stories in the local press, making the resistance against the Japanese seem greater than it really was. He concocted deviant rumors to undermine the authority of certain generals. He created diversions and invented imaginary informants to save the lives of the real ones. He was brilliant, Jo, tactically brilliant. And fearless. It's a mistake to pass judgment on a man like that.'

'I thought you wanted me to give up on him. Wasn't that why you went away?'

'It was.' He stared at a crack in the floor. The morning was closing in around them, the steady slur of cycle traffic already yielding to the horns of *tongas,* the wails of street vendors. He could feel and smell Joanna's presence beside him, even though they weren't touching. 'Do you remember in Kashgar,' he asked, 'Mrs Desai mentioned a man from the State Department? Name of Douglas Freeman.'

'Yes.' She sounded surprised, though her face told him nothing.

'I've turned up some information about him, as well. After the takeover, he was arrested and imprisoned in Alma-Ata, the same town where Aidan was in hospital.'

She was listening intently now. 'You don't think it's a coincidence.'

'It's only a hunch, but no. I don't. I think he might have played a hand in Aidan's strategy.' He paused. 'There's information we need from Washington, Jo. I've been called back to Sydney, anyway. I'll go on to the States from there.'

He took her hand. Her fingers were cold. 'We could go together.'

She looked up at him. 'Lawrence.' He didn't answer. 'We'd have to leave Kamla here. I couldn't do that to her.'

'No. I suppose not.'

'When will you go?'

'After Christmas.'

She nodded.

'Will you trust me, then?' he asked.

She squeezed his hand. 'Do I have a choice?'

4

To an outsider, it would have appeared much like those first weeks after our return from Sinkiang. Once again, each evening Lawrence joined us for dinner, then stayed on afterward talking with Mem. They would sit in the living room poring over papers and maps, drinking and talking and making notes long after they sent Simon and me up to bed. Sometimes we tiptoed back down to watch and listen from the bottom of the stairs. The nights now were cold, the cicadas quiet, and the breeze through the open window would stir Mem's hair. She and Lawrence had put away the chess set and used the game table for their studies. The lamplight fell in a pyramid, sparking against the small hairs on the backs of their hands and forearms as they talked. This talk, as before, was of China, Ambassador Minton, Mem's husband. But now when Mem spoke her husband's name – Aidan – it was as if he had just stepped from the room and would return any moment. Lawrence's hands moved restlessly over the stacks of papers, and for all the hours they spent together, he and Mem did not touch. They avoided each other's eyes.

I thought of the imaginary thread that had bound Mem and Lawrence and me together through the hardest, sweetest days of our trek, and as clearly as I sensed this thread finally had broken, I knew it was Mr Shaw's fault.

'What's wrong, Kammy?' Lawrence asked one afternoon when he picked us up at school and I came out ahead of Simon. 'You act as if you don't like me anymore.'

I shrugged. I shook my head. I looked away at the children streaming around us on bicycles or piling into the backs of black Ambassadors. They pretended to ignore us.

Lawrence gave me his crooked smile. 'No, you don't act that way, or no, you don't like me?'

'No,' I said frowning. 'I like you.'

He stuck out his right hand. 'Friends, then?'

Watching his palm, I placed mine against it. We shook hands formally, the way he did with the people he interviewed. I wanted him to reel me in, to wrap me in a breath-stopping hug and promise to keep me safe.

But just then Simon came running, and with a bound clutched Lawrence around the neck. They whirled, Lawrence making a great show of being strangled, of his desperation to throw Simon off. 'Uncle! Uncle!' he cried. 'You win!'

Simon saw no difference. Now that Lawrence was back their cricket games in the driveway could resume. Their Saturday matinees at the cinema. He introduced him proudly to his new school friends, and when they asked who exactly Lawrence *was,* Simon told them 'He's my other dad.'

I worried that he would be disappointed. Simon usually fell asleep as soon as his head hit the pillow, so he didn't realize how little really was the same. I thought I was doing him a favor when I kept him at the top of the stairs one night later than usual. Mem's and Lawrence's muffled voices moved out into the entryway and the front door opened and closed. I drew Simon back into our room as Mem's steps climbed the stairs alone.

'Remember when he used to stay the night?' I said.

'Why doesn't he anymore?'

'She won't let him.'

'Why not?' he said, his voice indignant.

'I don't know,' I answered truthfully.

There was a long silence. Then Simon said, 'You don't know that. Maybe he's just busy.'

I took a deep breath and relented. 'Yes,' I said. 'You're probably right.'

The day before Christmas we wreathed a stunted pine tree in garlands of dried marigolds. Lawrence had brought a box of silver stars, which Simon and I fastened to the branches. Mem played a song about snow and fire on the gramophone, and Simon announced he was cold, so he and Lawrence went into the kitchen to make something warm to drink. Mem and I finished decorating the tree, then she stood behind me with her cheek against my hair, admiring our handiwork.

'I'm sorry,' she said softly into my ear. 'I'm sorry none of this has turned out as it should. I wish . . . I wish I knew how to do better.'

I should have turned to her. She was asking me for comfort. But that was not how it sounded to me. No. To me the hush of her voice was like the fall of darkness. I could not move. Then Simon and Lawrence burst back into the room holding steaming cups of Horlicks. Mem's hands dropped away and Lawrence stepped forward. I smiled. I do not know why. My heart hurt, yet I smiled.

The next morning we exchanged gifts of cards and books and balls and hand-stamped writing paper that Simon and I had made in school. Mem gave me an ivory brush and comb, and Lawrence gave me a silver hand mirror. Simon's present from Lawrence was a cap pistol, and from Mem a box of magic tricks.

Mem and Lawrence exchanged their gifts last. Mem's to Lawrence was a small brown leather valise with lots of inside pockets and a crocodile handle. 'You're a writer,' Mem said. 'Writers carry briefcases.'

'Is that a rule?' he asked, smiling.

'It should be if it isn't.' She ran her hand over the shiny leather. 'This one is big enough for at least some of those books you insist on dragging all over the world.'

Simon poked me with his cap pistol and grinned.

'Open yours,' I said to Mem. Her gift had come in a box I recognized from the Taj Dress Shoppe on Lady Hardinge Road. Last year Lawrence had given her a beautiful pink cashmere sweater from this store.

This year's box produced a new pale blue pocketbook with a brass clasp and shoulder strap. 'It's lovely,' she said, looking at Lawrence. 'Thank you.'

'May I see?' I asked. Lawrence started to put up his hand, but Mem didn't notice. She passed me the purse and I immediately undid the clasp. I loved the snapping sound of Mem's purses, and the silk linings the good ones had. But there was something else inside this pocketbook. It stared up at me like a green tongue inside the gaping blue mouth. A check made out to Mem in the amount of 10,000 rupees.

I let out a gasp. It was not actual bills, of course, but even so, I had never seen such a sum. I happened to know that Nagu earned just thirty rupees in a month, so this was really a great deal of money. It occurred to me then that we perhaps depended on Lawrence in more ways than I was aware of.

I looked up. He was watching me closely, his eyes warning me to say nothing. At his nod I closed the purse and handed it back to Mem. Simon had distracted her. She had not heard my gasp. I understood that Lawrence would rather she discover his true gift in her own time.

That afternoon we went to the Plaza Cinema to see a film called *Lost Horizon,* about a group of *firenghi* who discover a perfect world called Shangri-la after their airplane crashes high in the mountains. On the way home, Simon asked if his father, too, might be living in Shangri-la.

No one answered him, so he persisted. Hadn't his father crashed in the mountains just like the people in the movie? And if he was in a place like that, could anyone blame him for not wanting to leave? Maybe his dad didn't *need* to be rescued. Maybe we should all go to Shangri-la.

He kept it up the whole way home, insisting that Shangri-la was a real place and not noticing as the silence grew louder and sharper. I could almost hear Mem grinding her teeth.

Finally she turned in her seat and said, 'Simon, that's enough.' But Simon for some reason just kept talking, on and on, and no one said anything more to him, but Mem nearly ran the car into a cow as she turned onto Ratendone Road, and as soon as we got out Lawrence took hold of Simon by the shoulders and gave him a shake. 'I have something to tell you, and I need you to stop.'

I knew instantly that whatever he had to tell us was not good news. Simon did, too.

We filed silently into the living room and sat down. Without so much as a glance at Mem, Lawrence told us he was going away again. He was leaving India in the morning. To meet his publisher in Australia, finish off his book. He would be back in a few months, but he could not tell us exactly when.

Months. Australia. He was going away again. I watched the color change in Simon's face. His skin turned milky white except for his freckles, which stood out like a spattering of brown ink across his nose. Suddenly he looked at me and began to cry. I realized I had made a grave mistake in telling him more than he could possibly fathom.

Mem reached to hold him, but he jumped up from the sofa and punched her in the neck. 'He hates you!' he screamed. 'It's all your fault!'

Then he ran upstairs, slamming the door to our room, leaving Mem with her hand folded over her throat, her right shoulder up to her ear, an expression on her face as if he had sliced her with a knife.

Lawrence went after Simon. Mem got up and poured herself

some whiskey. She stood with her back to me, staring out into the garden. I heard the murmur of Lawrence's voice above our heads, not a sound from Simon.

In a few minutes Lawrence returned alone. He put his arms around me and kissed my cheek. I breathed the spice smell of his shaving soap. I didn't want to let go, but he unwound my arms and gently pushed me away.

He and Mem looked at each other from their opposite sides of the room. He said he would write. She nodded. He said he had an idea, something that would help 'about Simon.' She told him we would manage. He said, well, anyway, if he could swing it he would surprise us all. Mem seemed suddenly to notice me standing to one side. She motioned me closer, and when I came, she slid an arm across my chest, resting her hand on my shoulder and drawing me back against her. In this way, I stood between them when Lawrence kissed her goodbye. He leaned over me, pressed his lips to her cheek, touched my hair, and was gone.

Mem and I ate dinner by ourselves that night. I stared into my book, she at her American newspaper. Simon refused to come downstairs.

Later, as we lay in our beds, I tried to soothe him with whispered tales of heroism and love. I told him the stories my flash house sister Mira once taught me. How the great Babur had conquered India by matchlock and elephant, and Humayun, his son, fell to his death while answering the muezzin's call to prayer. How Akbar made peace with the warring princes of Rajputana, and Shah Jahan built the Taj Mahal as an expression of love for his wife, only to die imprisoned by their son, the cruel and bloodthirsty Aurangzeb. I laid out his dreams the way I remembered others once seeding my own, not with stories of purity and light, but of worlds in which fortune and desire collide, and truth is shaped as much by loss as it is by faith.

I had told him the truth as I knew it. I could not take it back, nor could I extract the bitterness or disguise it as sweet. But I tried to reassure him he was not alone.

I reached across the gap between our beds, and after a moment he stretched his hand in reply. The bed frames had been pushed apart, so our fingertips did not quite meet. I expected him to crawl in with me then, and I would not have turned him out. Instead he sighed. He began to cry. He pulled back into himself and told me to stay away.

CHAPTER 12

1

One evening, about a week after Lawrence's departure, his 'surprise' turned up on Ratendone Road. Joanna did not at first recognize the gift, as it appeared in the form of an odd ferrety-looking young man dressed in British khaki shorts and an orange Madras shirt. His skin was molasses brown, his long black hair tied back with string, and the sharpness of his features reminded Joanna of the Los Angeles street hustlers that her mother had warned her to avoid when she was growing up. But he claimed Lawrence had sent him.

'Said to tell you I'm the new ayah.'

She peered at him through the half-light of the entryway. 'I beg your pardon?'

He passed her a chit: *This is Lazarus. He's a good man and will lend you a hand with the kiddies.*

'I don't understand. My children are old enough to look after themselves. Besides, ayahs are generally female.'

'Bloody hell, for what he paid me I'd wear a damn sari, but it hardly seems necessary. Lawrence said your boy likes the cinema and slingshots and cricket. The girl likes her books. Said both of 'em like swimming when the heat comes, and you could use some help getting them to and from places. I'm a bloody good driver, mechanic as well, and I'll keep an eye out, see they're safe. I'm new to Delhi, but I've been around India long enough to know the score.' He spoke with a broad British accent that was like an audible grin.

In truth, she was hardly likely to turn away help, in whatever form. Over the past days Simon's protest had only escalated. Yesterday evening he'd taken his BB gun out and shot a hole in the Austin's rear windshield. Fortunately, the car was parked and empty, but Simon refused to say whether it had happened accidentally or on purpose. You couldn't hold out a handful of sunshine to children, then suddenly snatch it back and expect them not to notice. Joanna wasn't sure just how brightly Lazarus was capable of shining, but his smile was a start.

'You say he's already paid you?'

'Right. Other sots might lie to you, take your money as well. But I consider Lawrence my friend, and I think he feels the same 'bout me. I'm watching out for his flat, if that tells you anything. You don't even have to put me up.'

'So this is a favor you're doing him.'

'Right. Just to help out while he's gone. Here, how's this? Consider me your man Friday, like in *Robinson Crusoe*.'

'You've read *Robinson Crusoe*?' Joanna was unable to conceal her surprise. With his persistent good humor and apparently limitless talents Lazarus would have fit right in on Crusoe's desert island.

'Read it in school. Dr Graham thought I'd identify 'cause I came from an island – Luzon in the Philippines – and I was shipwrecked as a boy. My parents drowned.'

It came back to her then, Lawrence telling her about this wartime orphan, half Portuguese, half Filipino, who'd wound up in Calcutta tuning pianos. Lazarus, as in raising the dead. A survivor, Lawrence had called him. 'Aren't we all?' Joanna had shot back. And Lawrence had skewered her with that look that was half admonition, half plea. 'Some are more talented than others,' he said. 'And those of us who are less able would do well to take a few lessons.'

So here, it seemed, was her lesson, wrapped in the guise of Lawrence's stand-in. Lazarus was at once obnoxious and irrepressibly likable. Over the days that followed they would discover he cheated at cards, roared at his own jokes, and deflected the inevitable slights he received from the servants (who perceived him as an Anglo-Indian and a usurper) with the practiced agility of a clown. But he wisely took a gradual approach with the children. Kwality ice cream and afternoon cricket games were no longer enough to

335

cheer even Simon, and Kamla barely looked up to be introduced to their new 'man Friday.'

Fortunately there was the cinema. This was not a part of Indian life that Joanna had enough attention or interest to fully appreciate, especially after the *Lost Horizon* fiasco, but Lazarus adored it. He could sing the scores to a dozen Bombay spectaculars, complete with the flashing eyes and swiveling hips of the dance accompaniments. He quoted lines from *Hamlet* and *Gone With the Wind* with equal enthusiasm and was delighted to learn that the Regal, Rivoli, Odeon, and Plaza cinema halls of Connaught Place all offered Hollywood fare. He and Simon took to spending every Saturday afternoon in these dark, stifling theaters, and soon he had Simon, too, once again whistling theme songs. Simon remained aggrieved with Lawrence. 'Why couldn't he have taken us with him?' he demanded over and over. But Lazarus was a distraction, and for that Joanna was grateful.

As for Kamla, it was difficult to say how much of her moodiness was due to Lawrence's absence. For weeks, even months, the girl had been preoccupied, aloof at times to the point of muteness. Joanna chalked it up to the approach of puberty. During meals she stared into her plate as if it would tell her fortune. In the car she insisted on taking the back seat, letting Simon sit up front, and the rest of the time she would curl up on her bed or the living room sofa reading the endless supply of books she brought home from the school library. Joanna could hardly remember the last time Kamla on her own had ventured close enough to hug. But then, the girl had always shown this capacity, a kind of heightened self-sufficiency and strength. She was another talented survivor, and under the circumstances, Joanna could hardly criticize her behavior. Withdrawal seemed a sensible defense.

If only she herself had that luxury. She had honored Mr Chou's request. She had not exactly lied to Lawrence, but evasion was a form of deceit. Bertie Solomon's warning had proven true – in part, at least. She couldn't trust him. Not with this. And especially not if he was right, and Aidan was just playing along with the Chinese in order to survive. She had to rely on what she remembered. What she believed. And that was Aidan's love for her and Simon. His last words to her. His last touch.

336

In fact, she was relieved when Lawrence left.

But the passage of time now gnawed at her. She'd reorganized Safe Haven so successfully that it ran like a machine, and the meetings and paperwork, the minor crises of the girls and the management of their education required her time but hardly her full attention. She kept tripping over the card Bertie Solomon had given her, which she left in her desk at work. She hadn't mentioned that, either, to Lawrence. A kind of fear, perhaps. Dread. And hope that Aidan's reply would eliminate the need for any more questions. But though Mr Chou promised he'd delivered her letter, no reply came.

The address on the card directed Joanna to the heart of Old Delhi – the maze of bazaar alleyways known as Chandni Chowk. The ancient streets were narrow and filthy, crowded with displays of silver and beads, mechanical toys, luridly colored soft drinks, bolts of cotton and silk, embroidered hats, packaged underwear, eyeglasses, hair tonic. People lived behind the storefronts and in upper-level apartments – you could see the terraces with their canvas awnings and lines of drying laundry, but given the red-light district's proximity, it did not surprise Joanna that most of the women here hid under *burqas* or were carefully shepherded by male relatives. Schoolgirls rode past in cycle rickshaws, three to a cab or with servants, but never alone or on foot. A rickshaw wouldn't have been a bad idea, as no car could possibly get through and Joanna had to park out by the Red Fort, but she hadn't realized how far she was going to have to walk. So she clutched her purse to her hip and her hat to her head, stepping between a man with a glass eye selling cauliflower to her right and a leper shrouded in dirty gauze stretching an oozing palm to her left. It was not yet ten but already she felt herself fading. She'd had to wrestle the car away from Lazarus this morning, insisting on dropping the children at school herself so she could come here alone. And now she half-regretted this – she could use his company in this place. But she couldn't risk the chance that Lazarus might report back to Lawrence. Also, she wasn't sure what she expected, or even what she hoped to find in this man, Douglas Freeman.

To the left of Nurwala's Sweet Shop, an unmarked door opened onto a steep, two-foot-wide stairway that smelled of urine and mold. There was no directory, no indication that anything other than apartments lay upstairs, but this seemed to be the right alleyway and the building that most closely matched the address. On the bottom step a little boy, maybe four with flat black eyes, sat shirtless in a pair of worn shorts, playing with a length of red string.

'Freeman *sahib*?'

The child gave her a gap-toothed smile and pointed up the stairs.

The scent of curry now laced through the stink. Maybe a hundred years ago some artisan had carved an ornate pattern of birds and ferns into the handrail. The paint had long since worn away. There was just one door on the landing. A small, brisk woman wearing horn-rimmed glasses and a turquoise sari greeted her at the second knock.

'International Vision?' Joanna said.

The woman peered at her suspiciously.

'Is Mr Freeman here?'

The woman let out a short peremptory breath and stood back for her to enter. 'Who is calling, please?' she asked. Joanna told her and added that Mrs Bertie Solomon had sent her. The woman left her in a gloomy cubicle where two young assistants sat on the floor before low writing desks. The girl, wrapped in a thin blue shawl against the chill of the unheated building, appeared to be working her way through a pile of invoices and receipts, while the young man entered figures in a ledger book. A third desk, presumably the older woman's, was stacked with closed manila folders. Pasteboard boxes full of pamphlets and softbound books filled what little floor space was left. The pamphlets proclaimed 'Livelihood Through Literacy!' and displayed photographs of International Vision at work through outdoor classes in villages and city bazaars.

Joanna stood, for there was nowhere to sit. The two assistants bent over their desks, studiously ignoring her.

'Please.' The woman reappeared, and Joanna followed her down a tiled hall past the kitchen.

Freeman's office was a bedless bedroom containing a wooden desk of Western height, two chairs, and a military green file cabinet. The exterior door and windows were open to the outer balcony, and a grimy breeze blew in streaks of lukewarm sunlight. He sat in one of these streaks but rose as she entered.

She was struck by how much thinner he was than she'd realized in their brief encounter that night at the *maidan*. A pale-skinned man with a dirty-blond crew cut, he actually looked like a recently released – or escaped – prisoner of war. His white short-sleeve shirt seemed to float on his shoulders, and the belt of his khaki trousers, though tightened to the extreme, drooped on his hipbones. The skin of his face was stretched over his jaws and cheeks, the dome of his forehead so tight it seemed polished. Burning blue eyes in this spare face gave him the look of a zealot, though his voice, when he spoke, was mild.

'How can I help you?' he asked, gesturing for her to take the chair next to his desk. There was nothing on the desk but a large black telephone.

She hesitated. 'I'm Joanna Shaw. Perhaps you don't remember. Bertie Solomon introduced us during the Ram Lila celebration.'

Not a flicker of recognition. 'Doug Freeman,' he said, offering his hand. A Midwestern accent, maybe Chicago. 'Sorry. I'd just arrived in Delhi then. The Solomons gave me the whirlwind tour, you know? I was a little overwhelmed.'

She smiled. 'India can do that. Never mind. I'm here on business, anyway.'

'Oh?'

She handed him her card from Salamat Jannat. 'I run a rescue home for young prostitutes. We're funded by the Indian government through the Social Welfare Committee. As you can imagine, it's not enough.' She was racing. Slow down.

He sat back in his chair. 'I can imagine.'

'Actually, before I make a fool of myself by suggesting something impossible, perhaps you could clarify exactly what International Vision does. Bertie said you do literacy work. Is that right?'

'That's right,' he said.

There was a timid knock, and the girl from outside brought in a tray with two tumblers of hot milk tea and a plate of sweet biscuits. To Joanna's relief, Douglas Freeman received the food with enthusiasm, promptly popping a biscuit into his mouth and washing it down with a long swallow of tea. It disturbed her that he was so much thinner – so much more visibly damaged by his time in the hands of the Communists – than Aidan's photographs showed *him* to be.

As if reading her mind, Freeman said, 'I'm just over a rotten bout of dysentery. Trying to fatten up.'

She smiled. 'What kind of literacy work, if you don't mind my asking?'

'Not at all. We work with labor groups and community leaders, get visiting teachers into the neighborhoods and factories. We support the teachers, help organize the classes, supply books and materials. It's very grass roots.'

Joanna nodded. Doug Freeman, she suspected, knew all about grass roots, but very little about real literacy work. 'It sounds perfect. Here's what I'm thinking. The girls in the red-light district are sorely in need of just the education you're describing. And we at Salamat Jannat are sorely in need of more eyes and ears in the district to help us identify the girls who've been trafficked into prostitution.' She reached into her purse and pulled out a copy of Bertie's article about Kamla. She tapped the photograph. 'This is one of the children we rescued from the district. She's an extraordinary case, of course. So extraordinary I decided to adopt her. She's now at the head of her class at the All-Nations School.'

He looked at the picture. 'She's very beautiful.'

'Yes.' She knew he had seen Kamla, seen Joanna strike her. And probably knew all about both of them. But he simply reached for another biscuit and waited for her to continue. What if Lawrence's intelligence about Freeman was wrong?

She said, 'The point is, there are hundreds of others like her out there, and we simply don't have the resources or personnel to identify all of them. Our rescue home primarily serves girls who are remanded through the courts, and too often these girls would frankly rather be back in the brothels than studying for exams. We need to reach girls like Kamla, who are still young enough, eager enough to see some possibility in life. That's why I thought we might team up with you.'

'Team up?'

'If you set up a class for the children of G. B. Road, you would get to know those children and their mothers – and earn their trust.

340

Then you could link them to us, and we would arrange the rest.'

'An interesting thought, Mrs . . .' He glanced at her uncertainly.

'Joanna.'

'Joanna. But we're stretched as tight as you. We're working with the street kids over by the bus terminal, and in some of the slums near the river. Maybe we'll catch some girls before they wind up in the red-light district, but as for setting up shop there, I'm afraid we'd run head-on into the police. They like their take, as I understand it, and they don't much cotton to anyone getting in the way. Imagine that's why you folks rely on the courts.'

'You've been well briefed.'

'Oh, I've spent enough time in Asia to know some things are the same wherever you go.'

She took a handkerchief from her purse and blotted the perspiration from her upper lip and throat. Then she removed her hat and gave her hair a calculated toss. Freeman's eyes followed her as she'd hoped they would. 'Where in Asia?' she asked.

'China mostly. Shanghai for a while. Later out west.'

'West?'

A delay, just long enough that she knew Lawrence had gotten this right. 'I spent a few months in Sinkiang before the Communist takeover.'

'What were you doing there?'

'I had a grant to study some of the border languages.' His bony face betrayed nothing.

'I'm almost afraid to ask this, but you didn't . . . by any remote chance, you didn't cross paths with my husband while you were in Sinkiang? He's a correspondent. Aidan Shaw. American, though he's half Chinese and mostly grew up in China.'

Douglas Freeman made a show of giving this question his full consideration. Then he answered, 'No. No, there weren't a lot of Americans in Sinkiang, and I think I remember every one I met.'

'Or a young woman? Blond. Her name was Alice James.'

That split-second delay again. This time she detected a flicker of disquiet. 'Now that, I *know* I'd remember,' he said.

'She was traveling with my husband,' Joanna said. 'She died in an accident not far from Tihwa. My husband disappeared around the same time.'

'My God! I'm sorry.' He shook his head. 'Sinkiang was a dangerous place.'

'How did you get out?'

'Oh, me. I was lucky.' His breathing sounded uneven. 'I flew out months before the takeover.' As he finished off his tea, his face flushed pink.

'Well,' Joanna said. 'I guess that's that, then. I apologize for taking your time. If you change your mind about working together, I hope you'll give me a call.'

Freeman cupped her card in his palm. After a moment he lifted his eyes, the blond fringe of his lashes lending a touch of innocence to his otherwise searing stare. 'Forgive me for asking,' he said, 'but, given what you've just told me, what keeps you here in India?'

Joanna hesitated, for the first time wondering if he might be sincere.

'I'm afraid perhaps I misled you a moment ago. As far as I'm concerned, my husband disappeared. But there are others who believe he's defected to the Chinese. I suppose you could say I'm ashamed to go back to the States until I've proven his innocence. With all the talk around Washington lately, maybe I'm even a little frightened.'

'How do you prove his innocence if you don't know where he is?'

'I keep asking questions, knocking on doors.' She met his eyes. Steady. 'I love my husband very much. And I'm very, very stubborn.'

Douglas Freeman pocketed her card and dropped his gaze, blinking twice before clapping his hands to his knees and standing up. 'Let me think about it, Joanna. I'd really like to help you out.'

'I hope you can,' she said, wishing she believed him.

2

Lazarus Figredo reminded me of the marmots we used to see along our trek popping up from underground tunnels in meadows or peering around boulders with their paws in the sun as we came down into the foothills. His skin was the color of coffee, his hair shiny as axle grease, and his nose was large and rounded, his restless hands always gesturing or flipping the cigarettes that he chain-smoked. I believed that Lawrence had sent this man to watch out for Mem and cheer up Simon. Perhaps he even imagined that Lazarus and I would 'hit it off.' We both were orphans, after all, both stateless mixed-blood misfits of the scheduled caste. We both were survivors. But that was just the thing. I knew what survival required, and what it destroyed. And so I mistrusted the glint in his eye, his ferocious good cheer, his wild and contradictory stories of childhood escape and rescue. Simon, of course, loved him on sight, and Mem soon came to rely on him as she herself slid back under her blanket of duties at Safe Haven, her renewed preoccupation with her husband. No one asked my opinion about Lazarus, and I did not volunteer it, but I knew that I would never place my confidence in this man.

From the first week after his arrival he would drive me and Simon to school. Sometimes he would stay to see us through the gate. More often he would clap Simon on the shoulder and tell us both, laughing, to work our 'bloody pants' off, then honk the horn and drive away, back home to pick up Mem. I'd walk Simon inside and leave him on the path to his class's bungalow as I turned toward my own. But one morning early in February, Teresa Ruíz, a rather stupid girl from South America, approached me on the path just as I was parting from Simon. I say she was stupid because she insisted that her father was considering whether to buy India. Now she tapped me on the shoulder and pointed back to the gate, twirling her finger as if I were her servant and she were sending me to fetch something. 'Your man wants you,' she said.

Lazarus must have forgotten to tell us some detail about our plans for the afternoon. I told Simon to go on his way and hurried back alone, fearful that this delay would make me late for class. When I reached the street, however, there were only the usual parents and servants hurrying tardy children. It was Teresa's joke, I thought, annoyed with myself for playing into her hands. Just then a bicycle rickshaw pulled up beside me.

The driver spoke my name. 'Your mother has sent for you,' he said. When I hesitated he continued, '*Memsahib* has important news. Good news. It must not wait.'

This was not the first time Mem had sent a rickshaw to the school. Before Lazarus came, she often sent Nagu this way when we forgot our lunch money. When she slept late or had an early meeting we would come on our own, and twice, when the Austin was in the repair shop, she had sent a rickshaw to bring us home. To send for us after the start of school was unusual, but I had watched other children be called away for family emergencies. That, I decided, must be what this was. Perhaps Mem's husband had returned. Or Lawrence was back. Perhaps the American Ambassador had decided to grant my visa. Perhaps we were going to move to America, and she needed my help packing right away. It had to be something she had learned after we left the house – something that couldn't wait for Lazarus to come back and turn around again. Good news, the driver said. I told him to wait while I fetched my brother. But no, he said, *memsahib* wanted Kamla only. I should have known better, yet I felt my heart soar with pleasure that she should want me alone, and chose to ignore my instincts.

But as we got under way, doubts began to set in. What if she was calling me back to tell me she could no longer keep me? I was nearly grown now, and she had given me advantages the other girls in her rescue home could hardly dream of. Maybe she had decided it was time for one of them to take my place. I recalled her letting the cook go only weeks before. 'It's not working out,' she told him quite simply, and he packed his bags and went. But *where* did he go? Where would I go? I put my hand to my cheek where she had once slapped me.

And that was the moment when I looked up and realized the rickshaw was traveling in the wrong direction. Not toward Ratendone Road at all. We were heading for Old Delhi. For G. B. Road.

Fortunately, there was a good deal of traffic, forcing the rickshaw to slow. At the next pause I prepared to jump out, but as soon as I moved, the driver looked back. He had long dusty black hair and a purple birthmark like a scald covering one side of his neck. 'If you try to escape we come after you. If you hide we take one of the sons of the bearer in the house where you live.' He rolled his head and a dreamy look entered his eyes. 'Or perhaps the American boy.'

'This is Lazarus's doing!' I cried out, desperate to blame.

But the driver ignored my outburst. He tossed a piece of newsprint back into my lap. It was the *Gazette* with Mrs Solomon's article, browning around the edges and stained with grease and tea. Those were my own eyes staring back at me, my own face cheek to cheek with Mem's. A son, Mrs Solomon had written, a little boy, who attends school with his new adopted sister, and they all live happily together. Then Surie had seen me, knew where I lived, and time had passed.

Now, quickly, I had to find a way out. I did not believe they would dare to harm Simon, but I knew the threat against Nagu's sons was perfectly real. Only last week, the *mali*'s cousin had been tracked to our compound and left with two crushed legs as punishment for his unpaid gambling debts. And Mem never even learned of it.

I demanded that the driver tell me where we were going. He grinned and swiveled his head. My old mother wanted to talk to me, he said. I owed her a great deal of money.

So Surie had reported to Indrani. And she doubtless to her friends the policemen. But this rickshaw boy was no hardened *goonda*...

We were nearing Raj Ghat and would soon turn onto G. B. Road. My thoughts tumbling now, I asked the boy his name. Jaggu, he answered boldly. I asked how much Indrani was paying him, and when his head wobbled at the question, I told him that if he pulled over I might make him a better arrangement. We stopped by the grassy embankment, and I offered to pay him double what he was getting from Indrani if he would serve as go-between instead of taking me to her in person. I pointed out that my *memsahib* would surely go after Indrani if she learned of this attempt to kidnap me, and Indrani then would take her revenge on him as well as on me. I explained to Jaggu that I could earn far more if I continued my studies (I remembered Bharati once telling me that rich men preferred and would pay a premium for educated girls), if I dressed in fine foreign clothes, and especially if I was not restricted by the squalor of the flash house. I persuaded him that I understood I could never escape Indrani but also that it was in her interest to leave me with the *firenghi*. Each fortnight he should meet me by

345

the entrance to Humayun's Tomb, an easy bicycle ride from Mem's house, and I would give him one hundred rupees for Indrani and twenty for himself. Even as I spoke these figures, the size of them alarmed me. The only money I possessed was given to me by Mem for lunch or to buy occasional trinkets at Khan Market. But I saw no other way.

The rickshaw driver was young and greedy. He accepted the arrangement, but before turning back to school, he unsheathed the knife from his belt. 'Just so that you understand.' He reached back and with the tip of the dagger plucked the top button from my blouse. Then he studied me, not lecherously, but with an eye so calculating that I shuddered. After a moment he used the same blade to stroke the birthmark along his neck. 'I have always thought of this as a curse,' Jaggu said. 'But your beauty is *your* curse. Isn't it?'

Strangely, although I had been told before that I was beautiful, this was the first time I believed it. The effect was not what he must have intended. For if beauty could be a curse, then, too, could power be. And one curse might well vanquish the other. 'Thank you for the compliment,' I said. 'Now would you kindly take me back to school?'

Lawrence was gone. Simon was a child. And even if Lazarus had not brought my downfall, I sensed that he would rather escort me to Indrani himself than risk his little finger defending me. I did think about turning to Mem. For days I thought about little else. Surely for this Mem could not blame me. She worked day in and day out for the welfare of girls who sold their bodies. She was mistress of Safe Haven, after all. But safety was her illusion, not ours. As Mrs Shaw she was still – perhaps more than ever – *firenghi*. Outsider. What could she truly understand in this? Had it not been due to her own action – that stupid, stupid interview – that Indrani knew where and how I was living? This had not stopped Indrani; no, in fact it must merely have whetted her greed. I remembered Bharati telling me of girls who escaped the flash house, moved to faraway places and lived for years in the care of husbands or well-meaning employers, only to be brutally mur-dered when their *gharwali* tracked them down. The *goondas* would tie up the girls' protectors, vandalize their homes. Here and now a threat had already been made against Simon. And with that unforgotten slap Mem had made it abundantly clear that her true allegiance was to Simon. If she learned of this threat, I did not doubt she would abandon me.

3

As Lawrence entered Battersby's new office, he took a quick inventory: arched windows, northern light, matching mahogany furniture and paneling, oriental carpet and club chairs. The vast desktop held nothing but a telephone. He said, 'Been demoted again, eh, Jack?'

Without rising, Battersby reached forward and received Lawrence's outstretched hand, rotating his wrist with a forceful flick. A condensed arm wrestle, which Jack invariably won.

'Have a nice time trekking the Himalayas?'

'Oh, yeah.' Lawrence flexed his fingers and settled himself in front of the desk. 'Fucking fantastic holiday, thanks.'

As Jack ran his tongue over his upper teeth, his mustache rippled. His hair had gone grayer than Lawrence realized in the darkness in Delhi. 'I should have reined you in months ago,' Battersby said.

'Why didn't you?'

'Because I wanted to give you enough bloody rope to hang yourself.'

'My blood or yours?'

'Look, there's a loose piston in Washington. This McCarthy bugger's turning the State Department inside out. CIA's next. Our mates are starting to fret about him connecting the dots to your joe.' He folded his hands in front of him. 'This is not a good time for them to be nervous, Larry. In case you've been too busy on holiday to read your briefing sheets, we're about to sign a treaty with the Yanks that the Prime Minister's rather keen on. Regional peace and partnership. Be a bloody shame if the ANZAC alliance was torpedoed over your fuck-up.'

'You told me the Yanks didn't know it was Aidan.'

'They figured it out.'

347

'I'll bet they did.' Lawrence looked pointedly at a photograph on the credenza, of Jack with his two young sons, taken in front of the Washington Monument. Jack's only interest in ANZAC was its effect on his future as Australia's first spymaster. Lawrence could practically hear him salivate as he spoke the letters, CIA.

Jack brought a pipe, ashtray, and pouch of tobacco from his desk drawer and began a preparation for smoking as elaborate as a Japanese tea ceremony. 'What'd you turn up on this bloke Eldon?'

'Might as well be a dog marking his territory from Singapore to Beirut. At every stop he whips out that "smuggled" candid of Aidan and Chou En-lai, talks about the terrible tragedy of his old war mate the turncoat. And he makes lots of stops, this Eldon. Buyers for Kodak all over the world. It's a bang-on cover.'

Jack struck a match and lit his pipe, puffing his weathered cheeks until the tobacco glowed and the smell of burned cherries filled the room. Then he picked up the phone and asked his secretary to bring in a couple of glasses. She obliged within the minute, a sturdy blonde with good legs and thick lips not unlike, if memory served, those of Jack's wife. Along with the glasses, she brought a bucket of ice and a bottle of Glenfiddich. Jack barely acknowledged her as she came and went.

'How far back have you traced him?' he asked, handing Lawrence his drink.

'When Aidan saved Eldon's life in Burma, they were both working for OWI. And when the CIA was formed in '47, guess who was standing in line with an application in his hot little fist?'

'Why would Central Intelligence *advertise* your man's defection when their State Department's marked it top secret?'

'The object is to protect Aidan's pose as a leftist. And make sure no one traces him back to his true source. Playing one hand against the other may be part of the exercise. They fed you his name, didn't they? He wasn't your idea at all.'

'What are you suggesting?'

'We were set up, Jack. We're the stupid younger brothers who were had by a turncoat. By routing through my friendship with Aidan, then setting up a smoke screen of accusation and denial within their own ranks, your mates at the old CIA have laundered themselves right out of the mission.'

'Which is?'

'He's a news writer. The Yanks knew all about that Soviet A-bomb test in Semipalatinsk. How? How did they know to send their B-29s on a flyover, getting aerial pictures at just the right time?'

'They're an intelligence machine, Larry. It's what they do.'

'Precisely. And for the moment I'm betting Aidan's a critical cog. Troop movements, new air bases, Soviet aid and advisors floating in over the Sinkiang border. Not to mention the Chinese hand in Korea and four hundred Americans trapped behind the Bamboo Curtain. Plenty to occupy a double agent, I'd say . . . He left behind an insurance policy with a disappearance clause that no commercial insurer in their right mind would agree to.'

'How so?'

'Death benefits payable after he'd been missing nine months. At the "Company's" discretion. This company happens to be the same firm that covers the CIA.' Lawrence continued talking as he opened his valise and placed a manila envelope on Jack's desk. 'Joanna, of course, would have had to declare him dead, which she couldn't bring herself to do, so now, as we all know, he's been proven alive.' He arranged ten news photographs for Jack's inspection, the results of a pre-Christmas search through the archives at the University of Delhi, which he'd managed to conduct without Joanna's knowledge. 'These are from various Chinese publications since the Communist takeover. Aidan's in every one, somewhere in the background. Note how the crowd is holding up banners, posters, the usual slogans. Our loyal cadre, right there with them.'

Jack pulled a magnifying glass from his drawer and briefly pored over the pictures. 'I don't read Chinese. What are you saying?'

'Hide in plain sight. I haven't cracked it yet, but I will.'

Jack lifted his glass noncommittally and drank. 'And the hell with his wife?'

'Perhaps out of necessity. I'm not sure if Aidan realized going in that he was going to *stay* in. His initial assignment may well have been simply to tail Alice James.'

'They were quick to pop the news of that crash.'

'Sometimes it's easier – cleaner – to bring someone back from the dead than to make them disappear among the living. If only Jo had played along.'

'Maybe.' Battersby leaned back in his chair. 'You're working too hard, Larry. Maybe you just don't want to admit you were had. Not me. Not us. You.'

'That's why I'm going stateside,' Lawrence said evenly.

'I warn you—'

'I know, the bloody ANZAC alliance.'

They drank in silence for several minutes. Jack seemed to be waiting. Finally, Lawrence said, 'Aidan's a mixed-breed. He can sustain loyalty to two opposing beliefs, ambitions, even women at once. Weller's wife actually quoted him . . . what was it? China Hands see the world in gray as opposed to red and white.'

'Opposing *women*?'

'Apparently he had a serious affair in China at the end of the war.'

Jack smiled at Lawrence. 'Who didn't?'

'Difference is, he told his wife.'

'Can't be much of a spy in that case.'

'He's also a reporter.' Now it was Lawrence's turn to smile. 'Like I said, he saw no contradiction between living a secret and telling the truth. But he didn't tell her the whole story. I did some checking. Turns out the other woman was Special Operations. Irish, but working for the Brits in Chungking. She ran afoul of some of the less sympathetic generals in Chiang Kai-shek's stable. Caught them selling arms to the Japs – theoretically for use against the Communists. Aidan's affair with her may or may not have been real. He may have simply been protecting her. Unfortunately for her, she didn't think she needed protecting. One night she went out by herself, and a couple of thugs dragged her into an alley. They left her paralyzed, unable to talk.' Lawrence wiped his palm on his trouser. 'She died back in Ireland a few months after the war ended.'

Jack's face appeared motionless through the blur of smoke. He took one last pull on his pipe and emptied the bowl with a smack on the edge of a silver ashtray. 'What's the wife doing this time around?'

Lawrence looked straight into Jack's eyes. 'Planning to divorce him.'

'You haven't shared your theory with her?'

'No.'

'And she hasn't tried to contact him through the Chinese?'

'She's understandably angry.'

'No benefit of the doubt? No impulse to stand by her man till death do them part?' Jack's tone was mocking. 'Ironic that just when she quits on him, you take up the cause.'

'We don't have quite the same investment.'

'Not anymore?'

'No.' He continued to hold Jack's gaze. 'Not anymore.'

'My condolences.' Battersby refilled their glasses. 'You realize you're making a better case against him than for him.'

'The Reds will be marking the same scoreboard, Jack. That's to his advantage as a double agent.'

'Talk to me about Alice James.'

'I think she was one of the Left's starry-eyed true believers, headed for the Soviet border with a trove of names and numbers she'd picked up in Washington.'

'And what do you think happened to all those names and numbers?'

'I'm betting she was clean by the time Aidan's rescuers reached the site.'

'Why *are* you working so hard to defend him?'

'Tell you the truth, Jack, I wish he had gone over. If I'm going to be made a fool of, I'd rather it were done all out. For real. This is like being stabbed in the ribs by one of your own teammates. Maybe the right side wins but you're lying bloody on the side of the field and all the glory's gone out of you.'

'Better side of valor's to expose his game, eh?'

'Could be this is all part and parcel of your bloody treaty negotiations, Jack. Price we pay, a little hazing to qualify for the fraternity.'

'What if you're wrong?'

'Then I'm in the wrong business, aren't I?'

Jack smiled. 'You don't seem to quite understand, Larry. The current regime Sydney-side isn't any keener on Communists than the Yanks are. And your affiliation with a known defector places you in a rather precarious position. I've been protecting you as best

I can, but it seems about time I got something I can really use in return.'

'I don't need your charity or your protection.'

'Oh, I think you do,' Battersby said. 'Fact is, you like playing my game. It suits you. And you suit me – that is, when you haven't got your head up your arse. You're a charmer, you are, and you speak in tongues. Those are two useful attributes for a spy. You also have an obstinate streak, which I admire. You're determined to see this theory of yours through, which is why I'm paying your way.'

He stood and handed Lawrence back his clippings. 'However. I don't have to tell you, these are serious charges. I don't like being played for a fool any more than you do, but the Yanks are technically our allies. Rather powerful allies.' He paused while Lawrence got to his feet. 'If you're wrong about this, Larry, and you go too far, we'll all be lying bloody on the side of the field. Some of us may not get up again.'

4

Though it was only two o'clock the sky was like gunpowder, the city beneath it subdued. The ancient compasses and sundials of the eighteenth-century observatory loomed like gargantuans from a Jules Verne novel. Rising to heights of up to fifty feet and styled from the most basic geometric shapes – triangles, circles, spheres, and squares – these red sandstone instruments were reputed to measure time, space, and the zodiac with exquisite precision. They also functioned as massive sculptures, with convex and concave and leaning surfaces that turned the vast court into a maze of screens against prying eyes.

Joanna drove on past Jantar Mantar and parked the Austin in front of the stores on the outer ring of Connaught Place. She pretended to window-shop for a few minutes, then drew her scarf up over her head and walked back the few blocks to the observatory. She had received a chit at work that morning, delivered by a boy no one knew. Unsigned, it stated this time, this meeting place, and read, 'The message you long await has arrived.'

An iron fence surrounded the park, broken by a single

unmanned gate. Inside, a handful of visitors strolled or sat or slept on the massive astrolabes. Through the networks of improbable stairways and deceptive porticoes, figures appeared and disappeared like phantoms. Joanna assumed she was looking for Mr Chou. She assumed she was being watched. She felt like a fool and, for the first time, saw the advantage of those black upside-down *burqas*.

She passed a young couple, bent-headed, murmuring, the girl in a jubilant orange and gold sari. Through the fence she could see two brown-shirted Indian policemen sauntering down the street, snapping *lathis* like riding crops against their thighs, an old man selling paperback books off a pavement blanket.

She ducked under an overhang and stepped through a doorway into a shadowed chamber, then around a corner and out the other side. Curved red walls formed an empty bowl under the silent sky. The city and its millions had completely disappeared.

A footstep sounded behind her. She turned.

He was dressed like an Indian. That is to say, he wore brown trousers, *chappals* on his feet, an orange and green plaid shirt, argyle sweater vest, and a red knit cap pulled low on his brow. Between his conspicuous attempt at disguise and her own relief, she couldn't help smiling.

'Mrs Shaw,' Chou said. 'I apologize for meeting like this. But I think it is better.'

'It doesn't matter. Has my husband answered?'

He nodded. 'It is being arranged. Come. Sit with me here.' He led her to a cement bench on the opposite side of the bowl.

'*What* is being arranged?' she asked.

'You wish to see him.'

'Yes! But . . .' She was being put off again. 'You said there was a message. I expected a letter . . .'

Chou spread his hands, touching his fingertips together. 'He thinks you will not understand. Words on paper are easily misinterpreted.'

Words on paper were Aidan's life. His refusal to write could also be misinterpreted. Or perhaps he was not being *allowed* to write.

'There is nothing to do just yet,' Chou said. 'It will take some weeks. I think not before April, but you must stay in Delhi until

353

you hear from me. When everything is ready I will send a chit, as I did today. If it does not state a meeting place, you come to our embassy.'

'What about my son? I haven't told him anything yet, but I'm sure my husband will want to see him.'

'I am afraid this will not be possible. I must remind you, no one may know. If your government learns of our plans, your husband's life may be endangered.'

A familiar chill of fury and fear traveled the length of her spine, but as usual it was arrested by the simple fact that she didn't know whom to be furious *at*. Any more than she knew where this threat of danger truly came from, or where it could lead.

'I understand,' she said miserably.

'Good, I will see you again in a few weeks, then.' He stood, but when she started to rise, he held out his palm. 'Please. Stay a few minutes. It is so peaceful here.'

She did as instructed. She didn't fear Chou. She didn't like or dislike him. Certainly she didn't believe that there was anything peaceful about this place. But the longer she sat staring at these high curved walls, the more difficult it became to move.

5

For two weeks I stalled and plotted and chewed my lips raw. I counted and recounted the total of change in my possession so many times that the paise shone clean, but no matter how I calculated, I had only ninety rupees, and I needed one hundred twenty. Finally, on the morning of my first appointed meeting with Jaggu, I sneaked into Mem's bedroom while she was downstairs finishing breakfast with Simon. I had decided to borrow just enough from the household money hidden in her desk to complete Jaggu's first payment, to buy another two weeks. With this breathing space, perhaps I would yet find the courage to confide in Mem.

I had to remove the entire drawer in order to reach the small black kidskin purse tucked into a rear corner. I did this hurriedly, and laid the drawer on the bed. The purse contained four twenty-rupee notes, but rather than risk taking more than I needed, I removed only one. The remainder I could borrow from Nagu.

A door slammed downstairs. I held my breath, but no footsteps followed. Without a sound I replaced the purse in its corner and settled the drawer back onto its runner. I did not mean to search Mem's things. The clutter of pencils and clips and blank stationery held no interest, in any case. But a familiar insignia on one of the other papers caught my eye. An American eagle. This same official seal marked the adoption forms Mr Weller had given us in Tihwa. For a moment I thought these were the same documents, but then I looked closer. Only the date and the official's signature and one other name had been filled in. The date marked was October 20, 1950, and the official signature belonged to Ambassador Minton. The form, I now saw, was a visa application for entrance to the United States of America. The lettering below the ambassador's signature read, 'Approved by.' The other name, written by some stranger on the line marked 'Applicant,' was my own.

I heard Mem's voice at the bottom of the stairs. Hardly caring now how much noise I made, I shoved the papers back in the drawer and the drawer back into the desk. I fled down the hall before Mem saw me, but my heart was raging. Three months had passed since this form was signed, yet she had never once mentioned it, never bothered to complete it. Certainly she had never cared to submit it to the embassy, even though it already had been *approved!*

I did not know what to think, or do. I tried to put the matter out of my head as I worked through my lessons at school that day, as I slid past the librarian's kindly eyes to my reading corner during lunch. Of course, I could neither read nor work nor put those papers out of my mind. Mem could take me to America now. In America I would be safe. No one from my past life could reach me there. But Mem did not want me in America. Most likely, she did not want me at all.

After school I borrowed the last ten rupees from Nagu, saying it was for a present for Mem. I rode my bicycle to Humayun's Tomb and found Jaggu whittling a shaft of wood with his long, foldout knife. I gave him the envelope of money, the agreed amount, and he grinned at me, flicking the knife closed. He was relieved. I could see it in his eyes. He was almost as frightened of Indrani's friends as I was.

But now my savings were gone, and I could no longer even fantasize about turning to Mem. If I kept stealing to pay my debts, she was certain to find out, and then she would surely toss me away. I would have no choice but to return to Indrani.

As I rode home I thought back to the girls I had met at the roundabout two years earlier. Everything I told Jaggu was true. I could earn plenty if I stood with the night birds, especially dressed in foreign clothing and speaking with an educated accent. Mem would never have to know. And if I succeeded, I could stay in school, continue living among the *firenghi*. I was smart, and I worked hard. All my teachers said so. This other business would not change that. One day, I might go to America on my own.

So it was decided. I would tell no one.

I was surprised to discover how much of my training from the flash house remained within me. Although I thought I had put them out of my mind, I now recalled with exquisite clarity the ways and wiles of my sisters, and the tricks they used to please their *babus*. I remembered the pretended abandon with which they smoked and drank, the languor with which each operated her body like an instrument that was an extension of herself and yet not herself. I remembered Bharati telling me that a woman's flesh, whether sacred or evil, will dictate her survival, and I returned over and over in my mind to the monument of the *angrezi*, those painted girls jingling their glass bangles and scenting the air with rosewater and jasmine. How they had soothed me with their attentions, the easy inclusiveness of their smiles. I had ignored the chill of misgiving that swept among them at the mention of Mrs Shaw. I left them for the illusion of rescue. Now I understood.

From watching my sisters, and especially from the true smiles I used to exchange with Mira, I knew that the girl who went forth that first night must be other than myself. Oh, she would possess and use my body, but she and I truly would never touch, or even look alike. So it was for this shadow that I lifted from Mem's closet the red evening dress in which I had once 'dressed up' as Princess Kamla of Kashgaria. It was for this make-believe Princess's disguise that I stole from Mem's dressing table her rejected pots of rouge and kohl sticks. For this harlot's protection that I wheedled a key and the use of his gardening box out of the *mali*, Musai. That night as I lay in bed waiting to be sure of Simon's heavy sleep breathing and double-checked the setting of the watch Lawrence had given me for my invented birthday, I decided to allow my shadow three hours, no more.

The vine that twisted upward to the terrace outside our bedroom was every bit as handy as the damsel's braid in the foreign fairy tale of Rapunzel that Mem once read to us, yet still, as I watched Princess Kamla – no, I decided, only Princess . . . Even as I watched this Princess, then, gingerly finding her footing among the trunk's tangles, as my mind's eye watched the pale swirl of her nightgown drifting to the ground, the ghost of her body stepping and wriggling into its darker skin, her head dipping as she twisted her hair and handled her face, I wondered at her confidence and stealth. The Princess was an escape artist.

The sky loomed powdery black that night, cold and filled with stars, though it smelled, as always, of dung fire. Occasionally, between the black branches of the plane trees above the compound walls, the moon would appear as a chalky smudge. Jackals screamed across the wild lands. And from the dark sprawls of tenement encampments tucked under bridges or behind ancient tombs rose the moans of the sick and dying. A few bicycles and rickshaws passed, one or two automobiles with their lights out. It took only about five minutes to ride by bicycle to the statue, that pale thumb of stone with features of a British hero – which one did not matter. A match flared, illuminating kohl-rimmed eyes, a lipsticked mouth. Flash and fade. The smoldering glow of the cigarette became one of several that hung in the black air like fireflies.

I gathered my skirt to step up onto the high curb. 'Hey, sister!' The women laughed and reached a hand to help.

A covered cycle rickshaw entered the roundabout. Its lamp went on, and the hard yellow beam caught the girls in poses that made me think of the calendar Simon's friend Brian loaned him. I had caught Simon looking at it only a month ago, and he had sworn me to secrecy, then shown me every page. As I studied the displays of legs and breasts, the thick pouting lips and eyelids darkened with collyrium, I had felt my own face and body lift in inward imitation. 'Mem would kill us if she found out,' I said, confused by the mixture of dread and desire the images aroused in me. 'Why?' Simon replied, though I sensed he was mouthing his friend's words. 'It's just harmless fun.'

I had neither the courage nor the heart to tell him the truth.

The girls in the roundabout tipped their heads and bared arms and legs. They clattered glass bangles and floated vermilion finger-nails, outlining the curves of their bosoms and hips. Some wore golden threaded saris with nothing underneath. Some wore skin-tight turquoise and green *choli* bodices lifted to expose charcoal crescents circumscribing their breasts. As the headlamp slowly circled, it seemed to snatch each woman in turn and cast her back into darkness. Then suddenly, as the rickshaw came around again, the flood beam fell on a tall girl with blue-rimmed eyes who pulled her red sari across her mouth and did a little dance with her hips. The oilcloth flap to the cab pulled back, and the vehicle stopped. She stepped closer to negotiate a price. The flap opened wider and she climbed inside. The lamp flickered off again, and the rickshaw slipped back into the darkness.

'Will she return tonight?' I asked a girl whose pockmarked skin had reminded me of orange peel in the headlights.

'Most likely, she will return in an hour. The hotel is not far.'

'Hotel?'

The voice of another, scratchy as a thornbush, called out, 'Yes, child, a grand hotel, with English beds and uniformed waiters and gramophones and punkahs flapping. Just you wait!' A wave of laughter rolled across the darkness, and someone plucked at my arm to move me back as a motorcar approached. But I stepped forward and posed like the rest. The car was a handsome black Morris touring sedan that smacked of money, and I did not intend to wait.

The sedan slowed to a stop in front of me. The pockmarked girl gave me a shove. 'Beginner's luck,' she said.

The passenger door opened. I hesitated. 'Beginner's luck,' the girl repeated. 'Go on, or I will.'

The sedan held one man only who drove himself and offered an hour's price for half that time. 'I know him,' one of the sisters assured me. 'He is interested because you are new. Go along, he's all right.' All I could see in the darkness was the size of him, which was puffed and stubby. I climbed in, and the car rolled away.

He smelled of hair pomade and a dinner steeped in garlic and curry. He asked for a name, and I told him, Princess. He did not offer his own. After that we drove in silence, turning only minutes later between two sandstone pillars topped by carved lions. I looked across the lawn and realized we had come to the Jai Mahal hotel. But this was not the entrance Mem and Lawrence used when they brought me and Simon to swim. Here no guards stood sentry, nor was there a single light in the large flat car park where we stopped. The hotel building, with its side verandas and hundreds of windows, twinkled just a few hundred feet away, but here the leaves of the trees formed a separate canopy, and as the man beside me clicked off the engine and dropped his hand to my knee I understood that the hotel might as well stand in another country.

There were perhaps half a dozen cars parked around us, identifiable only through the shimmer of their chrome, the occasional sulfurous burst of a match, the rocking of metal springs, or the explosion of a groan. Every so often a waiter would appear on the ground-lit path from the hotel kitchen holding a tray of bottles and glasses, but as he came down the darker steps and moved among the cars, the white of his jacket seemed to float through the blackness as if worn by an invisible man.

I remember these things as if I, too, were invisible. As if I were the Princess's shadow instead of the other way around. Other things I do not choose to remember at all.

CHAPTER 13

1

Lawrence reached Wisconsin in early February after flying in fits and starts for five days from Sydney. He had never been to America's Midwest before, and as he climbed from the taxicab on Milwaukee's north shore the cold literally took his breath away. Factoring in the effects of the chilling wind, the temperature plunged to twenty below zero. His wool overcoat, sweater, and thin leather gloves had been up to the job in San Francisco. Here, they might have been tissue paper.

'Better get yourself a hat,' the driver advised him. 'Heat rises, y' know.' Then he tipped his own red beret and drove off, leaving Lawrence bareheaded, teeth chattering, loath to breathe for fear his windpipe would freeze. The sky was like slate, the trees barren, and Lake Michigan, which he could see through tears of pain if he faced into the wind, looked like a vast plate of whipped ink. Who but Americans would consider this a livable climate?

Turning from the waterfront, he pulled a notepad out of his pocket to make sure the address he'd written down matched the tarnished brass numbers on the brick pillar in front of him. The house, an imposing if careworn Tudor, was fronted by an apron of brown lawn laced with snow and presided over by a too bright and shiny platoon of grinning ceramic trolls. Faded floral curtains hung in the windows. A late-model dark green Ford sat under the carport. Lawrence shoved his hands deeper into his pockets and stamped his feet up the wide veranda.

A dog yipped inside. 'Hush, Lily!' A woman's voice, fat and stern.

As the door opened, Lawrence saw the owner of the voice bent over, holding a squirming tan dachshund by the collar. She was thick-waisted, approaching middle age, with bobbed hair the same color as the dog's.

'Come in! Come in!' she ordered Lawrence before he had a chance to introduce himself. 'You'll catch your death out there.' She pushed the door shut with one sensibly shod foot. 'Excuse me, I'll just get this little pest out of our way. Go on into the living room, will you?'

She vanished down the dark center hallway, leaving Lawrence to seat himself on one of the overstuffed couches in the parlor off the entry. Between the fire in the grate and the radiator hissing in the corner it was almost as hot inside as it was cold out. He quickly shed his coat and gloves and blew his nose. An array of framed photographs lined the mantelpiece and bookshelves, but before he could examine them the woman was back, tugging on a maroon cardigan over her pastel green housedress and wheezing lightly.

'Mr Malcolm!'

'Mrs Darling?'

Her round face squeezed into a smile. 'It always sounds so silly when someone new says it. And in that nice accent, too.' She offered her hand. It was like shaking a lump of bread dough. 'Just call me Grace.'

'Lawrence,' he returned.

'Would you like some coffee? Mother'll be down in a minute. She was just getting some things together for you.'

He had called from San Francisco. They knew who he was. Eldon had told them. Lawrence said he would like to pay his respects. Of course. They understood.

Grace Darling was a short woman, as ill suited to her name as sweetbreads were to theirs. She barely came up to Lawrence's shoulder and gave off a faint, disagreeable odor, like machine oil.

'Coffee would be fine, thanks,' Lawrence said.

'Good. It's all ready. Why don't you have a look at the pictures, then? I put out all the ones I could find of Alice. Whatever else she may have been, she certainly was photogenic.'

And she scurried back, once again, into the bowels of the old house.

361

She was that, Lawrence thought, picking up one picture after another of Aidan's femme fatale. Dressed in jodhpurs and a man's shirt, riding boots and helmet, astride a magnificent palomino. Or costumed for a ball in a long glittering gown slit halfway up her thigh, her blond hair a temptress's pile of curls. As a Goldilocks baby reaching for an enormous soap bubble, mouth and arms stretched wide as if she meant to gobble it whole. As a girl Kamla's age in a navy and white uniform not so different from Kamla's school outfits, though Alice exuded a kind of carefree exuberance that Kamla surely had never known.

He saw Alice water-skiing, diving into pools, hiking in the mountains, and striding arm-in-arm with girlfriends down the crowded avenues of New York City. She was every bit as glamorous and gorgeous as Joanna could have imagined in her darkest dreams. The perfect wife's nightmare, Lawrence thought. A man's woman, as poor Akbar had said.

And yet, something about meeting these images of Alice James here in this strange musty house with Alice's most unlikely sister pottering in the background disturbed Lawrence in a way he couldn't put his finger on. It wasn't the mental specter of Alice's decomposing body. That, he'd prepared for. That, he'd experienced during the war, when visiting the parents of slain mates from the field. No, this was something else. Something more to do with Joanna than himself.

'Mr Malcolm,' said a quiet, elderly voice. He turned to face a woman who resembled neither Grace nor Alice yet could only be their mother. 'I'm Helen James.'

She deposited an armload of scrapbooks, school yearbooks, and bundled letters on the coffee table. 'I appreciate your coming. I also appreciate why you've come.' She beckoned him to sit down.

'I'm sorry,' he said. 'It's a long time after the fact.'

Helen James clasped her hands in the lap of her dark blue dress. Her white hair was done up in a chignon. A simple gold brooch gleamed at her throat. No makeup. No earrings. Oyster gray eyes that were sober without being cold. 'Once death has come and gone,' she said, 'the passage of time becomes irrelevant.'

Lawrence was spared the need for an immediate reply by the tromp of Grace's footsteps and the distribution of coffee cups and saucers and spoons and coasters and all the edible paraphernalia that women the world over insisted on adding to the basic element of caffeine. Alice's mother poured.

'So,' said Grace. 'You want to know more about Alice, I suppose? Everyone always does.'

'Everyone?' Lawrence asked.

'Well. Mr Eldon did. And the two men from the State Department.'

Helen sighed.

Lawrence waited to see if she would speak. She didn't. He asked, 'The men who informed you of Alice's death?'

'No. The ones who came after. The one who came to tell us just told us, that's all,' Grace said.

'I see.' Lawrence sipped his coffee, which somehow tasted both thick and bland.

Helen picked up her cup, not drinking, and held it as if to warm her hands. 'The two men who came later wanted to know if Alice was a Communist. They didn't say it in so many words, but they wanted to know who her friends had been, if we had any letters. They said they were from the State Department. I think they were probably FBI.'

'Mother! Do you really?'

'They didn't show you any identification?' Lawrence asked.

'Oh, they flashed some papers, you know how they do,' Grace said. 'But Mother was still too upset to pay much attention, and I didn't get here until they were half done – I don't live here, my house is up on Pleasant Street, and so when she called me I had to drop everything and ask my neighbor to watch the kids – I have a boy and a girl, ten and twelve, though they were younger then, of course.'

'Sure.' Lawrence turned to her mother. 'Why do you think they were FBI?'

'They wanted us to name names.'

Again, Grace jumped in. 'They asked about Alice's boyfriends and clubs, things like that. They *said* they were investigating her death, and why she'd gone to China, and maybe someone had been with her there – well, we knew someone *was* with her, of course. Mr Shaw. But they made it sound like, I don't know, maybe

363

someone was stalking her, or something. For Pete's sake, I bet you're right, Mother!'

Lawrence continued to look at Helen, who was worrying the plain gold band on her ring finger. 'Did they tell you they suspected Aidan of being a Communist, or did you only find that out when the journalists began calling?' He glanced at Grace. 'Joanna showed me your letter to her.'

A grunt from Grace. 'Yes. Well, I'm sorry she never answered.'

'I don't blame her,' said Helen.

There was a long silence during which Grace swallowed elaborately, then adjusted the antimacassar on the arm of her chair.

Helen said, 'No. They told us nothing about Mr Shaw. Only that another journalist had been traveling with her, and he now was missing in China. It was Mr Eldon who told us that you and Mrs Shaw suspected her husband was there at the time of the accident.'

'If you can call it an accident,' Grace said.

Lawrence sipped his coffee. The dog was pawing at a door somewhere in the back of the house.

'What else did Ben tell you?'

'That she was gone days, maybe weeks before you found her. And buried her. Thank you for that.'

'You have Joanna to thank, really.' Lawrence waited for Helen to question him. But she didn't.

'He wanted to know if Alice wrote us from China. They *all* wanted to know that.' Grace topped off her cup with cream. 'She didn't. Not a word.'

After another long pause Lawrence said, 'Aidan was my mate, so maybe I shouldn't comment. But I don't believe he was a Communist.'

'We've *read* his articles,' Grace said, drilling into him now with her narrow brown eyes. 'Maybe he didn't carry the card, but—'

'That's enough, Grace,' her mother said. 'I don't believe Mr Shaw was a Communist, either, Mr Malcolm. Any more than Alice was.'

'Oh, for crying out loud. You *always* covered up for her.' Grace leaned forward and flipped through the top scrapbook on the pile until she found a page of clippings under the banner *Belmont Sentinel*. 'These were articles Alice wrote for the school paper. Just listen. "Students Rally in Support of Industrial Workers of the

World," "Why Roosevelt Needs Stalin to Win the War," "This Girl's Guide to the Meaning of the *Internationale*," "Belmont Students Found Young Socialist Club." Alice dated the president of that club for two years, Mother. She *was* one of those founding members. I *told* you, and you just kept saying, oh, it's a phase, she's experimenting, she'll grow out of it and come to her senses. Well, she didn't. I'll bet she *did* join the Communist Party when she went off to that fancy liberal college you sent her to back East. You know that old boyfriend of hers, Fred Hurley, was blacklisted, don't you? He hightailed it over to France and became a musician or something. Probably playing "The Internationale" even as we speak!'

Grace thrust the scrapbook at Lawrence, though her argument was aimed at her mother.

Helen didn't react. She sat stirring her coffee with a little spoon, around and around in circles, the coffee surely stone cold by now. She hadn't taken a sip.

Finally Grace got up in a huff. 'Oh, I quit. I just quit. You'd think you were *glad* she died, you know? I mean, it's the Communism that killed her!' She put her hands on her hips and turned to Lawrence. 'She was heading for Russia. She called it the "back door." "If I can, I'm going to find a back door in and see what it's really like." That's what she said right before she left.' She fumbled through the bundle of letters until she found a pale blue aerogram, which she thrust at him. 'See for yourself!'

She cast one more long-suffering look at her mother and left the room. 'I'm coming, Lily!' she called down the hallway. 'Yes, yes, *there's* a good dog!'

Lawrence dropped his eyes to the letter.

Don't worry about me, Alice had written, not from China but from Kashmir. *I'm traveling of my own will and on my own steam. I'll be out of touch for some time, I think, and I'm not entirely sure where this trek over the mountains will land me, but I'm picking up all sorts of interesting material. People are extraordinarily helpful, and it's just the sort of adventure I need.*

What was it Weller called her? Eager beaver, cub reporter? Might not have been far off, from the sound of it. But why did she *need* an adventure?

'Midway through the war she wanted to join the Young Communists, but her father wouldn't hear of it.' Helen spoke calmly, as if Grace had never opened her mouth. 'Andrew – Mr James passed less than a year before Alice.'

'I'm sorry,' Lawrence said. 'That must have been terrible for you.'

'It was worse for Alice. She adored her father, and he loved her extravagantly.' She studied the cup in her hands as if wondering how it got there. She set it down on the table. Alice's fabulous face beamed at them from the photographs that Grace had arranged around the room – perversely blocking the pictures of her own children, which Lawrence only now detected lurking on the corners of the mantelpiece.

'You were a close friend of Mr Shaw?' Helen asked.

Lawrence nodded. Though he had turned his head he could feel her gray eyes resting on him, waiting. A door slammed at the back of the house.

'And Joanna Shaw,' he said. 'The reason I'm here—'

'Is to find out whether my daughter and Mrs Shaw's husband were lovers.'

Lawrence blinked at her. 'Actually—'

'Actually, it's a perfectly reasonable question. The answer is probably yes. Not that it makes a whit of difference now. But wives always want to know, don't they? No matter how long after the fact. Jealousy is far more insidious than betrayal.' She pinched the folds of her dress, arranging them over her knees. 'Are you *her* lover? Joanna Shaw's?'

'I – ' He caught himself. This was a woman who had known secrets. Their vapors still shrouded every corner of this house. But he sensed that she herself now rejected them. They'd become, like time, irrelevant. 'I have been,' he said. 'After we found Alice, it seemed – likely – that Aidan had been with her. That he must also be dead. But a few months ago Joanna learned he's still alive. Inside China.'

She slowly turned her eyes to the window. Not looking at him, she asked in a restrained voice, 'Has she contacted him?'

'No. I'm sorry. We've no hard evidence,' he lied. 'Only rumors of a sighting – in a prison up near the Soviet border.'

She considered this for a minute. Then said, 'So you gave her up. You gave each other up. She's still in love with him, I suppose. In spite of Alice.' Helen had turned her hands over, fingers outstretched in her lap, and was staring at her palms. Her pale lashes had darkened, wet, though Lawrence could not see actual tears.

'I don't think you should blame Alice for Aidan's actions.'

'I'm not blaming Alice for anything!' Helen James said hotly, whipping a white handkerchief from her dress pocket and stabbing at her eyes. 'She's dead and yet the three of you are alive—'

Her voice broke off. Lawrence, feeling unjustly accused, selected another scrapbook and began turning pages jammed with pictures from camp, birthday parties, family outings to the beach and mountains, Helen and Mr James with the classes they'd taught, hers around Simon's age and his in upper school. Andrew James, it appeared, had been a stout man with an appealing smile and good teeth, perhaps ten years older than his wife. His students tended to be laughing in their pictures with him. Helen's, though younger, leaned more toward valedictorian poses – chins in the air, heads turned in profile, eyes meeting the lens indirectly. As if she'd coached them. Even Grace, who seemed to have had both of her parents as teachers, adjusted her attitude to the preferred model. She looked ridiculous – overweight and pompous – in the portrait with Helen, but happily mischievous with her father. Only Alice seemed to disregard her parents' influence. In both her class pictures she stared defiantly into the lens, head cocked to one side, lips simultaneously pouting and smiling like a born seductress.

Grace's heavy footstep sounded again in the hall, and she appeared in the doorway dressed in a long black coat, striped muffler, red tam-o'-shanter, and green mittens holding the dachshund, also dressed in a dog's striped sweater. 'I have to go now. My children will be home soon. It's nice to meet you, Mr Malcolm. I'm sorry I couldn't be more help.'

'Actually, there is one more thing before you go.' He glanced from Grace to her mother. It was Grace who had written to Joanna. Grace who meticulously chronicled her grievances against her sister. Helen's self-appointed secretary. 'Ben Eldon,' he said. 'I'm traveling to D.C. next, and I'd like to look him up, but I seem to have misplaced his address. I can write Joanna, of course, but that will take weeks to turn around—'

'Oh, you don't have to do that!' Grace stepped to a small writing desk in the corner and fished around the drawer. 'Here. He left his card.'

Lawrence jotted down the address. A postal drop on D Street under the banner of Kodak. *Sales Representative, Asia.* It matched the card Eldon had left with Joanna. Neither listed an office or phone.

He handed the card back to Grace and told her she'd been very helpful. She flung a defiant, needy look at her mother and was gone.

Again, Helen began speaking as if Grace had never been there. 'Alice was so wild and free. She and I never really understood each other any more than she and Grace did. Only her father could talk to her, reason with her. Probably that was because he never made the mistake of trying to control her. After he died, she wanted to get as far away from here – from us – as she possibly could. She loved us. It wasn't that. But it was as if she viewed us as a kind of cage.'

She sighed and once again toyed with her wedding band. 'Politics were the least of it, Mr Malcolm. You understand?'

He felt his chest tighten. He reached through the distance that separated them and took Helen James's hands in his. 'I do,' he said. 'Believe me.'

They talked awhile longer. He read Alice's letters and looked through the rest of the scrapbooks. Then it was time to leave. The sun made a blur of white above the black tassel of tree branches stretched across the western horizon. In the opposite direction the lake had calmed to the color of sea glass. Helen came out with him to the end of the veranda. She had only a thin blue shawl around her, but she assured him she was used to the cold.

She shook her head at the brightly shining trolls standing watch over the driveway. 'Grace and her husband's Christmas present to Andrew the year before he died. Aren't they awful.' She smiled, tentatively, met his eyes. And they began to laugh. They laughed harder.

'Oh no!' she said, 'I'm starting to cry. I can't cry in this temperature. My tears will freeze!' She was laughing so hard she grasped his arm. He pulled her closer. He had no idea why they were laughing, but it seemed the most natural thing in the world. He wound his arm around her shoulders, and she warmed her face on the sleeve of his coat.

The tears and laughter subsided, and he guided her back to her front door.

She put up the back of her hand to her nose, her warm gray eyes looking out at him over her palm. 'Thank you, Mr Malcolm. Really.'

The door closed so quickly that he didn't have time to finish saying 'Lawrence.'

That night in his hotel room he wrote sixteen different accounts of his meeting with Helen James. He meant to report back to Joanna from every stop along this route of investigation. But none of the accounts seemed acceptable. How could he explain why he had exposed Joanna so utterly to this stranger? How could he be certain she would not find in Helen's story cause for despair instead of hope?

Finally he placed the attempts in his valise along with the rest of his notes. He turned out the light and lay watching the moon stitch in and out of the clouds. What had disturbed him in the James home, he now saw, was the fact that the portrait of Alice he'd formed there so closely resembled Joanna. But could he also find in Jo Helen James's capacity for understanding?

He wished the answer were yes. He hoped it might be, for Joanna's sake.

2

They each paid twenty rupees for the hour. This was a high rate, but the Princess's youth and blue eyes were charms in my favor. In the beams of the headlamps, I stood out among my new sisters. I went with two to three men each night. This way I had only to go one or two nights each week in order to meet my obligation to Jaggu, and only on nights when I did not have school

the following morning. I would make up the sleep through afternoon naps, and if Mem asked why I was suddenly so tired, I would
tell her I stayed up late doing homework.

Most of my customers resembled the first. Oh, they would be
fatter or slimmer, hairier or noisier, with thicker lips or fleshier
hands. Only a few could afford a motorcar and the protection of
the Jai Mahal, so most took me instead by cycle or scooter to some
secluded place – a public garden or construction site, or to a nearby
school where the *chowkidar* opened a room for the purpose in
exchange for a small payment. But in the darkness and with the
Princess as my mask, I paid scant attention. To me just one man
was significantly different from the rest. He claimed me on my
second night at the roundabout.

His car was neither handsome nor moneyed but a battered white
Ambassador. It circled the roundabout twice before it pulled over.
'You!' The driver leaned out and snapped his fingers, but when I
went closer I saw that the driver was a middle-aged Sikh, a servant
who barked his words. He named a price. I asked for more. The
driver started to berate me, but a voice from the backseat stopped
him. It was an old voice, breathless and coarse. It agreed to my
demand.

The old man was a gem dealer from Moradabad. His name was
Shrilal. As aged as I was young, he took me not to the blackness of
the hotel car park but to the end of Old Delhi, to a Chandni
Chowk flat that he kept for this purpose.

'We are like two ends of a scale, you and I,' Shrilal said, studying
me that first night by the orange light of a lamp swathed in silk. I
lowered the red dress from my shoulders and stood before him
naked. Then he laid me on the bed like one of his diamonds,
inspecting every facet, crevice, angle of my anatomy, running
withered hands over my flesh to search out the hidden flaws.

He had a long trickling beard and eyes from which the color had
drained so it seemed he must be blind, though he saw everything,
that one, sensed everything. When he touched me I thought of
photographs I had seen in Mem's magazines, of those black-and-
white maps called X-rays. Shrilal was not possessive, yet he wanted
to know who else rented my body, where they marked me, how
they entered me. He himself could not, you see. His decrepitude

did not permit him to avail himself of my youth. He could no longer penetrate the span of time and sex that lay between us. He could only pay and hunger for it, possessing a right he no longer had the physical power to exercise. But together, we balanced the scale.

He paid me well and afterward I knew he would come for me again.

Between customers, when the roundabout was quiet, I would glean bits of information about my new sisters. The pockmarked girl had run away from home after her father, who owned a successful cinema in Jaipur, beat her for refusing to marry her cousin. The tall girl with blue-rimmed eyes ('You are blessed,' she told me. 'I apply Krishna's color for luck, but you are born with it.') had a good-for-nothing husband who forced her to this work. Of the five or six other girls who came and went, two were widows whose husbands' families had turned them out. The others had fallen in love with men who became their pimps.

And yet, for all their sorrows, most of my new sisters possessed a cunning and strength that impressed me. They could pick out the high-paying customers simply by the register of the men's voices. Many were actresses capable of portraying hilarity, pathos, haughtiness, or submission, all with the flash of an eye. And when the pimps or police came circling, the girls would banter and soothe them as if they were favored customers.

Unlike the flash house where Indrani always negotiated with the police, the girls here divided the entertainment of police among themselves. Some refused, preferring to pay in rupees. Others didn't seem to mind, even had chosen favorites among the officers. For these were not the same police I had known in G. B. Road. The pockmarked girl, whose street name was Scarlett, explained that the deputies here showed respect because our clients were more prosperous. This roundabout was known for its night birds. Some men traveled from as far as Chandigarh just to taste 'our delights.' Many of the customers were government officers, even Members of Parliament. The police would not risk angering these men by roughing us up, so, while it was understood they had the power to arrest us – or to cause us otherwise to disappear – they appeared relaxed when they made their visits, and my sisters responded accordingly. None of these girls had ever heard of Inspector Golba. Not by name, anyway.

The police came my fourth night out. I hung back, hiding by the statue as two of the officers played their flashlights over my sisters, making a game of identifying any new bangles or nose rings, measuring to see who had gained weight – in other words, who had been prospering the most under their protection and thus who might owe them a little extra. The girls joked with them, teased them. Then I saw a third figure circling the others. He was thick through the middle, had a large round head, and gave off a faint odor of fish. I drew back behind the Englishman's statue and held my breath. I was afraid Mem's carnation scent would give me away, but just as he was about to turn in my direction, Scarlett began to laugh. 'We haven't seen you in a long time, sir!' She beckoned him to her and whispered in his ear. The widows took the arms of the two other officers and the six of them climbed into the lorry and drove away. When I next saw Scarlett I tried to thank her, but she shook her head. 'It was my turn. Yours will come. The police are a nuisance we share around, a dirty but necessary chore.'

But my turn had already come with Golba. What was he doing so far from his own district? In fact he had been here once before, over a year earlier, then as now asking if any new girls had been working the roundabout. Then the true answer had been no. This time Scarlett lied, but if he was searching for one in particular, this would put him off only so long. From that night on, I went with the first man who looked at me, regardless how much he offered. And when that battered white Ambassador appeared in the roundabout again, I all but ran to it calling Shrilal's name. I went with him as to a reprieve. I petted and sang to him, soothed his old feet. I touched his hair, his hands, his very eyelids as I had once spied Mem touching Lawrence. Now we set the next night for our meeting in advance.

Scarlett warned me, 'This old man will lose interest. He will die. They all do, you should not depend on him.' But she need not have worried. I already knew that no safe haven lasts forever. This Mrs Shaw had taught me.

⌣

Once a fortnight, as agreed, I met Jaggu at Humayun's Tomb and passed him a tiffin box stuffed with money. In return he brought me signed receipts like bank chits from Indrani. The mathematics I had learned at school failed to prepare me for that magical invention called interest, which increased with the passage of time so that I owed more after the first month than I had owed at the outset. But the first time I challenged Indrani's reckoning, Jaggu informed me that her old friend Golba was now Superintendent of Police for all of Delhi, and he had not forgotten how I once caused him to lose face.

I refused to believe this. Surely, if Golba were Superintendent, some sign of his status would have shown itself that night at the roundabout. And if he did know of my arrangement with Jaggu – especially if he were taking his own squeeze from the profits – would he not have asked Scarlett more particular questions?

'You are making it up,' I said. 'You think you can frighten me.'

Jaggu stroked his birthmark and gazed west to the smoke-stained sun. He spoke as if he had not heard me. 'Superintendent Golba told Indrani that your American mother has been bribing the magistrate to remand certain girls from the courts. So it seems that Mrs Shaw, too, breaks the law. It is rare for Indian police to arrest a foreigner, but such a scandal as this could make Golba quite famous if he were the one to bring the case.'

I did not know what to say to this. It had never occurred to me that Mem might break the law. But, of course, she had done so when she took me in. If Golba was to be believed. If Golba represented the law. I eyed two policemen standing across Mathura Road. They were laughing broadly at a little boy with a brown monkey squatting on his head.

'You must not try to escape,' Jaggu was saying, 'or change the terms of our arrangement, for if you do, Mrs Shaw and you both could suffer grave consequences.'

'Why does Golba not come to say these things to me himself?' I demanded, but my boldness was as false as my night bird name.

Jaggu laughed. 'He is far too busy planning his rise to Parliament! But he has only to lift his little finger.' He drew his own forefinger across his throat and widened his eyes.

Parliament! Oh, it sickened me, but I could just see him, his bulbous face staring out from posters around the city, his name blaring from loudspeakers, his presence forcing itself from every direction. I could just imagine him accusing Mem from the grandstand. This foreign woman breaking Indian law and meddling in India's internal affairs. Perhaps, after all, I was deluding myself, and it would be best for everyone if I simply returned to Indrani.

'Jaggu,' I asked, 'does Mira still stay with Indrani?'

'Mira?' He pursed his lips, no longer laughing. 'The quiet one?'

I nodded.

'She is dead many months now, that one. Some female sickness. She refused to work, and Indrani had her beaten. Then she refused to eat. Perhaps she starved to death.' He shrugged.

I could not breathe. Then I could not see. I turned away blinking back tears. I thought of Mira's secret smile, her sorrow and her tenderness. I had not recognized the strength of her courage.

No. There was no turning back.

At school I made certain to excel at my work so that Mem had no cause to challenge me. I spent lunch and recess in the library studying the spoiled *firenghi* girls as they retreated behind their glossy magazines. I recorded the curl of their lips, the disdain that prowled within their gaze. *Leave me alone!* they shouted without opening their mouths, and to my astonishment, everyone did. 'It's an *awful* age,' I heard their mothers complain in the car park as they waited for the daughters to emerge. 'It's an awful age,' I heard Mem say to Mrs Solomon as I passed the living room one day.

So I hid behind sleep and books and the world-weary mask of my awful age.

Much to my relief, Simon, too, left me alone now. With his friends Brian Wilcox and Frankie and Willy Mann, he was too busy finding trouble even to notice my awful age. They formed parties to wrangle mongooses in the desert or fire BB guns at snakes. They used magnifying glasses to set scorpions on fire. On weekends Lazarus would take them all to the cinema, where they saw *Yankee Doodle Dandy* and *Beau Geste* over and over again. Afterward they made nuisances of themselves at the record shops in Connaught Place, then went for ice cream at the Milk Bar. At dusk the boys would get up a game of cricket, or take turns tying, closeting, and handcuffing each other like Simon's hero Houdini.

Simon, who had once been so sweet and trusting, was now stealing packs of rubber bands, chewing gum, and pencils from Mittral's in Khan Market. I discovered this when I overheard Lazarus, of all people, dressing him down.

He was late to pick us up at school, and I'd gone back inside for a book I'd forgotten. When I came out Lazarus had arrived but everyone else was gone except for a cluster of Untouchable children huddled beside the car park gate. They were awaiting the leftover snacks and cast-off lunches the school sweeper passed on to them each evening. Lazarus allowed his voice to rise in the empty yard.

'I stole when I was your age because I bloody well had to,' he said. 'I stole things I needed, things I couldn't afford, not stupid odds and ends I'd just end up pissing away. You trying to get caught, Simon? Is that what you want?'

It was that moment of dusk when the sky seems to suck the last light from the ground and dangle it like a lure. Lazarus and Simon stood on the other side of the Austin as I approached. I could not hear Simon's answer, but through the car windows I made out the violet silhouette of his hanging head.

'You get in trouble, you know who's going to have to bloody answer for it.' The world revolved around Lazarus, at least in his opinion, and he had his own unpredictable way of inflicting discipline.

'Get in the backseat,' he said when he saw me. 'Simon, up front. It's time you learned to drive.'

Whether he was testing Simon's bad-boy instincts or just wanted to have a little fun with him I could not say, but Simon was a poor choice for the challenge. He was still, for all his recent bluff, a cautious, fearful child. This was Mem's car, and he did not have to ask what she would say if he drove it into a wall, with or without permission from Lazarus. 'I don't want to,' he said. 'Shouldn't we ask Mem first?'

'Did you ask Mem before you took those knickknacks from Mittral's?'

'No, but – ' Simon frowned at me as I came around the car.

Lazarus gave him a rough push with the flat of his hand and he crumpled into the driver's seat. 'You want to take a risk. So all right.'

Simon began to hiccup loudly. He hunched over the steering wheel, hiding his face.

Lazarus slammed the door, but the window was open and the hiccups kept coming, like yelps of pain. I stood facing Lazarus now, and I was as tall as he was. 'You wouldn't try such a thing if Lawrence were here!' I said.

He had no patience for me, either. Without a moment's hesitation he took hold of my ears and shook me hard, demanded to know who I thought I was. Before I could answer he told me. 'You bloody half-breed. Cheeky bitch. How dare you upset Simon so!'

Lazarus's skin stretched tight as polished wood across his cheeks, and his eyes flashed crisp black between sharp-cut lids. He could almost pass for a handsome man. I took this opportunity to say so, to his face, and he slapped me across mine. It was different from the time Mem slapped me. More like the shots the doctor gave us. I hardly felt it.

Simon had gone silent.

'Is this why Lawrence sent you?' I asked Lazarus. 'To bully us and slap us and push us around? I think we should write and tell him, don't you, Simon? Lazarus knows how to reach Lawrence. You're staying in his flat. I'll bet you read his mail and sleep in his bed. I'm surprised you don't wear his clothes. But you're nothing like him, you know, you never can be, for all your bloody this and that—'

He'd had enough. He pushed Simon over, leaving me to climb in back, and reclaimed the driver's seat. As we lurched forward he blasted the horn at the Harijan children who stood in their rags and festering sores, gawking and blocking our exit. When they failed to rouse themselves he screamed at them out the window, '*Apka bapka rasta hai!*'

The question struck me as so preposterous that I began to laugh. Simon looked back at me, his *firenghi* eyes bleak and bewildered.

'*Apka bapka rasta hai!*' Now the tears were slithering down my cheeks. 'Does your father own the road?' It was ludicrous. Those children didn't have fathers. They had nothing, nothing at all.

3

The original address Joanna had for Ben Eldon, the one she'd marked 'home' and kept in her bedroom drawer, led Lawrence to a small corner house in Georgetown, a few blocks off Wisconsin Avenue. Gray clapboard with white trim, solid drapes in the windows, well maintained, and generally speaking, unobtrusive. Lawrence played bumbling tourist, marching up and down 34th Street, peering at the house numbers. Cold enough in reality, he made a show of blowing on his hands, breathing clouds of steam.

It was three o'clock. Nothing moved in or around the house, but just in case, he only pretended to ring the bell. To the right of the entrance stood a tall bay window with heavy drapes drawn to a crack. The wedge of parlor visible through the crack glowed orange with the late sun, but was as anonymously furnished as a hotel. A rolled newspaper lay on the sofa. An empty hat stand stood in the corner. No logs filled the fireplace.

Around the corner Lawrence found an alley bordered by a tall brick wall and a freestanding garage. He paused at the entrance. A handyman was repairing a fence halfway down the alley and two couples came strolling along the sidewalk. He decided to return after dark.

Eldon's mailbox – the address on his card – turned out to be conveniently located in a small post office just three blocks from the CIA's E Street headquarters. The box sat midway down the wall of numbered compartments, adjacent to a section of larger units.

Lawrence approached the service window and asked to hire two boxes, a small and large one, 'Side by side, if possible.' The clerk glanced at him.

Lawrence gave a shame-faced shrug. The man was florid, overweight, looked like a lager drinker. 'I'm lazy. Every step counts.'

'And my old lady complains about me.' The man checked his chart. 'Well, you're in luck. I'll need a two-month deposit. Fill this out.'

Lawrence completed the forms, listing the Australian embassy as his business address, visa officer his position. 'I'm hopeless with combination locks,' he said.

'Sorry, it's all we got.'

'No worries. I'll just need a bit of practice is all.'

'Practice your heart out.'

'Got a lot of box holders here, then?'

'Nah. Central PO over near the railroad station, that's the one gets the business. Half the time nobody comes in here all day. I keep telling 'em they should close this branch, but them bigwigs up top don't take advice from grunts like me.'

'Well, that's too bad, mate. I can tell you've got management potential.'

The clerk handed Lawrence his receipt and the combinations to his new boxes. 'What the hell. Works for you.'

As a matter of fact, it did. His boxes were positioned directly above Ben Eldon's. He spent the next fifteen minutes unobserved, fumbling with his own locks, periodically snapping the doors open, then ineptly trying again. Meanwhile, he worked on Eldon's combination. He'd never been much for safecracking, but he knew the basic drill, could feel when the tumblers started to give, the drag when he'd turned the knob too far. He had Eldon's box open in eleven minutes. That was a personal record. Unfortunately, the box for the moment stood empty.

He found a coffee shop with a view of the CIA's front entrance and ate a supper of liver and onions while watching the traffic of golden boys stream in and out of the building. They ran to such a type, he thought, they might as well wear placards. Clean-cut, square-jawed, in fighting trim. In its four years of existence the agency had spawned enough of these young heroes that you could spot them all over the globe. Lucky for Eldon he'd been first in line. They'd never take him with that gimp leg now. As it was, it had to have limited his game – and his chances for promotion. He wouldn't be the first to compensate by overplaying his hand with his mates.

But Jack's warning stayed his own impulse to march directly into the dragon's den and demand the answers that he knew full well lay there. Even now the kitchen radio was blaring out the day's proceedings at the House Un-American Activities Committee.

Rumor had it all government offices – except, perhaps, the FBI – were bugged and all official phones wiretapped. No wonder Eldon operated out of a safe house.

Back at the bus stop on the corner of 34th and Q Streets, Lawrence pulled down his hat and turned up his coat collar and studied the sign above the bench. Buses on this line ran every half-hour. He sat down to wait. The house was still dark at nine o'clock when the bus pulled up. Lawrence got on. At the next stop he told the driver he'd left something behind, and hurried off again. He walked around the back of the block to the alley. The waning moon glowed just bright enough for him to inspect the padlock on the garage door. Another combination. Twice Lawrence heard footsteps and voices in the street, and flattened himself against the spine of hedge that grew up along the garage. Finally the lock sprang open. He raised the door and slipped inside, closing it softly behind him.

A large Buick sedan, several years old, just about filled the windowless garage. Lawrence switched on his flashlight. The car was a deep blue with whitewall tires, in good condition, though it wore a heavy layer of dust. Something about it seemed familiar. He tried the door and found it unlocked. The odometer told him only that the car had seen respectable use. The glove compartment was empty, as were the side pockets. No sign of registration. He checked the trunk and under the front seats, but it had been cleaned out. He was about to move on when he thought to pull the rear seat up and check for anything that might have fallen through the cracks. Whatever he expected to find, it wasn't animal crackers. But there they were. Tigers and elephants and monkeys and bears, most intact. They must have been pushed through the crack with some care, though now they were hard as stone.

And then he remembered. Joanna had told him their car in Washington was a blue Buick sedan. They'd been driving it that day in Rock Creek Park when Aidan warned her – 'no ordinary life.' They'd sold the car before coming to India, she said, but hadn't mentioned to whom. To Ben, then. Or maybe Aidan hadn't sold it at all but merely left it here for safekeeping.

He put a hand out and leaned hard against the door frame, feeling the cold metal through his coat. He could see Simon as a toddler sitting in the backseat while his parents, deep in conversation up front, failed to pay attention to him. He could see the boy holding his open carton of biscuits and secretly sliding one after the other between the cushions, like a dog burying his bones.

He closed his eyes. The face of the boy in his mind was not Simon, but Davey, playing in the backseat of the same car that would one day roll over him. *What matters most,* he thought.

'You bastard,' he said under his breath.

He returned the seat to its position, leaving Simon's zoo intact. He turned off the flashlight and left the garage. In the moonlight the small square lawn looked hard as pavement. The house was still dark. Lawrence tried the back door, then each window in turn. A walkway led along the side past an old coal chute. The circular metal hatch moved on a hinge. Lawrence's scalp was soaked with sweat under his hat brim. This was not his line. If he tried this, at best he'd be blackened with soot. He shone the flashlight down. The chute turned so that it was impossible to see the end. At worst he'd get stuck halfway. He bent closer trying to gauge whether the passage narrowed. Something glinted. He put out his hand and ran his fingers around the chute's lip. A chink had been cut through the sheet metal. In it nestled a brass door key.

The key opened the kitchen door. The drawn shades and drapes made the place almost black as that coal chute. Rather than risk a light, he opened the window coverings to let in the moon. It was enough. Bare walls. Empty counters. No flowers, no clutter, no homey touches. In the parlor that newspaper he'd seen earlier lay as before. It was dated February 20, 1951. Day before yesterday. Two others piled by the fireplace were dated respectively three days and two weeks earlier. One was a *Washington Post,* the other two *Washington Herald*s. No daily service here.

Upstairs consisted of a bath and two bedrooms, in one of which stood a small desk with a telephone and writing pad. Lawrence ran his fingertip lightly over the surface of the pad, then pocketed it. In the same fashion, he tested the blank sheets of stationery in the drawer, but left them as they were. The only book in the entire house was a telephone book. Not hollowed out to contain something else or dog-eared on strategic pages – just a phone book.

Time to leave, he told himself. But something held him. Their thoroughness had faltered in the car. And he had found the key. Ben had not told Joanna to change his 'home' address. That meant he – or someone he trusted – must still make regular visits here.

He was standing in one of the empty closets, flashlight playing over the ceiling, when he heard the front door downstairs click open. He turned out the light and froze.

The footsteps moved lightly. Only by placing his ear against the wall could Lawrence feel the vibration traveling across the parlor. It stopped directly below the closet where he was hiding. He stared at the phosphorescent hand on his watch. One second. Two. He had no weapon. He hadn't carried a gun since Sinkiang. The last time he'd squeezed a trigger was the day he shot Simon. Given that, he was probably better off relying on his wits and hands alone.

His arm went to sleep, and he reached out, touching his finger-tips to the opposite wall. The plaster seemed colder, denser than the other two walls. He realized he was touching the chimney. Another thirty seconds, and the floor downstairs creaked again.

His foot cramped. The pain shot up his instep. He shifted his weight as gradually as he could, but the floor moaned beneath him. Then his heartbeat drowned out any other sound.

For five minutes he remained, unmoving, like a child playing hide-and-seek. *Come out, come out, wherever you are!* The memories of Davey's and Simon's voices collided in his head just as their faces had earlier.

But no one did call out. No one came upstairs.

He opened the closet door. Stopping and starting, he inched his way back down to the parlor. The visitor must have left while Lawrence's own fear deafened him. Which meant that whoever it was had come in, crossed to the fireplace, stopped for a lengthy pause, and gone out again. He had not gone into the kitchen or out through the garage, and he had his own key, so had noticed nothing out of place.

Lawrence stood in front of the fireplace. The newspapers were as he'd left them. He ran his hand over the hearth, but the bricks held fast. Then he reached up inside the flue and felt for the handle to the damper. It was a long shot. Usually these things screamed when you opened them, and surely he would have heard that. But this one glided back as if greased.

And a small square envelope fluttered down, landing at Lawrence's feet.

All set for end of March. Innocents still abroad. Need to work out the pickup plan. Assume you prefer to handle this, but we need the details ASAP. I'm up to New York this weekend, but will leave place and time in box next week for us to meet.
    B.C.

Lawrence smoothed the paper out on his hotel bed. It was thick, expensive vellum, the message typed. B.C. On the fourth pass through all the names he and Joanna had tripped over during their search for Aidan, he thought of Bob Cross. The supposed consular attaché in Delhi. The one who pretended ignorance while pressing Jo to admit she knew Aidan was alive. The one neither Bertie Solomon nor his own Foreign Office had ever heard of.

He felt a hard knot in his belly. *Innocents still abroad.* If this all centered on Aidan, then those words could have only one meaning. They were using Joanna, too.

He placed the writing pad on the bedside table, angling the reading lamp. With a sideways pencil he made a rubbing. The imprint was so faint that he could make out only a few of the letters: W-a . . .e G . . .l . . . s . . .9-4-4 . . .d.

A radio in the room next door blurted out band music. A woman laughed.

Lawrence rewrote the letters and numbers on a separate sheet, marking the empty spaces with blanks. Wa_e G_l_s__944__d.

Not a telephone number. Not an address. A name, perhaps, but then what were the numbers, and that final 'd.'?

He stared at the puzzle until his eyes crossed. The knot in his stomach remained, only tightening as a man's voice joined the woman in the next room and the dance music gave way to moans of sex.

The next morning a spear of sunshine woke him at eight. He'd left the curtains open. He sat up, swearing, and his eyes fell on the fill-in-the-blanks.

'Wade-Giles 1944 edition,' he said out loud, with absolute certainty.

He splashed some water on his face, pushed his papers into his valise, and twenty minutes later was sitting in front of the Library of Congress sipping coffee from a paper cup as he waited for the doors to open.

He found the Asian Reading Room on the first floor, tucked off in a wing apart from the library's famous rotunda. At 9:00 a.m., he was the only customer, and the young Filipina librarian was quick to offer assistance. He asked her to point him toward the available Wade-Giles dictionaries. There was a full shelf and she left him to them. The only 1944 edition had been published by Oxford University Press. On its face, it appeared no different from the others on the shelf. Chinese characters were listed in alphabetical order according to their romanized Wade-Giles versions, each entry followed by definitions in English. But something had to be different about this particular volume. Something in the wording of the definitions, perhaps. Or possibly in the Chinese characters?

He settled down at a table at the far end of the room from the librarian and picked up a copy of the *Taipei Daily* that someone had left on the chair beside him. He spread it out on the table. Then he pulled the earliest of the clippings of Aidan from his valise and laid it on top of the paper, folding the page back to cover it. This way he could surreptitiously check the characters from the photograph while appearing to study the news.

During the war he'd learned to read enough Chinese that he could deconstruct most ideograms into their elemental radicals, and he understood that the omission or inversion of a single stroke could drastically change a word's meaning – or render it meaningless. His guess was that this particular dictionary contained some of those mistakes, and that Aidan was using these errors as code.

At the end of the dictionary he found his key – a seven-page index by radicals. Using this, he began translating the slogans on the placards around Aidan. *Cast away illusions, prepare for struggle!! Be a true revolutionary! Long live the great unity of the masses! Cherish every hill, every river, every tree and blade of grass in Korea!*

The slogans repeated, ten, twenty times in each picture. And the characters in Aidan's own hands matched – or very nearly matched – the crowd favorites. The variations looked accidental – the banners were all handmade, after all. But as Lawrence checked what, in effect, were misspellings against the 1944 dictionary, he discovered three elements in every banner: a word for an animal – dragon, bear, dog; a date – September 9, December 20, January 16; and a place name – Baoshan, Ningming, Fugong.

A current atlas of China showed all the place names as villages along the southern border, near Burma or Indochina. These must be drop points, and the animals the agents' code names. Hide in plain sight.

He turned finally to the most recent photograph, which he'd pulled the day before he left Delhi. It broke the pattern. No animal. No place. No date. The errors decoded into only two words: *disaster* and *door. Tsi men.*

'*Tsi men,*' Lawrence whispered to himself. It was after noon, and the reading room had filled up with bespectacled students working through dissertations and Asian elders come to read the Hong Kong and Tokyo news. 'Disaster's door.'

He closed his eyes, felt himself spinning, the dry heat from the radiator suffocating. He breathed out rapidly, swept his clippings into his valise, and dropped the Wade-Giles back into its place in the stacks.

He walked until he found a stationery shop and equipped himself with a box of plain, expensive vellum and matching envelopes. Then he walked into a coffee shop and forced down a sandwich and some tea while he deliberated what to write. *Will leave place and time in box.* The fact that Cross had told Eldon he'd be gone this weekend told Lawrence that Eldon was in town.

After lunch he found a store that sold office equipment. Computing machines, cash registers, typewriters. The boy clerk was helping two men in Borsalino hats who talked loudly about 'getting a deal' since they had thirty girls to keep busy, and that meant a lot of keyboards. Lawrence mumbled something about being a playwright and told the boy to take his time. Tapping on one typewriter after another, he moved his way down the line of display models to the end, where he pulled a piece of vellum from his supply and inserted it into a large Remington similar to Aidan's.

Need to talk. See you at the Jefferson Memorial. Saturday, 10 a.m.
B.C.

Brief. Vague. That jaunty 'see you.' Lawrence stared at what he'd typed, then removed the sheet and slid it into his coat pocket. He waved to the young overwhelmed clerk, saying he'd be back another time, and continued on his way to the D Street post office.

The sectioned box area was empty as before. Lawrence spun the dial on Eldon's compartment and placed his note inside. Then he retreated to a pub across the street and drank for two hours, waiting for Eldon to show himself.

It was Tuesday. If Cross had any reason to contact Eldon again before the weekend, or if Eldon failed to check his box, this ploy would collapse. But going back to the safe house was too risky. At five the post office closed.

The next morning Lawrence overslept. This time he'd closed the drapes before going to sleep, and the desk clerk had failed to ring his wake-up call. It was nine-thirty by the time he got to the post office, and Eldon's box was empty.

CHAPTER 14

1

The slap of the *tats* against our bedroom window was sharp and hot against the cool darkness. I could not see Simon's face, but I felt his eyes as I silenced the blinds. 'Hey!' He sat up, suddenly waking. 'What are you doing?

'Shh. Go back to sleep.' I crossed the room quickly and lay down on my bed, pulled the sheet tight to my chin.

But he wanted to know, 'Where were you?'

I turned my back to him and did not answer. I wore the smoke and dust of New Delhi night. I stank of sour sweat and men. I was grateful that we had put a stop to his visiting me in bed, but still he continued to whisper his demand, as if I had cheated him out of a treat. I slipped into a pretense of sleep-breathing. Finally he fell silent.

'I was hot,' I insisted when he questioned me the next day. 'I went out to look at the moon.'

'Why didn't you say so?'

'I was also tired.' I could not meet his eyes.

For the next week I sensed him lying in wait, measuring the nights by my presence. I grew impatient, then anxious for him to forget. If this went on, where would I get the money to pay Jaggu? Might Shrilal replace me?

My concern mounted until finally I moved my bed to the far end of the room, protesting to Mem a need for privacy. As usual, she wasn't really listening, but she said she understood, and I told myself I had outwitted Simon.

I was wrong.

2

The mashing of bedclothes alerted him, the rub of bare feet on the *dhurry* rug. Through cracked lids he watched Kamla shape her pillow beneath the blue cotton coverlet, then slip behind the *tats* and out onto the balcony.

He counted to five, pulled on his shorts, and peeked out after her. An old bony stalk of wisteria formed a ladder from the second-story bedroom down to the garden. She was already below. Through the darkness, he could just barely make her out beside the *mali*'s box where the two of them used to play hide-and-seek. He was too far away to guess her new game.

He heard the slip of the lock, the crunch of gravel as she cracked the gate and rolled her bicycle out, then he shinnied down the wisteria, and a minute later they were making their way up Ratendone Road, Kamla's long dress bunched to her knees, Simon a spy's length behind.

The sky this night was sepia, choked with dust and dung smoke. Wild dogs skulked in the shadows. The compound walls rose ghostly and white, while the dark shapes of tents and lean-to slums huddled like trolls in roadside ditches. Simon had never known New Delhi to feel so empty and eerie. He thought Kamla must hear him following behind her, but she never looked back.

Wasteland alternated with walls until they reached York Road, where the darkness stirred with a mean half-life. Shadows twitched in the center of the roundabout. Women's voices muttered.

At first he thought it was an encampment. He hung back, hiding behind a banyan tree as Kamla crossed the road. She gathered her skirt to step onto the high curb, then hauled her bike over the top. Women's voices greeted her in Hindi. Simon could no longer tell her apart.

Suddenly an automobile entered the roundabout. Its lights went on, and the hard yellow beams caught the women in poses that made him think of the calendars Brian Wilcox hid beneath his mattress. Brian, just last week, reaching, laughing, and grabbing him between the legs. 'You know what that's for?' Brian said with a squeeze, and answered his blank horror for him. 'You put it in her and pull it out, in and out,' as Frankie Mann slid his finger suggestively up and down between the pinup's legs. 'Oh,' Brian said as an afterthought, seeing Simon's bewilderment, 'but she must be naked down there and your little in-and-out worm as well.'

Now, like the women in the calendar, the darkened figures leaned and stretched, tipping heads and unfurling bared arms and legs. His breathing tightened as the headlights slowly circled the roundabout, catching each woman like an actress on a stage. Then suddenly, as the black Ambassador came around a second time, Simon saw Kamla enter the flood beams.

Her eyelids and brows were blackened so her skin seemed paler, eyes bluer than he'd ever seen them, and she wore, not her nightgown, but that long sleeveless gown of Mem's. It hung too long, too loose, but she had piled her black hair on top of her head and the blood-red silk seemed to glitter. She wore the throat open. Her back arched, bare arms lifted to shake on her bangles. She seemed to reach for the moon.

He could not see the driver as the Ambassador pulled over. A door opened and Kamla leaned inside. Across the width of street and sidewalk, from the gateway where he concealed himself, he could hear her voice, sounding sharp and foreign. Then she climbed in, the door slammed, and the car rolled away. The headlights snapped off.

Simon pushed his bicycle from behind the tree. He was breathing too loudly. There were no other cars or rickshaws now. The bicycle rattled as he hauled it over a root and back onto pavement.

'*Accha thora admi!*' Laughter from the roundabout as one of the girls there spotted him. Then the others joined in. '*Come back, little man!*'

Taunting, begging, waving their arms, now shrieking. '*I want one like that!*'

'*Could you give me a lift?*'

'*I like you!*'

Somehow he got up onto the seat and began pedaling furiously. The clamor followed like a wave at his back. He could hardly see, and his face felt as if it would explode before the laughter faded behind him. He thought for sure he had lost Kamla, but he wiped his eyes with his sleeve and kept going, if only to get away, and there, just a block ahead, was the car's round black hump turning off the main road.

Two stone pillars topped by carved lions marked the drive. Simon recognized the lions as the emblem of the Jai Mahal hotel. Lawrence used to bring them to the Jai Mahal to swim, though never through this back gate.

Outside, the street was strangely deserted. No beggars slept or camped so close to the hotel, yet there were no guards standing sentry, either. Nor was there a single light beyond the pillars. Simon pulled his bike back behind a hedge on the opposite corner. As he struggled to catch his breath, he watched two Ambassadors glide from the gate, another enter, identical. Above the walls the silhouetted trees formed a cage against the brown sky.

He wanted to go home. Instead he left the bike hidden behind the hedge and ran across the empty pavement, ducked inside the compound gate. The hotel itself, with its side verandas and hundreds of windows, twinkled in the distance, but here in the yard the cage of trees closed into a roof of darkness. The smell of frangipani burned his nostrils. His throat was coated with grit. He could make out the dozen or so cars parked in front of him only by the shimmer of chrome, the occasional sulfurous burst of a match. He couldn't tell one from the others, but he detected a waiter gliding among them, the white of his jacket floating as if worn by an invisible man. Suddenly over the banging of his own heart Simon heard a girl's stifled squeal. Then an engine turned over, roaring. A car rolled past and out the gate.

His muscles cramped. His cheeks were slick with tears, his shirt and shorts soaked through. He stood up and ground the sweat from his palms into his thighs. Another anonymous vehicle slid past, and he became conscious of the rising wind rattling the trees overhead. As he turned toward home the blowing sand felt like nails driving into his skin.

By morning Kamla lay once more in her bed, her hair like a shadow across her face. He stood over her staring into that shadow, trembling and unwilling to touch her. He waited for her to wake, half expecting and more than half wanting her to blurt out a confession or break down in tears. He waited a long time. She liked to sleep late these days.

When at last she opened her eyes, she laughed at the intensity with which he stood watching. Nothing in her expression showed shame or regret. She said nothing to explain herself, merely bathed and ate her usual breakfast of Weetabix and juice, then curled up with a book on her bed. Mem had gone out, the servants kept their distance. When she was not at school or sleeping, Kamla read.

Simon took his slingshot into the desert behind the house. He spent the morning shooting stones at disintegrating termite mounds and mongoose holes. Kamla had become a stranger. It seemed impossible that they had ever shared the same bed, the same games, the same stories and songs in the dark.

He remembered now one story she told him long ago about Kali dancing on her husband, Shiva's, dead body, swinging a severed head in one hand, her bloodied sword in the other. As the goddess of death, she warned him, Kali must destroy even the ones she loves, because nothing on earth is eternal.

Simon did not tell Mem what he had seen. He was afraid she would turn Kamla out, afraid, too, that she would punish him for sneaking after her. He could not bring himself to tell even Nagu or Dilip or Lazarus. Instead he finally decided to write to Lawrence. He picked a plain piece of notebook paper and set to work: 'Dear Lawrence, Something bad has happened.' But it was impossible to write exactly what had happened. So instead he begged simply, 'Please come back.'

Remembering that Kamla said Lazarus was able to contact Lawrence, he sealed the note in an envelope and gave it to Lazarus to send. As he waited for a reply, he continued to follow Kamla. One night, two, sometimes three in a single week she would steal out. He went as far as the roundabout, careful now to hide so that the other girls would not detect him, and watched until the first car or rickshaw took her away. He traced the heart shape of a pipal leaf with his fingertip in the darkness. He memorized the glitter of the girls' saris, their movements in the moonlight, the curves of their bodies when the headlamps caught them. He listened to the drone of the cicadas and smelled the heavy scent of expectancy that weighed on the city at night. He imagined he could hear the breathing of the millions who slept in the streets. Strangely, he never felt frightened. He remembered the waiter at the hotel, unseen but for his ghostly jacket and the glitter of his tray, and he felt he was like that, too – invisible. Incidental. He saw Kamla, however, as savagely at home in the street, as purposeful here as she'd seemed in the mountains going to search for her father.

Then one night he recognized a battered white car from a previous week. He heard an old man's wheezing, tremulous voice call out a made-up name. He heard Kamla laugh in reply, a shy, tinkling laugh that sounded fake yet was unmistakably Kamla. He watched her climb into that car for the second time. The door slammed. The car drove off. Somehow, with this repetition, this made-up laugh and name, he was sapped, the betrayal complete and finally outside him. He rode slowly home, feeling nothing.

3

By Saturday the weather had turned. The sun rose warm in a sky so clear it looked polished. Lawrence's hotel was a tourist dump near the Smithsonian, and by the time he'd walked the mile to the Tidal Basin he was down to shirtsleeves. He reached the Jefferson Memorial at nine and busied himself feeding his breakfast toast to the ducks that swam out front. Forty-five minutes later he looked across the water and saw a short, thin man in a khaki jacket limp across the bridge on the other side of the pool. The man's head was down, his arms swung straight. Each step seemed to require concentration.

Lawrence dusted off his hands and stood, turning casually as if to leave along the west side of the basin. Instead he doubled back inside the colonnade. He pulled a navy driver's cap over his head, threw his jacket over his shoulders, and joined a group of British couples admiring Mr Jefferson's earnest bronze countenance and the great man's sayings on the surrounding walls. 'If only he'd been on our side,' one of the women said with a sigh. 'The whole bloody business might have swung the other way.'

Lawrence hadn't counted on the pleasant weather, which in turn had brought out the tourists. He'd thought he might have this place to himself and take Eldon by surprise. But he could see Eldon now at the base of the steps in front of the memorial, one hand over his eyes, leaning his weight on the banister as he searched for Cross. Though his gaze did not pause, he stared directly at Lawrence. Could he make the match? Surely Eldon knew of him, but he wasn't expecting him here, and there was a chance he'd never seen a picture or perhaps even a description to tip him off.

After twenty minutes, when Eldon looked at his watch for the last time, the Brits were still jabbering and a French family had just arrived. He cast one more searching look around the premises and set off, continuing around the basin. Lawrence gave him a two-minute start.

They strolled at a leisurely pace, but soon Eldon began to rub his leg. He found a bench beside a stand of cherry trees that were about to burst into bloom and pulled a rolled newspaper from his jacket pocket. The trees shielded the bench from the park and road behind it. A curve in the shoreline of the pool likewise obstructed the view back to the memorial, and the knoll that encircled the basin formed a natural screen so that the only path visible was the empty one around the pool.

Lawrence picked up his stride as if to pass right by Eldon's bench, but when he came abreast he glanced down and swung suddenly around, laying one hand in an uncompromising grip on the other man's arm.

He could feel Eldon stiffen, but he didn't startle. His gaze left the newspaper slowly, traveling the length of Lawrence before reaching his eyes. Only then did a spasm of uncertainty cross his face. The mismatch had the power to throw even seasoned professionals off balance.

'I don't know you,' Eldon said. 'And I'd appreciate your removing your hand.'

'No worries.' Lawrence sat down, tightening his grip before he released it. 'You're Aidan Shaw's mate, Ben Eldon.'

He nodded, eyes impassive. 'Why are you following me?'

'Lawrence Malcolm.' Lawrence stuck out his hand.

Eldon lowered the paper and gave him a tepid shake.

'I'm here on Joanna's behalf, you might say. Ever since Jo told me you made a special trip to Delhi to give her the good news about her husband's defection I've been asking myself, now, why would he do that?'

Eldon considered him before speaking. 'Maybe I thought if she heard it from anybody else she wouldn't believe it.'

'You had a vested interest in her believing it, then?'

'I thought she should know the truth.' The tone was righteous, the inflection Southern.

'Truth! Well, that's bloody noble of you. Damn near broke her heart, you realize.'

'If anyone broke Joanna's heart, it was Aidan. I had nothing to do—'

'Didn't you?' Lawrence shifted his body. He was easily twice Eldon's size. 'I think you had everything to do with it.'

Eldon calmly pulled a pack of Beeman's gum from his shirt pocket and offered Lawrence a piece. He shook his head and Ben took one for himself. 'I always thought you Aussies were nuts.'

'Didn't stop you using us, did it, mate?'

'Using you!' Eldon paused, chewing, then continued in a lower voice. 'We threw you a bone. Your boss was so eager to play he was practically pissing in his pants. Secret intelligence, joint operations. All that jazz.'

'Battersby.'

'That's right. We didn't need you. Battersby came to us, and with Hoover breathing down our necks we decided it wasn't the worst idea to distance ourselves from a known leftist like Aidan Shaw. But make no mistake, you were nothing more than a convenience.'

'You Yanks are arrogant bastards, you know that?'

'I've been called worse.'

'What did Aidan know when he left Delhi?'

'Whatever you told him. No one else talked to him.'

Lawrence leaned closer and pressed his thumb into the soft flesh behind Eldon's collarbone. He had a scrawny build, and there was little muscle to resist the pressure.

'Having your leg blown off raises your threshold of pain,' Eldon said evenly.

'I'd like to blow your fucking head off,' said Lawrence. 'I don't mind that you played us as dimwits. I don't even mind that you conned Aidan—'

'No one conned Aidan. He volunteered. Saw his transfer to India as the perfect stepping-stone back into China. Just a hop, skip, and a jump, he said. I told him to keep his eyes and ears open, and the opportunity was sure to present itself. I was right, as it turned out.'

Suddenly Lawrence could see Aidan. Hear him. That haughty Brit accent that sounded put on. *Kashmir? Why the hell not? Bound to beat the bureau desk in Delhi.*

He removed his hand from Eldon's shoulder. His fingers were numb. Eldon had to be in pain, but he didn't budge.

'What's *destruction's door?*' Lawrence asked.

'I have no idea what you're talking about.'

'I broke the code,' Lawrence said. *'Tsi men.'*

Eldon let out an explosive laugh. *'Simon,* you mean? Sure you know who Simon is.'

Lawrence felt his heart snap.

'Don't worry. It has nothing to do with the boy. It's just a code name. He's sentimental, I guess.'

Sentimental.

Eldon lifted his face to the sun and half-closed his eyes. He was silent for a minute or two, then said, 'You don't even know your girl's been visiting our Communist friends, do you?'

'Joanna!'

'That's right. She's a trouper, Jo is. Never gives up. Blind faith, that's what I call it. I don't know what she thinks she'll get out of it, but doggone if she hasn't persuaded them to bring him out and see her one last time.' He cast Lawrence a sidelong glance.

Innocents still abroad. All set for end of March.

It was now February 27. Lawrence breathed a little. 'You don't know what she thinks she'll get out of it?'

'Oh, I can guess.'

Lawrence's arm shot out, slammed across Eldon's throat so hard and fast he could hear the spit clog his windpipe. 'Don't guess,' Lawrence warned him. 'Tell me what you *know.'*

Eldon's face turned white, his eyes glassy. His Adam's apple looked as if it had turned sideways. He coughed his gum onto the grass and a wad of blood after it. His hands never moved from his pants pockets, and he refused to look at Lawrence again. If he was

394

trained for combat you'd never know it, but he was a master at passive aggression.

'What I know,' Eldon said finally, 'is that Joanna and Aidan are alike. They both back themselves into corners, then find their own ways out. Difference is, Aidan thrives under pressure. I knew that when I saw the pictures he shot after he saved my life. If my camera had been a gun he'd have blown that whole village to smithereens. He set himself up, shooting his mouth off, writing those left-wing articles, only asking the logical questions later. Which side was he really on? The answer just so happened to dovetail perfectly with our needs.'

Eldon's eyes followed a family strolling along the opposite side of the basin. A couple with a young boy bouncing a basketball behind them.

'What are you getting out of it?' Lawrence asked.

'Depends.'

'On what?'

'Aidan, mostly. It's a guts play.'

'With the Chinese calling the shots?'

'Yup.'

'And he goes back in afterward.'

'That's the plan.'

'What about Jo?'

'What about her? She went to the Reds on her own. We had nothing to do with it.'

'You showed her the picture of Aidan alive.'

'We needed her to rattle the cage. It was too quiet. The Chinese were starting to doubt Aidan's credentials.'

'So this proves his stripes.' Lawrence felt the hot chill of rage pass through him again, but Eldon was right. It was Aidan who had betrayed Joanna. 'She doesn't *know*?'

'Better off if she doesn't.' Ben stretched his legs in front of him and clasped his hands behind his head. 'If I were you, I'd think very carefully before playing the hero and warning her. You won't be doing her or yourself any favor.' He paused. 'Mate.'

A school outing appeared down the path. Twenty little children skipping, holding hands, their teachers zigzagging behind them like sheepdogs. *What matters most*, Lawrence thought.

The first Friday in March arrived blazing hot and so dry my eyes felt parched. It was teachers' holiday, so we had no school, and Simon sulked all morning because Lazarus had taken the day off 'to see a sick pal' and Simon's friends had excluded him from a duck shooting expedition to Sultanpur with Brian Wilcox's father. Simon was sulky in general lately, especially when deprived of the pleasure of making trouble with his friends, and today even Dilip and Bhanu were away with Nagu visiting relatives. So poor Simon was stuck. Mem had stayed home with us but shut herself in her bedroom doing her work, and having spent most of the night with my old gent from Moradabad, I passed much of the day with my head beneath my pillow. Simon took out his frustration by playing the phonograph at top volume – Gene Krupa and his orchestra with a scratch smack in the middle of the drum solo.

I pressed the pillow tighter around my ears and stared into the pages of a book I lacked the concentration to read. Shrilal was lately paying me more and keeping me longer into the night. He had begun to talk of my coming to live with him. 'You will be my Manu and I your Gandhiji,' he proposed. I reminded him that Manu was the great Gandhi's grandniece, not some street girl he had picked up. 'Nevertheless,' said Shrilal, 'they shared a bed. They bathed each other. They were chaste together.' Much as this last element of his proposal appealed to me, I told him I must think long and hard before accepting his offer. For as attentive as he was, Shrilal's withered legs and arms, the pale flaccidity of his belly, and his old man's smell sickened me. Even the bang and screech of Gene Krupa was preferable to the prospect of this old man's constant companionship. Toward the middle of the afternoon I pried myself out of bed and had just joined Simon in the living room when Mem appeared.

'Come along,' she said, straining her voice over the phonograph. 'It's too hot, and the two of you are too aimless to spend another minute in this house. I have a meeting, but you can swim, and then afterward . . . I don't know, maybe we'll go for ice cream?' She seemed to be trying her best but, as usual, was doing several things at once – gathering up her purse and papers, looking for her hat, pulling the needle from Simon's record, and frowning. These days, always frowning.

Simon grunted from his perch on the couch. It wouldn't be fun without his friends or Lawrence. Mem pointed out that I was going, though I had not yet said I would. Simon didn't answer that, nor did he so much as glance my way, but after another minute or two he rose and went off in search of his rucksack.

That rucksack went with him everywhere these days. I did not know what he kept in it, but it made a loud clanking noise as we climbed into the car. 'What have you got?' I tried to tease him into good humor. 'Babur's saber and shield?'

He merely shrugged and stared out the window, wincing a little as the dusty heat blew into his eyes. A few moments later he turned to Mem. '*Where* are we going swimming?'

I had simply assumed we would go, as usual, to the Cecil, but when Mem answered, 'The Jai Mahal,' an unexpected thrill shot through me. The Jai Mahal's swimming pool lay just a few yards from the car park where I conducted my midnight trade. *Princess Kamla of Kashgaria,* I could hear Lawrence breathe in my ear. I would swim and dive like a *firenghi* guest. I would feel the sun wash my back. I would splash as if I hadn't a care, and no one, not even the invisible waiter who brought whiskey and cigarettes in the darkness, would recognize my face.

We pulled in between the two front lions and up a long curving drive to the Jai Mahal's main entrance. Mem turned the car over to one of the uniformed men who stood like sentries, then we marched in through the revolving door and down the marble corridor as if this were our home. I pulled myself up and looked directly into the eyes of every staff member I passed. The carefully groomed and made-up women behind the reception desk. The old man with a goiter on his neck who sold newspapers from a stand. The young manager with his side-combed hair and double-breasted English suit. The Sikh with a yellow turban and waxed mustache who peered at me through the window of his lobby jewelry shop. These were my colleagues, I thought, for did we not all work on the premises of the Jai Mahal? Did we not all perform services – entertain and make comfortable the paying guests? Surely these men and women knew about, and some doubtless profited from, the nightly commerce conducted behind the hotel. Yet here and now I was above them. I could tell as I studied their faces, not one suspected me.

Simon's bag thumped against his hip. He stuck out his tongue at a little girl, maybe two years old, who promptly lifted her dress and stuck out her belly back at him. Her mother, an Englishwoman to judge by her speech, scolded the girl but sent a killing look back at Simon and Mem.

Mem didn't notice. She was too busy looking about the lobby. As we passed through the wide glass doors into the garden the bar stood to our left, with umbrellas and tables and chairs on a terrace outside. The pool lay some distance across the lawn to our right. Mem's breath shook a little as she sighed. 'I'd better wait here. I'm supposed to be by the bar. You two go ahead to the pool. Behave yourselves, and don't go wandering off, Simon.' I looked to see if she meant this warning for me, a reminder of that night at the *maidan*, but no, she had waved her hand and dismissed us already. Her mind was on this meeting, her business.

I followed Simon across the lawn, a radiant green swell of grass bordered by marigolds. A wedding was to take place in the garden that night, and all tables and chairs had been removed to the lawn so the deck around the pool could be used for dancing. A band-stand rose behind the diving board, and large wooden trellises covered with lights and tinsel and white and red crepe paper flowers screened the deck from the hotel, but at the moment no one else was about, and this private swimming pool/dance hall seemed at once festive and eerie. As it should be, I thought. Tonight some virginal girl would be tied in marriage to her groom within shouting distance of the very activity that wives were supposed to dread most. And even as one part of me envied this girl, whom I could clearly envision in her gold-threaded sari, with ears and nose studded with diamonds and hands laced with henna designs, another part of me pitied her for the servitude she would be required to perform from this night forward. At least we night birds were compensated, and we had hope of freedom one day. Her only hope was that her husband would be a good man, that he would stand by her and not visit us or the flash house, not beat or rape her himself. Had she even met this man? Did she know the first thing about him? Did he care for her at all? These thoughts tumbled and pushed their way through my mind as I stood at the edge of the pool, removing the thin blue shift I had worn over my bathing suit.

'Race you,' Simon said, coming up behind me. He had stripped to his trunks and put on swim goggles. With the goggles he was bound to beat me.

'It's not fair,' I said.

'Who cares?' And with that he reached forward with both arms and pushed me into the water.

I fell sideways, snorting and thrashing. Simon dove in over my head and was off. In that split second we became brother and sister, children again. There was no one here but the two of us, and we could still pretend.

So we swam, from one end to the other and back again. Simon won. He had the advantage. But I was not far behind, I told myself, and I had what Lawrence used to call the handicap. That meant that I did not have the equipment. I did not have the training or skills, the native intelligence, the birthright. I did not have the advantage, and so I must claim my disadvantage and turn it into strength.

I remembered suddenly the day when Lawrence first explained this notion of handicap. He had taken us to a tournament at the golf course – this was just one year ago, not long after Mrs Solomon interviewed me for her article – and he was trying to explain how handicaps 'equal the playing field.' I could not understand this idea. Was not the playing field – in this case, the golf course – the same for all players? It was the players themselves who were unequal, no? And was it not the purpose of games to prove one player stronger and therefore unequal to the others? This idea of handicaps seemed so much nonsense to me. Certainly, it was not the way of the world. Who in this world ever gave the advantage to the poor, or the ignorant, or the weak? One was always having to prove oneself. Even beggars climbed over each other to claim the scraps of the rich. This equal playing field, this notion of fair play, I decided was a *firenghi* invention. It had only to do with games, and nothing to do with truth.

Now suddenly I did not even want the handicap. 'You win,' I told Simon. 'You have what you want.'

He had pushed his goggles up on his forehead like a second set of eyes. The strap turned his ears out so they looked even more like handles than usual. His face was red and wet from the race, as if he had been crying, and there was a kind of strain in his mouth as he looked at me, as the harshness of my voice penetrated. He said nothing, but cupped his hand and sliced it over the surface of the pool so that a skin of water rose to hit me with a slap.

It stung, but before I could retaliate, he swam away to the other end, climbed out and crouched with his back to me, busying himself with his rucksack. I thought of the clown, the underwater Shiva he had once played, and a piece of me wept for Simon. I wondered if the *firenghi* could see how they handicapped themselves?

I flipped onto my back and floated, staring into the sky. Threads of cloud lay across the heavens like strands on a balding man's skull. I had run my fingers over such strands, had inhaled the tonics that old men used in vain to preserve their youth, and felt the knots of bone and flesh that lay beneath the pretense. I had fixed my eyes on these threads in the darkness, making a game of their disarrangement as their proud possessors rode me on their laps.

The water held me. It lapped over my thighs and chest and face. It filled my ears and pores. It entered me like a gentle lover, like Shrilal might have, I thought, had he been a younger man – if youth can ever be gentle. The water entered me as the blood had left me when my first period arrived last month. Mem, very businesslike, had assured me that this simply meant I was a woman now. She gave me a supply of American-made pads and a belt and showed me how to wear the contraption, how to roll the pads in paper and discreetly throw them away. She touched my shoulder and asked if I was frightened. I shook my head. Any pain? I said no. She bit her lip and removed her eyes from me, then came back and said, 'Kamla, this is a good sign. It means that you are well, your body is healed. It means that someday you might have children.' She did not tell me what my night sister Scarlett told me, which is that once I started bleeding I must tell the men I had a disease so that they would wear a condom and I would not get pregnant. Mem gave me pads, Scarlett a supply of condoms. Scarlett said to think of this as the necessary equipment for my trade as a woman. My handicap, I thought now. My weakness turned in futility to advantage. The water was soothing as the blood.

Above me the clouds thickened with color until the sky seemed to drip magenta and gold. The sun had fallen below the fringe of palm trees that bordered the hotel property, and the pool now lay in a trapezoid of purple shadow. It was the mosquito hour. I dropped lower under my blanket of water, closing my eyes so that only my nose was exposed. It was a trick Lawrence had taught Simon and me. 'Drives the bugs batty,' he told us. 'They can't smell your skin or feel your heat. They can't get to you.'

This was what I was thinking when Simon landed on top of me.

Later I realized that he had been crouching at the end of the diving board, waiting for me to float beneath him. At that moment, however, I did not know where he came from, only that I felt his weight knock the air out of me, his legs wrap around my hips. They pulled inward and pushed me down. Water went up my nose. My ears filled with thrashing, and the chlorine stung my eyes so that I could make out only the darkness of his body against the brilliant sky. He was too heavy. I panicked and lifted my arm, trying to pull out from under him, but he grabbed me and I felt a snap of metal around my wrist. I got my head above water. He was riding me like a horse, leaning forward, now yanking my arm, for he wore the mate of my handcuff.

I realized he was speaking into my ear. 'I am the great Houdini.'

'Let me go!' I cried, flailing and trying to kick free. We were still in the middle of the deep end. Simon began to laugh. As I slipped under again, I felt his palm press against my right breast. He dragged our cuffed arms behind my back, cinching me against him. We sank.

Houdini, I remembered him telling me, could stay underwater for five minutes. Holding his breath had been one of Simon's favorite tricks long before he even heard of Houdini.

Our bodies righted themselves in the water, but his legs remained locked around me, and now he began to rub himself like a dog against my thigh. At last I understood the game he was playing. My

401

lungs burned. I was being pushed down, but I knew that in this particular contest Simon's powers of endurance were no match for mine. I closed my eyes and sent my thoughts back to the Shahidulla Gorge, to those tiny reaching hands, that blood-tinged foam. I remembered the sensation of escaping skin and life easing out of my grip. My sister Mira once told me that some Sikh women in the flash house slice their wrists with their *kara,* their metal bracelets, then hold their hands in a basin of water watching their blood drain away. She said she imagined this would be a peaceful way to die, and when she decided she'd had enough, this might be the path she would choose. And perhaps it had been. If I ceased to struggle, I told myself as the water around our handcuffed wrists began to cloud with red, I could escape as well.

But I felt Simon weakening. Beyond rubbing and kneading he didn't know what to do with my body, and, Houdini or no, he was losing air. I gave a great kick, shoved him with my free arm, and pulled with all my strength to drag us to the surface.

I took a gulp of air and was about to cry for help when I felt Simon's hand between my legs, a desperate, angry grabbing. I brought my knee up hard into his groin, a defense I had inadvertently discovered (and which cost me my hour's pay) several nights earlier in the cramped confines of a car not twenty feet from where we now fought. Simon's body clenched. I reached out and caught hold of the pool deck, dragging his folded weight. Another few inches and my foot found the shallow bottom.

Simon would not meet my eyes. When he had recovered his breath, he began wrestling with the cuffs and key he had hidden in his trunks. He swore words I did not think he knew. His impatience suggested this was all my fault. I did not make a sound. Finally he pulled in his thumb and wrenched his hand out, leaving me with his manacle dangling from my wrist.

'You'll be sorry,' he said, still not looking at me, and swam hard across the deep end. When he reached the ladder he swung himself up, grabbed his sack, and disappeared among the wedding decorations.

Looking up I realized the sky had changed. The streaks of pink and amber cloud had turned as dark as bruises and the air around them hardened to a flat, pale gray.

The terrace was crowded. After sending the children off to the pool Joanna had claimed a table on the outskirts, under a massive kapok tree. When the waiter came she reluctantly ordered a lemonade. She longed for a gin and tonic, but alcohol would be a mistake. She'd received the chit yesterday at work. It named this place, this time. Nothing more. She had no idea what to expect.

A few feet away a Sikh wearing a chartreuse turban and a beard rolled thick as a sausage sat poring over architectural plans with two Italian men. Four Scandinavians surrounded another table littered with tourist maps. These men occasionally glanced at Joanna and smiled. She faced her chair away from them. Through a flower–covered trellis she could just make out the forms of the children diving into the pool. It looked as if they were alone over there, but this was no cause for concern. Lawrence had taught them both to swim like otters.

The waiter delivered her lemon water. She pulled an *International Herald Tribune* from her bag and stared at the headlines. REDS IN STATE? one banner trumpeted. SENATORS TO HEAR FROM SPY'S EX-WIFE announced another. She turned the pages in desperation until she reached a column headed PREPARING YOUR GARDEN FOR SPRING PLANTING, with a companion photograph of a field of blooming tulips. She pretended utter absorption.

'Excuse me, *memsahib?*'

She looked up into the beaming face of her waiter. He held a silver tray on which lay a small square envelope. 'Mrs Joanna Shaw?'

She nodded.

'Please.' He wiggled his head. 'A messenger is just now bringing this chit for you.'

She took the envelope and fumbled in her purse for a tip, then watched the waiter return to the bar. A glance around the terrace told her the other men, too, had lost interest in her. She shifted her chair back toward the empty lawn.

Dear Mrs Shaw,
I apologize that I am unable to convey this message in

*person, however, the meeting you have requested is now
arranged for tomorrow at 3:00 p.m.*

All other details remain as we have discussed.

I trust you to keep this confidential.

Your friend, Mr C.

Tomorrow! After all the waiting, the suddenness stunned her.
Tomorrow.

In a daze, she refolded the note and tucked it away in her purse.
Then she caught the waiter's eye. This time she ordered whiskey,
and when it came she drank it fast.

Somehow more time had passed than she realized. The sky was
streaked with eggplant black. Small white lights had gone on in the
trees, and Kamla and Simon were out of the pool, already changed
and moving in opposite directions as a group of musicians cut
between them hauling trumpets and drums. There was to be a
wedding tonight, the waiter said as she paid her check.

A great celebration.

CHAPTER 15

1

Lawrence staggered into his Delhi flat at two in the morning. It had taken the better part of a week to fly back from Washington, and he still hadn't decided how to warn Joanna – how to minimize the damage. But late March was yet a ways off, and for the moment all he could think about was sleep. As he flipped on the light, however, Lazarus sat up blinking in the only bed available.

His own fault: He hadn't bothered to send a warning that he was coming back.

Lazarus leapt to attention. But the bedclothes did not stop moving. At first Lawrence thought his exhaustion was playing tricks on him. Lazarus grinned. Lawrence stepped past him and tore off the sheet.

A young boy who could not have been older than twelve reared up biting the air in laughter. His skin and hair white as coconut flesh, he was dressed in a *dhoti* and one of Lawrence's castoff undershirts. '*Salaam*, mistah!' the albino cackled, and sprang like a frog to the floor.

Lazarus showered abuse on the boy as if he'd had no idea he was there, and within seconds had him out and down the stairs. He returned buttoning his shirt and tightening the drawstring of his pants, his face an almost convincing imitation of outrage. The undershirt was crumpled in his right hand. His left thumped his breast. 'Bloody little bugger. He claimed the Red Cross led him to me, some rot about our being cousins—'

'Don't waste your breath.' Lawrence sank into the old draggled armchair. The room looked as cluttered and anonymous as ever but reeked of sex and sandalwood cologne. He paused, then slowly lifted his eyes. 'If you've touched Simon or Kamla like that I swear I'll rip your heart out.'

'Bloody hell!' Lazarus staggered backward as if from a physical blow. 'I love those kids like my own brother and sister.'

'That's what I'm afraid of.' But he wasn't, really. Lazarus knew how to play both ends against the middle. In the lingo of Asia, Simon and Kamla represented his 'rice bowl,' and he was hardly likely to risk shitting where he ate – whatever his other perversions.

With eager officiousness Lazarus whipped off the bedding and smoothed on a clean set of linens. 'I've taken bloody good care of the lot of them, if I do say so myself.'

'Have you?' Lawrence noticed a pile of letters strewn across the writing desk. He'd instructed Lazarus to bundle his mail and forward it, care of External Affairs, but he'd received only one dispatch – while in Sydney, and none of it worth the postage. 'Hand me those, would you?'

Lazarus cleared his throat and rolled his shoulders backward. 'I was just about to send them off to you. Bloody good thing I didn't, or they'd've been lost weeks in transit.'

He scooped up the envelopes and delivered them with a defensive sigh. The same old assortment of notices and chits, plus a flurry of invitations to dance performances and drum recitals sponsored by the Australian High Commission wives' auxiliary. It looked like Lawrence's unofficial tenure in Delhi had somehow put him on the official hit list. He tossed all but three of the envelopes aside. These were marked in a child's hand, which he recognized at once as Simon's, though it slanted erratically, and the pencil had dug grooves into the paper. The envelopes bore no stamps, no addresses, only Lawrence's name.

Lazarus had collected his belongings, scattered around the room. Now he stood with his arms full. 'Guess I'll be shoving off, then.'

'When did Simon give you these?'

'Different times. I don't remember.'

Lawrence tore the bottom envelope first and scanned the ragged lines:

Something bad has happened. I don't know where you are, but Lazarus says he can get this letter to you. This thing, it's bad. I can't tell you what. I can't tell anybody, but maybe if you come back I'll tell you then. Maybe you can fix it. So will you come back now?

  Simon.

'What did he say?' Lawrence demanded.

'Nothing.'

'Was he upset?'

Lazarus shrugged one shoulder. 'If he had been, I'd have hurried it off to you, wouldn't I?'

'Would you?' Lawrence tore open the other two letters. 'Even if it meant upsetting your rice bowl?'

'I said I would!'

The other notes were shorter. *I guess you're never coming back,* read the second. *You're just like my father,* read the third.

'How long have you been sitting on these?' he asked again.

Lazarus shifted his load from one arm to the other. 'Few weeks.'

'How many weeks?'

'I dunno. Maybe four. Five.'

'You promised the boy, didn't you? You promised to get these to me.'

'He's a bloody kid. What's it matter?'

'Get out.'

'Now, Mr Malcolm—'

'I said clear out. Before I break your skull.'

But Lazarus wouldn't leave it. He jutted his chin and planted his hands on his hips. 'You owe me. I did everything you told me and more.'

Lawrence stood up. He was shaking. He had never misjudged anyone as badly as he had this stinking rodent.

Lazarus wisely backed into the vestibule. The darkness swallowed him, but a minute later, his voice rang up the stairwell, 'Those are two bloody juvenile delinquents, you ask me.'

Lawrence slammed the door.

Something bad has happened. You're just like my father.

Conceivably this was all a ruse to get him back. But the hand-writing unnerved Lawrence. Though Simon's penmanship would never win any prizes, it had always been conscientious, more loping than galloping, more circular than angled, and at least attempting to line up straight. The writing in these notes all but slid off the page.

He debated whether to approach Joanna first. Whatever had happened, Simon seemed to have decided that Lawrence was the one person he could trust. Thanks to Lazarus, that trust by now was probably gone, but if not . . . well, he intended to honor it as best he could. His own business with Joanna could wait until he got this squared away.

He shut off the light and lay down on the bed. His head was pounding, his throat raw. He tried to remember what day it was, but the effort only made his head throb more. He stopped trying.

It was two in the afternoon when he woke up. Saturday. The hot air roiled with yellow dust, and outside the whole city seemed to be struggling to rouse itself after the midday rest. Lawrence had to wake a trishaw driver in order to buy a ride to Ratendone Road.

He got down in the shade of a large plane tree opposite the house. Over the compound wall he could see the *tats* lowered like eyelids. Nothing moved.

He used his key to open the gate and made his way up the driveway. Joanna's car was gone. He continued to the garage-turned-servants' quarters where he heard a radio chattering. Nagu's sons, Dilip and Bhanu, were doing their schoolwork in the low square room they shared with their father. They looked mildly surprised to find Lawrence in their doorway, but not particularly interested.

'Do you know where Simon is?' he asked them.

Bhanu, the younger boy, scowled as his brother said he'd seen Simon heading out into the alley behind the compound. But, he quickly added, they had no idea what he was doing there.

'Is he alone?' Lawrence asked.

Dilip shrugged, smoothing the pages of his textbook.

'He in some kind of trouble?'

The boys exchanged glances. 'I think you had best ask him that question,' Dilip answered. 'He has other friends now. And we do not have time for his games.'

Lawrence left them busily manipulating their sums and let himself out the rear gate. This put him at the midpoint of the narrow dirt alley, which curved in a long semicircle. To his right Lawrence could see to the street, where a cluster of men squatted, smoking and chatting and chewing their *paan* in the shade of the tall compound walls. They were the neighborhood *chowkidar*, watchmen whose job it was to keep ruffians away. Thanks to them, only residents of the houses that backed onto the alley had access to it.

Around the bend to Lawrence's left, out of the watchmen's sight and earshot, stood a vacant building that once had housed a dairy. Simon was down on his haunches in front of it. He would have seen Lawrence had he looked up, but he was busy searching for stones, his slingshot looped over his wrist. Several windows of the dairy had been shot out already, as well as most of the streetlights that lined the alley. Simon worked with a jerking motion of his hands, mumbling to himself. When he stood to fire, his jaw tensed. He was only a few feet from his target, one of the remaining intact overhead lights, and his arm cranked back farther than necessary. As the stone hit its mark, glass showered like sparks. The rickety pole quivered. Simon registered no satisfaction, was fishing in his shorts pocket for another rock when Lawrence called to him.

'You're making a pretty mess.' He sauntered closer.

Simon's mouth opened and shut. He was skinnier, more wiry than he had been at Christmastime. Dust caked his hair, arms, and sandaled feet. The child had gone out of his eyes. 'I don't care,' he said at last.

'How many more to go?' Lawrence asked, squinting at the line of street lamps.

Simon didn't answer.

'Mind if I try?'

The boy shrugged. Lawrence had given him this slingshot, made from a whittled neem branch and a strip of bicycle inner tube. When they first came back to Delhi, he'd taken him out into the wilds to practice shooting at the anthills and termite mounds that rose like castles out of the sand.

Lawrence held out his hand and Simon put the slingshot into it. Lawrence waggled his fingers. Simon handed him a stone from his pocket.

A fringe of glass still clung to the lamp Simon had just shattered. Lawrence took aim at the fixture's lip. Like bowling a split, it was more difficult to shake the dregs free than to shoot out the center. He angled himself so the rock ricocheted within the metal housing. The remaining glass fell down.

'I didn't get your letters, Simon. Lazarus – ' He stopped himself. The boy hardly needed one more betrayal heaped onto his growing pile. 'He told me when I got back last night that he'd sent them, but he must have put the wrong address. It doesn't matter. I'm here now, you can tell me yourself what they said.'

He stepped closer, opening his arm for a hug. But Simon didn't move. He stared at the slingshot in Lawrence's hand.

'It doesn't matter.' The boy repeated his words back to him.

'I didn't mean it like tha—'

'You're too late,' Simon said bluntly.

'Now, hold on, son.'

'I'm not your son.' He lifted his eyes, gazed unwaveringly into Lawrence's own split pair.

'No,' Lawrence admitted when he could find his voice. 'I'm sorry.'

Simon's thin chest rose and fell quickly with his breathing. Then he said, 'She's sneaking out.'

Lawrence hesitated. 'Mem?' he asked gently.

But Simon's head snapped up. His eyes burned. 'You and Mem think she's such a good girl, reading all the time, skipping ahead in school. You don't know anything.'

'Simon, what are you talking about?'

'She goes out.' He opened his palm and made a circular motion in front of his face. 'She stole Mem's lipstick and things, her red dress. Every Saturday, sometimes even on school nights. She goes with men. *Old* men. Older than my father. It's disgusting!'

Lawrence grasped him by the shoulders and faced him squarely. Simon was shivering so violently his teeth sounded like a wood-pecker. 'I followed her.'

Lawrence stayed silent then, listening. When the boy had talked himself out Lawrence held him for a long time, resting his chin against the sandy hair, staring into the vacant building.

'I'll take care of Kamla,' he said at last. 'I'll talk to Mem . . . Everything will be all right. Simon, I promise you.'

'How?' Simon wrenched himself free. 'Mem's not even here. And Kamla won't admit anything.'

'We'll see about that. Where is Mem?'

'Out.'

'Did she say when she was coming back?'

He shook his head. 'You shouldn't have gone away.'

'I know. I'm sorry.' He extended the slingshot, handle first, but Simon refused to take it.

'You promised,' he said. Then he turned abruptly and left the alley, slamming the gate behind him.

2

B road daylight. No subterfuge. She nosed the Austin right up to the gate. The guard had changed. This one was beefy, with a block head and square mouth, his cap's red star pushed high on his brow. She started to tell him she had an appointment with Mr Chou, but the gate opened before she'd finished the sentence. Another guard waved her on, around to the back of the mansion, out of view from the street. And a third appeared as she parked and stepped out. This one she recognized as the pinch-faced boy who had manned the gate last time. She tried to smile, as much to test herself as him, but they both failed. He looked past her, through her, would not meet her eyes, and while she managed to rearrange her mouth, the warmth of a smile was beyond her.

She followed him across an enclosed dirt yard and up two steps, through a rear door that was peeling mustard-tinted paint and into a dingy corridor. No carpets covered the dark stone floor. Not even posters of the proletariat on the walls. She glimpsed a couple of large communal offices through open doorways – men and women alike dressed in the same dull blue uniforms as the guards. It was stifling inside and smelled of cigarette smoke and rancid oil. Finally they reached the square green room where Chou had received her before. A ten-foot-high portrait of Mao Tse-tung now hung above the empty fireplace. And at least half the chairs against the wall were occupied.

Her eyes flew from one drably dressed figure to another. Briefly she registered Chou's face lifting in her direction, an older man with long pouches beneath his eyes, a middle-aged woman with her hair pulled severely into a knot, and a younger man and woman holding tablets of paper and pencils. She looked to the doorway in the opposite wall. Would he come through there, then? Fleetingly, she wondered if this was some kind of trick, but she forced back the surge of panic as Chou moved toward her.

'Mrs Shaw,' he said. 'You received my instructions.'

'Where is my husband?'

He patted the air with both hands. 'One moment, please. I wish first to introduce you to our comrades who have helped to make this meeting possible.' The older man and woman set aside their mugs of tea as Chou steered her toward them. 'Comrade Gao.' The elderly man grinned unexpectedly and thrust out his hand. She took it, felt his bones grip her, and shook. Comrade Yu, the woman, merely nodded.

'Comrade Gao was with Chairman Mao on the Long March,' Chou explained, glancing significantly at the enormous face with half-closed eyes peering down at them from the portrait. Chou's tone suggested this information should hearten her.

Somehow Joanna managed to sit down, to accept the tea a young serving girl thrust into her hands.

'Comrade Yu is deputy consul.' The woman had a squint in one eye that made her look as if she were winking at Joanna. Under almost any other circumstances, it would have seemed funny. But she realized now that if and when this reunion occurred, it would be worse than none at all. These were to be their witnesses.

Her attention phased in and out as Chou went on singing the praises of these two heroes of the Revolution. Periodically she bent her head and murmured how grateful she was. There were a couple of volleys of Mandarin among the three of them, which Chou did not bother to translate, then at last he raised his hand. The guard disappeared, and moments later the opposite door opened.

Joanna's breath caught in her throat.

She'd half expected shackles and chains, but Aidan stood on the threshold without any visible sign of restraint. He was dressed like the others, in a dusty blue worker's jacket and formless pants, his black hair roughly cropped and parted nearly in the middle. His arms hung at his sides. He was clean-shaven, neither thinner nor heavier than when she'd last seen him. Just as he'd appeared in the photographs. His green eyes moved over her face without even a trace of emotion.

'Please.' Chou sliced the air with an upturned palm.

Aidan stepped forward, limping slightly. Joanna started up toward him, but his gaze stopped her. It was hard – and narrow as that of a disciplined soldier. That must be it, she thought. They'd brainwashed him!

The guard pushed an empty chair to face Joanna's, almost close enough that their knees touched when they sat down. The proximity was too much. She leaned forward recklessly and touched her fingers to Aidan's cheek.

As if in some ghastly dream state, he took her wrist and calmly returned it to her lap, then released her. 'I'm sorry I didn't write,' he began without ceremony. 'It seemed the kindest way.'

But the sound of his voice, the touch of his skin only unleashed another wave of despair. 'Kind?' She stared at him.

'To disappear.'

'We thought you were *dead.*'

'I hoped you would,' he said flatly.

'But Simon . . .'

'It's not all about you, Joanna!'

'I'm not talking about me.'

'Not you *or* Simon. Anyway, you had Lawrence.'

She was conscious of the quiet stealthily curling around them. The slide of lead against the recorders' tablets. The strike of a match as the older man lit a cigarette. Over Aidan's left shoulder she saw the old woman frown at Chou.

Joanna took hold of herself. 'What's that supposed to mean?'

His gaze wavered. He shrugged. 'He was smitten with you the first time he laid eyes on you.'

'I never thought twice about Lawrence!'

'More the fool you.'

She felt a cold stabbing pain through her middle. 'When did you become so cruel?'

'Not cruel, Jo. Honest.' He smiled to the others. 'My comrades understand. There are higher principles than love, even than family.'

'What principles!'

'Revolution. Progress. The triumph of the masses. You have no idea what the people of China have suffered – under Chiang, the Japanese, the imperialist powers. There is nothing more compelling than the liberation of an entire nation. A chance opened for me to be part of it, and I seized it.' He swallowed and moistened his lips. A muscle twitched along his jaw.

She dropped her voice, less than a whisper. 'I don't believe you.'

'Why not?' he answered loudly. 'I've written about nothing else since the war.' And then, 'Or didn't you notice?'

She blinked back a hot rush of tears. 'I *know* every word you ever wrote, Aidan. I *know* what you believe!'

'Evidently, that's not true. Or we wouldn't be here now.'

Joanna looked frantically around the room. The faces staring back gave her nothing, except one. Chou sighed, shaking his head. She returned to Aidan. 'Mr Chou said they would have allowed me and Simon to join you in China.'

'Did he? I suppose he also explained that I refused.'

She didn't answer.

'Are you going to make me spell that out, as well?'

She wanted to say, *You're protecting us.* Instead, she asked, 'Is it because of Alice James?'

'Alice is dead, Joanna. I know you know all about that.'

There was another long silence as she tried to decipher what he was telling her. Just what *did* she know about Alice? And how did he know what she knew? 'Why must we talk with these people staring at us? Why won't they leave us alone?'

'It's just like the night we met,' he said quietly.

The suggestion of sentiment in his voice brought her up short. 'What are you talking about?'

'The hall of mirrors. Perhaps you should have paid more attention. We were never really alone.'

She met his eyes.

'For years you've seen what you wanted to see, Jo. Believed what you wanted to believe. I tried to warn you, but you thought it was just intellectual conversation.'

They were talking in code, but it ran so close to the truth that the lines overlapped.

'Why did you marry me?' she asked.

'Because you wanted it so badly. And your innocence charmed me.' He leaned back in his chair, distancing himself. 'What matters most,' he said carefully, 'is larger than any one, or two, or three of us. Humans are no different than ants. We live, we work, we breed, we die individually, but together we can move mountains. I'm helping to move that mountain.'

'What about love?'

His eyes burned into her. 'I love the Party. I love the State. I love the Revolution.'

She dug her thumbnail into her palm. One minute she was sure this was all a ruse. In the next, his ruthlessness seemed so genuine that she could not recognize him. The two old comrades smiled, apparently also persuaded.

'You sound like a windup doll,' Joanna said softly.

'And you ask why I didn't want you in Beijing.' He shook his head. 'Jealousy does not become you, Joanna.'

'Why didn't you simply write and ask for a divorce?'

'Because I know you. I was trying to avoid this.'

'That insurance policy. You *wanted* me to declare you dead.'

His jaw tightened. 'I told you. It seemed the kindest—'

She leaned forward and hit him with such force that her palm and his cheek turned the same flaming pink. It was a desperate measure. And it failed.

Aidan didn't even flinch. He glanced at the others, as if to put them at their ease. 'Think what you want. You always have.'

She began to shake. 'I loved you so much, Aidan. Why do you spit in my face?'

But he was rising, pulling away from her. 'I don't think there's anything more to say. If you want me to sign something, I will.'

'You're prepared to never see Simon again?'

He halted and looked to Chou as if remembering something, then reached into his jacket pocket and brought out a small red book. The picture on the bound cover showed a Chinese boy wearing a red and white checked shirt and red bandanna, carrying a rifle over one shoulder. The title was printed in Chinese. 'It's called *The Youngest Pioneer*,' Aidan said. 'Tell him I hope when he's older and the world is a different place we will see each other again. In the meantime, tell him this is how I think of him. As a young pioneer.'

She restrained the impulse to throw the book in his face. 'What exactly do I tell him you mean by that?'

His expression stiffened. 'You never knew your parents, Joanna. And the imperialist assassins killed mine. I suppose in a way everything I'm doing is to avenge my family's death. It seems to me, by comparison, Simon is lucky.'

'Lucky.'

'Marry Lawrence, Joanna. He'll take care of you and Simon both.'

'I don't need anyone to take care of me!'

'That's what I thought.' He spoke so flatly the words seemed blunted. For an instant Joanna thought she detected genuine regret beneath the mask. But Aidan refused to look at her. Instead he turned to Chou and nodded. The others stood.

She wiped her eyes with the back of her wrist and pushed herself to her feet.

Aidan extended his hand. She remembered the touch of his fingers on her cheek, the soft pressure of his voice the morning he left her. *I love you. You know that.* The wedding band that had pressed against her fingertip that morning was now gone.

She searched his eyes one last time. They were green and cloudy as a stagnant pool. She couldn't begin to penetrate them.

She turned and walked away. Only when she reached Chou standing at the door did she stop to collect herself. Chou didn't say anything, but his silence was gentle, patient. Like Lawrence, he had done everything she asked. She had no one to blame but herself.

'If I bring you the divorce papers . . .' she said.

'I will see that they reach him,' Chou promised. 'Take care of yourself, Mrs Shaw.'

Without looking back she retraced her steps down the corridor past the thin-faced guard and somehow got her car started, maneuvered it back onto the street. But she covered only a block or two before she had to pull over. Her head was reeling. She had chills. She rolled down the window and let the warm air pour in.

Around her the evening descended like war. Voices plucked at her out of the blackened eyes of decaying buildings. Naked bulbs powered by chattering generators fired light over sidewalk displays of tribal artifacts and dirty fruit. Bullock carts dragged past, and men with their heads wrapped in dingy shawls rode three or four to a bicycle. A snake charmer sitting cross-legged next to the car lifted the hat off his basket and laughed.

3

L awrence waited until eleven-thirty, then left his flat and walked over to Connaught Place. Beneath a cuticle moon a half-dozen cycle rickshaw drivers stood smoking and rolling *paan* as they waited for night trade. He bypassed those who knew him and chose instead a fellow he'd never seen before. He kept his face averted. As he named his destination and dropped the oilcloth barrier between them, he could feel the man grin.

Less than five minutes later they entered the roundabout where Simon said he would find her. He leaned forward and pushed back the rickshaw's oilcloth siding. The driver stopped pedaling, snapped on his headlamp, and they glided forward, freeze-framing girls in the usual burlesque of seduction. Lawrence swallowed the scents of coconut oil and frangipani they'd laced into their hair, the musk with which they'd oiled their skin, the dung smoke that enveloped them. They wore parrot blues and greens, flamingo pinks, and canary orange. They chewed *paan* and flicked cigarettes. They wore makeup like grotesque dolls. He searched each face, each figure. They circled the roundabout twice.

'You like I stop?' the driver asked.

'No. No, I don't –' But then the hedges by the statue parted. He spotted the red dress. He'd last seen it on Joanna in another life, at a reception he'd attended with her and Aidan shortly after his arrival in Delhi. The same crimson color and mandarin collar . . . now it hung on its wearer like an overcoat.

The driver, detecting Lawrence's sudden interest, slowed to a stop as the girl came forward. She stooped to see inside the cab and abruptly looked away. But not fast enough.

'Get in,' he said in a voice so foreign that she had to glance back, and then he had her, his hand wrapping her slender arm like an iron cuff.

He barked out his address to the driver, and they rode without speaking, she erect, almost haughty, balancing herself with hands by her sides on the patched leather seat. When they rounded a corner or hit a rut, he could sense her body tensing, compensating to avoid contact. He could see just enough through the enclosed darkness to know she'd made a mess of her paint. Her face looked submerged, eyes and mouth drawn in loose waves. The carnation smell of Jo's cologne on her skin sickened him.

When they reached his building he paid the driver, adding the usual surcharge. Then he led her up the rickety stairs to his apartment through a darkness so absolute that he was forced to take her hand. She misunderstood – or miscalculated – and began rubbing the tip of her thumb against the center of his palm. The motion unleashed a sensation like rage but not rage that rippled up his arm and radiated through the core of his body. He flung her hand aside and let her find her own way. When he had gotten the door open and they stood beneath that brutal overhead light, his heart was flailing.

He poured out a shot of whiskey, ignoring the reproach in Kamla's eyes, and swallowed it quickly.

'All right,' he said at last and pointed to the tattered armchair. 'Sit there.' Meanwhile he continued to stand, shambling around the room with his arms folded across his chest until at last he ducked into the bathroom and came out with a damp towel. 'Get rid of that stuff. Then maybe I can talk to you.'

She sighed heavily and put her face in the towel. When she removed it the effect was worse. He knew she was contriving now to make him touch her. He took the towel and scrubbed hard enough that by rights he should at the same time punish her and feel nothing himself. But even through the coarse wet weave he was aware of the smallness of her nose, the shallowness of those wide eyes in their sockets, the height and breadth of her cheekbones.

When the cloth fell away those eyes blazed up at him, and she was a child again. A child dressed in her mother's clothing.

He rummaged in his packing crate wardrobe for a clean *kurta–pyjama,* then sent her to the bathroom to wash herself and change. When she emerged, her hair was down, black sheets of it pouring over her shoulders, and her body seemed even slighter in the drooping mannish white garment. She handed him Jo's red dress folded. It reeked of stale onion, tobacco, whiskey, and the ocean bottom stench of sex all teased through with Jo's astringent perfume. He took it onto the balcony, dropped it into the metal brazier, and set it alight, watched as the flames died to ash.

'How long?' he said coming back in, then abruptly, 'No. No, we'll get to that. You'd better tell me why, first.'

So she told him about Surie and the rickshaw boy, and her debt to her old *gharwali.* 'I speak English. I have schooling.' She gestured toward the balcony. 'In this dress I attract high-paying customers. In two, three nights I earn what the others make in seven.'

Her voice was high and clear and struck a note of defiance not unlike Joanna's. Numb, he asked if she was hungry. She shook her head and folded herself into the chair, pulling one knee up and clasping hands around her naked ankle. She stared at him, daring him. He looked away.

'What do you owe?' he said finally.

She named a figure at once obscenely low and high. If he'd been here . . .

'Why didn't you ask Mem for help?'

'Why did you not return me to her just now?'

They glared at each other, forty to thirteen, light to dark, male to female and all bets off. He peeled away his cotton jacket and plunged his fists into his trouser pockets. He wanted another drink but stopped himself. If he had another drink he might not stop himself.

'I don't know,' he lied.

'*I* know,' she said.

He looked at her sharply. She didn't move, only looked right back at him with those somber aquamarine eyes framed by straight black lashes. She had scrubbed her body as he'd scrubbed her face, so hard that the skin was inflamed, so deeply that the scent of all others was expunged and only her own remained. She smelled warm and pungent, aromatic and sweet, a smell like that of some essential oil, treasured spice, a commodity over which men killed each other along the fabled Silk Road.

'I know,' she repeated. 'You do not trust her.'

His mouth was dry. He sat down so hard that the wooden frame of the *charpoy* bruised the back of his legs. A sudden eruption of cicadas drowned out the murmuring night.

'What are you talking about?' he asked.

'She does not tell the truth.' She folded her arms. Her jaw tightened.

'To you?'

'She says the American Ambassador will not allow me in America, but this is not true. I have seen the forms. He has signed them already – *Approved*, they say. And she hides them in her desk. Since October, Lawrence. We might have gone to America *last year*. Then none of this would have happened.'

'Now, Kammy. There are other considerations – ' But even as he began the apology, he thought of Joanna's lies to him. About Kamla. About her own bullheaded actions. He wanted to protect her, was trying to, but the girl was right.

Kamla said, 'I know. Her *husband*.'

Careful. 'Has she been talking about him?'

'Not to us. She says nothing to us. But her silence is all about him.'

'Tell me.'

'Lately she is like – ' She looked around the room for inspiration, and her eyes fixed on the photograph of Davey, which he'd set on the bedside table that evening. She didn't directly acknowledge the picture, but her voice softened. She nodded. 'She is like a ghost. We speak and she does not hear us. We ask a question. She does not reply. She enters a door, then turns and walks out again. Before, she would get angry with me. Now she does not even see me. I think she would not notice if I disappeared. She would not care.'

'That's not true.'

'I think she does not even care about you anymore, Lawrence.' Kamla knelt on the floor in front of him, placed her palms on his knees. The intensity of her gaze made him feel as if he were unraveling.

'You say she's been like this lately,' he said. 'How long do you mean?'

'It has been ever since you left. But worse these past few days. And tonight . . .'

'Tonight?'

She dropped her hands to her sides. 'She returned home after dark and went straight to her room. I went in to her at about eight o'clock. Simon had been eating candy all evening – so much he was vomiting in the bathroom. I thought she should know.' She swallowed. 'The truth is, I was afraid he would not be able to sleep, and then I could not go out. I hoped she would take him into her room to sleep with her. But she lay on the bed just staring at the ceiling. Her face was white as the pillow. I asked if she was ill. She didn't answer. I told her about Simon, but she did not even lift her head, and when she finally did speak I hardly recognized her voice. "I don't know what to do," she said, and it was as if she were talking to herself. "I destroy everything I touch." These were her very words.'

Kamla sat back on her ankles. A question hung in the silence. Lawrence knew then, Joanna had no idea. The Americans must have had the date wrong. Only one thing could knock Jo down that far.

He hadn't gotten here in time.

Kamla stood up and turned off the harsh overhead light. Lawrence didn't stop her. He was only dimly aware of her returning to his side, drawing her legs up under her. She moved behind him and touched his shoulder. He shook his head, but her touch became more insistent. She placed her fingertips against his chest, lifted the hem of his shirtsleeve to kiss the roughened skin of an elbow. Through the *kurta*'s thin muslin, he felt the barely formed curvature of her breast brush against him as she strung her arms around his neck. She had the fraudulent delicacy of a strand of steel. The persistence of a shadow.

For an instant he wanted to throw her across the room. Then he caught her hands and, turning, held her palms together.

He looked again at the child beside him and curled her into his arms.

421

'Oh, Kammy,' he said, rocking backward. 'What in God's name have we done?'

<h1 style="text-align:center">4</h1>

The sound was like fleas trapped inside her skull. Or the firing of a distant cap gun. *Rat-tat-rat-tat.* The pill she'd taken made her brain feel swollen, her lids too heavy to lift. *Rat-tat-a-tat-rat-tat.* A dog barked in the street.

She rolled over, cracked her eyes. Darkness covered the room like a wool blanket. The clock by her bed read one-thirty. *Rat-tat-rat-tat.* The scratch-knocking continued, ricocheting through the sleeping house. Insistent. Bewildering. An image of Aidan's hardened face spun across her mind. She should never have gone after him. No. She should never have married him. But it was over now.

She pushed her legs to the edge of the mattress, got herself upright, her robe haphazardly wrapped around her, and threw back the mosquito net. She was too numb to care. She just wanted that sound to stop.

She walked barefoot down the unlit stairs. Before she reached the bottom it occurred to her to wonder where Nagu was. How the caller could reach the front door without raising Musai to unlock the gate. Why the children hadn't heard it first. A sliver of anxiety shot through her as the knocking stopped.

She inched open the door. A tall man in shirtsleeves stood listening, face averted. The low outside light glinted off the pale hair on the back of his raised hand. Then he turned to her. Douglas Freeman.

'I'm sorry,' he said.

'How did you get in the gate?'

'It was unlocked.'

'Oh.' She stood mutely staring at him.

'Could I come in?'

She nodded her head. Then she swung the door wider. As he stepped past her, she noticed her own bare feet, the crisscross of her sandals ghost-printed over the tops. They looked so white against the dark slate floor.

When she raised her head Freeman was standing in the entrance to the dining room fumbling for a light. She went on in, located the table with her hands, and sat down. He found the switch and the room leapt painfully into view. 'Please don't,' she said. 'There's a lamp in the corner. It's not so bright.' He put that on instead, and the low oily glow puddled across the lower half of the room.

He sat down to her left, catty-corner. Since they last met the cadaver had been replaced by a long spare man wearing khaki pants and rolled-up shirtsleeves. He carried a brown leather briefcase. His blue eyes were almost as vivid as Kamla's.

He cleared his throat. 'I'm sorry,' he said again, 'to disturb you like this. We just learned of your meeting with Aidan. We didn't expect it so soon. They caught us off guard.'

He stopped, searching her for a reaction. But she didn't have one. At least not one that connected to any recognizable emotion. Aidan had drained her of emotion. Only her mind was waking up.

'Did you follow me?' she asked.

'No. We had an inside source.'

There was that exaggerated *we* again. As if he were reading from a cue card. 'Chou,' she said.

He hesitated. 'I can't tell you who it was. But we didn't need to follow you . . . We didn't think we did.'

'When did you think it would happen?'

'The end of the month. That's what Aidan was told.'

'How do you know what he was told?'

Freeman narrowed his eyes, examining her.

A clump of her hair swung forward. She yanked it back behind her ear. So hard her eyes watered. 'What did you come here to tell me?'

'He played through, then.' He reached out with a pitying look, and for a third time said, 'I'm sorry.'

'Get out of here,' she said.

'Please, Joanna.'

'Get out!'

But she didn't have the strength to stand and force him. Without taking his eyes off her he reached down and unclasped his briefcase.

He slid a small beaten-up envelope across, then he got up and moved the little lamp from the sideboard onto the table. 'Before you say anything else,' he said, 'please read this.' On the envelope were written her name and the Ratendone Road address in Aidan's straight, angular hand.

When she didn't move, Freeman lifted the flap for her. It was not the first time it had been opened. The stationery bore the mark of the Indian consulate, Kashgar. He smoothed the sheets until they lay flat in front of her, then he said, 'Can I get you something to drink?'

She barely heard him.

Kashgar, May 20, 1949

Dearest Joanna,

It's been well over a month since you last heard from your wandering husband, and if you're not ready to throw him over yet, then you're not the woman I married. Please believe me, if I could have written before this, I would have, but this is the first chance I've had since Kashmir for a secure delivery, and at that, so much of this little adventure is undecided that I can lay out only the barest of its bones. Doug's a good man. I'm sure he'll get this to you if he can, but it's a long way from me to you, and anything could happen in between. I have to be careful, Jo. And one way or another, you have to trust me.

Where to begin? I love you. How's that for a start? I miss you and Simon more than you will probably believe. I even miss Lawrence's ugly mug. He deserves an apology, too. If he's still there in Delhi with you, tell him I got waylaid, but I'll make it up to him.

All that notwithstanding, I have a bad feeling that certain rumors are going to precede my return to Delhi. Rumors about the company I'm currently keeping, both personally and politically. Name: Alice James. Age: 23. Politics: Decidedly left of center.

Yes, my darling, it was this 'other woman' who waylaid me, but before you jump to the predictable conclusions, please just hear me out. I was told Alice was going into China hell-bent on exposing the Nationalists' crimes against humanity. Which included, she was heard to say, extortion and torture. The burning of villages. Mass graves and midnight execution squads. Yawn, yawn. It may be old news to you and me, but she had all the markings of a young crusader, utterly convinced that her particular pen was mightier than the sword. (Believe it or not, my own tirades pale by comparison with hers.) While in Srinagar I was tapped by forces who must, for now, remain nameless, to go after her and knock some sense into her pretty blond head, lest said sword slit her throat. This, as it turned out, was not as simple as it sounds. Her guide was substantially wilier than the fellow I hired at the last minute, and we played a game of cat-and-mouse all the way over the mountains. When I finally caught up with her two days ago in a town called Khargalik (a quaint little place that looks and smells like the Middle Ages), she threw such a tantrum I thought we'd both be arrested, which in these parts could mean having our tongues cut out.

Yes, well, as far as Alice is concerned, you have nothing to worry about. I want you to know that. If I had my way I'd have put a leash on her, dragged her bodily back over the mountains, and dumped her on the first plane home.

Nothing doing. Easier to collar a cobra than turn this girl around. Besides, I've decided it'll be quicker and easier to accompany her as far as Tihwa, where there's an aerodrome, and try to fly out rather than trek another six weeks back from here. So that's my game plan. With a little luck and a lot of persuasion, I might get back to Delhi in another two weeks. In the meantime, there's enough traffic around these parts, some of it almost what you might call civilized, that the aforementioned rumors are a distinct possibility. I'm hoping this note will defuse them, at least until I can get back and recover your good graces in a more intimate fashion.

However . . . there could be another twist in this road before I head for home, and part of my reason for writing is to prepare you for that, as well. Fact is, the winds of change are blowing even harder and faster over here than I realized sitting back in Delhi. I'd feel a pretty sad sack if I up and left without giving this change its due. I've replenished my resources so I could stay on in Sinkiang another month or two if the situation warrants.

That's why I say, the adventure is undecided. A lot depends on the wind.

I don't want to alarm you, Joanna, but in case time stretches and I don't write again, I've asked Doug to stay in touch with you, to lend you and Simon a hand if need be. I'd like to think Lawrence would hang by you, as well. I'd like to think you'll still be sitting tight in Delhi, beavering away at your good works and keeping the faith in my return . . . At the same time, I recognize that if this disappearing act goes on too long, it will start to pall. If you do decide to pack up and head home, I certainly won't blame you. I'd ask only that you let somebody obvious – the American embassy, or the powers that be at the Herald – know where I can find you. Also, you should know that I took out a bit of extra insurance, again, just in case. If you haven't tripped over it already, I left the policy in a box on the shelf in my closet. It's paid up. The other item in that box belongs to Lawrence. Please return it with my apologies. Tell him I'm such a novice, I felt safer without it.

There. I've said the nasty. I promise when I get back I'll improve on this pathetic attempt at explanation. In the meantime, you must believe that I do love you and Simon. Whatever else you may hear, Jo, know this much is true.

You are in my heart and my dreams. Forever.

Aidan

Douglas Freeman leaned forward. He pushed a glass filled with amber liquid into her hands. 'I found the Scotch. Drink some.'

She stared at him.

'I had to convince you. Everything he said to you this afternoon was a lie. He's a double agent, Joanna. For us.'

Her voice crawled out of her. 'He gave this to you *two years* ago.'

'He didn't know the full plan then. Actually none of us did, but I had an inkling. It would have been too risky to send this.'

'He trusted you to tell me.'

'And then – ' He lifted his own glass to his mouth. His neck rippled as he swallowed. 'This letter sat in safekeeping until just recently. But not my safekeeping. You see, I didn't actually fly out

426

of China, the way I told you. I spent about a year in prison in the same town where Aidan wound up.'

'Alma-Ata,' she said. 'I know.'

He was silent.

She tasted the Scotch, concentrating on the sensation of heat flowing down her throat, up into her skull. 'Is that when you ordered him to stay?'

'There were no orders. If anything, when push came to shove, it was the other way around. Aidan organized my escape. He made a friend in the hospital whose brother worked in the prison. But the quid pro quo was, he would stay on. If he hadn't, our friends would have been killed.'

She closed the collar of her robe, pulling it tight around her throat.

Freeman said, 'You have to understand. There are always contingency plans. Sometimes they take on a life of their own.'

'Like life insurance policies.' She drank. 'Like divorce.' Then she drank again right down to the bottom. 'It's so quiet in the middle of the night. We could be anywhere.'

'Joanna. I need something from you.'

It dawned on her then, as he refilled her glass from a bottle of Johnnie Walker that seemed to have materialized out of nowhere. Freeman had been searching the room all this time. His eyes darted from the sideboard to the window ledge, through the kitchen door. He had gotten up while she was absorbed in the letter, had roamed through her living room and probably the hall. Perhaps he had even gone upstairs.

'When Aidan saw you,' he said. 'He gave you a book.'

The sudden burst of comprehension was like an explosion in the back of her head. Aidan would use anyone, trample anyone. *By comparison, Simon is lucky.* He honestly believed that.

Freeman spoke softly, gently, as if the whole house might fall if he weren't very careful. 'There's something extremely important inside that book. We'll just take it out and give the book back. It will be as if I never came here—'

She interrupted, 'Do you honestly expect me to think he's a hero?'

His mouth hung open. Then he closed it and rubbed the back of his neck. 'I certainly understand—'

'Do you? Do you have any idea?'

'I think so,' he said. He squinted at the ceiling. 'I had the same life insurance policy, Joanna. My wife declared me dead on the day, and married my brother the following week. While I was sitting in a Soviet prison, dreaming about making love to her.'

'Blind faith is expensive, Mr Freeman.'

'Doug.'

She took a sip from her glass then held it against her forehead. The condensation cooled her skin. A jackal wailed far in the distance. It sounded like a crying baby.

'Who's he saving now?' she asked.

He shifted in his seat. Eventually he said, 'I can't give you any details.'

'I have a certain leverage,' she said. 'I was prepared to burn that damn book when I got home this evening. I still could.'

'You don't want to do that.'

'Tell me why not.'

'A plane was shot down last fall. In Manchuria. Some good men were captured.'

'Good white men or good yellow men?'

He frowned. 'The yellow ones were executed as soon as they were caught.'

'I see. Too bad for them.'

'Please, Joanna.'

But the Scotch had gone straight to the top of her skull. She realized she hadn't eaten in two days. And now she was drunk.

'So whatever Aidan hid in this book helps you get them back. Then what?'

'That depends on the war. And Aidan.'

'He doesn't want to come out, does he?'

He smiled. 'I wish I could tell you we'd had long heart-to-heart chats. But you're the only person I know who's seen him.'

'It didn't feel like he was acting.'

'That's the mark of a good actor, isn't it?'

'Actor? Or spy?' She laid her hands flat on the table, pressing her fingertips into the unyielding surface. 'Tell me something . . . Doug. If I hadn't gone to the Chinese. If I hadn't wanted so badly to see him, would he have come out anyway? For you?'

'Probably not. It was very risky.' He took a deep breath. 'I know it's practically impossible to believe, but I think he wanted to see you every bit as much as you wanted to see him. Even under these circumstances.'

'But your operation . . . ?'

He shrugged too casually. 'There are safer ways to smuggle information out.'

She closed her eyes. Waited for the room to stop spinning. Finally, she stood.

'Stay here. I'll bring you the book.' She walked past him into the hallway and began slowly climbing the stairs.

5

Lawrence had insisted I cover my face.

'No one must recognize you,' he said. 'Just for tonight, you're in *purdah*.'

'No one can see,' I protested. 'The moon is slim tonight, and besides, the rickshaw man has seen me already.'

He answered by draping a long black shawl over my head and shoulders. Then he took my hand and led me out of his flat. I stumbled in the unlit stairwell, but his arm was steady, pulling me up, holding me back. Outside, he pressed me against the wall, then walked alone some distance down the street to a row of sleeping rickshaw drivers. He woke one of them, and the man mounted his bicycle as Lawrence climbed into the rickshaw. I stepped from the shadows as they passed, and Lawrence instructed the man to pause. He asked if I would join him, as if he had never seen me before. Then he told the man to take us as far as Lodi Gardens.

We did not speak. We did not touch. There was some shame between us that I did not fully understand, but I knew it was not my own.

At the entrance to the gardens we waited for the driver to ride away, then turned back toward Ratendone Road. The night was clear, filled with stars and a lowering moon like a scythe. Dawn was still distant enough that we encountered no one but a few mangy *pi* dogs. I let the shawl drop from my face.

We could see the house when Lawrence finally spoke.

'You have to promise me,' he said.

'Promise?'

'I'll pay them off. I'll see that they never come after you again. I'll get you out of here, but you have to promise me you'll never sell yourself again. And you must tell no one about tonight.'

My heart rose in my throat. We had come to the gate, which stood ajar, as I must have left it. A breeze rustled the leaves, and one of the *pi* dogs roaming behind us nosed closer now, as if expecting us to toss him scraps. I looked up at the shadow-shape of the house, the pale box of its walls, the darker squares marking rooms I knew better than my name. Windows through which I had made my escapes. Windows through which I had spied.

Suddenly my voice flew out of me, like the ball in the photograph of Lawrence's son, tossed by an unseen hand. 'Will you marry me, then?'

You see, I was still, even in that one last moment, a child. I saw and I heard, yet truly I understood only my own selfish greed.

He stopped walking. 'What on earth?' He sounded as if he might laugh, and I turned to him touching his cheek, willing him to lift me again like a child but to love me like a woman.

I heard a cough, then a strangled cry. A small dark figure stumbled into the road.

'Simon.' Lawrence recognized him first.

'I followed you.' Simon's voice climbed quickly to a high-pitched whine. 'You said you'd bring her home, but I followed you.'

'Hey, now, laddie.' Lawrence raised one hand and with the other gently pressed me away. 'It's not like you think.'

'I waited . . . and waited.'

I saw that Simon's hand was outstretched, but it was too dark for me to see why. The quiet seemed to close around us, catching whispers in its folds. A snuffling. The sigh of dust underfoot. Lawrence took a step toward Simon. 'Easy, son,' he said, low and soft. 'Why don't you give me—'

Just then one of the dogs gave a deafening bark and lunged

toward us. It was like an explosion off to my right, the noise and movement so unexpected that I leapt backward. But in that same instant I saw a jerking flash by Simon's hand and heard a second noise – a loud, startled pop.

The next thing I knew I was drenched and falling. Lawrence's weight came after me, then rolled so that I lay against him, tangled in his arms. Too stunned to move, I heard a mewling, tasted smoke and blood and earth. My body throbbed, but not with pain. I raised up on one elbow and placed a hand on Lawrence's chest. His heart pounded against his ribs, the force of his pulse pushing me away. I drew back and a fountain erupted between us, rising as high as my shoulder.

I reached with both hands to stop the flow, but Lawrence gripped my arm. 'Blame me,' he whispered. 'Somehow . . . Blame me.'

In the darkness I saw his soft gray eye turn toward Simon, who stood whimpering blindly, 'I didn't mean to!' Lawrence's blood drenched my palms, the force of his heartbeat overpowering me.

Simon stood almost close enough to touch – close enough now that I could make out the gun still clumsily wrapped in his hands. Lawrence's fingers tightened and his face twitched, eyes squeezing shut. His chest rose as he drew in a breath, but when he let it out his grip relaxed. The fountain of blood subsided.

Simon knelt in the dust, sobbing now and holding his head. He had dropped the gun. Lawrence felt so warm. I wanted to lie back down beside him, but a door slammed, and I heard footsteps in the driveway, Mem's panic calling our names.

Blame me.

I let Lawrence go. My hands were covered in blood. I rubbed them in the dirt, then crawled forward. 'Simon,' I said. 'I'm taking the gun.'

I picked it up, felt its weight, the length of its barrel. This was the gun Simon had been too fearful to touch. The gun like a cowboy's pistol. The gun belonging to Mem's husband, who had, after all, brought our world to an end.

I stroked the pistol against the hem of my *kurta,* cleaning away Simon's marks. The *pi* dogs had fallen back at the shot but now were circling again, sniffing Lawrence's blood. I wrapped my fingers around the trigger and took aim at the closest one. It had a long, pointed snout.

I squeezed. The dog fell, whining. I shot again and killed him.

A man appeared in the open gate. He had pale hair and stood tall as Lawrence. I could not see him clearly enough to know that I had seen him before. For a moment I thought he was Lawrence's ghost.

Then Mem came behind him. She started toward Simon. She saw me and stopped. Slowly her face turned toward Lawrence's body.

And she began to scream. The sound filled her throat, raw and ragged, with pauses like hiccups as she caught her breath, then started up again. The cries built quickly to a wracking, explosive howl that seemed to take over the night. It was like an animal dying, but refusing to die, summoning the last pure breath of life. I had never imagined Mem capable of producing such sound.

It shook the very ground beneath our feet.

6

We had heard a voice – a familiar voice. Someone at the gate. We tried to wake Mem, but she was hard asleep – she often took a sleeping pill before bedtime. If it was Lawrence we knew she would want us to let him in, and we were almost certain we heard Lawrence's voice. We hoped it was Lawrence, as he had been away many weeks. Still, this was India and one had to be careful, so Simon grabbed his cap gun to summon the servants, in case we were mistaken.

Simon knew where Musai hid the key, and when we reached the gate we heard Lawrence again, his Australian accent marking him as surely as a beam of light, though it was so dark we still could not see him, and he stood so far back we could not make out what he was saying. We opened the gate, but instead of Lawrence, a pariah dog confronted us. The animal was moving closer, growling, mad. I knew such dogs are often rabid.

I told Simon to fire his pistol, to frighten the creature away. But then the dog barked and Simon was too frightened to move, so I grabbed the gun from him and shot in the direction of the beast. The sound was much larger than I expected. I had never fired a gun

before. The noise echoed in my ears, but the dog kept coming. I fired
again, and again. At last the dog fell, and I realized Simon was
sobbing. Only then did I see what I had done.

Fifty years later, I can still hear myself weave this lie as I am
taken into custody. I can see the shafts of sunrise swimming with
dust and hear the thickened music of doubt in the policemen's
Indian English accents. I can see Nagu's and Musai's sad, bewildered faces, the boys Dilip and Bhanu huddling in the background
as the white cloth falls over Lawrence's body and Simon burrows
mutely into his mother's arms. I can feel her agonized gaze bore
into me to this very day.

The last echo of my childhood died with Lawrence. I had no more
time for grief than I had for fantasies of justice. The same declara-
tion that protected Simon would condemn him to a life of torment.
I knew this as surely as I knew that it had also destroyed the last
bonds of trust between Mem and me. I owed her and Simon and
Lawrence so much. This final act was the only way left for me to
repay them, but it meant that from this moment on, they must
disown me.

Before my first day in custody ended I succeeded in smuggling a
message out through one of the women detention house guards.
The following night I was awakened by a hand pressed over my
mouth. For an instant I was back at Safe Haven, and Lawrence was
breathing in my ear, promising to fly me away. Then the cloud of
memory shifted. I smelled fish and onions and the sweat of skin. I
was pulled up, shoved, began moving forward through darkness as
thick as blood. My captor walked behind me. One door opened,
then another. I saw four flat blue-gray strips of sky with a sliver of
moon in one corner. Then the hands of the stranger released me.
His voice instructed me to keep walking, warned me not to look
back.

I reached the street before I heard the final door slam shut.

And then another opened.

A battered white Ambassador stood waiting for me at the corner.

EPILOGUE
Washington, DC

APRIL 2001

I kept my promise to Lawrence.

I had chosen my next rescuer well. Shrilal understood that we were engaged in the fairest of trades. Youth for age. Freedom for safety. Comfort for generosity. And ultimately, life for death.

This was the nature of our marriage. It lasted for more than ten years and left me a wealthy young widow attending university in England. I did my dissertation on the Great Game, and eventually finished the book Lawrence had started. I hand-delivered it to his old mate, Rodney Tynsdale. It was published under my pseudonym in Sydney and London and became a classroom text. I assigned the proceeds to Safe Haven – now run by an all-Indian staff – in memory of Lawrence.

At Mem's insistence, after my escape, Lawrence's death was recorded as an accident. I had read this in the *Hindu Times* as Shrilal and I were traveling as far from Delhi as that old white Ambassador could carry us. But while in fact his death was an accident, I knew the truth. We had all played a hand in his dying. Through blind faith and bewildered longing, through that craving for some impossible goodness, we had turned against one another, and Lawrence paid the ultimate price.

What mattered most in the end was not right or wrong. It was not politics or fidelity or even understanding. Certainly it was not the act of rescue. It was simply our mutual ineptitude at love.

I became a historian. I studied war, making espionage my specialty. Last year, I was putting the finishing touches on a review of American intelligence operations in Asia when I learned that Aidan Shaw had been arrested in Shanghai early in 1952 following a successful US rescue of two captured CIA operatives off the coast of Shandong. He spent the next twenty years in a Chinese prison and died, according to the Chinese, by slashing his throat with an American-made razor in 1973. Joanna Shaw had never been allowed to visit him. Nor had she divorced him.

This past April a star in Aidan's name was to be placed on the CIA's Wall of Honor at the agency's headquarters in Langley, Virginia. Through the London university where I now teach, I managed to obtain permission to attend the commemoration.

The day was cold, clammy. I arrived at 11:00 a.m. and was ushered to the upper tier of the enormous marble lobby. The folding chairs in the main hall below were reserved for family members. Those families were just beginning to drift in. They wore gray and black. Some carried lilies or single roses to lay at the base of the engraved wall. My escort, a young African-American man with a honeyed voice, explained that many of these families had waited decades for the agency to recognize the sacrifice of their loved ones. Even now, some of those agents who were honored by stars on the wall could not be publicly named.

I listened to his talk of secrecy with only half an ear. I did not know whether Mem would come. I did not even know if she was alive. I had made no previous attempt to find her. My own name, my identity, my entire world had changed since last I'd seen her. As the lobby filled with silent mourners, I looked down over the balcony railing and wondered if I would recognize her.

But then I saw them.

She entered under her own power, though she leaned on a three-sided walker. Her hands were bare, white-knuckled, and mottled by age, a gold band on her left ring finger. Her hair, now snowy white, was braided into a shining crown on top of her head. She wore a long dark blue dress with simple gold earrings. Her face was tipped down, away from me, but I recognized those mango-shaped ears, the width of her cheekbones, the angle of her nose. The years had scored many lines in her skin, and she wore none of the garish paint so many privileged women use to try to disguise their age. There was, indeed, a softness about her, an air of acquiescence that might have dissuaded me that this was really Mrs Shaw.

Except that Simon was by her side. Simon grown to middle age. I

438

almost laughed. He wore a camel hair coat and brown felt hat. When he removed the hat I was stunned to see he'd lost most of his hair, though what remained on the sides of his head and in his scrubby mustache was the same sandy brown color I remembered. And his ears, now veined a purplish pink, still stuck out like teacup handles. He touched his fingers to Mem's lower back, as if afraid she might topple if he let her go. And he talked across her as they found their seats, to the man who had entered with them.

This man was tall, lanky, with flowing silver hair. The size and age Lawrence would have been had he survived to this day. With a shock I realized this same man had been with Mem the night Lawrence died. The man I'd briefly mistaken for Lawrence's ghost.

Douglas Freeman held a bouquet of blue gladioli and Simon a framed photograph. They seated themselves almost directly below me, so that as Simon laid the picture across his knees the image smiled in full view. Others gathered here had brought single portraits of their dead, but there were two in the picture Simon held. I recognized it from our days on Ratendone Road. This was one of the photographs Mem could never bring herself to put away.

More than fifty years later, Lawrence and Aidan were still grinning from the back of the elephant they'd ridden across Burma.

The service began. 'We stand together before this sacred wall of stars, united in fellowship to remember . . .'

Mem stretched one hand to the son on her left, the other to the man now on her right. Her eyes closed.

The program was brief. When the roll call came and Aidan Shaw's name was spoken, I watched Mem and Simon bow their heads. They held the photograph between them. And then Simon did something that set my heart free.

He lifted his head and stared straight at me as if he had known all along I would be there. Without removing his eyes, he reached a hand to Mem's arm. She raised her face to follow his gaze, and it seemed to me I was seeing her through a sequence of subtly shifting mirrors. Her brows lifted, erasing the creases of age. Her mouth formed a perfect O, and then her eyes pooled with tears. The tender drone of grief and honor welled around us like a suspension of time.

But time had not stopped for me. Not in the way that I sensed it had for Mem and Simon. Nor in the way that Lawrence would so ardently have resisted. The irony came as a bittersweet dawning.

I was the lucky one.

I waited for the shock to subside from Mem's eyes. Then I raised my hand and smiled.

ACKNOWLEDGMENTS

This book has godparents around the globe. First among them are my parents, Jane and Maurice, and my brother, Marc, whom I thank for their enduring love and memories and for making India and China two of my homes of the heart.

I am also indebted to the following generous individuals whose insights and advice helped to shape this story: In New Delhi, Jacquelin and Ranjit Singh; Bandana, Akash, and Prem Sen; Gopal and Smriti Jain; Som and Suman Benegal; Jahani Wassi; Usha Ramanathan; Jerry Pinto at UNICEF; Ratna Kapur with the Center for Feminist Legal Research; Sudeep Chakravarti; Promilla Kapur; Mohini Giri of the National Commission on Women; and Jyotsna Chatterji of the Joint Women's Programme. In Chandigarh, G.S. and Minoo Chani. In Mumbai, Dev and Anuradha Parikh Benegal; Priti Patkar at PRERANA; Mrs Vipula Kadri; and Shabana Azmi. And all through India, Shadi Ram Shama. My thanks to Geoffrey and Diane Ward, Tom and Jonathan Keehn, and Sharon Jay for helping to make many of the above connections. And for the acute details of American life in India circa 1951 I could have no richer source than the letters of Martha Keehn. She is deeply missed.

A number of fellow writers and readers have contributed information, advice, expertise, and invaluable encouragement during the five years it took to complete this novel. I am grateful to Kylie Moloney, Reference Librarian of the National Library of Australia, and Robert Akeroyd for assisting my researches into the birth of Australia's intelligence services; to Linda Ashour, Wendy Belcher, Deborah Pyper Brault, Susan Chehak, Eric Edson, Mark Lee, Arnold Margolin, and Leslie Monsour for offering critical honesty as well as unwavering friendship; to Erika Steiger, Judy Soo-Hoo, and Sarah Jacobus for their attention to detail; to Ritu Menon, Kamla Bhasin, and Peter Rand for extending their considerable knowledge to a total stranger; and to Michelle Matthews for so gamely adding cartography to her burgeoning repertoire.

As every author knows, the publication of a book is a team effort. Caryn Karmatz Rudy, Molly Chehak, Fred Chase, Harvey-Jane Kowal, Nancy Wiese, Jamie Raab, Maureen Egen, Laurence Kirshbaum, and the rest of the superlative team at Warner Books – I thank you for your excellence and for believing in me.

A career in letters, too, is a team effort, and I cannot imagine a better 'captain' than my agent of more than twenty years now, Richard Pine. I owe a debt of gratitude also to the other members of the Pine Agency, especially Lori Andiman, Sara Piel, and the late but fondly remembered Arthur Pine.

Finally, there is that sticky issue of the writer's 'real' life. I am more than lucky and more than grateful to share this life with three magnificent men. Graham, Daniel, Marty – I love you all madly.